SURVAINE

GEN-HEIRS: THE GUARDIANS OF SZIVERIA
BOOK 6

SARAH WESTILL

SURVAINE

Gen-Heirs: The Guardians of Sziveria – Book 6

Copyright 2023 by Sarah Westill

ISBN 978-1-955293-13-6

Cover Design by For the Muse Designs

OTHER TITLES BY SARAH WESTILL

The Guardians of Sziveria

(in reading order)

Levkaseon – A Prequel

Wintersfall

Raiventon

Kynhaven

Asherwick

Ericksen - A Wintervail Special

Survaine

Wolvenguard (winter 2023)

Bella and the Beast Master

(A Gen-Heirs World Novella Series)

Frozen Flowers Fallen

Perfect Melody Silenced

Dreams Never Seen (summer 2023)

For world maps and to stay up-to-date on the latest
information, be sure to visit www.sarahwestill.com

DEDICATION

*To the dreamers who become risk-takers.
Every goal has to start with a leap of faith.
Here's to the ones who take it.*

CONTENT WARNING:

THIS BOOK CONTAINS MATURE CONTENT,
INCLUDING BUT NOT LIMITED TO –

Consensual sex (non-graphic)
Action violence

Reader discretion is advised.

WELCOME TO THE GEN-HEIRS WORLD

In the distant future, a major cataclysmic event not only reshaped the world as humanity knew it, but left entire lands uninhabitable. As generations of survivors struggled to endure a fight for territory and resources, humanity regressed into what became known as The Primal Years. A dark and dangerous time that lasted for centuries.

Slowly, civilizations formed in the new nations. Limited means of transportation and communication began to develop in a resource-poor world. Powerful countries arose known as Sziveria, Ruthenia, Italyssa, Westica, and Cairo. New cultures, with their own standards of honor, became global powerhouses.

By 830 Post-Cataclysmic Event (PCE), strong talents are now inherited traits, passed down through genetics. The recipients of an unavoidable hereditary legacy are known as Gen-Heirs. Trains, ships, carriages and if one can afford them, small magnetically powered vehicles move people. Radios are the only means of quick communication besides handwritten messages. Heated water is a luxury. Extreme drops in temperature and harsh arctic winds have forced most food growth indoors, in greenhouses. A dangerously lethal virus known as Human Rabies Syndrome (HRS) plagues the globe. The inhabited world is growing at a slow rate, each unique country striving to exist in harsher, cold climates, and those who survive have become ruthless in their quest to thrive in this new, forsaken world...

PROLOGUE

Haven City, Sziveria
 June 3rd, 830 P.C.E (Post-cataclysmic Event)

THE WOMAN HUDDLED ON THE WRONG SIDE OF THE BRIDGE guardrail almost went unseen. She was little more than a black shadow against an even darker river flowing below. If she hadn't moved, Caidon wouldn't have noticed her. But she did. A slight shift closer to the ledge she barely fit on. And he stopped.

She hadn't realized she was no longer alone, giving him a chance to strategize. If a river fifty feet beneath seemed a better option than life, things weren't looking too great for her. He approached slowly, not wanting to spook her, an action that may send her plummeting before he had a chance to diffuse whatever situation she seemed to have found herself in. Providing he could say anything useful. He didn't understand people, and didn't have much in common with most.

I

A gentle mist floated in a haze through the meager street lamps. The night was thankfully warm for the season and his hands didn't stick from ice build up to the rail when he leaned to looked over. She hadn't moved anymore, just seemed to stare at nothing. Closer, and with enough light reaching them, he could make out the smooth angles of her face and dark curls tamed by water. She was young and pale and too curled up for him to know much else.

"How old are you?" he asked, leaning casually onto the rail, his gaze on the foggy void beyond.

Her gasp made him tense. "Who are you?"

Still staring out, he clasped his hands together. "Caidon Survaine."

When she remained silent, he glanced down at her. "This is where you answer my question because I answered yours. How old are you?"

If possible, she shrank more into herself. "Nineteen. Why are you asking me that?"

Caidon considered her reply. "Nineteen. Young. Lots of possibility still. Are you all by yourself? No family?"

"I have family. I have… my brother."

"Is your brother a good man?"

She glanced at him, a quick cut of her eyes and lift of her shoulders. "My brother is an enforceman for Haven City Enforcement Services. A prefect."

Caidon opened his hands in supplication. "Okay, he protects people." He looked at her and waited until she met his gaze. "Does he protect those at home?"

She blinked and quickly looked away. "Yes, my brother is a good man."

"What is your name?"

A breeze blew up from the river. The chilled edge carried the scent of stale water and algae. She pressed closer to the rail, her fingers wrapping around a bar at her shoulders. "How old are you?"

"Twenty-five."

Her fingers flexed on the rail. "Ramsey."

"Is that a first or last name?"

"First."

"How intriguing."

"Many people seem to think so."

Caidon lowered himself onto the wet cement, his shoulder near hers. "So, Ramsey, who is nineteen, with the good brother, why are you on the wrong side of the bridge?"

When she went to pull her hand free, he covered her cold fingers with his. She trembled under his touch. "I'm... scared."

The tremor in her voice made him tighten his grip. He considered their conversation until this point, limited as it'd been. Since she'd climbed over the rail and settled herself on the other side, he didn't think she was scared of her current position. No, something else had her running. "Why? Will your brother not help you?"

"My brother can't help me," she said, her voice cracking. Against his shoulder, he felt more than heard her deep inhale. "He's more likely to do something stupid."

He shifted closer, until his head was near hers. "Like you're about to?"

"At least I'll only hurt myself."

"Is that what you think?" he asked quietly. She

loved her brother. He could work with that. "There is no hurt for you here, either. Only an end. They might find your body before you reach the Black Ocean. Give your brother something to bury, at least."

The gentle burble of water sweeping between pilons filled the quiet night. The distant, unhurried clop of hooves and clatter of wheels told him they wouldn't be alone on the bridge for much longer.

"Perhaps," he said, "you'd consider giving me your brother's name. I can at least do him the courtesy of letting him know what happened to his sister. As an enforceman, he'll search the city for you, I'm sure."

"You aren't going to try to talk me out of this?" she asked sharply.

"Were you hoping some stranger would walk by and stop you?"

"I don't know," she said in a mixture of wonder and a hint of anger. "I didn't *want* to be here at all."

"Then don't be," he said with a biting edge. A challenge for her to obey.

Tense seconds passed, and then she shifted, and Caidon moved with her, ensuring she didn't fall when she stood. "Help me over?" she asked, completely calm, as if she sat on the wrong side of safety every day. Maybe she did for all he knew.

Caidon grasped her elbow and held out his other hand to steady her if she couldn't make it over on her own. One leg swung over the rail, she balanced using her palm and teetered precariously. She pivoted, reaching out blindly, her tongue stuck out the corner of her mouth. While a figure of grace she was not, there was no mistaking her stunning beauty.

Somehow, he managed to grasp her hand while staring. She lifted her face to him, and the glow of the nearest street lamp caught in her violet eyes. With the familiar sensation of time slowing, coalescing around him, the very droplets in the air hanging mid-fall, he looked over her round face. Regal, exotic, unique… they all applied. He wanted to memorize the smooth angles of her cheeks and jaw. Trace the delicate slope of her nose. Lick the water from her full lips. Caidon blinked at the foreign burst of desire. Lust and romance had no place in his life, and he took great care to keep both tightly reigned.

The harsh clatter of the approaching carriage pulled him back to reality. Caidon inhaled and rushed to help her down before they gained unwanted attention. She squeaked and gripped his shoulders. Her feet tangled in the wet folds of her skirt. Fabric ripped, and she tumbled against his chest.

"Shoot," she muttered, lifting the saturated black length. "I liked this skirt."

"I'd hope so," Caidon said, "since you'd planned on it being the last thing you wore."

"Ha, ha," she said in sarcasm. "I wasn't going to jump. I just needed…" She shrugged and straightened. He swallowed the disappointment of losing her soft curves. "Some time to think. This bridge is pretty far from everything, but not too far from my house."

"Pretty risky."

She shrugged. "Maybe." When he lifted a brow, she rolled her eyes and tsked. "Okay fine, so I didn't make the smartest choice to wallow in self-pity. I'm okay now."

"Yeah?"

"Yes."

The carriage ambled by, the heavy, wooden cab rocking gently behind the slow-walking horse. The driver lifted a hand in greeting, but didn't stop. Either off duty, or he already had a fare. Caidon watched the coach fade into the mist and redirected his attention to the barely visible three-story building on the corner across from the bridge.

"I'm staying there, in that hotel. The owner keeps her kitchen open all night, and a fire burning in the lobby. Do you want to go warm up, or do you want me to walk you home?" he asked, pointing at the corner.

She looked at the building, then over her shoulder in the opposite direction, then back. Pressing her lips together, she met his gaze. "Just the lobby?"

"Yes."

Crossing her arms over her small chest, she nodded. "Okay, that sounds nice. Thank you."

The urge to slide his arm around her waist had him shoving his hands into his pockets and falling in step beside her. He wasn't tall or overly built, but beside her, he very much felt like a man. While she had full hips, her waist was narrow, and her breasts small. He figured he outweighed her by fifty pounds, maybe more. Black curls fell in clumps around her shoulders and down her back, soaked with water. Dry, he imagined they were chaos. What had he been thinking wanting to spend more time with her? Nothing good would come of learning more about this enigma of a woman.

And yet, he held the door open for her when they arrived. He settled her on the couch with a blanket, and then went to get her something warm to drink. When he returned, two steaming cups in hand, he found her curled up and staring into the massive fire. Angling himself on the couch so he could still see the doors and stairs, he relaxed and allowed himself to look once again.

She turned and met his gaze, a small smile curving her tempting mouth. "You're staring."

He shrugged and kept looking. "Not often I find something worth staring at."

A subtle flush blossomed across her cheeks. "Well, aren't you a charmer?"

"Not usually."

A delicate, black brow lifted. "No?"

"Nope."

She returned to watching the dancing flames. Silence descended around them, only disrupted by the pop and hiss of burning logs. The moving shadows caught on her drying curls, and as he'd suspected, they were wild. Her chin rested on her drawn knees, the blanket over her shoulders acting like a cloak.

"Why did you stop on the bridge?" she whispered. "Why did you help me?"

"Would you have preferred I left you there?" he asked, genuinely curious.

"No." She scrunched her nose. "At least, I don't think so."

"Things are so bad?"

Her chin dropped further between her knees. "Yes."

Caidon waited. He was a patient hunter, an ingrained ability of his inherited talent.

"My name is Ramsey Hunter." When he didn't

respond how she seemed to expect he would, she turned her head, laying her cheek on her knees. Her hair fell in a cascade across her back, and he tightened his grip on the rear of the couch. "Don't you read the papers?"

"Not unless I have to. Have you been in them?"

She nodded. "I helped send a very bad man to prison."

"That's a good thing."

"Most people didn't seem to think so," she said softly. "I've lost all my friends." Her left hand slipped free from the blanket. In the amber light, he could see the pale band around her wrist where a thick bracelet had once been. A promise band. "And *he* left. Decided I wasn't worth the trouble."

Caidon leaned forward and slid his fingers between hers. A sizzle of awareness raced up his arm. Like a magnet, he shifted closer until his hip pressed to hers. His arm stretched out behind her, cocooning her into his side. "I guess he did you a favor then. Marriage contracts aren't for the weak."

"You've been married?" she asked, her eyes bright.

"No, not me." He pulled her hand into his chest. "Not yet."

"I wasn't sure if I was ready." Her fingers tightened around his. "Now, I guess it doesn't matter."

"He wasn't the reason you were contemplating the river to sweep away your worries."

Her gaze fell to their clasped hands. "He was part of it, yes. My parents were in Monaco Sands when the hurricane hit. You know the one? From two months ago?"

"I heard about it."

She nodded. Tears shimmered in her eyes. "I wanted my mom, and she wasn't here. Won't ever be here again. My brother can't help. He's so… proud of me, for standing up against Joel Blackbain and fighting for all the girls he assaulted. I didn't know Blackbain was keeping half of Haven City wealthy. With him in prison, he won't be able to do business."

"I should hope not. And if money was more important to everyone than a rapist receiving justice, then why would you want to be around those people?"

"I don't, I just…." She took a shaky breath. "I didn't expect to be shunned, you know? And…" She sighed and looked away, a flush darkening her face. "Ditched. He made so many promises. You aren't supposed to break those." Her face dropped to her knees. "I can't believe I'm telling you all this."

Caidon gave in to the urge and swept curls from her face, his fingers lingering in the silken length. "I'm glad you told me."

She settled her cheek onto her knees again, her hand flexing in his. "So, tell me something about you."

"I received a ranked guardian position today."

Shock widened her eyes. "Really? Wow… congratulations." Then her gaze shuttered. "Be careful who you make friends with."

"I won't be staying in Sziveria. I sail out tomorrow."

"Where are you going?"

He shrugged. "Don't know yet."

Understanding dawned in her gaze. "Oh, you signed on with the FIO then, didn't you?"

"Yes."

She pressed her lips together. "I guess we won't have much to talk about."

He caressed another ringlet behind her ear. "You can keep telling me about you."

"I'm boring."

"You're pretty interesting from where I'm sitting."

She laughed a sweet musical sound. "Not a charmer? What a liar you're turning out to be."

Caidon leaned in until his nose nearly touched hers, knowing he was getting too close, knowing better than to learn anything more about the vulnerable beauty. The compulsion outweighed his common sense. A first, and he couldn't seem to care. Not tonight. "I leave tomorrow. I don't know when I'll return home. Give me something good to remember. Talk to me, Ramsey Hunter."

"Okay," she said quietly and relaxed back, closer to him.

As she spoke random bits of information about herself, getting lost in memories with her parents because it was all she had anymore, Caidon shifted until he held her fully in his arms. He couldn't make himself stop touching her. Small caresses where she'd let him. He knew he was a poor substitute for the man she needed, the one who should have been strong enough to hold her in the midst of her sorrow. Gladly, he took the man's place, soaking in a moment he knew he'd never share again. Just existing. Learning. An indulgence he didn't deserve with a woman he could never hope to have.

"What rank were you endowed with?" she asked, her fingers sliding through his in a caress that left desire knotting in his gut.

"Master guardian," he answered.

"Whose seat were you assigned?"

He twisted a curl around one of his fingers. "No ones. It's in-name only. I'm not filling a seat in the House of Laws, nor will I have one once I'm done working for the FIO."

She shifted until she faced him but didn't move away. One of her knees rested on his thigh, the blanket pooling on both their laps. "I didn't know they could do that. I mean, I knew they could create new seats, but not temporary, and without an option for how you serve, in the house or in-service to the country."

Caidon wondered if she'd let him slip his hand under her rain-dampened skirt. Touch her bare calf. Continue up to her thigh. If she'd be warm to his touch, or cool from the wet fabric against her skin. "I'm a unique situation."

"A unique *Sziverian government* situation," she clarified.

Then she looked around, as if assuring herself they were truly alone. The night had faded to early morning. Perhaps some stragglers would venture in, but Caidon figured not.

Ramsey leaned closer, and beyond the scent of rain still lingering on her skin, he caught a faint hint of lavender and vanilla. Warm, calm, and inviting. He wanted to press his face into the curve of her neck. How in the inhabited world was this woman, whom he'd only known for hours now, able to make him forget every carefully laid barricade he'd erected to keep from wanting anyone? She'd been nothing more than a shadow on a bridge, and yet here he sat, having a conversation he should not be having, distracted into needing things he should not be needing.

"Can you tell me? Why they made such an exception for you? Why you can't do something as easy as sit in a chair and help pass or amend laws but are required to serve your nation to have a ranking?" she asked, her gaze searching.

Suspicion took root in Caidon, and he narrowed his eyes. "You are inquisitive by nature, aren't you? That's the reason you're in the papers. You learned, or saw, something and couldn't help but look deeper."

Her cheeks flushed as she blew air into them and glanced at the weakening fire. "So my brother tells me. Though he said he blamed our very strong justice gene."

He smiled and brushed hair over her shoulder so he could see her face fully. "Ah, but I have a suspicious feeling it goes well beyond righting wrongs."

Red suffused her entire face, and she audibly swallowed, remaining silent, her attention forward. How intriguing.

Caidon brushed his fingers along the softness of her neck. "What have you done, Ramsey Hunter?"

She squared her shoulders and faced him once again. "An answer for an answer."

"Sounds fair," he agreed, then guessed, "and you want to know what I do for the FIO."

"Yes."

Curiosity and amusement shone from her eyes. Whatever work she believed he did, had zero effect on her. Caidon frowned, realizing he didn't want to change her perception. He didn't want her to look at him in fear, or horror. And if she knew his genetically inherited ability to connect on a cellular level with a gun, therefore making *him* the perfect weapon, she might. For some reason, he wanted her to be different, like his mother, who could accept a monster for a mate. Since Caidon only had tonight, he wouldn't take his chances.

Smiling with the sadness he couldn't bury, he put some distance between them. "Perhaps another night."

"Ah," she said, pulling the blanket tighter around herself. "Not a good job, then."

"No," he said softly.

She glanced past him and scooted to the edge of the couch. "I should probably be getting home. My brother keeps odd hours, and if he realizes I'm gone...."

"He'll have his entire division out looking for you," Caidon finished for her.

"Yes," she said, chuckling. "Probably. And since you outrank my brother, who is a key guardian, I don't want to cause any trouble."

"Your brother is an enforceman. Key guardian or not, everyone has to obey his order if he opts to give one, me included."

She slipped the blanket off and folded it carefully. "Not many guardians feel that way."

Rising with a frown, he held his hand out. "Only nineteen and already jaded."

"I suppose helping convict a ranked guardian of multiple counts of rape, when he's apparently managed to be ignored for years, will do that to a girl," she said dryly, accepting his help.

And what would she say if she knew she held the hand of a man who killed in service to their country? Would he be placed in the same category? A guardian who didn't truly guard much of anything... Caidon kept the struggles internal, ensuring his expression revealed nothing as he helped her stand. His father had warned him of the lonely path to becoming an assassin, and the decision hadn't been an easy one for Caidon. He alone would have to live with the consequences.

Cold air swirled past when he opened the door. Ramsey shivered, causing Caidon to hesitate.

"What's wrong?" Ramsey asked.

"If you wait here for a minute, I'll run up and get you a jacket. You can't walk home in damp clothes without anything else to keep you warm."

She shrugged. "I'll be okay."

"I'll be right back."

Not allowing her a chance to argue, Caidon ran up the stairs to his room. He grabbed the jacket he'd worn yesterday, locked back up, and returned to her side. Laughter danced in her eyes. Smiling, she shook her head and accepted the jacket.

"I was contemplating jumping off a bridge when you found me. I wasn't concerned about the cold then, I'm not now," she said, slipping into the too-large covering.

Caidon waited for her to walk past him into the now icy night. "You wouldn't have jumped."

"You don't think so?"

He matched her shorter stride on the glistening sidewalk, shoving his hands deep into his pockets. "No. You would have thought of your brother and changed your mind on your own."

"I hadn't," she said so quietly the soft burble of water under the bridge almost took the words away. "Thought about him. I don't know if I would have. I was too lost in my own self-misery to consider beyond everything I lost so quickly."

An unwarranted and unexpected sliver of jealousy

made Caidon frown. "You loved your former promised?"

"I'm not sure." She wrapped the coat around her and crossed her arms. "I think I liked the idea of him. Of the security. All my frien—" She sighed and shook her head. "All the girls I know are married and seem to be happy."

"So young?" he asked in shock.

"Well, sure. I mean, they're only yearlong contracts, or maybe up to three years, but why wait? It's the safest way to have a relationship."

The words hung in the air between them. A reminder, he supposed for them both, that having a sexual liaison outside the safety of a marriage contract could prove deadly. Human rabies syndrome was passed on through sex in its dormant stage. Within two weeks, the virus would go active and turn its victim into the equivalent of a zombie for a couple hours, forcing the infected to seek out other hosts by biting. A monogamous relationship safeguarded both parties. The commitment could be one year or a lifetime, depending on the couple.

"Plus," she said, "sometimes the marriage can elevate one's social standing. The next contract could be to someone with more wealth, more power, or whatever."

"Is that what you were doing?"

"No, but I think maybe he was," she said, her focus somewhere off in the distance. "When he told me he wouldn't be honoring his promises to me, he also let me know he was marrying a primary guardianess. When my father died, my brother inherited his seat as Key Guardian Asherwick. Unless something awful happens to Jonathon, Tobyn had no hope of having access to my family ranking."

"He couldn't have found another woman to marry so soon."

"No, likely not. I'm sure he'd been wooing her for some time. My… scandal was the excuse he needed to end things."

Shops gave way to neat rows of two-story brick houses on either side of the wide road. No lights burned in the windows. A few houses had greenhouses higher than the house's roofline. Caidon took in the tranquil, safe atmosphere. "It wasn't your scandal."

"To some, daring to go against a ranked guardian, a figure in society, was a disgrace. I betrayed one of our own."

Caidon rolled his shoulders in discomfort. *This* was the world he'd just signed into? Thank goodness he was leaving in a couple hours. "Good thing you were saved from learning his true nature until after you were stuck in a contract with him, hmm?"

Laughing, she tugged on his forearm and pulled his hand free. She laced their fingers together and slipped their joined hands into the oversized coat pocket at her hip. The action created an intimacy and a sense of comfort he wanted to fall into. How could anyone have let this woman go?

"I hadn't looked at it like that," she said, her fingers tightening around his. "But I think you're right. I bet he would have been looking to trade up even if he'd married me."

"He would have been a fool," Caidon said before he could stop.

She laughed again and bumped her shoulder into

his. "You don't know me well enough to know. He could have made a very wise decision."

Regret filled Caidon. He'd never have the opportunity to know. Never get the chance to learn what kind of match she'd be for him. If a year would be too long or not long enough. He kept silent, not wanting to give voice to the disappointment unfurling inside. Thankfully, Ramsey didn't push for further conversation. He didn't know whether his silence at her response upset her or not. Decided not knowing was for the best.

They turned a corner, and she squeezed his hand again. "That's my house, the third one on the right."

Caidon noted all the dark windows. "Your brother still appears to be oblivious to your disappearance."

"Small favors," she said, chuckling. "I have to go in through the greenhouse. I have a key hidden under a small rock at the back door."

"Sneak out often, do you?" he asked, casting her a sideways glance, hating the curl of jealousy that once again snuck up on him. There were limited reasons she'd have ventured off in the middle of the night, and her former promised was one.

"A few times. Jonathon would have a fit if he knew I kept a key hidden. He takes our security very seriously."

Caidon breathed cold air in deep. "Understandable when you see the worst of your society."

"I know, and I probably will take the key in with me tonight." She stopped at the small alley that ran between houses and gazed up at the dark, cloudy sky. "I don't really have a need for it anymore."

The murmured words confirmed his suspicions. She'd taken off in the night to see her lover. Past lover.

He pushed away the urge to learn where the man lived. When he'd decided to follow in his father's path, he'd made a vow to only accept assignments of those deserving a fatal sentence. A broken heart, while a travesty, didn't usually warrant death. Nor did jealousy.

"I'll walk you to the door," he said, stepping into the alley.

She led him to a gate in a tall wooden fence, which left just enough room to open the greenhouse door. Darkness loomed inside, the house cutting off any residual light from the street and the clouds too thick for much moonlight to filter through. Caidon paused, listening, a habit he couldn't afford to break. The musky scent of earth and a sharp tang of fertilizer filled the moist air. Something small scuttled in the brush next to the door. Ramsey yelped and grabbed his arm, pressing into his back.

"Oh summer sun, what is that?" she squeaked, ruffling the hair at the back of his neck.

Caidon pulled her the rest of the way into the glass structure, trying to ignore how good his arm around her waist and her body fitting to his felt. "Probably a mouse, or small bird, wanting to get out and explore for the night or back to its family."

She tensed further. "A mouse?"

Caidon laughed. "It won't hurt you."

"Killer mice, they could exist," she said, easing around to the other side of him. "We do live in a strange world."

Ramsey guided the way, her hand wrapped around his. Even in the dark, she seemed to know where to step to keep from tripping or walking on precious plants. Another testament to her *few* nights of sneaking out.

Three narrow stone stairs led to the back door, and beside them, she released his hand to tilt up a small stone.

"Ah ha!" she declared, rising with her hand fisted. "He hasn't discovered it. I always worry Jonathon will figure out my little secret and leave me locked out in the greenhouse all night."

"He'd do that to you?"

"Sure. Well, maybe." She laughed on a huff. "Okay, probably not. But he'd make me think he would." She turned to face him. "If you had a sister, would you torture her in such a way?"

"I have four," he said. "And I don't know. I'd like to think they'd be more careful with their safety."

She groaned. "Not you, too. If they are adults, they are capable of making adult decisions, I promise."

"None of them are adults yet, of which my father is thankful."

"Really? I wish we had more time. I bet there's a story there. Why you're very grown, and yet your sisters are not."

Caidon couldn't help but reach out and brush a knuckle across her jaw. "Not really. When my parents met, my father still had an obligation to his ruler. My mother wouldn't allow him to her bed if there was a chance of conceiving another child. She told him when he was home to raise them, they could make more babies."

"Well," she said, "he took her seriously, didn't he? Four daughters."

"I think it was a matter of him being thankful she'd waited."

"She loved him."

"Very much."

"I wonder what such love feels like," she said quietly.

His chest constricted, and he dropped his hand. "You'll learn someday."

"I wouldn't think less of you." She stepped into his space, her hands pressing to his chest. "If I knew whatever it is you do for the nation."

Caidon fisted his hands to keep from wrapping her in his arms. "You say that…"

"No, it's true. You're a good man, Caidon Survaine. Whatever choice you made to become a master guardian, an important rank, is one we must have great need for."

"A good man?" he asked with a head shake. "To repeat your earlier statement, you don't know me."

She moved in closer, and despite knowing he should, he didn't move away. "A bad man wouldn't have helped a woman unable to see beyond her own misery. A bad man wouldn't have sat on a couch and listened to silly memories, doing nothing more. A bad man wouldn't have walked me home without expectation."

"Why would I expect something?" he asked and then snapped his head back, staring down at her shadowed face. "You… you have been pressured into doing more than you wished by someone?"

"I was curious," she said carefully, "and he was convincing in his reasons."

"You mean convincing in his *expectations*," Caidon said, anger tinging his voice.

Her cool fingers traced his jaw, catching on the stubble. "See? A good man. You care about the past, now gone, never to occur again. I learned. I won't be so naïve next time."

Next time. He didn't want her to have a next time, unless it involved him. And how ridiculous was *that* thought?

"I should warn you," she said, breaking into his wayward reflections, "I am curious now."

Caidon barely had time to blink before her lips, soft and yielding, pressed to his. Teasing, her mouth sought more, and Caidon stood frozen, his heart pounding in an uncomfortable mixture of anticipation and remorse. He wanted more than he could ever hope for. He could give this girl nothing of himself and had no future to offer. Grabbing her shoulders, he took a bracing step away, breaking the courage of her kiss.

"No," he whispered.

"Why?"

A dozen reasons swam through his mind. All of them valid. None of them worth losing the kiss he knew he'd carry with him for months, if not years. Taking a deep breath, he leaned in close, sinking his fingers into the thick curls at the base of her neck. He crowded her, forcing her to step back into the brick wall.

"You want me to kiss you, *zlanishka*?" he asked on a growl, his nose touching hers, his body pressing her to the wall. "I don't think anyone has kissed you the way I will."

Her swallow was audible in the quiet greenhouse. "You expect me to say no to that?"

Without hesitation, Caidon took her mouth. To his shock and the delight of the Ruthenian side that ruled him, she offered no resistance, opening to his onslaught with a murmur of welcome. Of desire. Caidon's tongue swept inside to claim. To possess. Hunting for every secret passion she'd reveal in the stolen moment. Sweetness exploded across his senses, from her scent, her taste, to the feminine curves crushed against his body. All of them competed with the whisper of *more* in his blood. A demand he found he had no control to ignore.

His mouth slanted over hers as he kissed her, and kissed her, and *kissed her*. He broke the embrace only long enough to lift her higher, to be able to feel the *more* his body required. She made no argument. Her legs wrapped tight around his hips, and her hands sought with the same urgency riding him. The tangled fabric of her damp skirt did little to hinder his questing touch. Only when her firm thighs were under his palms did he reign in some semblance of control, knowing to go any further would risk too much.

Ramsey squirmed, a hard shift of her hips into his arousal, an answering shudder racing through her body. Caidon knew by instinct the faint motions felt good to them both, and he was undecided about making her stop. By her quickening movements, the shift in their breathing, and the building inside him, he was seconds from coming, and she'd likely take the journey with him. She knew more about intimacy than he did, a self-imposed decision he'd made when he chose his career. If he allowed himself to give into the temptation, she'd show him what he had to lose. The cost of his future.

He pressed harder and tightened the grip on her thighs, forcing her to stop. No. This was not the time, and he would rather this not be the place. She cried out in denial, and he deepened the kiss, then pulled back.

He wanted her. And he'd have her. But only when he could have all of her, and she could have all of him.

"Wait for me," he rasped. "Will you? I don't know how long I'll be gone. Could be a year, could be ten. Wait for me, Ramsey. Promise me."

She pressed her forehead to his, her body trembling, her gasps mingling with his. "Yes."

1

Five years later…
Haven City, Sziveria
March 25th, 835 PCE

RAMSEY HAD NEVER CONSIDERED HERSELF ONE TO SUFFER A fool. Yet here she sat, staring at the biggest one of all, still listening to his ridiculous proposition, her mouth hanging open. Perhaps, she mused, her shock left her speechless, unable to toss the man out on his butt. Or, the more likely reason, she was very much alone. Jonathon and his wife Sylphine were stuck in Italyssa on some legal technicality Ramsey didn't quite understand. They were both frustrated and radioed daily to talk to their adopted son, who still lacked the necessary paperwork to leave Sziveria. When her unwelcome guest stopped speaking, he stared at her expectantly, without a hint of embarrassment.

"I think my offer is rather generous," Tobyn Fenster,

Primary Guardian Dziekane by marriage, said in all seriousness.

Ramsey blinked. "Does your wife know you're here?"

Finally, he had the gall to at least look away. "Miriam suggested the arrangement. She birthed our second son a month ago. As per our contract, as long as my lover uses an ovulation bracelet and signs a companion agreement, I can enter into an exclusive relationship outside of our contract for the next three years."

"And you chose me?" Ramsey asked, her heart pounding in anger and humiliation.

"Of course. I mean, you're still unmarried and haven't even been courted again since our time together." He offered her a smile of pity that did nothing for his thin, pale face. "I knew you cared for me. I regret I failed to realize how much."

Ramsey looked away, disgust burning in her stomach. "There is nothing to regret, aside from you breaking a promise. Which I can now admit, I'm thankful for. I reject your proposition, Tobyn." She stood, shaking out her skirt. "You may leave now."

He remained seated, his wiry frame leaning back in a relaxed pose on the small couch. "Why would I want to do that? We haven't reached an agreement yet."

"And we aren't going to," she ground out. "I said no."

His dark brown eyes narrowed. "I don't think you're appreciating what I'm offering here. Along with money, you'll be seen in society again with a man of power on your arm."

A laugh escaped before she could contain it. "A man

of power? Is that how you see yourself? You look pretty, well, not even that really... on your wife's arm. However, she's always had someone prettier, hasn't she? Is that what this is about? You want someone pretty, too?"

Red suffused his cheeks. The Primary Guardianess Dziekane had never hidden the fact that she loved someone other than Tobyn, only bringing her husband when the occasional warranted his presence. Otherwise, her long-time partner was always on her arm, a beautiful gen-common man with rich, dark skin who made Miriam the envy of many. An opportunity the shrewd guardianess never failed to employ. Ramsey suspected if Miriam hadn't wanted children guaranteed to inherit her talent, and therefore her ranked guardian position, the couple would have contracted.

Tobyn touched a manicured hand to his neatly styled pale, brown hair. "I'm sure you remember my telling you the arrangement I made with Miriam was practical, for both of us. I told you it wasn't a love match. I wanted what she had to offer and was perfectly fine with her lover, and her lover was fine with me. They knew of a couple who attempted, shall we say, other methods of producing genetically gifted off-spring that had disastrous consequences. Being up front about our marriage, expectations, and true-loves has been a benefit for all of us. Miriam wants to try for a daughter in a few years, and so we shall.

"Sziverian law mandates we remain married for eighteen years after any of our children are born. It's only natural I'd choose to find another monogamous relationship to be part of as well," he continued to explain as if anything he said would change her mind.

"Since they now don't care if their relationship produces a pregnancy, I have decided I don't want any children by another, and Miriam would prefer that as well. I will make sure you're protected by only visiting during your non-fertile weeks."

"I will not be your whore," Ramsey said through clenched teeth, her hands fisting at her sides. "I already asked you to leave. Now please go."

"M-my..." He stared up at her in shock and then sighed and shook his head. "Oh, my lovely Ramsey, you mistake my desires. No, never my whore." Standing, he reached for her, and Ramsey shifted closer to the doorway to the foyer. "Did you not hear me say truelove? Don't you remember what we had together? How good we were? How much you wanted me, us?"

Not half as much as she learned she *could* want a man. Tobyn wouldn't even be a sad substitute. He'd be a total and complete disappointment. She knew that now. She'd tasted true passion. Had experienced a desire that still had the power to make her yearn. No, she figured he'd been kicked from the proverbial martial bed now that his usefulness had been met and wouldn't be welcome for another three years. And Ramsey suspected that was only if Miriam and her lover didn't conceive within that window. Apparently, he wasn't willing to go without sex. And he figured, wrongly, Ramsey would be desperate enough for his returned affections, thinking *love* still held a place in her for him. Forced reflection so many years ago on a misty bridge had revealed no love had ever been present.

"You made your choice," she spat and stalked from the room. "I'm not going to be your..." She waved a dismissive hand. "Whatever you think to call me in place of whore."

He stopped in the doorway, his face still flushed. A spark of anger flared in his eyes. "Look, we both know no one is going to align themselves with you. You're going to be stuck in this house until your brother asks you to leave because he has to have the room for his family. And really, why would you want to intrude, anyway? I am offering you a house, a stipend, and a full wardrobe suitable for attending all manner of social events. Don't be a fool and reject this opportunity."

Ramsey forced away the hurt his words caused. The truth in the uncertainty of her future. That in the end, she'd be good for nothing more than a paid companion. Though, if she had to face such a future, she'd rather raise someone else's children than give away her body. "You mean Primary Guardianess Dziekane is offering me all those things. You have no money of your own, Tobyn."

He inclined his head and straightened his taupe, silk embroidered jacket. "Yes. She wants to see me satisfied. She's a good woman."

"More like a thankful woman," Ramsey snapped. "Answer an ad in *The Havener* for women seeking just such a union."

Much to her disappointment, he didn't rise to the insult. "I would prefer someone I know I'm already… compatible with."

"We are *not* compatible! We never were!" She went to the door and flung it open. Cool air rushed into the house. "I learned quickly whatever it was we had wasn't worth a repeat. I appreciate you saving me the mistake a contract between us would have been."

His gaze narrowed on her again. "You are already in such a relationship, aren't you? Who is he? I'll go speak to him at once and buy out your agreement with him."

Tears of outrage burned her eyes. Her nails bit into her palms. "I am no one's paid companion, *guardian*," she spat, her voice trembling. "I *have* promised to marry a very powerful man. I suggest, once again, that you leave."

He shook his head, the pity returning to the thin angles of his face. "You don't have to make anything up, Ramsey. You forget, I remember how you were rejected, the ridicule you still receive. That you won't even go anywhere unless it's with your brother or his heiress wife." He took her hand. "I can help make all that go away. I can help bring you back into society, and then maybe you truly will find a powerful man to marry. Let me do that for you, it's the least I can offer."

Ramsey snatched her hand away and took a step back before she smacked him. "No. I'm not lying."

His focus shifted to her left wrist. "I see no promise band."

"There was no time to exchange them before he had to leave on mission for the FIO."

"A likely story."

She lifted her chin. "Not a story, and I owe you no further explanation. Out of my house."

A commotion at the top of the stairs diverted her attention. The safety gate rattled, and Parker, her nephew, let loose an annoyed shout. "I want down! Down!"

Sighing, she turned her attention back to the more annoying situation in her house. "If you could leave now, that'd be great."

Tobyn blinked and stumbled back, his pallor turning an alarming shade of white. "How old is that child?"

"He's almost four," she answered, holding the door open further.

Parker threw something over the gate. The object clattered down the stairs in an unidentifiable blur. The horror on Tobyn's face as he looked between her and the boy almost made her laugh. She had a second of wanting to be cruel. Parker's sandy hair and hazel eyes could certainly be taken for Tobyn's line if one failed to look closely. Parker was darker complected and considerably better looking, even at three than the man reeling feet away.

"He is not yours," Ramsey assured. "Despite you not bothering to make sure I wasn't pregnant before ending our engagement, I did not conceive by you. Of which I am forever grateful. This is Jonathon's son. Now, leave."

Apparently, just the thought of possibly having an illegitimate child was enough to finally scare him off. Had Ramsey known, she would have brought Parker down earlier. Tobyn fled from the house, his heeled boots clacking on the steps to the walkway.

"I hope to never see you again!" she called cheerfully and slammed the door closed. Hands on her hips, she turned to face her nephew, who held another toy over the gate. "Now, let's see to you, little man."

TWO WEEKS LATER...

• • •

CAIDON FOUND HIMSELF STOPPING OUTSIDE THE BUSY Haven City MagnaRail station, taking in the tall buildings, streets crowded with carriages, the smaller and far fewer very expensive magnetic-engine powered Ariot's, and the brave occasional bicyclist. People moved in a surging crowd along the wide sidewalk, entering or exiting the massive structure behind him. Cabbies shouted their fares, trying to outdo one another to claim a customer.

Just as he'd done at Port Anchor, he observed the crowd around him, searching for anyone out of place or who seemed to be waiting. From his peripheral, he noted a man leaning casually against the wall, smoking, a dark jacket cinched tight to keep out the chill still in the early spring air. Smoke streamed from the man's nostrils as he straightened and slipped into the crowd. Caidon took a deep breath, the spice of the smoker's cigarette mingled with horse stench and the various, interchangeable scents humanity produced.

Smoker man made the mistake of glancing over his shoulder, his gaze lingering a little too long on Caidon. Careful to keep his attention on the row of cabbies, Caidon hitched the strap of his rifle case higher on his shoulder and tightened his grip on his duffel bag. So, he'd guessed correctly. He'd been expected, but not in an official Sziverian capacity, as the letter he carried in his pocket claimed. A ruse he'd suspected from the second he'd read the orders.

Mindful of the crowd and the two he'd identified following behind, Caidon set off down the sidewalk. At the first popular eatery he came to, he slipped inside and waited in the too-long line. At his turn, he placed an order and then found an empty spot along the back wall. A constant flow of customers moved through the establishment. Caidon observed, patient. When his two tagalongs arrived, he ducked through the back door and disappeared in the rush of foot traffic before they could pick him out in the teeming business.

On foot, he took a convoluted route to the FIO building. A hulking ten-story cement structure, unimaginative, yet a testament to the early days of Sziveria clawing her way from the primal years into a semblance of civilization. A wide, circular drive curved in front of cement stairs the width of the building. Hired carriages, and more impressive ones belonging to ranked guardians, along with a few parked Ariot's, crowded the thoroughfare. Caidon bypassed the main entry in favor of the employee entrance for non-guardian, clerical personnel.

Inside, he made quick work of blending in, finding a large rolling mail cart to place his gear in before heading upstairs, pushing the cart. On the fifth floor, he traversed the maze of cubicles and corridors until he located the office he needed. Hefting out his belongings, he abandoned the cart in an unoccupied room nearby and slipped into office. He used his foot to close the door, dropped his gear in an out of the way corner, and settled in behind the desk. He removed the orders from inside his jacket and unfolded them, knowing better than to read them again. A clear head was needed, not a haze of anger that would cloud his judgement.

Almost an hour later, the door opened without a knock. Tall, broad-shouldered, with a physique that betrayed the guardian did more than sit behind a desk all day, Ryan Voklane entered, tapping a folder against his thigh. His pale, silvery-blue eyes landed on Caidon, and he froze, the door half open. Caidon lifted a brow but remained behind the desk.

Voklane took a careful step the rest of the way into the office and closed the door but made no further effort to come closer to Caidon. "Master Guardian Survaine, this is… unexpected. I thought you were in Cairo."

"I'm glad to hear my appearance is a surprise to you," Caidon said evenly, tapping the folded papers on the desk surface. "Someone is playing with your guardians, Voklane."

"You aren't *my* anything," Ryan said with a frown.

Caidon smiled. "Whatever you say."

Crossing the distance to the desk, Ryan accepted the papers Caidon held up. "What's this?"

"Orders I will not be following. I was hoping you could tell me why, or how, I'd received them." Caidon allowed Ryan a few quiet seconds to look over the document before asking, "Who wants Ramsey Hunter dead, and why are they asking me to do it?"

2

CAIDON WAITED PATIENTLY WHILE RYAN SAT IN FRONT OF the desk and looked over the paperwork. An expression of pained anger and disbelief crossed over the guardian's features. Slowly, Ryan shook his head.

"This is... wrong." Ryan glanced up. "Who gave you these orders?"

Caidon shrugged and rolled a pen back and forth on the desk. "It was waiting in an envelope under my hotel door. Not usual, but not the first time you've chosen to deliver an assignment in that manner."

"You know who Miss Hunter is?" Ryan asked, his shrewd gaze narrowed.

"Yes." Caidon paused with the pen mid-roll. "Has she managed to piss more people off in the last five years?"

Ryan carefully refolded the papers. "No, but a lot has happened."

"The only man I could think of who would want her dead is in prison and not in any position of power. Of course, that doesn't mean he can't get to someone who is, which I'm assuming he's done here. But why? And who would have anything to gain by helping a convict on his vendetta path?"

Silence.

Caidon slumped back on a curse-filled sigh. "A lot has happened, you say."

"Joel Blackbain is no longer a prisoner of Stonebreak. We don't, in fact, know *where* he is currently," Ryan said quietly. "He's been gone for at least two years, possibly more. I'm not sure why he would have chosen now to see to Miss Hunter's demise."

Caidon let the information filter through his conscience. "Who released him?"

"No one specifically. Arch Guardian Praekasdian's family has been under extreme duress for years. His oldest daughter is now safe, married to Primary Guardian Kynhaven. Praekasdian's sequestered his wife and young daughter in the Northern Boundary. We were made aware of his forced participation in the release of hundreds, if not thousands, of Sziverian prisoners. We're still uncovering the complete number."

"Joel Blackbain was among them?"

"Yes. A prisoner transfer that never took place. He just… disappeared. On a ship bound for who knows where with hundreds of his fellow inmates." Ryan stood and went to the wide window that overlooked the city below. "As for why he waited, it could be he hadn't proven his loyalty or hadn't amassed the power yet, or hadn't learned how we function here at the FIO to be able to produce a forged set of orders. I'm more disturbed by the fact that he knew you and what you do specifically, if this is his doing."

"Who I am and what I do isn't a secret," Caidon felt

the need to point out. "I was being pursued for my talent when you reached out to me to do guardian work."

"I know." Ryan clasped his hands behind his back and continued to gaze outside. "Where you are, what has been asked of you while you're there, is only ever known to myself and Arch Guardian Synintel. So, how did Blackbain find you?"

"He couldn't have known I'd be acquainted with Miss Hunter."

Ryan glanced at him, the quick motion questioning, his body tense. Caidon knew the guardian wanted to ask, practically vibrated with the need for information, but since Caidon hadn't offered, Ryan wouldn't inquire further.

"He also," Ryan said, "wouldn't have known of our arrangement and that you'd never agree to remove anyone on Sziverian soil. Not unless they were so intent on evil we had no other option except to seek out your assistance."

"And, from my understanding, you have another that could handle that well enough for you."

A long exhale left Ryan. "Yes and no. She's currently stuck in Italyssa, and she's eight months pregnant. She's married to Wintersfall."

"Well, that'd be ironic, Blackbain asking his sister-in-law to remove his mortal enemy. Why is she stuck in Italyssa? We're at peace with them, and last I knew, they could handle their own small problems."

"She went with Sean to help Jonathon Hunter."

Caidon laughed long and hard. "So, Ramsey Hunter is alone, and your other sharpshooter, who is also a Blackbain and is clearly friends with the Hunter's, and therefore poses a threat to this little operation, is conveniently stuck out of country. Oh, my friend, you have been outmaneuvered."

"I would have to agree," Ryan said. "The moment the channel was safe enough to cross, you were contacted, and they were detained."

"They've been detained?"

"Not in a prison or anything, but they can't leave. Some odd bureaucratic nonsense. Sylphine Hunter, the heiress to Sun Wind Trade, can't even use a ship from her father's fleet. They aren't letting any of them depart."

"You could demand their return in an official capacity, you know," Caidon said.

"And if it comes to that, I will. It was some ridiculous primal law that sent the Hunters there, I assumed some stupid law was in their way for this too. I was hoping Sylphine and her father would be able to keep it from becoming an international incident." Ryan puffed out his cheeks and huffed. "I was obviously mistaken."

"Well, not an incident yet."

Ryan shook his head. "Ramsey Hunter is one lucky woman. She knows both my assassins, and neither seem to be willing to anonymously remove her. If you were a different man, she'd be dead, and you'd be gone in the wind before her brother even knew where to start looking."

"An enforceman, right?" Caidon asked, recalling what little Ramsey had said about him on that fateful night so many years ago.

"A master tribunni and the lead investigator for violent crimes with the East Street Division," Ryan confirmed.

"Does he know about Joel Blackbain?"

"Yes, he's who told me."

Caidon frowned. "But he left his sister alone anyway?"

"He was injured in Italyssa, and the channel became impassable while he recovered. No one does much of anything during the winter, she's been safe. Until now." Ryan turned to face him. "You should know once they realize you didn't follow their fabricated orders, they'll send someone else."

"They have someone else?" Caidon asked, surprised.

"Yes, but they aren't nearly as good."

"A bullet is a bullet. Fire enough rounds, and eventually, you'll hit the mark," Caidon stated dryly.

"And that's pretty much what they've been doing." Ryan's brows pinched together. "I think maybe they wanted to send a message. My guardian teams, no matter how loyal, can be maneuvered by them if they wish, without the guardian even knowing they're working for the wrong side."

Caidon straightened, a sense of alarm racing up his spine. "Who is *they*?"

Ryan's jaw tensed. "They call themselves the V Alliance, and for the past six years, that we know of, they've been trying very hard to take over key aspects of our leadership. They've come alarmingly close on several occasions."

"And in the case of Praekasdian, they've succeeded, yes?"

"They couldn't replace him, so they did the next best thing and threatened him with coercion," Ryan clarified.

Caidon shrugged. "They achieved a goal, regardless of the manner. Who else do you suspect?"

"They've made attempts at the Synintel and Immetana arch guardianships, and were able to successfully turn the Enbrackon shield guardianship, but we handled that one." He rolled his shoulders. "We're pretty sure they've managed to take to the Reconimica arch guardianship."

Caidon didn't hide his shock. "Finance? Ambitious."

"Yes. We've warned the queen-elect and her security chief, Shield Guardian Taerraine. Queen Elect Arnita wished the V Alliance to think we're ignorant of the treason, so we've made no moves to change anything."

"Taerraine is still trustworthy?" A touch of anxiety tingled along his nerves at the idea of the queen-elect's head of security being compromised.

"Yes, last I checked."

"Someone has an interest in this. I was followed from the rail station." Caidon leaned forward and rested his elbows on his knees. "And you're telling me once they realize I didn't obey, they'll send someone else?"

"I think they may attempt something, yes. But who knows? This may have just been a bragging event, something to prove their power, that I, or rather Synintel, doesn't have the upper hand," Ryan said, returning to look out of the window.

Caidon figured Voklane had it correct by assuming the V Alliance was making the statement personal but remained silent. "I need a basic marriage contract, and my file amended to include travel with a spouse. Make us a team if you must."

Ryan sucked in a breath. "I made a promise to her

brother she wouldn't get involved in anything to do with the government."

"Why is that?"

"I don't know the extent, but she may have a linguistic talent. She's never been tested, and as far as her brother knows, she didn't display any hint of the ability until recently."

Caidon considered the information. "Interesting. And her brother is concerned?"

"He has a right to be. Any of the branches, from us here at First Intelligence to Immigration and Import. Even the National Investigative Division can use someone with that talent. It's rare, and if it's strong…"

"She could be a codebreaker. A pattern finder," Caidon said softly.

"Yes."

"You would not object to her going with me on assignments," Caidon guessed.

"If her talent is what her brother fears, she'd be one of the biggest assets I could place with you."

Caidon's mind sorted through yet more information. Ryan's surprise at him knowing Ramsey was genuine. This wasn't some convoluted setup to get the Hunter woman to work with him. Despite the benefit to the FIO, Ryan had nothing to do with Caidon returning home. Caidon trusted Ryan that much. However, Caidon's association with Ramsey was a rock on the proverbial train track for whoever wanted her dead.

"You let me deal with the brother," Caidon said. "We both know I'm her safest option right now. Does anyone else know about her talent?"

"Only the sister-in-law."

Caidon nodded. "Okay, good. Let's try to keep it that way."

"That's been the plan." Ryan went to a center filing cabinet along his office wall. "Here's the contract."

Caidon bit back a sarcastic comment on why the liaison for the Arch Guardian Synintel would keep a stock of marriage contracts. Sadly, it wasn't a secret that the FIO, and even on occasion the SNID, used them to strengthen, or even force, guardians into teams together. At the moment, he needed to be thankful for the shadow tactics. They were working in his favor. He accepted the paper, looked it over to make sure there weren't any hidden surprises, and then folded and tucked it into his pocket.

Ryan crossed his arms and leaned against the filing cabinets. "Do you think she'll sign it?"

Ramsey's whispered promise, breathless from their restrained passion, slid through his mind on a sensual wave. "Yes, she'll sign."

3

EXHAUSTED, RAMSEY CLOSED THE DOOR WITH A WINCE and then waited, barely breathing, to make sure Parker didn't wail in protest. Again. For what felt like the tenth time in twenty minutes. When she'd agreed to take on the little person, she'd figured she'd be on her own for a few weeks. Not six months. Blissful silence filled the house, and Ramsey pressed a thankful hand to the door and turned away.

She knew Jonathon wasn't to blame, and on nights like tonight, when her patience was sorely tested, she had to squish the guilt at her frustration. Along with the urge to cry. Single-parenting wasn't for the weak. Breathing out a breath of relief, Ramsey undid the row of buttons along the front of her gown on the way to her room. A long, hot bath would go far to help relieve the stress of dealing with a belligerent toddler. How exactly did one handle a screaming, object throwing, cuteness-turned-monster anyway? Books did not exist on the subject, and if they did, they were useless. The few acquaintances she had simply patted her shoulder and said the age will pass by faster than she'll realize. Not helpful.

Ramsey shed her clothes all the way to her bathroom. A single lamp burned on her bedside table, not doing much to illuminate her spacious bedroom. However, the low light provided a peaceful ambience she sorely needed. The queen size bed was unmade, the soft pink sheets twisted and rumpled underneath a pastel quilt. She passed by her cluttered work desk. Books lay open, half covered by notes and riddles she still attempted to solve. She ran her bath while she finished undressing. The fragrant, soothing notes of her vanilla lavender soap filled the small bathroom.

Sinking into the hot water, she sighed and let the heat ease away her tension. She remained until the water grew tepid and her fingers and toes pruned. Using her toes, she pulled the plug and then stood, reaching for a large, fluffy towel. Wrapped in the cloth, she ran a comb through her thick, damp curls. She dropped the comb on her desk and began braiding her hair on the way to her dresser across the room.

A shadow moved near the window on her left wall. Ramsey froze, her hands buried in her hair. She clamped her elbows down tight to keep the towel in place, chancing a slow turn. The figure stepped into the shallow fall of light, and Ramsey blinked. *Surely not…*

In the passing years since she'd uttered an impulsive promise, she'd imagined Caidon Survaine's arrival back into her life. From the mundane chance encounter on the street to the most erotic fantasy of him slipping into her bed in the middle of the night. Never had she envisioned she'd be taken unawares amid her evening routine, in nothing but a towel, no less.

And, oh summer sun, he looked *good*.

Black hair, off his collar and ears, longer on top, left to do whatever it wanted. Emerald eyes looked her over, from her bare feet to her bare shoulders. The faintest curve tilted the corner of his mouth, his bottom lip fuller than his top. The weak light accented the strong angles of his jaw and cheeks, and the deep set of his eyes. He was larger than she remembered, thicker in the shoulders, but not overly tall. She recalled when she'd kissed him, all she'd had to do was rise on her toes.

At the memory of his body pressed to hers, of the desire that had flared too easily between them, a strange tug in her chest had her stumbling a step toward him. His gaze narrowed and his muscles tensed.

"This is unexpected," he said quietly.

"I should say," Ramsey said, having to exert a strange sense of will to keep from going any closer to him. "You are the last person I expected to sneak through my window."

If possible, he seemed to still further. "You were expecting someone else to sneak into your bedroom?"

She clutched at the top of her towel. "Don't be ridiculous, of course not. What is unanticipated about this to you?"

"Our bond."

Bond? She blinked. "What are you talking about?"

"I was warned about forging a bond, but I thought I'd have to..." A pained expression twisted his face. "Mate first."

"Mate?" She scrunched her nose. "What an archaic word."

"It's the less crude option of what I wanted to say."

Her mind filled in the word he could have used, and she cleared her throat, unsure how to take the thrilling little zing that shot through her body. "Oh."

He jerked forward, grunting harshly. Jaw tight, he took a step back as though his feet were in something thick. "Definitely did not expect this," he said between clenched teeth.

Ramsey clutched the towel tighter. "What's happening?"

"I'm half-Ruthenian."

"I know a full-blooded Ruthenian, and this doesn't happen to her."

He gripped the edge of the window frame. "The bonding is different for every couple, therefore not spoken of in any great detail. My father told me it exists and may be something I'd have to deal with, since he forged one with my mother. Apparently, like Gen-Heir talents, bonding types can be hereditary, but still an unknown as for how it'll behave."

"And you think we have this bonding?" Ramsey asked carefully.

"I can't understand how, but yes." He gripped the frame until his knuckles turned white and she feared he'd crack the wood. "Give me a minute."

So many questions filtered through her mind, from his mysterious presence in her bedroom, to how, after not having seen each other for five years, could they be bonded in any manner? She ignored them all and inched closer to the dresser. "Can I get dressed while you do whatever it is you need to do?"

"Please."

Ramsey pulled a long cotton nightgown from a middle drawer, and yanked her robe off a hook on the way back to the bathroom. She dressed quickly, and finished braiding her hair. When she emerged, Caidon sat in a rocking chair in front of the window, his hands braced on his knees, intense concentration pinching his handsome features. After a quick glance around, she decided to sit on the edge of her bed.

"Why are you here?" she asked. "Why did you sneak into my room?"

"I didn't want anyone to see me," he said, eyes closed. "And I'm here because you are in danger."

Frowning, she drew her feet underneath herself and settled more comfortably on the mound of jumbled bedding. "Danger? I've been alone for months without any issue."

She decided the idiotic attempt to secure her into a companionship agreement by her ex-promised wasn't worth mentioning. The proposition was humiliating but not a threat. Except perhaps to her ego. Fabric rustled, and seconds later, a folded piece of paper extended from his fingers. Ramsey leaned over and plucked the sheet free. He didn't so much as twitch while she scanned the document.

Her heart kicked a hard thump in her chest, and she took a slow breath. "Is this real?"

"Very."

Slowly, she lowered the creased page to her lap and pressed her palms into the soft mattress. The orders held multiple implications. "This was given to you? To carry out as an assignment?"

"Yes," he answered without any hesitation.

Ramsey took some comfort in his choosing not to lie. "The not so pleasant work for the FIO that you do, you are an assassin?"

He inclined his head, his gaze meeting hers from the slightly bowed position. "Did you mean what you said that night so many years ago?"

I wouldn't think less of you… Ramsey drew her knees up and wrapped her arms around her legs. Resting her chin on her knees, she ignored the crinkle of the paper and stared at Caidon. Pensive. Expectant. Nervous. All things he didn't hide, though she figured he probably could have if he chose to. Once again, he opted not to allow any lies between them. A curious flare burst in her chest, and the tug from earlier returned, no less subtle and almost sending her tumbling from the bed. He was there, palm pressed to her shoulder, stopping her mid-lurch.

His face appeared in her field of sight, searching. "Okay?"

She nodded and relaxed back. "Yes. What's going on? What was that?"

"The bond. I felt it that time, though, from your end. We'll have to learn this thing so one of us doesn't meet an untimely end by surprising us all the time."

"This will happen forever?" she asked, eyes wide. "I mean, what is going on?"

"I already told you, I don't know much. A mating bond between couples is unique, and my father wouldn't tell me anything more than to be careful who I chose to take to my bed. Very careful."

Ramsey scooted back, confused by his words and flustered by his nearness. The enticing scent of leather, smoke, and sandalwood had her almost forgetting she needed to concentrate. "This could happen to you with anyone?"

He thrust both hands into his hair and turned from

her. "I don't know. I didn't grow up in my father's land, and like I said, he wasn't very forthcoming with information."

Pursing her lips, she tapped a finger to her chin. "Information. I can get that tomorrow. We'll figure out what's happening between us later. Help me understand who would want you to kill me? And why use you?"

"They don't know about that night almost six years ago," he said quietly, returning to the safety of the rocking chair.

Ramsey swallowed, her heart rate kicking again. "You would have then? Followed the order?"

"No. Again, they don't know anything about me." He didn't expand further.

"Who are they?"

He shrugged. "I have no idea. Ryan Voklane thinks maybe a group called the V Alliance. Or, could be someone acting alone with strong contacts in the FIO."

Ramsey drew her legs up once more, and bounced her chin on her knees. "Did Guardian Voklane have any suspects?"

"One." He took a deep breath and Ramsey knew, deep down, she wasn't going to like his answer. "Joel Blackbain."

"Jonathon told me he'd managed to escape." The anxiety she'd been expecting never arose. Instead, she stared at Caidon, finding with him in the room fear didn't quite fit.

"Yes, they suspect. And he'd have reason to want you dead."

Ramsey thought back to the vile, hate-filled, venom-spewing man who'd been dragged away with a guilty verdict at his accusation hearing. A shudder ran through her at all the things he'd promised to inflict on her. Dead or alive, he'd said it mattered not. "Perhaps if prison changed him, yes. Otherwise, I think he'd prefer me delivered before him. Very much alive. Joel Blackbain... he's not a good person."

"Maybe now that he's free, your death would suffice his need for revenge."

"I have no idea how a madman thinks." She hugged her knees tighter. "Is that why you're here? To warn me?"

He relaxed back in the chair and sent it rocking. The wood groaned and squeaked under his weight. "Not exactly. But if I were, would you listen?"

"Yes, but it wouldn't do me much good since joining my brother in Italyssa would be my best option, and right now, I'm stuck here."

"Why?"

"Six months ago, Jonathon adopted an orphan he rescued from a crime scene. The boy's father had intended to sell him to a trafficker and had managed to have all records of the child erased. Parker still doesn't exist, according to Sziveria, except for in his late mother's employment records. Until I have paperwork for him, he can't leave," she explained, rubbing her forehead at the familiar ache her nephew's situation caused. "Securing documentation for him is proving more difficult than anticipated."

The rocking chair fell silent. "He's here now? This child?"

Ramsey nodded. "Yes, sleeping in the next room over. For now, anyway."

"Another surprising problem," he muttered, rising.

"What is the reason you came, if not to kill me or warn me instead?"

He glanced at her, his mouth twisted in annoyance. "You know I could never harm you."

Ramsey dropped her legs back to the bed and shifted, following his progress across her spacious room from her position in the middle of the bed. "Actually, I knew you for only a couple hours, one night, years ago. I know nothing about you."

He stopped at her desk, picked up a small porcelain figurine, inspected it for a moment before placing it back in the exact same position and moving on to something else. "And yet, you waited."

A truth she couldn't deny and a reason she didn't dare to put a voice to. Since he'd somehow, beyond all reason, *felt* her earlier emotional pull, Ramsey carefully suppressed what she couldn't afford him to know. Not exactly a lie, she convinced herself, more an omission of reaction.

Leisurely he set another knickknack on a shelf above her desk filled with silly little trinkets. "What if I were to tell you I've come to collect on that promise?"

Ramsey's heart did a hard flip in her chest. She swallowed against the tide of excitement laced with nervousness. Oh, shoot, she grimaced at the trickle of longing she couldn't hide. This time, however, she didn't launch toward him, nor did he to her. The only hint he *might* have felt anything was the quirk of his brow. She definitely needed to learn about whatever was happening between them.

"And if I've changed my mind?" she asked after a deep breath.

He propped himself against her desk, crossing his

ankles and bracing on his palms. "I would never force you into anything."

Good to know. Even better to know he meant the words. The truth somehow reverberated through her, a soft flutter warming her stomach.

"Have you?" he asked. When she didn't answer right away, he elaborated, "Changed your mind?"

She shook her head. "Is that foolish?"

He reached into his jacket and pulled out another folded sheet. "It's just a year. I promise I'll keep you safe."

Disappointment filled her. Slowly, she scooted off the bed. "That's why you're here, isn't it? Just to keep me safe."

He turned, pushing things around on her desk until he found a pen. "Mostly, yes. There are things in my life, places I go, things I have to do, that I'd rather spare you from."

"Now, I've become part of them."

"Yes."

An apology almost left her. However, she hadn't done anything wrong. Not that she knew of, and she certainly hadn't asked him to be her noble hero. "I'll be okay, you know. My brother can take care of me, and he's made powerful friends."

He glanced over his shoulder while his hands smoothed the paper open on her desk. "Will you go live with these powerful friends whenever your brother is away from home for more than a day? Will they teach you what to watch for to make sure you aren't being followed or have a scope sighted on you? Will they go with you when you leave the house to ensure no one can walk off with you?"

"And you're going to do this?" she asked, waving her hand around. "Follow me around like some guard dog? Don't you have a job to do? An important one? With a master guardian rank attached to it?"

He leaned forward until he was eye-level with her, the faint lamplight catching on the vivid green of his irises. "Yes, and guess whose master guardian I'm going to be?"

RAMSEY HAD ALWAYS FIGURED IF SHE MARRIED, THE EVENT would be similar to her first promise ceremony. A pretty dress, friends, family, food, and merriment. Love. Only things seemed to be reversed. She'd had the romantic ceremony and no contract. Now she had a contract and no ceremony. The love part... well, maybe. Someday. If they had the time to make the seed of emotion grow into something beautiful.

She stared at the rough, scratched words Caidon had scrawled before leaving her alone to make her decision. He had told her either way, he'd be staying. At least until she decided or found another, safer place to live while she waited for Jonathon to return. Her fingers brushed the corners of the paper as she read the terms. One year, written in numerical form in the space provided with one stipulation. Wherever he went, she accompanied.

Ramsey glanced at the small world map tacked on the wall below her shelves. So much unknown, uninhabitable, yet so much still to be seen. Cultures she'd only read about. She brushed a finger along a jagged section of coast along Thanzia, wondering if the water was ever warm in the Sea of Italyssa like the stories she'd heard. The rich and diverse culture of Vativarsa, where the women were so beautiful men were known to never leave after venturing to their shores. Or the proud and rigidly structured society of Ruthenia, where part of Caidon's ancestry lived.

Her attention shifted back to the single year he'd allowed them. Chewing on her lip, she considered adding an accompanying zero. No way would a year be enough. Not to discover the complicated man she had a feeling he was or the broad world they'd traverse in their short time together. A decade probably wouldn't be enough. But she didn't have anything to offer except following him around like a puppy. If he'd wanted more time with her, he'd have put in a different number. Sighing, she lifted the tip of the pen and left the number alone.

At the bottom, Ramsey signed her name with a flourish. There. She was officially his. For a year, anyway.

When Caidon didn't return to her room for an answer or to tell her his plans for the night, she figured he'd taken her offer seriously to use Jonathon's room. The housekeeper that came three days a week had kept the room clean, and Ramsey certainly wasn't ready to share her space yet.

She doused her light and crawled into cold sheets, and stared at the ceiling. Puffing air through her cheeks, she bounced her arms on the fluffy down of her comforter. Sleep eluded her except for in small doses, her mind too full. When the soft gray of dawn slowly glowed in her room, she gave up. Once the sun fully broke the horizon, Parker would be up and ready to go. After dressing in a long cream, silk gown with flowers and a vibrant blue sash around the waist, she went downstairs to start breakfast.

Slipping into an apron, she began her morning ritual. Crayons set out on the dining room table with clean sheets of letter practicing, followed by preparing coffee and setting out everything she'd need to cook a simple breakfast. The squeal of a child had her rushing from the kitchen minutes later. Caidon bounded down the stairs with Parker hanging upside down, his head bumping the center of Caidon's stomach.

"This urchin jumped on me," Caidon proclaimed, flipping Parker and setting him on the ground in an unbroken swoosh of motion. "And smacked my face. Do you know why?"

Parker laughed and jumped, almost falling. "Oh, oh! Again! Do it again!"

"No, why?" she asked.

Parker continued to hop, arms stretched high above his head, his fingers bunching in the rumbled fabric of Caidon's shirt. "Because I wasn't Jonathon, but I was in his bed, and that apparently was bad enough to warrant a slap."

His eyes twinkled while he explained torment at the hands of a three-year-old in complete seriousness. Ramsey stared, wondering what the protocol for this was. An apology? A faint red mark still marred his cheek, where a tiny hand had landed with enough force to leave evidence. Parker's insistence changed from excited to annoyed. He jumped and huffed out a whine.

Caidon batted the child's hands away. "Stop that."

Realizing there was no more fun to be had, Parker sat on the floor and wailed. Ramsey grimaced as embarrassment flamed her cheeks. She reached for Parker, and Caidon grasped her upper arm mid-stride, forcing her to change direction away from her screaming nephew.

"Leave him. He'll be fine."

"But—"

"No. He's having a tantrum, it'll end soon enough," he said, guiding her back into the kitchen.

Caidon's explanation finally filtered through her sleep-deprived brain, and she sagged into a seat. "He came into the bedroom with you this morning?"

"Yes."

"Shoot," she whispered. "He's been checking Jonathon's room every day, expecting him home. He must have been so excited when he saw you."

Caidon shrugged and opened cupboards. "He's a kid, they're resilient, he'll be fine. He dealt with his disappointment." He pointed at the spot on his face. "See?"

Ramsey glared in irritation. "And you are an expert on children?"

Having found a coffee cup, he set it on the counter next to the stove and held up a hand with his thumb tucked in. "Four sisters. Four. I was almost eleven when the first of the hellion siblings arrived. The youngest was two when I left home."

Rising, Ramsey smoothed her hand down the front of her apron. While she didn't need to explain anything to him, she found herself bristling in her own defense. "Parker has been through a lot, and he's not finished yet. When I hand him off to my brother, he'll have to adjust yet again. I try to limit his stress."

"And that's admirable," Caidon said, spooning sugar into an empty cup. "But there's a difference between safety and allowing him to be a brat. No one likes a brat. Letting him handle his disappointment at my no is okay."

As if to prove his point, Parker walked in, rubbing at his puffy eyes. "I'm hungry."

"Yeah?" Caidon asked, glancing over his shoulder. "Me too. What are you going to make us?"

Parker's hands froze, bunched on his cheeks. "I can cook something?"

Ramsey waved her hands. "No, no, no, absolutely not. Uncle Caidon was playing. I'm making breakfast, same as every morning, while you work on your letters."

He groaned and stomped his foot. "No."

Ramsey clenched her jaw and gave him her best you-will-mind-or-else stare. He grunted, slapped at the air, but climbed onto a chair without another argument. Ha! Point for her. Then she sighed at having to keep score to help make herself feel more in control of a situation she was woefully inadequate to still be taking on. No, she thought with a jaded twist of her lips, an assassin appeared more capable of taking care of her charge. The weight of failure threatened to pull her under again, a constant clawing shadow she fought more often than not lately.

Caidon reached for the coffee, glancing over his shoulder. "Uncle Caidon?"

Ramsey shrugged and went to the dry storage cabinet for eggs and bread. "I signed the contract, so that makes you family now."

He tensed, the action so fleeting she wondered if she'd imagine it, as he continued to pour his coffee. "Did you make any changes or additions?"

Ramsey swallowed, slowly setting ingredients on the counter. "No."

"You were okay with everything? With traveling with me? It won't be an easy life." He leaned against the counter and blew softly into the steaming liquid.

She forced herself not to react to the sense of relief. He hadn't changed his mind, hadn't decided a life dragging her around the inhabited world would over-complicate things. "I've never been outside of Haven City."

"You will see more than you wish to," he said softly as he passed her on the way to the table.

Ramsey paused halfway to cracking an egg on the edge of the counter. "Surely the world isn't filled with nothing but horror?"

"No," he said, sitting in the chair next to Parker. "There are many amazing sites to see. Waterfalls, lush forests so thick with green you can get lost thirty steps in. Great expanses of mountains made of nothing but sand. Old wonders, so old beyond the cataclysm, the cultures don't know anything about them other than they still stand. A testament to the ingenuity of humanity and our inability to give up our place on this planet."

"And yet?" she asked, returning to the breakfast preparations.

He shrugged and pushed the handle of the coffee cup back and forth between his thumb and index finger. "There is a lot of bad. A lot of… evil. The land between Imperial Qu'In and Vativarsa is occupied by a tribal people so violent traversing by land is impossible. The borders of both countries are heavily fortified, and yet the tribes are persistent in their raids and often succeed. Many areas bordering UZ's have this same problem."

Curious and a little awed, not having read any news of such civilizations, she held a bowl in her arms and turned so she could see him while working. "People living in the Uninhabited Zones? Thriving there?"

"More they are people who haven't been formally recognized. So, while they have a land, a country even if you will, a name for themselves, no one will give them the honor of a distinct nation, or people."

"Why?"

"Usually because they are living a way of life many countries have left behind."

Ramsey frowned. "They exist as if the primal years are still happening?"

"They never left them," Caidon confirmed. "And they have no desire to move into a more civilized way of life, having existed on blood and violence for centuries."

"And Sziveria offers assistance to nations who skirmish with these tribes?" The pot clattered on the cast iron stove top as she situated it over a heating burner.

"Depends on the interests, both political and economical."

Ramsey sighed at the sudden knot in her stomach. She dumped small slices of fruit into the batter and tried to beat the frustration away. "Power and money, ever reasons to send men to their deaths."

"Or kill for it," he said quietly.

The soft rattle of Parker dropping a crayon made Ramsey shake her head and bite back any further conversation on the topic. "I hope you like fried fruit bread."

"I love fwied fwoot bwead!" Parker proclaimed, another crayon smacking to the table. "My favorite."

When Caidon didn't answer, Ramsey looked over her shoulder. A thin sheen of oil sizzled in the pan. He stared at her, head tilted, his handsome face drawn in concentration. Oh, summer sun, she could stare at him all day. Ramsey found herself transfixed. Reality slammed home. Caidon Survaine sat at her dining room table. In her house. As her husband. Oil popped, and she quickly looked away, forcing herself to breathe. Carefully, she controlled her thoughts, not wanting the odd thread between them to flare to life.

"After we eat, I need to go to the bookstore," Ramsey said, slowly dropping a spoonful of batter into the pan.

"Okay," Caidon said. "How do you normally handle going somewhere? I didn't see a carriage house, and the Ariot isn't big enough for all of us."

"I radio a service to pick us up. The Ariot isn't for our personal use, it belongs to HCES, for Jonathon to drive when he's on duty." She flipped the small cakes over. "We couldn't afford one for ourselves, and I don't know how to drive one anyway."

"Your brother never taught you?" he asked curiously.

The sweet scent of sugar and fruit filled the air. "No, because we'll never own one, so why bother?"

"In case of an emergency?"

Ramsey shrugged and plated everyone's meals. "If something happened here to make Jonathon incapacitated, chances are I would be as well."

A calculated gleam narrowed his eyes as she set the

plate before him. "You have an answer for everything, don't you?"

Parker clapped in delight. "Hooray, my favorite!"

"Probably," she answered and took her seat across from Caidon. Then she cast him a playful smile. "Too bad you're stuck with me now."

4

Caidon took in the poorly lit interior of Mr. Harold's Book Emporium. The odd, musky quality of air that filled any bookstore, regardless of location, swirled with dust motes. The ivory of Ramsey's skirt disappeared as she rounded one of the aisles of bookshelves, ushering an excited Parker to the Children's Corner. An attended area for kids to safely remain while their parents browsed the three floors' worth of books.

Caidon waited near the front desk, where a young man with a headful of thick, bright red curls seemed to want to crawl into the novel clutched in both his hands. The clerk had been eager to see Ramsey, but had blanched when Caidon stepped in behind her. Usually, Caidon controlled his expressions better. This time, he must have failed. Not good. Feelings, especially ones strong enough to be seen by others, weren't something he could afford.

This morning had thrown him. A little boy, an innocent life, a nephew he was now as responsible for as the wife who'd been waiting downstairs. Where she'd fed him. The whole domesticity of it all left him off balance.

The soft fall of booted feet announced Ramsey's return before she appeared down a wide aisle. She smiled at him, and his chest constricted. Her attention shifted to the man behind the counter, and Caidon had to shove away the rise of jealousy.

"Toby," Ramsey greeted, looping her arm around Caidon's, "where would we find a book on Ruthenian mate bonding?"

Toby's skin flushed to rival his hair color. "Um, either in the foreign books upstairs or…" He pressed a fist to his mouth and cleared his throat. "You know."

A long sigh left Ramsey. "I'm not even going to bother with upstairs. Why do I always end up in the lusty book section?" she muttered to herself.

Caidon raised a brow. "The what?"

Her hand slid down to wind around his. Warmth seeped up his arm. She tugged. "Come on, it's this way. Thank you, Toby."

He tried not to notice how right her hand felt in his or how walking next to her felt natural. A red curtain hung from the entry Ramsey walked toward. She pushed the thick fabric to the side, revealing a room full of browsing patrons. No one spoke or even acknowledged their presence as they passed by.

"Do you read Ruthenian?" Ramsey asked, pulling him deeper into the room toward a sign hanging from the ceiling that read *Reference*.

"I can read in several languages." A lewd title caught his attention, and he almost stopped in his tracks.

She led them to what he'd gathered was the only

part of the room not occupied by anyone. The small oasis seemed almost private. An alcove created by shelving arrangements. "Oh good, that's good. I will look on this side for anything written in Sziverian, you look over on that case in the foreign titles."

Several shelves later, he kept from tossing a useless, near-pornographic title across the room in his frustration. If his father had bothered to teach him more, they wouldn't be searching through inappropriate material to find out information about something in his lineage. Ramsey sat on the floor with books piled around her. She flipped through pages, engrossed, her head turning left while she rotated a book to the right. An elegant, black brow rose then she snorted and tossed the book over her shoulder, muttering something under her breath. The vivid gold title gleamed along a crimson-bound book, *Positions to Master Her Pleasure*. Clearly, the contents hadn't appealed to her. Nothing thrummed along their delicate mating bond, not like last night.

Caidon turned his back to her, not wanting to dwell on the night before. How her desire floated on a thin thread into him, settling in his nerves, igniting something primal. At one point, she'd attempted to forge a stronger connection, though he didn't think she was aware of the endeavor. Other emotions hadn't filtered between them. Not yet, anyway. If Caidon were careful, perhaps they never would.

A faint pulse of heat zipped through his veins, accelerating his heart and heightening his awareness. He spun and stared down at Ramsey. Her cheeks were flushed, and she slowly turned a page, squirming slightly. Caidon leaned down and snatched the thin book from her. She pressed her hands into her thighs and stared up at him, pupils so dilated they nearly took over the violet of her eyes.

Curious at how this book could have excited her where the other had failed, he flipped the cover over. *A Woman's Guide to Safe Indulgences.* He opened to a random page and almost dropped the book at a graphic depiction of a nude woman sitting over a man's face. A turn of the page revealed detailed instructions for the partner. Another page explained the advantages of mutual masturbation, providing an artfully expressed example. Every page told, in words or pictures, how to have a safe sexual experience, without being exposed to the deadly human rabies syndrome virus by not engaging in actual sex.

The publication date revealed the first edition to have been printed shortly after the initial outbreak over sixty years ago. Before contracts had become normal and people needed *something* to help them feel in control of their sexuality. Now, short-term marriage contracts kept people in safe relationships, free to explore their boundaries. However, the appeal to discover pleasures at the hands of another for a quick moment in time continued to entice some. Prostitution still thrived. Affairs still occurred. And HRS still plagued the inhabited world. Temptation would always remain. He could appreciate a book that allowed a relatively safe method for a woman to explore her horizons. Found it interesting and a whole lot arousing, Ramsey did too. Looking up, he met her curious stare.

"You like this?" he asked softly, turning the book to face her.

"I didn't know... about some of the things in there," she said in a near whisper. Her chest moved in rapid, shallow breaths. "I like the thought of doing them with you."

A pulse moved through him, like warm honey, sweet and coating. He gasped and settled his weight to keep from moving closer to her. Suspicion welled inside him at the calculating gleam in her gaze. He bit his tongue to keep in a sharp curse. Sweat beaded along his hairline and across his back. The woman was dangerous to his razor-thin self-control. By the way she bit her lip, she knew as much.

"We need to find that book," he said between clenched teeth.

She twisted and picked up two titles, one in each hand. Holding them up, she looked between them. "I found two choices. We have either, *The Female's Territory: The Curious Bonding of Ruthenian Couples for Life. A Scientific Inquiry* or *Neither Lust nor Love: The Lie of a Ruthenian's Sexual-Bondage Examined.*"

Caidon recoiled and twisted his face in disgust at the second one. "We are not bound to our sexual appetites."

Ramsey titled her head. "No?" She flipped the book around. "What about love? According to this book, that is a lie in your relationships, too."

"My parents are very much in love, and they aren't living a lie."

She considered both books. "One is written by a man from Westica. A scientist who has made it his life's work to study the marriage rituals of the inhabited world cultures. And the other, also by a man. It's his only publication though."

"I bet he was turned away by a Ruthenian woman because she couldn't form a bond with him. It's very important from my understanding," Caidon explained, proud of himself for not reaching across the short distance to snatch another book away.

A feminine hum accompanied the turning of pages. "Yes, it seems without the bond, conception is rare, if not impossible, for a Ruthenian female."

"Which book revealed that?"

"*The Female's Territory*," she answered. "It appears to be scientific and logical. Do you think it'll help us?"

"More than a spurned lover's diatribe, I'm sure."

Ramsey made no move to leave the floor, once again observing him in a manner that he began to fear meant mischief. "Are you sure about the bond not being more of a bondage situation for you?"

Caidon swallowed against a sudden nervous lump in his throat. What was she up to? And how did a harmless young woman reduce him to a level of uncertainty he'd never experienced before? "Would it matter? Our contract is signed and filed now."

She rose from the floor in a sensual unfolding of limbs and female curves. A glint of determination shone in her eyes and tensed her jaw. "Perhaps," she said in a husky tone, "when I learn you want me, I'd like to know you find me desirable, and it's not simply some biological urge you can't control."

The sticky sweetness crept through his veins again. A warm flow of feminine power. She watched him closely, and Caidon fought to pull a solid breath. The female's territory indeed. "What are you doing?"

On a look of curiosity, she raised the *Neither Lust nor Love* book and moved it back and forth. "Maybe we should get this one, too. For arguments sake."

Caidon closed his eyes, searched deep, and slowly

forced the odd sensation away. Ramsey still watched him carefully when he regarded her once more. "Look, I know we don't know what the bond means or how it works yet, but how I feel about you, or how I may feel about you in the future, won't be involuntary for either of us. Okay?"

Doubt shone in her eyes, and turned her mouth, but she nodded. "I'm not sure how I feel about being able to… influence you. That's what it's like, isn't it?"

Caidon looked around to make sure no one was listening. The reference section continued to keep them hidden, and so far, none of the other patrons had sought out the nook. "I wouldn't say influence." He considered the awareness she stirred in him without a touch. "More an impression of your willingness."

"My willingness," she said, piqued.

"You asked," he reminded her. "And I answered. Do you feel anything from me?"

"Not emotions. It's more like a pull." She transferred the books to one hand. With a fist to her chest, she pretended to tug on something. "Like a magnet yanking me to you."

"And you can control this?"

She shook her head. "I don't think control, but it appears to happen when I'm…" She glanced at the book he still held and licked her lips. Her cheeks flamed. "Aroused."

The single word caused a brush, like a breeze along his skin, and he focused on the sensation. How peculiar. "You think of something that excites you, and it affects me?"

"I hope one of these books provides some sort of answer, but yes. It seems I can manipulate *something* between us if I focus my thoughts in a specific manner," she agreed, not meeting his stare.

By the deepened flush on her cheeks and neck, he knew the concession had cost her. "I appreciate your honesty."

She took a deep breath and turned. "You haven't lied to me, so I owe you the same courtesy."

Caidon went to set the woman's guide down, but before he could, Ramsey plucked it from his hold and added it to her growing collection. The thought of her being forward enough to do any of the suggestions in the book left his pants fitting much too tight. They hadn't discussed the perimeters of their marriage. He hadn't wanted to pressure her. Caidon had also learned to live by the motto he couldn't miss what he didn't know. And right now, he didn't know Ramsey beyond a passionate kiss so many years ago. He couldn't imagine intimacy doing more than creating all sorts of issues he didn't want to deal with.

Even now, he struggled not to haul her up against the nearest secluded wall and find out *how* excited the book and thoughts of him had really made her. How much worse would his control be if he *knew*? Learned precisely how she felt under his fingers, how she responded to his touch. He flexed his hands to help ease some tension. No. He couldn't afford the distraction she was sure to cause. Or the cost to her when she realized she couldn't see past the killer she'd married.

THE SCENT OF FRIED HERB PORK, SALT AND PEPPER potatoes, and seasoned baked vegetables floated in the air. Caidon stared down at the plate Ramsey had once again placed before him, neatly arranged and delicious looking. In a seat beside Ramsey, Parker ignored his fork in favor of his fingers, popping a small chunk of meat into his mouth. The chiding Ramsey gave fell on deaf little ears. Caidon took a deep breath, wondering at the equal parts panic and contentment that fought within him.

"Is something wrong?" Ramsey asked when she noticed he wasn't eating.

Caidon picked up his fork and shook his head. "No. It's just been a long time since I've tasted something from home."

"Your mother cooked?"

"Yes, my father did too, whenever he missed Ruthenia." He smiled at old memories. "In the end, we had a good mix of two cultures at most meals."

Another attempt to get Parker to use his utensil failed. The boy giggled and poked a finger into a soft potato piece. Caidon clenched his jaw to keep from laughing. Ramsey heaved a sigh and then turned her attention back to Caidon.

"Were you satisfied with my brother's security around the house?" she asked.

"Everything but the key you said you'd never leave out again."

Ramsey smiled. "He'll be happy to know that. And I'm guessing my key is how you managed to get in undetected last night?"

"I didn't replace it," Caidon said with a small smile. "Have you heard from your brother today?"

Her gaze shifted to the doorway. Any thread of amusement faded from her pretty face. "No, and I tried radioing before I started dinner. Nothing. I'm worried.

The last time I went days without hearing from him, he'd been shot."

The concern she displayed spread to him. Caidon knew all too well how fragile a human was, how easily one could be snuffed from existence. What would she do if something had happened to Jonathon? What would he do? He glanced over at Parker, innocent and oblivious to the distressed adults. Without question, he knew Ramsey wouldn't give up the boy. Nor could he ask that of her. Her brother had made him a Hunter, and Ramsey would honor the promise. Caidon would as well, regardless of the cost. He wanted to reach across the distance and touch her in reassurance, but he had nothing to offer. Promising that Jonathon was okay might be a lie. Since he'd never offered comfort before, he wasn't sure how.

A situation being entirely out of his control left him troubled. Reminding him that depending on others, and being depended upon, was something he'd avoided for a reason. Now, for a year at least, he had to provide for this small family. And as he lifted his focus, his gaze connecting with Ramsey's still worried one, he wondered if a year would be long enough.

"Voklane told me the Blackbain's are still in Italyssa with him. I can tell Ryan what's going on and see if he can learn anything. Not being able to reach a guardian team leader isn't a good thing," Caidon said.

Ramsey pushed food around on her plate. "Thank you. If I can't reach him tomorrow, I may ask you to."

"There is no may," he said. "The FIO can't lose contact with a guardian."

"Does your family live in Haven City?"

The question took him by surprise. "Yes, we lived in an apartment outside Old City Ruins."

"Do they still live there?"

He shrugged. "As far as I know."

Disbelief widened her eyes. "You don't know?"

"I haven't spoken to them since I was given my ranking and assignment." He gathered the rest of his food into one neat pile in the center of his plate. "Safer that way."

The stricken look on her face made his chest constrict. She finally seemed to realize what life with him would be like, what she'd have to give up. "It's only for a year," he assured her quietly.

"No one should live without their family," she whispered, her hand reaching the short distance across the table to wrap around his wrist. "I'm sure they'd agree, they'd rather take the chance than hurt not knowing."

The warmth of her touch spread across his arm, along with the realization she hadn't been upset for herself. But for him. He swallowed and shifted until his hand wrapped around hers. "I'd rather they not know than be targeted because I missed them too much."

"Thank goodness my brother never felt that way," she said, her fingers wrapping tightly around his.

"He doesn't kill people," Caidon felt the need to quietly point out.

Sadness reflected in her eyes, and turned down her mouth. "Nope. He only sends them, or their family member, to prison. A vendetta need not have such a powerful reason to rise in the heart of someone who would become an enemy."

No, he supposed not, especially considering she

made a fierce adversary by simply testifying against a man. "I'm going to keep you safe."

"I know. And I didn't even kill anyone," she said with a flippant shrug, pulling her hand free. "You don't need to hide from your family anymore. Contacting them, at least now, won't put them in any greater danger than just being related to you."

"All done!" Parker said with a clap. "Bath time now! With the bubbles."

Ramsey pushed away from the table and then hesitated. Caidon gathered the plates together. "I'll take care of the kitchen. You take care of the kid."

She laughed. "All right, but we need to talk after he's in bed. I finished one of the books while you were scrutinizing the house from the attic to the greenhouse."

And why did that information both excite and terrify him?

5

THE LUSH WARMTH OF THE GREENHOUSE WRAPPED RAMSEY in a comforting balm of muggy earth scented air. A bedroom for the upcoming conversation was too intimate. Too tempting. The room she'd been propositioned in left her feeling too vulnerable. The greenhouse was her domain, her safe haven, so here was where she'd tell Caidon what she'd been able to learn about the bond forming between them.

Her husband had revealed a lot at dinner. Probably more than he'd wished to. Already, she schemed for a way to get him to his family. She couldn't imagine having to make a decision that cut off the ability to see the people who loved you most. At some point, probably the moment Parker could legally travel, Caidon would have them on a ship bound for Italyssa and then wherever Sziveria needed to send her guardian. No way would she allow Caidon to go on another mission without seeing his family.

At the squeak of hinges, Ramsey straightened her back to stifle the fluttering in her belly. Somehow, she managed not to fidget. She took a long, calming breath and forced herself to focus on the objective. Allowing them both to be aware of the very real predicament they found themselves in. Strength and masculine power flowed from every inch of him as he strode from the shadows into the shallow light of the hanging lamp she'd lit behind the bench. Her breath caught, somewhere between wonder that he was *hers* and the curiosity of how it must feel to have such confidence.

Ramsey swallowed and forced all emotion away. She didn't want to influence him even a little. Not right now, anyway. He hesitated when he spotted how close they'd have to sit, and Ramsey scooted to make more room for his much larger frame. His fingers tapped along his thighs, and he glanced around, apparently not satisfied with the minuscule distance she'd provided. He disappeared into the shadows and then returned with a chair in hand. Disappointed, she sighed.

"I don't bite," she said.

"Maybe I do." A thrill zipped through her body, going deeper as he brushed his fingers along her hand clenched in her skirt. "And neither of us is ready for that. Not yet."

Implying perhaps someday, they would be. "I don't want a sterile marriage."

A dim smile crossed his lips. "Isn't the guy supposed to say that?"

Frustrated, she clenched her skirt tighter. "I'm serious. But…"

"But the bond between us," he guessed.

In the darkness, his hair was the same shade as the inky shadows swallowing all form and light behind him. The hard lines of his face were all the harsher in the weak glow, and the urge to trace them, memorize each curve had her perching on the edge of the seat. Rough growth along his jaw and cheeks from not having shaved since morning made her lose the battle, too captivated by the promise of his textures. She touched from his temple to his jaw. Shocked when he stilled and let her.

"If I were Ruthenian," she murmured, leaning closer, caressing under his chin to the strong cords of his neck, where his pulse beat a solid rhythm underneath her touch, "you'd be able to know how I was feeling right now. Like a sympath. The author surmised the mate-bond is what launched the genetic ability. A rare variant in offspring that isn't tied to a bond, except for that of all humanity. You will miss out on so much if you don't shut down the start of our connection."

He closed his eyes, bracing his palms on the chair arms. "Assuming I could figure out how to, why would I?"

"Because if you don't take a Ruthenian as your mate, you will give up a lot." The admission cost her. A small pain bloomed in her chest. "Regardless of how much time we're together, anything forged between us would be a shadow of what you could have, what you could experience."

The chair groaned under his weight as he leaned away from her. "I will never go to Ruthenia to look for a spouse. I'm Sziverian, a guardian of this nation. I won't be missing anything, because I won't know any different." His piercing, emerald gaze caught her. Held. The air around her thickened until she could barely breathe. "And I don't want anyone else."

She swallowed and rubbed damp palms on her thighs. "Okay."

"Tell me what you've learned."

The request wasn't a demand but an encouragement steeped in interest. Ramsey could relate. She couldn't read the pages of the scientific inquiry fast enough. She licked her lips and focused on the dark path of packed earth beneath her feet.

"While the bond is unique, as you were told, it's still genetic in nature. However, your parents bonded, you and I will as well. It's unlikely any children we produce will carry the genome, though," she said.

He tilted his head and regarded her. "Why is that?"

Ramsey shrugged. "He wasn't sure, but he guessed by the third generation, the dilution of the pure Ruthenian heritage was likely the culprit. Then again, based on lore, legend, or fact, depending on who you spoke to, all Gen-Heirs can trace their family line back to Ruthenia. At what point the ability is lost to physically bond with a partner is speculation. Not many couples outside of Ruthenia that he found were willing to discuss something they perceived as very personal."

"And in Ruthenia, it's so common why wouldn't anyone talk about it?" he surmised.

"Correct." She shimmied, straightening her spine for courage. "With two Ruthenians, they both bring something into the partnership. If he can sense emotions with his connection, then she will be able to as well. If she transfer's thoughts, he can too. The only one that doesn't go both ways appears to be tattoos, and that's with the beast master genome only. Whoever holds the more dominant beast master gene for that is the only one, the other partner loses their ink, but gains the dominants markings."

His brows rose at the information. "How interesting. And what's between us? How does it work?"

She rubbed her hands along her thighs again. "Well, it's a lot simpler. Vague emotions. Shouldn't be anything more than that."

"Vague? Nothing has been vague so far. I've known pretty much exactly how you're feeling at specific times."

"Yes, well," she said, ignoring the flare of heat across her cheeks all the way to her ears. "If things go further, you may get more, and I might be able to feel something from you, too."

He rubbed a knuckle under his chin. "Unless I somehow stop it from forming."

"Yes."

"Did the book say how?"

Ramsey shoved the hurt deep down, knowing him preventing any further linking between them was for the best. He deserved a better mate. One he could fully bond with and who would be a more equal match. Her usefulness was limited to cooking and, hopefully, the eventual pleasure she could provide.

Past experience had left her with enough knowledge to know she'd please him, even if she found sex somewhat of a disappointment. While she'd known her first time would be awful, all the other times she'd ventured into Tobyn's bed had been equally lacking. No matter what she did or didn't do, the result was always the same. A frustrated sense of unfulfillment. A bunch of huffing, sweat, and a satisfied man.

Then five years ago, a man had pushed her against a

wall, kissed her in a manner she'd never been kissed before, and brought her precariously close to *something* marvelous. All without more than his lips on hers and his hips pressed between their clothed bodies. Sex with Caidon would be *different*. She knew this for a fact. Every cell in her body agreed. Ramsey wanted to crawl onto his lap, meld her mouth to his and see if all that tight control was an act. See if he burned as hot as she did. If she chipped away at his resolve through the fine thread linking them together, she figured she'd succeed. But that would be wrong, and not him wanting her, but rather him giving in to an urge she forced.

Ramsey took a deep, steadying breath. She'd have him. She would. Just not tonight. "I can show you the chapter. I'm not sure. It didn't make sense to me, but I'm not Ruthenian."

Another reason to see his parents. His father was pure-blooded and should have told his son more than he had. Part of her wondered if he hadn't because he figured perhaps at half-blood, without another Ruthenian, the bond would be too weak to even notice. The book mentioned such as well.

"I do know," she said, "the female initiates and the male accepts or rejects. Keeps the female from being bound against her will. A tactic developed by necessity or on purpose by the first generation of Ruthenians, the author wasn't sure. No one in the country would give him access to the primal year's records."

"That is interesting." He relaxed further back in the chair, one leg stretching out toward her. "I wonder why the woman couldn't reject."

"Probably a dominance thing. From my understanding, if the legends are correct, Ruthenian is a nation built on the genes of engineered humans. The men were likely all extremely alpha."

"The women, too. From what my father says, Ruthenia doesn't have many submissive females."

"Still, a man can have a lot more mass over a woman and can make her do things she doesn't want." Ramsey closed her eyes against dark memories of just how much power a man could impose. She'd bore witness to the ravages of a man who didn't see a woman as something worth protecting. "I'm rather thankful for the insight of past scientists to leave the control to the woman, if such is the case."

"Will it become permanent, or is it something that I can reject at any time?"

Ramsey swallowed. She didn't really want to reveal the truth to him, afraid of the direction the knowledge would take them. Or rather, what she may have to give up. However, Caidon had made clear he'd not be in a marriage based on lies or deception. "Permanence is created by intimacy. Once it's forged completely, there is no going back."

His fingers drummed on the chair arm. "So, if we aren't intimate…"

Since she'd already made her feelings known on where she stood about their relationship, she remained silent, letting him work things out on his own.

"Are there any other changes after sex, besides the strength of our bond?" he asked.

"One." She cleared her throat and pushed her toe into the packed earth. "You'll know when I'm fertile."

"Ah. Yes. I remember hearing something about that." A small smile toyed at his lips. "Both blessing and curse. From what I recall of my parents, you'll be rather irresistible to me."

"The book said as much, too."

"Did the book tell you why?"

Ramsey tucked a curl behind her ear. "Something about Ruthenian women being able to reject the genetic material supplied by the men. The more he gives when she's fertile, the higher chance she'll accept."

"Such is not the case for Sziverian women." He offered another shallow smile. "The unions tend to lead to larger families."

Ramsey cleared her throat. "Yes, well, we'll have to figure something out, I suppose. A family isn't something I imagine you'll want just yet."

"What about you? What do you want?" he asked gently.

Ramsey glanced at the second floor, where Parker rested. "I think I'm okay with no kids for a while."

"I would say an ovulation bracelet like most women wear would work, but since I'll know your window personally, I don't know if you'll need one."

Excitement fluttered in her chest. She wished she could crawl into his head and know what he was thinking. "Maybe just to know when it's approaching, to be safer?"

He held his palms up. "That's up to you."

Deciding to test him, Ramsey narrowed her gaze and searched his face. "And would you be okay traveling around with a baby or two?"

Even in the faint light, his skin visibly paled. "No, it's not possible."

"I thought not. Perhaps you should begin looking at this situation as an *us*. *We* need to make decisions together since the outcome affects us both, not just one of us."

An expression she couldn't place shadowed across his face. He shifted and looked away from her. "I do everything alone."

Tenderness and compassion slid through her. Ramsey shifted from the bench to her knees before him, not caring about the dirt. She pressed her palms onto his thighs, unsurprised to find them strong and warm beneath the soft fabric of his pants. His fingers curled into the arms of the chair until his knuckles turned white.

"Do you want to remain alone?" she asked when his eyes finally met hers.

"Someone wants you dead. Whether I want to remain alone is irrelevant," he huffed.

Ramsey frowned and shoved upward, rising. "No, it's not. If my being with you is going to be some burden you shoulder, I'd rather take my chances here."

Since the death of her parents, and the shunning of society, Ramsey had been a duty to her brother. A little sister he couldn't break free from because she had nowhere else to go. No skills, no gifts or talents, nothing to help her make a way. She wouldn't be the same to a spouse. The year commitment would pass like water through her fingers and be nothing to him. Especially if he didn't have to worry about dragging her around.

"I said the wrong thing," he said, more as if to himself than to her. Then he let out a long breath and stood. "Life with you will not be lonely, boring, or any of things I've endured since I made the choice to become an assassin. And I think I will prefer the new life we will make."

"Really?" Ramsey asked, hating how pathetic her voice sounded.

He shifted forward, hesitated, and then took a step back. "Yes. But this," he motioned to the space between them, "is all new to me. I have no idea how to be a husband, or a good partner. I *will* say the wrong things. Often. But you will be safe."

What about loved? The question hovered in her mind, much too bold to be spoken. Instead, she nodded and offered a weak smile. "I think patience will be our key word."

"Patience," he said, testing the word. "Yes, patience will be good."

6

No scents of food or coffee greeted Caidon when he stepped from his room. After awakening for four days in the Hunter residence, he'd already become accustomed to Ramsey's easy routine. Only this morning, something was off. The strong impulse to get his handgun had him fisting his hands. With a kid in the house, he wouldn't risk a stray bullet. He was trained in hand combat. While he wasn't as quick as an interceptor, he didn't need to be since he'd likely never face one. The supernaturally fast Gen-Heir talent was so uncommon as to rarely be a concern in his line of work.

Creeping into the hall from Jonathon's room, he strained to discern any sound. Soft voices, one chiding and the other small and unhappy made him relax. At the top of the stairs, he froze, taking in Ramsey and Parker. Both were dressed, ready to go in front of the door. Ramsey even had a purse dangling from her forearm. A bright yellow number that somehow matched the short-sleeved, navy dress with little embroidered pale blue and yellow flowers. Caidon glanced down at his bare feet and lifted his toes.

"Are we going somewhere?" he called down.

Ramsey jerked her head up. "Yes. We'll walk to a café to get some food and then hail a cab."

"Where are we going?"

"You'll have to give the address. We're going to see your family," she stated as if it were a perfectly normal thing for them to do.

Caidon stiffened. "No."

She straightened her spine and lifted her chin. Defiance shone bright in her violet eyes. "Yes. I've thought a lot about this, and you deserve to see them, and they deserve to know you're safe and healthy."

Caidon shook his head and took a step back. "No. My father—"

"Will be glad to see his oldest son," she interrupted before he could finish the excuse, fire glinting in her beautiful gaze.

Parker hummed and spun in circles, oblivious to the tense air between the two adults. Caidon took a slow, centering breath and turned on his heel, heading back to the room to put on his shoes. He wouldn't win this battle. Maybe he'd get lucky, and his family wouldn't be home. After over five years, he wasn't sure what he'd say. His father knew the reason for his absence, but he was sure his mother didn't, and his father wouldn't have enlightened her.

He yanked on socks and boots, grabbed a light jacket for the still-cool morning, and took the stairs down at a rapid trot. Parker hopped from one thick plank of wood to another, his small hand clasped in Ramsey's, shoes now on his feet.

"Where we going again?" he asked between jumps.

"Where *are* we going? To visit Uncle Caidon's family," Ramsey answered with a patience Caidon admired.

Her gaze caught his, and he motioned for her to exit the house. He locked up after them and followed at a more leisurely pace behind, his attention constantly shifting to the quiet homes, the glittery shadows between them, and the slow mixture of Ariots and carriages easing down the street on the still frosty, brick road. Nothing seemed out of place, and no inner alarms sounded. Parker skipped alongside Ramsey, safely kept from the street on her right side. Once again, a startling fist tightened in his chest.

Mine, his heart whispered.

Liability, his mind countered.

He ignored them both, focusing instead on their surroundings and all the dangers she'd never thought of, had never needed to worry about. Since she was his to care for now, he'd teach her, but not today.

A chilly breeze gusted by, carrying the aroma of wood fire, baking bread, and smoking meats. Parker's small body shuddered in an exaggerated show of cold. His muffled words floated by Caidon, unheard except for their displeasure. Ramsey's made an equally embellished motion toward the group of buildings on the corner, where a short line formed. The boy's attention had moved on, however, and before Caidon could call out a warning, Parker sprung. Two little booted feet slammed down into a puddle. Muddy water splashed around him on a squeal, and Ramsey shrieked, jumping to the side.

Caidon lunged, wrapping an arm around her torso, pulling in the opposite direction to keep her from tumbling into the road. Parker continued to laugh and jump in the seemingly endless supply of shallow water. Ramsey gripped Caidon's forearm, the fabric of his clothing shielding the worst bite of her nails. Underneath his hold, her chest worked overtime to draw air. The rapid pound of her heart under his palm warned him a little too late where his hand had come to rest.

Soft female flesh and the warmth of her body almost distracted him enough to forget the small crowd who had taken an interest in the family drama playing out before them. Caidon carefully set her away and took Parker's cold hand.

"That's enough," he said. The authority in his voice allowed no argument, and the boy responded by going still and slowly stepping from the puddle. Water pooled under his feet and dripped from his pants. "Apologize."

Parker's bottom lip quivered when he met Ramsey's stare. "Sorry, Auntie."

With a hand pressed to her belly, she frowned and met Caidon's eyes. "Well," she huffed, "at least we're already married, and I don't have to worry about impressing your parents."

Caidon swept his gaze down her body, ignoring how his stomach tightened at how the dress molded to her breasts and accented the subtle curve of her stomach and flare of her hips. Dark brown water beaded on the skirt and rolled to drip onto the sidewalk, soaking into the folds in other places, ruining the once pretty print. She'd probably never be able to get the fabric clean again.

"You have no need to impress anyone," he stated softly. "And you're beautiful, muddy or not."

"Careful," she said, her gaze going smoky. The thin

thread between them blazed. "I might consider adding two zeroes to that one year you scribbled on our contract."

A hundred years. Forever. A lifetime contract.

Yes.

The Ruthenian in him roared with approval. Ruthenian's joined for life, and she'd chosen him. Over the past few days, he'd researched right alongside her and learned the honor she'd bestowed when she'd forged the bond. The treasure she could become. If he accepted. He swallowed and looked away, composing himself.

"I'm sorry," she said, releasing a shuddering breath. "I need to figure this out. I keep forcing my feelings on you. I apologize."

"If you could feel *me*, you wouldn't be apologizing," he growled.

Pink blossomed across her cheeks. Her mouth opened and then snapped closed. She looked away and nodded. "Okay." She squeezed her eyes closed and nodded again. "All right, how about we eat and find a ride?"

Caidon motioned for her to choose one of the many seemingly popular choices before them.

Parker grunted and pulled, trying to get free, his other hand reaching for Ramsey. "I'm sorry, Auntie."

Ramsey took his free hand but made no attempt to do anything more. "We'll talk about your misbehavior tonight."

"No yummies?" he whined.

Ramsey's mouth pressed into an unhappy line. "Probably not." When he sucked in a breath as if to wail, Ramsey lifted up her hand. "Don't even think about it, child, or it's an hour earlier to bed for you in addition to no yummies."

The boy's lips pursed in anger. His nostrils flared. He yanked his hand away from her and stomped. "I don't like you."

"Well, that's okay," Ramsey said, stopping at the end of a line. "I still love you."

Caidon picked the boy up and settled him comfortably on his hip. Despite having been around small kids, he still marveled at how tiny a life could be. How fragile and precious. "You ruined your Aunt Ramsey's dress, you know."

"Yeah." He rubbed his nose on Caidon's shoulder. "I'm sorry."

"I think," Caidon said quietly between them, "that a missed dessert is fair, don't you?"

Parker turned his face away, making a noise of equal parts anger, disgust, and resignation only a kid could pull off.

Caidon shifted his attention to Ramsey and found her watching thoughtfully. "What?"

She shook her head and looked away. "Nothing."

The line moved forward until they were inside the modest building. Caidon set Parker down and read him the menu Ramsey had procured for them. A glass front counter displayed an arrangement of delicious breakfast options, from sweet to savory. Parker ignored the menu for the visual options, pointing to five in rapid excitement.

Ramsey smiled and leaned close. "Before Jonathon, he'd never been to a café before. I always love watching him, and it's an effort not to buy everything he wants."

"It's almost an hour ride to my family," Caidon said. "Food may help make it more fun."

"I brought a few toys in my bag." She held up the little yellow purse, and Caidon raised a brow. She laughed. "They're small. A wooden pony and Ariot. But okay, I'll let him pick three instead of one."

At the counter, they made their selections and left with two bags of food. One filled with pastries and another with fried meats wrapped in waxy paper to keep them warm and mostly leak-proof. Parker clapped in happiness and danced, reaching for the bag held far from his grasp. Caidon smiled as he ushered the small family out of the crowded shop.

Ramsey hailed a carriage after letting several pass by, and Caidon noted it was a higher end service. Inside thick red carpet covered the floor, and the seats were padded with clean folded blankets. The driver even hopped down to help them in and make sure they were comfortable before beginning their journey. Too excited to wait, Parker made happy noises at the bag, his feet kicking the wooden bench, alternating between his three choices until Ramsey just handed him one.

Parker wore more than he ate and by the end of the ride, had managed to make every surface he climbed and played on sticky. He alternated between playing on the carpet with his toys, climbing on the seats to look out the windows, and when both those things bored him, he'd sit on one of their laps. He'd begun to doze when they finally pulled up to the eight-story apartment building Caidon had been raised in.

At the sidewalk, Ramsey shielded her eyes from the mid-morning sun and took in the cinderblock and cement building. He knew what she saw. Ancient to the point of almost being derelict. The complex was, in fact, on the outer edges of the Old City Ruins, a section of Haven City no one except the bravest ventured into.

Years of smoke curling from woodstove pipes between filthy rectangle windows left black soot stains. The structure, like the abandoned ruins beyond, was built when the newly arrived citizens of Sziveria were struggling to survive in their new land. Families that could afford to demolish a portion of their dwelling to create a greenhouse for the brutal winters had done so, leaving oddly shaped, random shimmering glass facings scattered amongst the cement walls. The area was quiet. No vendors hoping to lure in sales. No carriages except the one they'd rode in on. Only the occasional bird song, dog barking, and rustle of wind broke up the eerie stillness.

"You… grew up here?" Ramsey asked in hushed tones. Even Parker was silent, clinging to her leg.

For a moment, Caidon considered letting her believe they were so far apart in social class as to be incompatible. Lies, however, weren't something he spouted, and he wasn't going to start now. Especially when he'd already declared their relationship to be built on truth. "I was born here. The building is much more than it seems, and it turns out, the perfect cover for a former assassin in hiding."

Skepticism twisted Ramsey's face. "Much more, how?"

He motioned to the two wide front doors as the carriage ambled off, leaving them alone with a deeper sensation of abandonment. Ramsey glanced at the retreating ride.

"It's okay, we're safe," Caidon assured. "I can

explain more inside."

Taking Parker's hand, she led the way into the building. Once inside, she stopped and looked at the opulent interior. "What…"

Caidon smiled. "As I said, more. The building is old, an original from the first settlers to Haven City, precious to the families who can trace their lineage through the apartments. My mother's family has lived in unit five-seventeen for nine generations. One of my sisters will likely inherit it from her. When an owner dies, and no one is left to take over, the apartments can sell for more than your house. Their historical value alone makes them appealing."

The two bottom floors of the building were left open. Snow often accumulated in the winter months, making first floor apartments too dark in the winter for occupation. Or, if they were created, were inexpensive and appealed only to the strongest of those who could survive the sun deprivation in their home brought on by feet of snow. The architects of *this* building ensured no one had to make such a choice. Several other apartments in the city were the same, often turning the bottom floors into a greenhouse. The feel was close, but with only regular windows, it lacked the flood of light necessary for large trees and more sun-hungry plants. Still, pots dripping with flowers and vines hung from the ceiling.

A small creek that had likely been present when the building had been erected flowed in a winding path, disappearing around a corner in the E-shaped construct, where it went outside, only to reappear along its natural path somewhere else on the bottom level. The gentle burble of water added to the serene atmosphere, along with the rocked pathways lined with shade happy plants along the creeks edge. Benches and tables welcomed those wishing an extended escape.

Caidon led them to a footbridge that crossed in front of the wing his family resided in. Over the generations, his mother's family had acquired two additional neighboring units, making the once two-bedroom apartment big enough for a very large family or another household, whichever the future generations would need. Since his mother, Maressa, had married a Ruthenian, having a space large enough for the family they produced had turned out to be a blessing.

The stairway was as silent as the street had been. He led them to the seventh story, the door opening into a dark wood-planked floor with soft gray walls. A table with fresh flowers, flanked by lanterns on the walls above, was positioned at every third door. Dark framed paintings of natural wonders found in Sziveria, from the Tabria Mountains to the ocean cliffs in the south, lined the corridor. Parker insisted on stopping to look at a particularly vivid image of the Stonebreak Ice Fields at sunrise, the pinks, oranges, and muted blues reflecting on the pristine ice and snow drifts. Neither Caidon nor Ramsey had ever been to see them in person, so couldn't answer any of his questions beyond what they'd been taught in geography lessons. Ramsey stopped to peer at a fog-shrouded body of water, and Caidon noted the plaque beneath labeled it Wintersfall Lake.

"Is it petty of me to hope Joel Blackbain never gets

to see this lake again?" she asked, her voice a mere whisper in the noiseless hall.

Caidon stared at the detailed rendition done in a muted blue palette. Splashes of gold hinted at the sun struggling to be seen through the gloom, giving the image a sense of hope. "It's not his anymore, and never will be, even if something happens to his brother."

She nodded, and with an effort that seemed to border on physical, forced herself away from the painting. Caidon pressed a hand into the small of her back. Beneath his touch, her muscles relaxed, and she moved closer until their hips brushed with each step. At the second to last door on the left, he knocked. Before he could complete a second rap, the door yanked open. Green eyes he'd inherited stared at him in disbelief. Without warning, Caidon was pulled into a fierce hug by Christopher Survaine.

When his father finally pulled back, he took Caidon's face in both hands and searched. "Five years."

Caidon frowned, wrapping his hands around Christopher's still strong forearms. The sound of his father's voice, thick with his Ruthenian heritage, had a strange effect on him. Caidon hadn't realized how much he'd missed home until he was standing at the threshold. "I work for the FIO. I couldn't safely communicate."

Christopher nodded and dropped his hold. "Yes, I know. A master guardian with our name. A position of secrecy and power." He shook his head and held the door open. "Come in, come in. My lamenting will solve nothing."

"Working great on the guilt level, though," Caidon said, grinning.

"Ah," Christopher laughed. "Well, there is that, I suppose. Less than you deserve."

The quiet apartment stilled Caidon's progression into the apartment. He frowned. "Where is everyone?"

Christopher closed and locked the door behind Parker and Ramsey. He brushed past them and led them into the spacious living room. "Ruthenia with your *daki* and *baki*. Your mother and sisters are no longer safe in this country."

His grandparents had been surprisingly thrilled with his father's large family. Had Christopher married a Ruthenian, he'd have been lucky to produce two children. Five would have been impossible.

Christopher glanced at Ramsey and Parker with curiosity but said nothing, instead answering Caidon's unasked question. "Someone is hunting the families of known assassins. Alexandrov Nachemir's youngest daughter and wife were murdered a couple years ago. Henry Castien's young son and wife were killed last fall, and his teenage daughter was kidnapped. While I've forbidden your sisters to touch a gun, I can't risk someone thinking they have my genetic ability despite not knowing. You inherited it, so it's not a stretch to believe one of them has too."

Caidon's frown deepened. He tried to remember if Voklane had said anything about Castien's daughter. "Did they get the girl back?"

"Yes, she was rescued, along with dozens of other children," Christopher answered.

Ramsey looked up at his words. "I remember that. I helped them learn they were looking for more than just the missing girl, perhaps many missing children, which they found. But none of this made any type of news."

Christopher merely smiled. His emerald gaze met Caidon's. "You have brought me something special, *dak*?"

Caidon nodded and took a deep breath. "This is Ramsey, my wife, and her nephew, Parker Hunter."

7

RAMSEY'S BREATH BURNED IN HER LUNGS WHILE SHE waited for her father-in-law's reaction to the news of her marriage to his only son. Christopher Survaine had passed on more than his Gen-Heir talent to his progeny. In thirty years, Ramsey knew exactly what her husband would look like. And wow, she could find no fault in the passage of time. The genes in the Survaine family were certainly more than a skill.

The thick black hair falling to his collar in the back, around his ears, and almost into his eyes held no gray. Intelligent green eyes, the same startling shade he'd given to his son, looked at her closely. Signs of age added interesting lines around his mouth, eyes, and across what she could see of his forehead. He was clean-shaven, his skin a richer caramel than Caidon's, accented nicely by the sky-blue shirt and tan slacks he wore. Crossing his arms over a broad chest, he angled his head and cut her a shallow smile.

"Life is not easy married to an assassin," Christopher said.

"I know, but I'll be with him for a while, so that'll help," she answered.

Christopher's attention snapped to his son. Caidon gave a barely discernible shake of his head. His father's gaze moved to Parker, still glued to Ramsey's thigh, trying to be smaller than he was. Strangers were never his favorite.

Dropping to his haunches, Christopher waited until Parker met his stare. "Would you like to see our playroom? Lots of toys, building blocks, and dress-up clothes I think you would enjoy."

Parker looked up at Ramsey, his curious yet hesitant gaze asking permission without words. Ramsey stroked her fingers down his small head and smiled. "Do you want to go see the toys?" At his nod, she broadened her smile to encourage his natural inquisitiveness and provide confidence. "Then go. We'll be right here the whole time. Just remember to treat everything nice."

"I will," he promised with a hop and followed behind Christopher.

Moments later, Christopher returned. The muffled sounds of imagination filled the hall behind him. Her father-in-law gestured for them to sit in the living room. "He'll be content long enough for us to have an adult conversation, I believe."

"Oh, good," Ramsey said, taking a seat across from him. Caidon sat beside her but kept a careful distance, so they didn't touch. She tried not to let the action annoy her. By the quirk of his father's brow, she'd failed.

"It's for the best," Christopher said, his voice tinged with regret. He turned his attention to his son. "I take it you've had a sense of bonding, then?"

"I disagree," Ramsey cut in before Caidon could answer. "I think it's our marriage, and we can decide what's best."

"And do you know what life traveling with an assassin will be like?" Christopher asked, his tone curious. "Did you think about how difficult it'll be for Caidon to be bonded and sharing space with you?"

Ramsey had never been one to shy away from a challenge, and she wouldn't start now, even if it meant upsetting a man she should be trying to impress. "We've been trying to learn what we can. And I didn't have a choice in traveling with him, so whatever challenges we face, we'll face together."

"Someone falsified a kill-order," Caidon explained. "I asked my leader. He had several ideas for who and why, but nothing concrete."

Christopher looked between the two of them. "So, you married her?"

Caidon settled back on the couch, sighing. "I met Ramsey five years ago. I knew who she was before the order came in."

"And I know I'm extremely lucky for that," Ramsey chimed, fisting her hands in her lap to keep from reaching for him.

Christopher cast her a sideways stare. "Doubtful, girly. My son has a rule, and he would not have broken it for you. I believe you have always been safe." After a brief pause, he added, "From him, at least."

Intrigue made Ramsey glance Caidon's way, wondering what his rule entailed. Honor amongst assassins? The concept almost made her giggle. However, the realization of how very little she knew the man she'd bound herself to caused all humor to fade.

"Either way," Caidon said, "she's with me for the duration. I don't know how long that will be. All our research says whatever bond we forge will be the same one you have with Ma."

Christopher rubbed his thumb and middle finger against his temples. "I was hoping you wouldn't get it, being only half Ruthenian."

"Apparently, my children won't have it," Caidon shrugged, "but who knows. The evidence isn't clear."

His father looked between the two of them, a hint of a smile on his lips. "My grandchildren. What a thing to consider."

Caidon glanced at her, a shadow flickering across his eyes. "Can I deny the bond?"

Ramsey's heart clenched, and she swallowed. She turned her focus to the rest of the room, taking in the cozy mismatched collection of furniture and decorations. From the colorful woven, almost threadbare rug under the scarred coffee table to the porcelain figurines, that showed evidence of having been salvaged from the remnants of an ancient society off the shores of whatever land had a penchant for dancers. The space was large, if a little cramped with bookcases, tables, lamps, and chests. Through a wide archway, she could make out the dining room and doors to a nice sized greenhouse.

A large mural of a tree branching off into dozens of limbs on the wall leading to the dining room had Ramsey standing. In her peripheral hearing, she tried to ignore Christopher's answer.

"She's Sziverian, so the bond is a little different. If it's anything like your Ma's, it's more heightened instinct, a leftover from a past generation being Ruthenian. A claiming, if you will. The only way to deny it is to leave," he said with a hint of sadness. "Something I could not do."

Ramsey forced a surge of emotion down. If they were to have hope of an honest relationship, Caidon had to choose her, choose them. Not forced into any union or bonding. Until the threat against her was nullified, Caidon had promised to remain at her side. What happened between now and then... well, hopefully forever. But she would not coerce the outcome, no matter how desperately she wanted him.

Their conversation turned quiet, personal. Ramsey took a deep breath and looked over the detailed, sprawling beauty of a family tree. At the very top, a couple was listed, and from there, generations blossomed and thrived. A gold thread from the original owners to the next kept up with the owners of the apartment and, therefore, the keepers of the family history. Ramsey searched for Caidon, finding him along a golden line to his mother, Maressa Thornley Survaine. Someday a golden thread would lead to one of the sisters, continuing a tradition that would perhaps include her and Caidon's recorded progeny.

Little feet pounded on the hardwood behind her. Ramsey turned and smiled as Parker rounded the hall corner, a small log house clutched in his hands. "Auntie! Auntie! Look what I—" A corner of the rug caught his toes, and he lurched forward. Blocks flew and landed with a clatter, bursting the small house apart and sliding pieces across the floor. He landed hard on his stomach, his elbows skidding along the carpeting.

"Oh, here we go," Christopher chimed, leaping over the back of the couch and picking Parker up off the floor. When the child failed to breathe, his face purple and frozen mid-cry, Christopher gently blew. On a noisy inhale, Parker let loose a scream. Christopher sat on the arm of the couch, perching a gasping, mewling child on his thigh. "Okay, you're okay. You're fine."

Parker lifted his arms, showing off skinned elbows. Fat tears tracked down his round cheeks. Then he pointed to his broken creation. "My house broke."

"Sure did, but you can build it again." Christopher set Parker on the floor in front of the scattered logs. "Here, I'll help."

The urge to intervene had Ramsey turning her back to the scene. Parker wasn't freaking out, screaming, or pitching a fit. If she inserted herself into the equation, he probably would change gears and remember having a tantrum was how he normally dealt with disappointment. Cheeks flaming with self-failure, she returned her attention to the artistic genealogical diagram.

"My father has five children," Caidon said softly, coming to stand beside her, hands clasped behind his back. "Five."

"I am drowning in how to raise him," Ramsey whispered, hating the burn of tears. "I'm afraid I'm ruining him for Jonathon."

Caidon moved closer, and much to her shock, his fingers twined between hers. "Loving a child is never a mistake. Will never cause harm."

Ramsey remained silent, looking back over the beauty of a family not just surviving but flourishing in their world. The heart-warming murmur of an adult playing with a child helped ground her but did nothing to ease the ache of uselessness. She squeezed his hand.

"My father said we can keep things from getting too

intense while we're together on my assignments by keeping our distance," he whispered. "I'm not asking for long."

A rush of frustration at his words curbed any hope. She didn't want to wait. "How long is that to you?"

He shrugged, his arms sliding along hers. "I don't know, until we get a feel for how we'll work out the particulars while traveling together."

Ramsey pulled her hand free and wrapped her arms around herself. "We'll talk more at the house."

Happy clapping made Ramsey turn. Parker jumped in excitement and pointed at the once again finished house. "Look, Auntie! See!"

"I do see," she exclaimed with excitement. "Wonderful job, Parker. What do you say for the help?"

Parker turned to Christopher. "Thank you!"

Christopher inclined his head. "Anytime, little man. You will take good care of your aunt, *dak*?"

Parker scrunched his nose. "What is *dak*?"

"It means yes."

Parker smiled and nodded. "Yes." He pointed a thumb at his chest. "I'm a big boy, I help her cook and wash dishes."

"Excellent." Christopher gave Parker a gentle cuff on his upper arm. "I knew you could be counted on."

Ramsey held out her hand and wiggled her fingers. Parker obediently slipped his small hand into hers. "Time to go."

"Why?"

Words failed her. She glanced to Caidon for help. Did he want to leave? Her discomfort was not his, and he hadn't visited with his father in over five years. Despite having only come at her insistence, she didn't want to cut their time together short. Who knew when they'd get the opportunity again? Caidon shoved his hands into his pockets and looked at his father, still sitting on the floor.

"We can stay a little longer," Caidon said.

Christopher began to rise. "I'll make us something to eat."

Ramsey motioned for him to stay. "No, I'll do that. You two visit some more."

CAIDON WAITED UNTIL RAMSEY AND PARKER DISAPPEARED into the other room before he held a hand down for his father. With a grunt, Christopher grabbed Caidon's hand and hauled himself up.

"She will cause you no end of trouble," his father warned, his Ruthenian accent thick. "Defiant, head-strong, like my Maressa."

Caidon propped himself against the nearest book-case and looked up at the decorative tile ceiling. "She's it for me, *Ahtyshka*. There has been no one else. There will be no one else."

"I understand." Christopher blew out a long breath. "And I am glad you have accepted her. I fear I made a mess of your mother and I's beginning. That she forgave me is something I am thankful for every day. I had hoped you'd be spared the… discomfort of a bond you have no choice in."

"I have a choice. As you said, I could walk away, and the bond would fade."

"There will come a time when it won't." Caidon dropped his head and met his father's intense stare. "No matter how far you go, she will still be present."

Christopher touched a fist to his chest. "Here. Inescapable."

After having lived life alone, on his own terms, his own way, the thought of never feeling *alone* was daunting. He figured, on some level, he knew he'd be a disappointment. As a loner, he didn't have the first clue how to be part of something, especially something important like marriage.

The moment he'd learned how valuable his skill was, he'd walked from this apartment and into the cold world of contract killing. Literally. Little warmth remained in the inhabited places of the world, both in humanity and in the environment. Only a handful of countries had shown an ability to live in a civilized manner, and in some instances, even that was a stretch. Ruthenia had a rigid structure, and they treated outsiders with contempt. To marry outside of their culture was almost a crime. The thought made him look closer at his father.

"You must have really worried to send Ma and the girls to Ruthenia," Caidon said.

His *ahtyshka* looked away, rubbing his palms on his thighs. "A family by the name of Ralston has changed things. Most of their children are powerful beast masters, all born here in Sziveria to a Sziverian *makyshka*."

"Their *ahtyshka* is Ruthenian?"

Christopher nodded. "*Dak.*"

Caidon considered what his father was trying to say without saying it. "There are many formidable beast masters in Ruthenia. Why would half-breeds change things?"

"Ruthenian born beast masters are not so great

anymore, it seems. The blood is too saturated with competing genes. New blood, clean of an overabundance of power, has allowed the Ruthenian half to thrive." Christopher let loose another sigh. "From what I have heard, they have not seen strength of control of this nature since the first recorded generation. It has changed things."

An almost sad smile graced his father's lips. "You are likely more powerful than I ever had a chance to be, thanks to your mother's blood."

Caidon didn't like the thought of being *more* than his father, who was a legend in his own right. That sort of attention put too big a target on him. Potentially made wanna-be assassins want to challenge him in hopes of securing their position on the ladder of greatness. He already had a large enough focus on him simply by being a Survaine.

"Hopefully, no one considers that," Caidon muttered.

His fathers glanced in the direction Ramsey had disappeared. "Are you certain traveling with a bride is wise? Have you *really* thought about it?"

"I will not lose her," Caidon whispered, everything in him tightening. "Left here, whoever wants her dead will learn what I've done and send someone else. They may still, but I'll be there to keep her safe."

"Or you will die trying," his father said grimly.

Caidon shrugged. "Then I do."

"Very well. As I said earlier, if you stay your course, the bond between you will become permanent. After that happens, you'll know when she's in her ovulation phase." Christopher ran both hands through his hair. "I'll tell you now, it's going to be rough the first couple months because you won't be used to the changes your own body goes through to match her fertility. If you aren't strong, she *will* end up pregnant."

The rough start his parents had endured when his mother had inadvertently forged a bond with his father hadn't been a secret of his childhood. As a custom, and perhaps more so because of the strength of an established bond, Christopher and Maressa had little choice but to make their relationship work or remain alone for the rest of their lives. Caidon didn't want such a beginning for his own bond. Knowing ahead what to expect, the good and the bad would hopefully make the transition a bit smoother for his marriage.

"Will I be the only one influenced by the connection?" Caidon asked, resting his elbows on his knees and clasping his hands.

"This I cannot tell you. While it's perhaps true how the bond affects couples is an inherited trait through the male family line, it is still unique to each couple. Your mother knows when I'm close. She'd often meet me in the street or downstairs in the lobby park. What your Ramsey will be able to do?" He lifted a hand in question. "You both will learn in time."

8

Warm afternoon sun helped burn away some of Ramsey's anxiety. Since leaving his family home, Caidon had said very little. She wondered if not being able to see his mother and sisters bothered him or if it was something to do about the conversation with his father, likely concerning the mating bond. Ramsey admitted she'd put him in a difficult position. The bond made things tricky, and she'd muddied the waters further by insisting on a physical relationship.

Glancing covertly over at him, at how his clothes revealed a honed, fit body with each smooth, confident step he took, oh yes, she *wanted*. However, now she worried perhaps she was the only one. Aside from the brief glimpses of heat she'd caught in his emerald eyes, he hadn't kissed her, hadn't even really touched her. Ramsey chewed on her bottom lip and guided Parker around a puddle. Should she do something to learn if he desired her?

Pedestrians milled all around, the sidewalk growing

busier as the lunch crowd hurried to get to eateries or complete chores on the short break. Carriages crawled by behind slow, sedate horses while the infrequent Ariot driver, impatient in their quicker vehicle, sought safe ways to pass. The occasional brave bicyclist zipped between the traffic. They were walking home the rest of the way home, having to give up the carriage ride when Parker had made it clear he was finished being cooped inside. Working out some excess energy was preferable to a tantrum.

"Will your father be joining the rest of your family now that you've seen him?" Ramsey asked, tightening her hold on Parker's wrist when he attempted to run off.

"I'm not sure. He'd mentioned trying to reach out to the shooters who've lost family to an assassin targeting them. He wants my ma and sisters to be able to return home, safely. They can't do that until the mystery of who is hurting our families is discovered."

Ramsey frowned. "That could take a very long time."

His gaze swept the sidewalk, the street, and even seemed to look up and around. Ramsey wondered if he was looking for something or if the action was more of a habit. "Yes. He'll likely spend most of the year in Ruthenia, since it's icebound for more months than not. The bond doesn't allow him to be away from my mother for too long."

"Will we be like that?" Ramsey asked curiously. "Unable to remain apart?"

He shrugged, slipping a hand into his pants pocket, his focus still shifting to take in everything around them. "I'm not sure. My father said some things will be the same as his, while others will be completely unique to us. We will learn them in time."

"Well," she huffed, unable to hide her disappointment, "I had hoped to learn more. At least you were able to see him."

"Yes. Thank you for that," he said softly.

Suddenly the small space between them seemed too far. Ramsey slid her arm through his and settled her hip against him, their thighs brushing with each step. The small action sent tiny thrills through her belly. "Of course."

Parker hopped over a section of cracked brick, asking, "Can we make cream noodles for dinner?"

"With peppers?" Caidon asked in an almost wistful tone. "I haven't had that in… a long time."

"I have some fresh peppers in the greenhouse, actually. That sounds like a great plan, Parker. We'll need noodles, though," Ramsey said.

"Yay! Cream noodles, cream noodles, cream noodles…" he chanted over and over again with each hop over broken bricks.

Caidon shifted his arm until her hand slid down and twined between his fingers. They reached the little corner grocer nearest to the house. Ramsey picked up a small hand basket when they walked through the door. Before they checked out, the little basket would be full. Once again, she was struck by the normalcy, the rightness, of doing something so routine with Caidon at her side.

He took over handling Parker while Ramsey pulled items off the shelves and placed them in her basket. The two disappeared to somewhere else, though the shop was small enough for Parker's excited words to carry. A new flavor of sweet biscuits grabbed her attention. She snagged the little wax paper wrapped snack and read the neatly printed card secured by twine.

"Ramsey." A surprised, familiar male voice snapped her attention from the biscuits.

Blinking in shock and not a small bit of horror, Ramsey somehow managed not to drop the package. "Tobyn, what are you doing here? This market is far from your house."

A jar of red jelly was clutched in his hand. He shook his head and tightened his fingers around the glass until she feared the container would burst. "No one makes berry preserves like Mrs. Hollister."

That was true. Suddenly not hungry, Ramsey set the crackers on the nearest shelf. "Well, enjoy."

She turned to leave, but his hand snaked out and grabbed her elbow. He moved in close, the slightly floral, faintly nutty scent of him flowed over her, making her nose wrinkle in distaste. "Have you given anymore thought to my proposal?"

Anger and disbelief burned her cheeks. She yanked her arm free and put distance between them. "I am *married*."

Tobyn's head snapped back as if she'd struck him. "Married? When did that happen? I visited you last week!"

"I told you I was promised. We've contracted."

His dark gaze narrowed, looking over her left wrist and hand, which she knew to be bare of any indications of her married status. "Why must you lie? I understand the word no, even if you are making a mistake." He closed the space between them, a finger brushing under her chin. Heat blazed in his eyes as they wandered from her face down her body. Ramsey swept his hand away and resisted using the basket to cover herself, feeling oddly exposed despite her clothing. "I will be good to you like I was before."

Ramsey *hated* that she'd shared something with Tobyn she hadn't yet experienced with Caidon. She hated Tobyn had such memories of her, which were apparently far better than any she had of him. Didn't it figure? She wanted to forget the way he sounded puffing over her, how he felt losing himself in her body. And all he wanted was to use her again, only paying her this time. Acid churned in her stomach, and she quickly turned on her heel, needing away from him before she lost her lunch on the Hollister's store aisle.

Turning the corner, she almost ran over Parker holding up a jar of ginger peaches. Using the shelf, she stopped herself, but not before jostling into Parker's shoulder. Caidon reacted swiftly, catching the jar mid-arc, his vivid gaze meeting hers.

"What's wrong?" he asked, reshelving the jar. Parker made a sound of distress, his little hands reaching back for the peaches.

"Were you going to let him get those?" Ramsey asked, hoping with every cell of her being, Tobyn had disappeared, and she could forget the shameful exchange.

Caidon's eyes narrowed. "I hadn't decided. Now, what happened?"

Ramsey placed the peaches in the basket and slipped past. "I have everything we need, so we can pay and head home."

"Ramsey," Caidon said, almost too quiet to be heard, nearly a warning.

Squeezing her eyes shut, she stilled, hating the mortification sliding through her. Would Caidon view her in the same useless light if they became intimate? Nothing more than a warm body to satisfy his lust, good for little else? "I just saw someone I wish I hadn't, that's all. Can we go?"

His hand brushed along her lower back and then disappeared as he moved past, leaving Parker with her. "Who?"

"No one. Really," Ramsey rushed to say, catching him and taking his hand. "Please, leave it alone."

"This person bothered you." His tone implied the offense was enough to warrant action.

"People are going to bother me. You can't take them all on."

He arched a black brow.

Ramsey laughed and let out a nervous breath. "You can't."

Caidon said nothing, simply turned, and headed to the front of the store. Ramsey grasped Parker's hand and placed her items on the small checkout counter. A young woman tallied their total, packing everything into a paper bag while Ramsey counted out the raimarks. Caidon took the bag, glancing around before heading to the door. Relief rushed through her when she didn't spot Tobyn.

On the walk home, Parker chattered and asked an endless barrage of questions, with little patience to wait for an answer. At the house, Ramsey sent the boys to the greenhouse to pick the fresh ingredients she'd need for the pasta while she handled the rest. A tension vibrated from Caidon during their meal, but Ramsey remained quiet, likely knowing the cause. Well, too bad, he could sulk. She still wasn't going to talk about the encounter. She wanted to forget the whole thing had even happened.

After dinner, Ramsey took care of Parker while Caidon handled the cleanup for dinner. Bathed, read to, and allowed quiet playtime, Ramsey locked the child gate before heading down the stairs. Halfway to the first floor, she froze.

Caidon wasn't alone.

Tobyn Fenster stood in the foyer, arms crossed, belligerence darkening his thin face. Standing beside Caidon, he looked almost skeletal. Weak. How had Ramsey ever seen something attractive in him? Tobyn seemed to be taking advantage of the fact that he stood almost a head taller than Caidon, looking down his nose at him with a sense of power. As though he had every right to come into *her* home and have authority. Tension coiled every muscle in Caidon's frame. Their words were muffled by the distance, and Ramsey knew if she didn't do something, Tobyn might not walk away. Ramsey rushed down the remaining steps, catching Tobyn's attention.

"Finally!" Tobyn exclaimed, raising his arms in a dramatic fashion. "This has gone far enough. You didn't have to convince some man to be here pretending to be your husband."

"There was no convincing," Caidon replied softly. "I am her husband, and you need to leave."

Tobyn glared and leaned in close to Caidon. "I'm not going anywhere. I'm not the fake in this house, you are."

• • •

A RED HAZE HOVERED OVER CAIDON'S VISION. HE WANTED to lash out, slam this joke of a man against a wall, and snarl. The beast of his Ruthenian side wanted to do worse. Ramsey seemed to sense his inner struggle. She laid a cool hand on his forearm, her shoulders squared.

"Mr. Fenster—"

"It's *Mr. Fenster* now?" the man snapped, his dark eyes bright with anger. "It wasn't Mr. Fenster when—"

Ramsey shoved two hands into Fenster's chest, hard. The action took the man by surprise, and he stumbled backward into the door. "My husband told you to leave our house. You are now trespassing, and anything that happens to you will be legally justified at an accusation hearing."

Fenster sneered, looking first at Ramsey, then at Caidon. While Caidon didn't have the man's height, he had muscle mass on him and training. He could wipe the floor with the scab and not break a sweat. Stress lined Ramsey's face and tightened her body. Caidon wanted the man gone. He grabbed the front of Fenster's neatly-pressed white shirt and yanked him away from the door. Ramsey filled the void, opening the door to the outside. Cool air rushed in. The clatter of wooden wheels on brick and the gentle hum of an Ariot passing by flowed in on the breeze.

"I am a primary guardian! You can't treat me this way!" Fenster howled, trying to twist free of Caidon's hold.

"And I'm a master guardian," Caidon growled. "*You* can't enter this home without permission, which you were never granted."

Fenster stumbled under the weight of Caidon's hold

while being forced toward the door. "I've never seen you before. You're lying, you aren't a master guardian."

Caidon barked out a laugh, waiting until Ramsey cleared the doorway before releasing his hold on a shove. Fenster floundered backward, arms windmilling to keep from falling. "I'm with First Intelligence. I don't go to social events."

Fenster's eyes widened, looking away before Caidon could catch any emotion. When his focus returned, venom filled his gaze and twisted his lean face. "You may be higher ranking, and you *may* be her husband, but you'll never get from her what I did."

The primary guardian's attention swiveled to Ramsey. Lust and possession burned in his stare. "You'll never know how tight she was her first time. How her nails felt digging into your arms from the pain of a first lover. You'll never be to her what I was."

"Stay away from me," Ramsey said, voice shaking. "You are *nothing* to me."

"That wasn't what you said the night you begged me to take you," he smirked.

"I didn't beg you for anything," she snarked right back. "I was eighteen and curious. You were an experience, and now you are a memory. And not a great one."

The thought of this man touching anywhere on Ramsey, let alone taking her body in the most primal of ways, had Caidon calculating distance and time. Four-point-six seconds to his room. Fifteen-point-three seconds to assemble his rifle. Three-point-nine seconds to get in position at the nearest window overlooking the street. Patience while he waited for the perfect moment – when the carriage pulled up, and Fenster opened the door. The bullet to his brain would send him forward, toppling into the vehicle. The driver wouldn't be any wiser until they arrived at the destination to discover the corpse for a fare.

But that would be a cold kill. No purpose except to make him feel better, to enact a sense of revenge for something he had no right to feel possessive over. He didn't own Ramsey, hadn't even known her when she'd been intimate with another. Even though taking this idiots life would settle his beast, he'd sworn long ago to only be executioner to the guilty. To eliminate those too wicked to live amongst the struggling remnants of humanity. So far, Fenster was nothing more than a bully. A sulking one if Caidon read the situation correctly.

Not wasting another breath, he slammed the door closed in Fenster's face, engaging the locks with more effort than necessary to make sure their securing into place was heard. The rapid fall of Ramsey's feet on the stairs echoed around the small foyer before he turned around. Sighing, he watched the tail end of her skirt disappear around the corner of the upstairs. Their relationship was still too new, too untested for him to follow.

Instead, he finished tidying up downstairs and then went to the room he'd borrowed. Unpacking his rifles, he took the time to clean and repack the weapons. Only after he'd heard Parker's door close for the night, followed by Ramsey's, letting silence completely settle over the house, did he venture to her room. Soundlessly, he opened her door and eased inside. Absorbed in something at her desk, she didn't notice the quiet *snick* of the latch closing them in together. For a moment, Caidon basked in the pleasure of watching her.

The only source of light from her desk lamp caught and disappeared along her figure, played over the texture of inky curls pulled into a messy *something* atop her head. Transfixed, Caidon allowed his gaze to wander, to discern every highlighted curve. The modest globes of her breasts pressed tight to the thin silk of her nightgown. The fabric cascaded along her gently rounded stomach and pooled between her full thighs. The seat obscured his view of her backside, which he knew to be as lush and round as the rest of her.

Desire coiled warm and thick inside him. He wanted to sweep the errant curls from her neck and breathe her in before tasting her skin. Would she prefer a gentle sweep of his tongue or a more aggressive nip of his teeth? Both? Caidon suppressed a shudder. *He'd* like to do both. Conquering the urge, he sat on her bed. The faint squeak of springs finally alerted her to his presence. She spun around, grabbing the back of the dainty white chair. A heated flush bloomed across her cheeks, and she swiveled back around.

"Can we have this conversation tomorrow?" she asked, her words strained.

"No."

Ramsey gasped and twisted to face him again. "No?"

"We can discuss something else first, but one way or another, we will talk about that man named Fenster," Caidon said softly.

She took a shaky breath and returned to the desk. "Do you know any Markinish?"

Caidon joined her, looking over her shoulder at the

collection of what looked like shipping manifests. "Markinish is a very complicated language."

"I know, there are dozens of dialects for one country. I found a book that had the five most common, but whoever is using the language for a code on these documents is either using a combination of multiple dialects or a dialect I haven't found a translation for."

A vague memory of Voklane mentioning Ramsey's genetic gift for language, which would also lend itself to breaking codes, surfaced. "How long have you been working on this?"

She braced an elbow on the desk and dropped her chin on her palm. "Months. It's so frustrating. Some of the characters I immediately recognize and understand, only they're paired with something that doesn't make sense or I've never seen, so I figure perhaps that same character has an entirely different meaning in a dialect I haven't yet found."

"How many months, specifically?"

"Since before Jonathon left, so seven months? Maybe eight? Last fall."

Caidon pressed a finger onto a sheet and pulled it closer. He tapped a rhythm in thought. "What do you think these are involved in to investigate them?"

Ramsey closed two open books and then gathered all the loose pages together. "Sylphine, Jonathon's wife, believed a shipping company from her country may have been involved in kidnapping people from here and trafficking them. All these manifests have to do with his shipping company."

"There's no other proof?"

She looked away, licking her lips. "Well, only what we heard them say when they attempted to take us."

The distraction of her tongue leaving a wet trail across her lips almost made him miss the importance of her words. "Take you?"

Ramsey waved her hand. "Yes, it was all very ridiculous. Someone thought they could gain power by forcing Sylphine into marriage. But she'd already contracted with my brother, and this guy, Leone Cyrano, decided he was going to take her anyway. I just happened to be with her at the time, and they decided I'd be a bonus."

Caidon scrubbed his hands down his face. "You were almost kidnapped into human slavery, and… you think it's nothing?"

A new flush crept along her cheeks. "Well, not nothing. But I'm not going to fixate on it. I helped find a probable shipment of children before Wintervail last winter. I know this isn't nothing, which is why I'm trying to break the code."

"You think it's still happening?" he asked in shock. "Even though they've been caught?"

"I think we'd be foolish to think such a lucrative means of trade has just ended. As I said, the actual proof is in these manifests and a few others I've been handed since the ports opened with the spring thaw. There is no other proof. Cyrano is still able to use our ports, so there wasn't enough evidence to do anything."

Caidon frowned. "What about your testimony about the attempted kidnapping?"

Ramsey shrugged. "There wasn't a hearing. And Sylphine hasn't been able to leave Italyssa to push Sziveria harder to keep Cyrano from our ports. As the liaison for Sun Wind Trade, she has an immense amount of political power considering her father's company is one of the largest shipping fleets in the inhabited world."

Caidon didn't like the connections he was making. "And when did Fenster start coming around again?"

She cleared her throat and stood, putting space between them. "Just last week. Actually… the same day you arrived."

"And what did he say he was here for?" Caidon asked, trying to stay neutral, thinking he failed when Ramsey grimaced.

She angled away from him, her arms wrapping around her waist. "The reason is irrelevant to all of this. He won't be returning."

"I'm not so sure of that," Caidon murmured, slipping a manifest from the top of the pile closer. "How many people know of your language gift?"

"My what?" she asked, blinking.

He held up the thin, yellow paper. "Your Gen-Heir talent."

Her lips pressed into a thin line as she looked away. "I don't have a Gen-Heir talent."

Caidon closed the distance between them. He took her cheeks in his hands and stared deep into her eyes. Stunning lavender with violet accents added depth and dimension, like a perfect specimen of faceted amethyst. No shades of blue, gray, brown, or green mingled in the beautiful hue. "You do. An amazing one, I believe. How are you unaware of that?"

"Languages coming easy to me doesn't mean anything. I know others who speak multiple languages. It's not a genetically inherited gift."

"How does it work?" he asked, refusing to give up.

Her fingers wrapped around his wrists. "What do you mean?"

"When you translate something for the first time, what do you do? How does it work?"

The tip of her tongue touched her bottom lip, and Caidon had to keep from running his thumb across the glistening trail left behind. "If I'm familiar with the language, I touched the paper it's written on, and the words just… make sense."

"What about hearing a language?" He caressed his thumbs along the sides of her cheeks.

"I have found if I read it first, I can understand it spoken."

Amazed, he smiled. "Incredible."

She pulled away and went to the half shelves in a little reading nook across the room. Her fingers brushed along spines as she bent over and searched. "You spoke a word to me five years ago, and I found a Ruthenian to Sziverian dictionary. I've been trying to learn what I can, but the most common language I hear in Haven City is Italyssian or Gaulish, which I find so interesting, considering how many Ruthenian's seem to have migrated here over the last couple of decades. Ruthenia is, after all, our closest neighbor."

Caidon returned to his seat on the bed. "Yes, and during particularly harsh winters, when the Northern Pass freezes, those who are brave could sled or walk across the ice between the countries."

A visible shiver trembled through her body. "I'll leave that to those more adventurous than myself."

Book in hand, she joined him on the edge of the mattress. Caidon took the translation dictionary from her hands and flipped through the pages. "You've read over this?"

She nodded, tucking an errant curl behind her ear. "Yes. And after our visit to the bookstore, I wanted to learn more."

"So according to your theory, when I speak, even though you've never spoken my father's tongue, you'll be able to understand me."

Taking a deep breath, she rubbed her hands on her thighs. "That seems to be how it works, yes."

"And you don't believe you have a Gen-Heir talent?" he asked, unable to comprehend her skepticism.

"I haven't manifested any touched-based talents, and when my parents tested me for a logic-based talent my sixteenth year, I didn't meet the requirements," she stated evenly. "They said I have no discernable inherited gift."

Caidon thrummed his fingers on top of the book. "What would you call being able to touch a paper and have the language suddenly make sense?"

"Only if I've been exposed to the language before," she corrected.

"Exposed, not fluent, correct?"

She squirmed. "Well, yes."

"Makes sense. Your brain must understand what you're seeing. But exposure and fluency are two completely different things. That you basically become fluent *after* mere exposure..." He shook his head. "I think your talent is so rare, they don't even know how to test for it."

"Okay, maybe," she said. "But to be honest, I've only had the understanding thing happen once with

Italyssian, and I'd had quite a bit of exposure because of Sylphine. She was constantly muttering in her language and translating for me when I asked."

Caidon turned to face her on the bed, drawing his leg up. He tossed the book away and braced his hands on his thighs. "Okay, what is it going to take for me to prove you can do this?"

"Prove?" she asked in confusion. "There is nothing to prove, I know what I can do."

"Do you really?" He stood and went to the book-shelf. "Do you have any straight Ruthenian books?"

"One, but I can't read it yet. I haven't studied the dictionary enough," she answered. "Doesn't that prove your theory wrong?"

Caidon searched the titles. "Not necessarily. I bet you can read more than you think, but I want to try something."

He found the book and smiled, recognizing the title. A fictional adventure, one of the stories his father had given to him to read when he'd been learning. Opening to a random page, he handed it to her.

Frowning, she accepted the book, laying it in her lap. She touched both hands to the pages. "I recognize small words, but I can't make sense of the entire page."

Caidon moved over her, bracing his hands on the mattress on either side of her thighs. She gasped and leaned back, eyes wide. Following her, he pressed his cheek to hers, closing his eyes against the softness of her skin, he whispered, *"Dsi sokrovard. Dsi krahet'sna zre vsayach, amtoya Tsa kuytem chvasno."*

9

YOU ARE A TREASURE. YOU ARE BEAUTIFUL AND AMAZING, everything I ever wanted. Caidon's words ripped through Ramsey like a gale-force wind. Breathless, she closed her eyes against the burn of tears. She almost grabbed for him when he pulled away, his touch leaving a tingling path along her jaw.

"Touch the book," he said softly.

Fingers trembling, Ramsey somehow forced herself to focus on the open pages before her. Pressing her hands to the edges, she looked down and sucked in a sharp breath. Every word made sense, read with an ease as if she'd been born into the language.

"Wh… how?" she gasped out.

His fingers caressed under her chin, forcing her face up to meet his stare. "You are a genetic heir. Do you believe me now?"

Ramsey had the sudden urge to shove the book away and crawl under her blankets. An odd sense of fear formed like a storm in her stomach. "What does this mean?"

125

"Nothing, unless you want it to. I think your brother figured it out."

Shocked, Ramsey stared at him. "What? And he didn't tell me? Why would he do that?"

He crouched down in her front of her, closing the book. "He told Ryan Voklane not to utilize you for First Intelligence. I think, if I had to guess, he was scared your gift could place you in danger."

Ramsey looked away, anger replacing uncertainty. "That wasn't his choice."

"Perhaps, but I think he was right. Your talent is remarkable. With enough time and understanding, you can break a code like that," he said snapping his fingers. "If an enemy discovered your talent?" He shook his head, his frown dark. "You'd be in immense danger."

Ramsey chewed on her bottom lip. "Isn't that my decision to make, though?"

"I'm only speculating, but I can understand where your brother was coming from. I'm not entirely certain your secret isn't out, and if that's the case, then he was right to be concerned."

"What do you mean?"

He folded his arms on her legs, his weight braced on her thighs. The action was familiar, almost intimate. Ramsey wanted to slide her hands into his dark hair and pull him closer. His brilliant, green eyes searched her face as if calculating how else to unravel the boring little world she thought she'd existed within. Now, she was potentially embroiled in the same shadowy world of espionage and death he dealt in daily. All because she wanted to find a way to be helpful and solve a mystery no one else seemed capable of resolving.

"I assumed the false orders to eliminate you were from a known enemy," he said.

"Joel Blackbain," Ramsey filled in the only enemy she figured she'd ever made prior to Tobyn Fenster after today.

"Correct. But what if it's your talent? Your ability to decipher the indecipherable? If this group, this V Alliance, has somehow learned about you, they'd go to extreme efforts to keep their secrets safe."

"There's no indication Leone Cyrano was working with anyone," Ramsey said, pressing her hands to her belly to keep from touching him.

"Who do you think was going to take on that shipment you helped interpret for Ryan Voklane?" Caidon asked.

She squeezed her eyes closed and covered her face. *Of course!* How had she not made that same connection? "And you think someone learned about that?"

"I think it's a possibility we can't ignore. I need to talk to Voklane and get more information, find out how anyone could have learned about your talent."

She scoffed and dragged her hands down her cheeks. "Especially since I didn't even know."

"Someone knew," he said softly. "Maybe those men who tried to take you?"

Ramsey shook her head. "They probably figured Sylphine taught me their language. She's lived with us whenever she visits for years now."

A flash of something dark flickered in his eyes. "And Fenster?"

They'd made their way back to the topic of conversation she'd been hoping to avoid. The humiliation of being propositioned for her body by a man who had once claimed she meant something, who had professed to love her. Ramsey wasn't sure how to put the awful situation into coherent words. Maybe fast, like pulling off cooled wax from her skin.

"I hadn't seen him in over five years, not until he showed up here last week." She wished there was more space between them, the mortification of what she was about to admit made her skin burn. "He wanted to know if I'd be interested in being his, um, mistress."

Caidon went very still. "He was one of the reasons you were at the bridge the night we met?"

"Yes," she whispered, seeing no purpose in lying. She'd laid her heart bare for him that night. He deserved nothing less now as her husband.

He rose until he leaned over her, his hands sliding to her hips. A dangerous glint brightened his gaze. "Tell me, did he ever take you in this bed?"

Desire warred with a sliver of alarm. Not for her personal safety but for Caidon's reaction to her answer. One she hated to give. Swallowing, she looked away toward the window she'd held open for her ex to sneak out of when her brother had arrived home in the early hours of the morning.

"Once," she answered in a whisper. "He left me a week later for the woman he's now married to."

"After your parents died, right?" His cheek brushed against hers, his lips a whisper away from her ear.

Goosebumps erupted over her skin as his breath teased her. Ramsey kept her attention on the window, resisting the temptation to turn her head and place her mouth on his. "Yes. I was upset and… weak."

"Not weak," he whispered, his lips brushing along her ear. "Vulnerable. Emotionally exposed from a loss he should have been there for, not taken advantage of instead."

"You are making me insane," she murmured, wrapping her hands around his corded forearms.

"No more than you are making me." He kissed the corner of her jaw. His tongue flicked out, and she gasped at the sensual sensation. "You have no idea what it's doing to me to know another man has been in this room with you."

Old heartache blossomed in her chest. The tears threatening broke and raced tracks down her cheeks. "I was so stupid. I thought he loved me. Learning he used me to gain attention in the ranked guardian world, walking away after taking what he wanted, I felt useless."

Caidon leaned back and brushed her tears away with his thumbs. "You should have punched him in the face when he asked you to be his mistress. If I see him again, I won't restrain myself."

"I wanted to," she admitted. "But I'm alone, and while he's not big, he's still stronger than me. I don't know him like I thought I did and couldn't get myself into a situation I might not be able to walk away from. Not with Parker in the house."

"You're not alone anymore."

A shallow smile bubbled up inside her, along with a soft chuckle. "I will feel free to punch him at will if there is a next time and let you deal with the fallout."

"Good."

Ramsey wrapped her arms around his shoulders and pulled. His eyes widened before he tumbled onto her. Smiling, she laid back, accepting his weight over her. "You know you're not alone anymore either, right?" she whispered into his ear.

His face buried in the crook of her neck. The heavy sound of him breathing deep had her hands fisting in the fabric of his shirt. He shifted his weight, laying so his thigh pressed between hers, the mattress depressing where he settled along her side.

"I want to erase his memory from this room," he murmured along her jaw, his tongue leaving a wet path.

Oh yes, she wanted that too, even if it were impossible. Sadly, regardless of what either of them did, the memories of her bad decision concerning her first lover would remain. But her second lover would be different. Ramsey knew, deep in her heart, loving Caidon would never be a mistake.

Arching her body into his, she slid her hands into his hair and sought out his mouth. She *needed* to know if the kiss she'd used for every fantasy in the last five years was a figment of her imagination or everything she'd remembered. He wasted no time with coaxing, instead sliding his tongue along the seam of her lips, demanding entrance. Ramsey opened, a gasp of surprise morphing into a moan as his tongue glided across hers and explored every secret of her mouth.

Ramsey's heart thundered in her chest. Her breath grew ragged. Her body turned hot and demanding. The sensual kiss turned into something more, an almost claiming, though she figured she was staking her territory as much as him. The spiderweb thin tug in her chest grew, drawing her like a magnet until she wanted to crawl into his skin. Desperate, she tugged at his shirt, pulling buttons free, until her palm glided along bare flesh and rippling muscle. He groaned into her mouth at the contact, and little bursts of pleasure snaked through her body.

Pulling her mouth free, she dragged in a deep breath, wondering at the sensation. The full length of his frame pressed into her side, his pelvis at her hip left no mistake he was equally affected. Ramsey resisted the strong compulsion to reach down and explore the hard proof of his desire, even if only through his pants. In the end, the struggle proved useless, her fingers learning every warm inch of his side on her journey south. His hands pushed the thin layer of silk up until he met her bare hip. Ramsey pressed into his touch, her head falling back as his mouth left a wet trail across her throat and collarbone.

An impatient need had her twisting beneath his hand, trying with everything to get his touch to the place damp and yearning for relief. Not that she knew exactly what he could possibly do since she hadn't ever managed to figure it out herself. And she'd tried. Repeatedly. With frustrating, inadequate results. She'd chased the mythical orgasm down many a rabbit hole, unashamed to admit she'd even sought out instruction from books similar to the one she'd bought outlining sexual pleasures without actual sex. Her body, however, didn't seem to think Caidon would fail, her impatience turning to outright desperation.

Near frantic in her craving to feel his touch, Ramsey wrapped her fingers around the waist of his pants and tugged, forcing his hips closer to hers and his body almost between her legs. He didn't resist, easing himself between her now parted thighs with another sexy groan that left her breathless. Ramsey lifted her lower body to meet his, an intense sliver of pleasure radiating from her center as she pressed into his erection trapped behind his pants. He bucked against her, and any coherent thought she may have managed to hold fled.

"I… need to…" he breathed against her chest, his mouth roaming further until he encountered her breast. Meanwhile, his hand slipped between their lower bodies, and Ramsey almost screamed.

"Yes," she panted. Oh, on everything beautiful in the inhabited world, whatever he wanted at this point, her answer would be a resounding *yes*.

Through the silk of her nightgown, he pulled her nipple into his mouth while his fingers glided over her slicked flesh. More gently than she cared for, and yet with a finesse that felt too good to protest, he caressed her inside and out, never spending more than a fleeting moment in any one spot. She writhed and whimpered. With every twist of her hips, the slide of his touch changed, deepened, until she begged, on the cusp. His free hand released her breasts from their silken prison, and his mouth enclosed around her nipple once again, lightly sucking and biting. The combination proved to be her undoing. She arched off the bed as pleasure exploded through her.

Reality returned to her slowly. First, the weight of his body still over hers, followed by his complete lack of movement. Blinking, she lifted her head and found him staring at her with an intensity that stole her breath once again.

"What?" she whispered, afraid perhaps her enthusiasm had been too much.

"I want you all to myself," he growled, the depth of his words reverberating through her torso.

Ramsey hooked her feet over his thighs and grasped his jaw in her hands, bringing his face closer. "I am only yours."

He braced his weight on one arm. His fingers, still trapped between their bodies, slid deeper inside her. She gasped, unable to stop her hips from rising. "No. This. I want you this way for *me*. Only ever for me. How can I give you what he never has?"

Ramsey moved her grip to his shoulders and rose enough to bring her lips to his throat. She breathed in the scent of him and licked the salt from his skin. "You already gave me what he never could."

His mouth crashed over hers, a possessive, open-mouthed kiss that flitted away her remaining concentration. The gentleness of his touch fled, replaced with an urgent, demanding force she couldn't hold out from. A second orgasm flowed through her body like a strong ocean wave. She ripped her mouth away on a shattered cry, his name broken into near incoherent syllables.

Spent, Ramsey's arms dropped from his shoulders as she gulped in lungsful of air. Caidon rested his forehead on her chest, a bead of sweat trickling over her collarbone. Staring up at the faint shadows on her ceiling, she wondered how much better making love would be if this was his foreplay. Frustrated she hadn't bothered to keep an ovulation bracelet to track her cycle, she sighed and hoped he'd be willing to fool around until they could safely discover more of each other.

"My turn," she said.

He lifted his head and frowned. "What do you mean?"

Smiling, she lifted her hips into the bulge still

trapped between them. "Now I get a turn to make you mine."

She shoved on his shoulders, flipping their positions. His hands gripped her thighs, straddling his stomach, and he stared up at her, eyes wide. Ramsey tucked tangled curls behind her ear and grinned. Sliding down, she rubbed herself against him, pressing her palms into his chest. "Tell me, how can I give *you* what no one else ever has?"

A faint flush darkened his cheeks. "No one has ever given me anything. You are… my everything."

10

Caidon watched her carefully, figuring he should probably be embarrassed by his revelation, but finding only a sense of contentment that Ramsey would be his sole lover. A rightness. He'd never wanted anyone the way he wanted her, had never desired with the intensity she alone brought to life. The slick heat of her still coated his fingers, now cooling, though he figured the memory never would. Her uninhibited response had almost been his undoing.

Somehow, he'd managed to hold on to a thin thread of sanity and reason, knowing while she'd welcome him taking her in the heat of the moment, a potential pregnancy would be met with less enthusiasm. At least for now, because Caidon knew without a doubt he wanted to see her round and fertile with his baby. When she didn't have a possible psychotic escaped felon after her or a secret organization hoping to keep her from discovering a dirty secret. Now was definitely *not* the time to be irresponsible.

She straightened, settling more comfortably over his

stomach. "Wait… *never*? As in, not ever? With anyone? How is that possible?"

He quirked a brow, unable to stop his hands from continuing to explore the silken lengths of her legs. The shimmery fabric of her nightgown pooled on his torso, leaving her calves and thighs bare. "Easy."

Disbelief continued to show on her face. She waved a hand around. "But you're… you know."

Contemplating her fractured train of thought, he shook his head. "No, I'm not sure I know. I'm what?"

"How did you keep women from throwing themselves at you?" she asked, clearly exasperated.

"I don't encounter many women. I work alone. Travel alone. And if anyone had enough time to pay me any attention, I've failed at my job. Anonymous sex is dangerous for multiple reasons, especially in my line of work."

"But… no one? Ever? You did go through teenage years, didn't you?"

He laughed. "Yes, but the first woman who propositioned me liked young boys, virgins, and when I realized I'd be nothing but a body being used, I decided if I ever slept with someone, they'd mean something to me."

She blew out a huff, disrupting inky curls around her face. "Well, talk about pressure."

Looking over her beautifully flushed body, he let loose a lazy smile. "I think if anyone should be concerned, it's me. After all, I have no idea what I'm doing."

"Could have fooled me," she muttered.

"It was the bond," he admitted. "I don't know how to explain it other than I could *feel* what you liked."

"How intriguing." Her tongue slipped between her lips, curled back into her mouth, bringing her bottom lip with. Caidon watched the sensual movements with a deepening hunger.

"I wonder," she said, her fingers tracing down his chest. "If I'll feel it too, with you?"

"I don't know."

She wiggled lower, her mouth brushing his stomach. Caidon lifted his shoulders so he could see her southward progress. "What are you doing?"

All she offered was a wicked smile before undoing the buttons of his pants. "I'm curious."

His aching erection sprang free from the confines of his pants. Ramsey wasted no more time on words, simply engulfing him into the hot, wet confines of her mouth. Caidon choked on air and collapsed onto the bed as ridiculous levels of pleasure bombarded him. She stroked and sucked, and before he realized it, his fingers were buried deep into her soft curls, holding on for dear life as she brought him to unimaginable carnal heights. Desperately, he tried to hold out, tried to pull free when the sizzle of his impending orgasm gathered tightly inside him. But she'd have none of it, and on a broken, growled shout, he arched off the bed and released into her mouth. Panting, he collapsed.

She folded her arms across his hips, a mischievous light dancing in her eyes. "The experiment was a success, I think. The sensation was faint, but I definitely felt something when I did things you liked. I wonder if it'll grow stronger."

All Caidon's muscles went lax, and he dropped an arm over his eyes. "Everything you just did I clearly enjoyed."

She traced a figure on his stomach above his belly button. "Yes, but I'm positive there were things I did you liked more. You responded differently. I'm excited to play around with our bond."

Caidon laughed through a groan. "I don't know what to say to that."

"You're a lucky husband?" she ventured, her fingers continuing a soft teasing motion.

He caught her hand and tugged, pulling her up until he could kiss her palm. "I was that already."

"Ah," she laughed and straddled his ribs. Leaning over, she captured his face between her hands and pressed a lingering kiss to his lips. "Then I'm a lucky wife."

RAMSEY STRETCHED, FEELING COMPLETELY MARVELOUS IN the warming light of morning. For too many years, she'd wondered how good physical pleasure really could be. After all, some were willing to risk contracting human rabies syndrome just to obtain a sexual release. Knowing now how delightful she could feel, she understood a bit better the temptation. Rising from the basil plant she'd been pulling leaves from to make spiced beans and potatoes for breakfast, she breathed in the damp, earthen air in the greenhouse and smiled.

Last night Caidon had shown her so much more than the awakening of her body as a woman. Ramsey still struggled to believe she may, in fact, be a genetic heir. She wished her parents were still alive for her to ask who in their family tree may have been a natural-born, Gen-Heir linguist. Years of thinking herself inept shadowed her excitement. She didn't honestly know if this gift had any practical uses other than being able to work as a translator. Caidon had mentioned something about breaking codes, but what did she know about that? Sighing, she bent over and pulled a few oregano leaves, and pinched off a small sprig of rosemary.

Air shifted behind her, and before she could turn, someone slammed into her back, sending her careening forward across a mounded row. Her skirt caught between her legs as her feet stuck into the yielding dirt, and she crashed into the next mound. Soft earth absorbed her weight. Small, delicate stalks and leaves crushed beneath her hands and stomach. She cried out in a mixture of shock and loss of her fragile growing plants. A heavy mass settled over her. Fingers wrapped around her neck and held her cheek against the gritty soil.

"I gave you every opportunity to make the decision on your own," Tobyn sneered into her ear.

"It's not a choice if you're going to force me in the end," she managed, her breath stirring loose bits of debris near her mouth and nose.

The full length of his body settled over hers, pushing her torso deeper into the risen soil. Stems and small rocks pricked through her dress and into her stomach, thighs, and chest. She grimaced and tried to keep from struggling, already able to feel the evidence of his arousal pressing against her rear.

"We both know I won't have to force you to do anything." He gently ground his hips to hers, and Ramsey's breath stuck in her throat. "I've always been able to convince you."

"There will be no convincing," Ramsey bit out between her clenched teeth. "Ever."

He shifted off her but left her no time to do something about the realization. His fingers dug into her upper arms as he hauled her up and propelled her forward. She collided with the glass wall, green and dingy from years of neglect. Adequate light still filtered in to keep her plants alive, and until her face was pressed into the filthy surface, that had been good enough. Now, she wished she'd been a better greenhouse keeper.

"I saw you," he whispered, his hands sliding from her arms to her hips. "With *him*. Last night."

Heat burst across Ramsey's cheeks, equal to the horror widening her eyes. "H-how?"

"I was about to sneak in the same way I always had in the past. I still remember the odd little quirk of your window lock that made it so easy to get past."

Ramsey squeezed her eyes shut. She'd forgotten about that.

"Then he walked in. So, I waited and ended up getting a naughty show equal to any curtain couple act I've been to."

The dark room adult-only entertainment name was familiar to Ramsey. But not something she'd ever heard about outside of the whispered name behind flipping fans and giggles of young girls who tried to imagine such a thing and likely failed in reality. Ramsey loathed something so personal and special between her and Caidon had been reduced to a dirty curtain show in Tobyn's eyes.

"How dare you." Her voice, like her body, trembled with anger.

"Oh, I dared to do so much more than watch," he

whispered. "I had no idea you liked to use your mouth. I am eager to know the real feel."

Bile burned a path to her throat. "If you put anything in my mouth, you won't have it as part of your body any longer."

Tobyn seemed determined to test her rejection. He stuck two fingers into her mouth, sliding along her tongue and bottom teeth. Ramsey didn't hesitate. She bit down. Hard. His bellow echoed around the glass enclosure. Using the distraction to her advantage, she jabbed an elbow into his side and wedged her foot between his legs, and lifted her heel, connecting with the sensitive flesh between. He gagged and sank to the ground. Ramsey picked up her skirt and dashed to the house stairs.

A blur of motion had her skidding to a stop. Yellow and white papers fluttered into the air. Caidon tackled another man to the ground at the bottom of the stairs. They rolled in the dirt, Caidon wrapped around some stranger. The unfamiliar man flailed, landing a lucky enough blow to get away. He scrambled from the ground and shoved Ramsey hard on his way by. She lost her balance and landed on her butt, skidding across the earthen aisle. Sure, why not, her gown was already destroyed on the front.

Giving up completely, she threw her arms wide and laid all the way back. Pale, twinkling light streamed in through the algae-coated windows above. From her peripheral, she managed to make out the unknown man towing a still whimpering Tobyn out of the greenhouse. Caidon made it to the side entrance before he seemed to realize she hadn't moved. He gave up pursuit and ran to her side.

"Where are you hurt?" He fell to his knees, his hands roving over her legs and sides.

"I'm not," she said, sighing. His concern, and his touch, felt so, *so* good.

Needing something other than the sensation of Tobyn's fingers in her mouth, Ramsey grasped the front of Caidon's shirt and pulled him closer. She brushed her lips across his and opened when his tongue probed for more. All too soon, he ended the kiss, groaning.

"Parker," he said against her mouth, pulling another kiss from her.

She returned it with a moan of disappointment. "Okay, go. I'm fine. I'll get myself up."

"You sure you're okay?"

"Yes." To make her point, she rose and brushed dirt and leaves from her hair.

"I don't think we can stay here anymore."

She followed his gaze to the mess of papers littering the front of the steps. "Are those my manifests?"

"Yes, he, whoever he was, attempted to steal them. I caught him when I heard Tobyn scream. What did you do, by the way?" he asked, helping her stand.

"I bit him and kicked him in the balls."

"What did he do to deserve that?" He glanced to where Tobyn had had her pinned against the glass.

She pressed her lips together and focused on shaking her skirts clean.

"Ramsey?" he growled.

"Hmm?"

"What did he do?"

She sighed and pulled a twig from her hair. "Nothing, because I didn't let him. Jonathon made sure I knew all the ways to take down a man. Nails, teeth, feet, he said all of them worked."

He stared at her for a moment, his eyes dark with anger, his nostrils flaring as if trying to pick up a lie. "All right. Do you know of a place you can stay?"

Ramsey stopped mid-pluck of removing a leaf from her curls. "You won't be with us?"

"I need to talk to Voklane and figure out how to get us out of the country."

"But, Parker," Ramsey said, a sliver of panic blooming in her chest.

"I know." Caidon rubbed her back, then changed to dusting her off. "We won't go anywhere without him. But while I'm gone, I need to know you both are somewhere safe."

"I can make some radio calls. I know people."

He smiled. "I figured."

11

THE SHRILL SOUND OF CHILDREN PLAYING MADE DELANEE Ralston rub her temples. Not that she didn't love children. She did. With her being number eight out of eleven offspring, kids were a fact of life. Nieces, nephews, and in today's odd mixture, friends of the family's progeny were included in the chaotic mixture of preteens to infants. A loud, happy whirlwind of noise that made getting anything accomplished near impossible. Her *bakishka* was in bliss if the happy smile on her aged face was any indication.

Madeleine Fenwick waved a hand that, even at seventy-two, looked healthy and unspotted by age. "Soon, one of your brood will be in this mix, Delanee dear."

"*Baki*, that would require a man in my life, of which we both know I have not even a candidate."

"If you'd quite rejecting all the suitors…" She waved a hand again and left the rest hanging in the air.

Delanee couldn't stop the glare, disrespectful or not. "I'm not the one who is rejecting anyone."

144

Madeleine tsked and went back to observing the playing gaggle of little people like a queen overseeing her favorite subjects. Which Delanee figured was about right. "Oh, child, if you'd stop bringing home simpering fools, perhaps I'd be a little less particular. I am, after all, *the* matchmaker in this city. I think I'll know when you bring home someone unsuitable."

Okay, so Delanee had to admit she preferred men less dominant than herself. She didn't want some alpha male like her brother's ordering her about or thinking her female form meant delicate instead of the strength she knew she harbored. As the daughter of an impressive beast master and intelligent SNID investigator, Delanee was no weakling. She had had enough of being seen as inferior by her managing editor at the *Haven City Chronicle* because of her age, let alone her gender. Being seen in such a light by her potential mate was unacceptable.

Baki Madeleine held to the innate belief Delanee needed someone powerful, who would be an equal force to her authority. Delanee snorted to herself. Not going to happen.

Ever.

As usual, her *baki* seemed to know Delanee's train of thoughts if the narrowing of her eyes were any indication. "Your fear will leave you lonely."

"Better lonely than a prisoner," Delanee said with a brittle smile.

Madeleine sighed sadly and shook her head. "You think I'd ever allow you to marry such a ghastly partner?"

No, her grandmother had not approved of the near disaster Delanee had almost found herself in because she'd believed her emotions over her head. Never again. Thankfully, she'd seen the light before the scab had been able to take more than her heart. "Like my brother, I don't need any help."

An imperial brow raised. "You think I didn't have a say in Deverick's choice of a wife? I met with Sadie the moment he declared his intent."

Not wanting to discuss her marital status, or the lack of, Delanee glanced over her shoulder at the closed door to the small radio room. "Do you think Miss Hunter was able to reach her brother?"

Madeleine picked up a stuffed pink bear and handed it to her fussy toddler great-grandson, who squealed in happiness and slammed the toy into the floor with wild abandon. "She's been in there long enough, so it's likely."

Under normal circumstances, Delanee would be using Ramsey Hunter's misfortune as reading fodder for the population of Haven City. The sister of a key guardian, who also happened to be a well-respected master tribunii for HCES, being in danger was the type of juicy story her editor salivated over. The story had literally walked into her living room, and it wasn't the first time. But Delanee respected Ramsey, felt her a kindred spirit. Since she didn't have many females she could call friend, she wasn't willing to sacrifice the one she had for an income.

A brisk knock sounded on the door, which opened before either she or her grandmother could rise. Two men entered, one tall, pale, and broad, the other darker, a bit shorter, but just as impressive build-wise. Both frowned and oozed the same dominance she recognized in her half-Ruthenian brothers. Her grandmother looked each man over, her wing-backed, white wicker chair once again reminding Delanee of an unconventional throne.

"Guardian Voklane," Madeleine said with a nod to the tall, pale man. Then she looked to the shorter, darker male. "Master Guardian Survaine."

Equal expressions of shock crossed over their handsome faces. Delanee swallowed. The tall one, in particular, left her feeling oddly breathless. His light blond hair, paired with silvery-blue eyes, a color she figured could be found in the ice fields, was striking in skin so much paler than hers she wanted to wrap her hand around his thick forearm and see the difference herself. The rich caramel shade of the man her grandmother had identified as Survaine was close enough to her own tea-with-cream complexion not to cause any sort of curiosity.

When the cute munchkin named Parker jumped up from the rug and ran to Survaine, Delanee almost let loose a breath of relief. *He* was Ramsey's husband, not the one named Voklane. And why did Delanee care? She'd ponder that later, if ever. Dangerous territory she had no business wandering into. Thankfully, the tall stranger's gaze passed by her without any interest. She told herself this was a good thing. She didn't want, nor need, the attention of an impressive guardian.

"Mrs. Fenwick," Voklane said, his voice deep and smooth. "I appreciate you letting the Survaines stay here for the night."

Her grandmother waved the gratitude away. "Child, Ramsey is a dear girl, and her little nephew doesn't get the chance to play with other kids unless he's here. She's always welcome. She knows that."

Voklane's focus shifted to Parker, who'd begun to jump in an attempt to be picked up. "Yes, well, all the same, the FIO thanks you. Miss Hun—, I mean Master Guardianess Survaine, is important."

"They're all important," Delanee said, her chin raised in challenge. "All the guardians, and the spouses who support them."

The unranked guardian simply looked at her, his chiseled face devoid of emotion. "Yes, but some have rarer gifts than others."

"And yet they're sacrificed all the same," she said with a syrupy smile.

"Something you would know personally about?" he asked softly.

Delanee glared and shifted in discomfort. "Not myself, no."

"Conducted some interviews then?" When she remained silent, he arched a blond brow. "Did research and wrote an article?" She ground her teeth, still without an answer to his questioning.

He shook his head. "No? Then how can you possibly know of any sacrifice *we* have made?"

"You or them, the sacrifice is made all the same, yes?" she asked, refusing to back down.

"A sacrifice for one's country is worth the expense for the benefit of the many," Survaine answered quietly. His hand cupped the top of Parker's small head. "I gladly continue to make it, as I know many others do as well. For you. For my wife. For this child and all the others in this room."

"And I appreciate your willingness to serve in a guardian role," Delanee acknowledged. "But not everyone is given such a choice."

Voklane's gaze narrowed. "No one in your family was ever forced to do anything."

"Fifteen isn't exactly an age one can make much of a decision."

"Does your brother know you feel he was treated so unfairly?"

He crossed his arms over an impressive chest, which she tried to ignore about as much as she attempted not to notice how his long-sleeved, black sweater pulled tight over muscular biceps. Failed completely and had to swallow against the sudden dryness in her throat. Darn it! Heat flared in her cheeks, and she allowed her attention to be pulled to a screaming little girl, the niece of a downstairs neighbor.

"My brother is one of the rare, one of the powerful. How he feels is likely irrelevant to you," she said. "All of my brothers are."

His smile was cold and smugger than she cared for. "As are you, yes?"

A sliver of fear pierced her chest. How could he possibly know that? No one knew except her father. She licked her lips. "I have no idea what you're talking about. I'm a journalist. Not exactly a talent the FIO recruits."

He nodded, something she felt in her bones was for her alone, a message he'd let her secret drop. "Keep protecting your family, Delanee Ralston. Despite being an arch guardian, I'm sure your brother, and the ones in lesser ranks, appreciate you on their side, ensuring their rights."

Her anxiety didn't lessen, but she did nod in recognition of his statement. "I will, don't worry."

He smiled again. The action only slightly above chilly this time. "I won't."

"Okay, this is all I could find," Ryan said, dropping stacks of books on a huge desk in front of Ramsey. "I'll be in Synintel's office if you need me."

Sitting forward, Ramsey opened the top book and examined the first couple of pages. She set the book to the side and went to the next. They'd taken over the library at Synintel's house, having left the happy chaos of Madeleine's apartment for the quieter residence of an arch guardian. While Ramsey wanted to be impressed and a little intimidated, she didn't have time. Their MagnaRail train south to Port Anchor, left in just under six hours. Ryan needed as many manifests as she could manage to translate in that time.

Now knowing she needed to hear, as well as be exposed to the written language to completely understand it, had Ramsey doubting her ability to help. While they could perhaps find a person who spoke a dialect, or maybe two, finding the dozen Ramsey suspected were being used to code the manifests was impossible given the time restriction. But she'd do her best. Ryan had pointed out no one who received the manifests spoke the language and likely had some sort of decipher. All she had to do was make sense of what she was looking at. She figured mentioning she'd been failing so far would be a waste of time, so she kept the frustration to herself.

Caidon seemed to sense her discontent. He came up behind her and massaged her neck until she relaxed. Leaning over her, he pulled the book closer, then he whispered into her ear the pronunciations broken down underneath each character. The page she touched revealed itself, and she gasped. "Tell me which ones you need, and I'll do this for you," he continued to whisper, his warm breath causing curious things to happen inside her.

"This is incredible," she murmured, turning pages while searching for familiar symbols.

"Yes, you are," he agreed, his fingers still working magic on the back of her neck.

Parker played on a rug surrounded by books, loose papers with some crayons, and a few wooden toy trains. For the moment, he appeared content, and Ramsey hoped he remained occupied. Their luggage was stacked next to the door with all their travel documents. Ramsey chose not to think beyond needing to get to the train station on time. Travel anxiety was a real thing in her family since most of the members who'd attempted to leave the shores of Sziveria hadn't ever returned. Jonathon's current dilemma seemed proof of familial misfortune.

Turning back to the distraction of her task, she flipped through pages, searching quickly. "How can you pronounce them accurately?"

"I've been to Mark Inland a few times. I know how the words should sound, even if I'm not sure what they mean. The dialects may all be different, but the overall sound is consistent throughout the country."

She found three and pointed. He said them, and they seemed to unravel before her eyes to become understandable like any other words she could read. Excited, she pulled several manifests forward and found she could write a word under some of the characters with confidence. Soon, a clear message formed on one of the manifests. Ramsey figured she could fill in the missing words to make a coherent sentence, but she didn't want to chance any of her guesses being wrong. After flipping through several more books, she found what she needed and had a small stack of completely translated messages for Ryan.

Caidon picked them up and looked them over, slowly moving between the pages. A low curse left him, only loud enough for her to perceive. "I need to find Voklane. I'll be back. Keep working on what you can mark if you need my help on anything."

Parker rose from the rug and fussed when Caidon told him to stay put and keep playing. Ramsey used the age-old tool of bribery to calm him down, reminding him to be good for the surprise he had coming. Near meltdown averted, she went back to researching and decoding.

The men returned minutes later. Ryan's face contorted in anger, while Caidon's held little emotional clues. The masked assassin was back in place. Ramsey dropped her chin on her palm and couldn't stop the inward smile of mischief. He was different around her. Unguarded. Open. And in her bedroom, he'd revealed a passionate nature she couldn't wait to unravel further. The memory of him hard, straining under the sensual assault of her tongue, experiencing for the first time what no one else had given to him, had her pulse rising. His gaze narrowed, and she cleared her throat and her mind. Though, the mischievous knowledge of knowing he could *feel* the direction of her thoughts through their bond made a secret smile quirk on her lips.

"Can you create a key based on what you've

managed so far?" Ryan asked.

"I think so."

"Once they learn you know how to read their messages, they'll go to something new," Caidon warned.

"I know, but it'll take them awhile to figure out we've managed to break their code. They haven't changed it yet in six months, and since we know they discovered the Hunters were investigating, they must have had suspicions. Codes take time to develop. I'm sure they're working on something now, but for a little longer, we can count on these and maybe, finally, get ahead," Ryan said.

Ramsey laid the remaining manifests in a line beside her. "How often are you finding them?"

"Nothing over the winter, obviously, but I found eight last month and two so far this month."

Searching over the still-coded documents, she chewed on her lip and pulled a clean sheet of paper forward. She separated three manifests from the others. "I think these are simply changing ports, hoping to remain undetected while docked and receiving new manifests. The messages state what's to be placed on the new documentation."

"What was on them before?"

"Let's see, this one says rice, cotton, and… I don't know how to say this… pee-ah-nut?" She looked at the men.

Caidon cracked a smile. "Peanut. It's a common food in almost all of South America, Westica, Miami Island and Monaco Sands. It doesn't produce a lot for the space it requires to grow, so it stays pretty local in its markets, being too expensive to export to most shores."

"It's a delicacy, then?" Ramsey asked.

"Here? Yes, if you can afford the import."

She tapped the table in thought. "The alterations being asked to be made changes the rice to wheat, and the peanut to pinto beans, cotton remains the same."

"Rice and peanuts are high end products, whereas wheat and pinto tend to be more shelf-stable and accessible. Wonder which was correct?" Caidon picked up the manifest she'd been looking over.

"Where did they come from and where are they going, and was anything delivered here or loaded before departure? That's what I want to know," Ryan said.

"You'd have to have seen the ship in question to know all that. Does Immigration and Import inspect ships?" Ramsey asked.

"Not ones that are simply here to resupply as this one was. It's easy income for the country. They're supposed to stay offshore and send a small crew to purchase supplies. It's easy for someone to be waiting to exchange the manifests."

"Why turn in the copy of the false manifest, then? Why not just get the new one and throw this one out?"

Caidon pointed to a series of numbers in the upper left corner. "The resources code. These resources were accounted for by whoever uses this number. There must be a paper trail. The new manifest would have a new code, so it looks like— to—" He searched over the paper. "Westica, the shipment of rice and peanuts was accepted by Sziveria."

"Who does that impact?" Ramsey asked, wondering how a small shipment of any type of resource could do much in the grand scheme of things.

"I don't handle anything having to do with import or export," Ryan said. "The rice, we use enough here that losing a shipment may have a small effect on supply. The peanuts? Someone was expecting those."

Caidon frowned. "And someone lost a serious amount of raimarks when they didn't arrive."

"I wonder if the same shipping company is involved in all of these or if it's multiple," Ryan mused, flipping between all the papers Ramsey had translated.

"I wish Sylphine was here. She may be able to tell." Ramsey tapped a yellow page closest to her. "I know the ones I was originally working on were all part of Leone Cyrano's small fleet, that's why I was helping."

"I'm going to get these to Arch Guardian Immetana. She'll know the best way to research and make it look routine instead of suspicious. Enough people have died already protecting this secret. We have to be careful. Another reason I'm making sure you're getting to your brother."

"She's fine with me," Caidon said.

"Her brother doesn't know you," Ryan said evenly, though if the tense way he held himself were any indication, calm wasn't his state of mind. "Asherwick didn't want her involved in any of this mess, and yet here we are, and she's chin deep in it. So yes, I'm sending her to him, where he can see she's perfectly safe."

Confused, Ramsey tilted her head and regarded Ryan. "Caidon mentioned Jonathon asking you not to involve me in anything. When did he do this?"

"Months ago, before he left for Italyssa."

Annoyance flashed through Ramsey. Her fingers curled into a fist. Confirmation that instead of trusting her to decide, her brother had coddled her and taken away the choice for her. Because once upon a time, jumping in to help others had cost her more than she could almost handle.

"He loves you," Caidon said, his words quiet, meant only for her despite the company as if knowing where her anger stemmed from.

"And as I told you before, he had no right to make a decision for me without even asking," she replied, taking a deep breath in hopes of soothing herself. "I know he meant well, but at some point, he has to realize I'm all grown up and understand mistakes, even if I have to make them to learn."

Caidon brushed her hair from her neck and caressed a path across. "You've made plenty of decisions without him the last half year. You'll get your chance to confront him soon."

Ramsey let loose a shaky sigh and focused on his gentle touch. "I don't know if I want to confront him."

"Then don't be angry."

The extent Jonathon had gone to try to ensure she stayed out of the guardian role buried deep in her blood frustrated her. She couldn't help her feelings. Knowing his head would likely pop free of his body when he'd learned she'd not only helped solve a dangerous mystery but had married in his absence made a vindictive smile uncurl within her. Let him try to stop her destiny now. Her shoulders rolled under Caidon's continued ministrations. She had another fighter in her corner. One who hadn't tried to do anything more than help her learn who *she* was. So far, she liked the new Ramsey.

"That look is making me nervous," Ryan said, sighing.

"Will you let us know if you find anything else?" Ramsey asked, ignoring his uneasiness. She picked up a pen to start creating a legend for the rest of the manifests. If he didn't want to come between two siblings, he shouldn't have agreed to anything Jonathon asked.

"I just hope there isn't a code within a code," Ryan said with a head shake.

"Like rice really means pale people and wheat golden skin?" Caidon asked, his hand falling away.

Ryan sighed. "Yeah."

Ramsey sat back, disgust and horror moving through her, taking away any lingering irritation. "Well, isn't that an awful thought?"

"But accurate," Ryan stated. "Like I said, I'll talk to Immetana, get her impressions."

"I hope this helps." Ramsey flipped through book pages and wrote more notes.

"Already has. And yes, if I'm able to reach you in Italyssa, I'll let you know if I make any new discoveries," Ryan assured.

An odd expression crossed over Caidon's face, but he remained silent. Curiosity made Ramsey want to ask what was on Caidon's mind, but she decided to wait until he wouldn't possibly have to lie. She finished writing out the decryption key while the men left the room. Parker came over and drove his trains all over the surface, making happy noises that had nothing to do with what a train actually sounded like. Ramsey smiled. Soon he'd know, and she wondered if he'd adjust his noise-making accordingly. Much like Ramsey had never heard ship's horn because she'd never ventured near any water large enough to hold one, Parker had never been outside the immediate city to hear a train. She wondered if he'd be excited or frightened by the loud mass of steel. Perhaps a bit of both. They'd find out soon enough.

She finished the translation index and hoped, based on her findings, another person would be able to figure out any characters she hadn't encountered if new manifests arrived during their absence. If she had enough time to research, maybe a pattern would emerge that helped narrow down how they were choosing which characters to use.

After stacking the books and straightening the papers, she helped Parker clean up his toys, placing everything in a small travel bag Caidon had found for him. She fitted it over his shoulders when Caidon returned, sans Ryan. He held folded papers in his hand.

"Parker's legal documentation was just delivered. We're officially free to travel," he said, holding up the bundle.

"I thought we were going regardless," she said, straightening.

"We were, but now they'll be no issues. Asherwick can return with his wife and his son."

Ramsey's heart turned in her chest. She held her hand out, and Caidon slipped the documents onto her palm. After unfolding them, she sniffled back the burn of tears as she took in Parker's record of birth. "They listed Jonathon and Sylphine. Why? His mother died protecting him, she deserves to be on his record."

"Ryan said it was easier since his original record was lost, and there's no proof of his mother ever having had him." Caidon brushed his fingers through Parker's hair. "Asherwick's wife won't have any legal issues now either, caring for him. He's loved and safe, Ramsey.

That's what matters. If keeping his birth mother alive in his heart is important, trust your brother to see to that."

Ramsey refolded the records and placed them in an accessible yet safe location in her shoulder bag with all their other necessary papers, like their tickets. "If he has an issue, he can take it up with Voklane, I suppose."

"He can," Caidon agreed.

Another bout of nervousness fluttered in her stomach and lodged air in her throat. She was ready to see her brother and sister-in-law. So ready. But she'd never left Haven City. Since the sprawling city had everything she ever needed, she never felt as if she'd been missing much. Now, not only was she leaving, but she was going to a new country. A new culture that didn't even speak her language. Of course, she knew theirs.

"It's going to be fine," Caidon assured, wrapping his arms around her waist and pulling her back into his strong chest. "We'll be safe. Parker is going to have a great time, and so will you."

"A train and a ship… I've never been on either," she confessed. "What if I get sick?"

He released her and picked up their bags. "Then I'll hold your hair. Come on, the MagnaRail departs in an hour. We'll be lucky to make the final call."

Not comforted by his rather straightforward, unconcerned words, world traveler that he was, Ramsey held tight to Parker's hand and tried to convince herself the adventure awaiting held more excitement than uncertainty. Knowing she had failed as her heart hammered and her throat turned dry. Scared or not, prepared or not, life was about to become very different. She hoped for the better.

12

The moment Ramsey stepped off the ship onto the dock, she almost sank to her knees. Brilliant sun shone down in sweltering beams on them. Birds squawked and dove into sparkling, aquamarine waters so clear and beautiful it almost hurt to look upon. Color burst in any direction she looked while shielding her eyes from the glaring light. Even in the dead of summer, she didn't think the sun was so ruthless back home.

Parker scrunched his nose and lifted his shirt to show his round belly. "I'm hot."

Ramsey pushed his shirt back down. "Me too, but our clothes stay on."

"They aren't," he whined, pointing to a group of women walking along the docks, laughing in animated conversation.

Vibrant, intricately embroidered fabric crossed over their breasts and tied at their backs to trail in colorful flutters behind them. Equally splendid, loose, almost sheer skirts covered their legs, leaving their midsection and most of their back bare. Sandals adorned their feet, showing ankle bracelets and painted toes encircled with rings. Three of the women had a vast array of clipped decorations throughout their hair, marking them single. The others only had a few, likely their favorites, along with their promise band connected to their marriage ring by a thin silver chain. Their golden skin gleamed in the late spring sun. They were stunning and exotic, and Ramsey suddenly felt very out of place.

She pulled on the neckline of her floral print gown, which covered her from neck to ankle, more out of necessity in the colder climate of Sziveria than for modesty. Though, as she gazed around at the revealing fashion, she couldn't imagine any woman in Sziveria being comfortable showing so much skin. Then again, except for one month a year, they'd be too cold to last long outside of any indoor function. Thankfully, Ramsey noted she wasn't alone in her over-dressed status. Other women strolled from the ship, many popping open little lacy umbrellas, unconcerned about their attire.

Caidon took her elbow and guided her down the wide dock to where their luggage was being unloaded from a narrow opening near the bottom of the ship by workers. Everything except their small carry-ons and a long case he'd kept in their berth, or slung across his back at all times, needed to be collected. Parker whined and yanked his shirt up again. This time he didn't stop, pulling it free and flinging it between the railings into the water before Ramsey could snatch it from the air. An excited group of birds dove for the solid orange color, only to screech in dismay when they learned they'd been tricked.

Parker laughed and waved his hands, having

learned on the channel voyage if he threw food in the air, he'd make new friends. Sometimes his fingers were enough for the desperate creatures to investigate. "Here birdy, birdies."

Tired from being unable to sleep with the constant motion of the ship and Parker kicking his small feet into her all night, every single night, Ramsey decided to let him walk around half-naked. The energy to fight with him didn't exist. Hopefully, the sun wouldn't burn him too badly on their trip to the Seartavos residence. She had no idea how far it was from their location, but the island wasn't large.

Caidon, apparently used to the dismal depths of travel fatigue, frowned at Parker as the child rubbed his belly in triumph before disappearing into the throng of pedestrians meandering along the docks and shops directly across. Unlike most ports that were seedy and rundown, Italyssian ports were welcoming, full of vitality, an example of the culture visitors were soon to be immersed in.

Ramsey grabbed Parker's arm before he could chase after Caidon. She sat on their luggage, hoping her husband would come back for them, yet unable to muster much energy to really care. Caidon returned, carrying a small, pale yellow linen sleeveless tunic. He put it on Parker, who let loose a scream, complete with huge tears. Travel fatigue seemed to have claimed another victim.

Yawning, Ramsey looked around for a means of transport and saw only the occasional bike among the foot traffic. "I'm going to sleep for a week when we get to my brother. How exactly are we supposed to get there, though?"

"A cart we can hire should be a few blocks from here," he answered, motioning for her to rise from their luggage.

"A cart?" She blinked. "Not a carriage?"

"Roads aren't big enough for much more than a single horse cart or bikes."

"Will we all fit in one?"

"Yes, we'll be fine."

Fine turned out to be Caidon up front with the driver, while Ramsey held onto Parker in the back and made sure their luggage didn't bounce free. Thankfully, the older man guiding a mule along a rutted shell-lined road spoke enough Sziverian that Caidon was able to handle directions. Ramsey filled in where necessary but was too tired to do much more than idly watch the beautiful vineyards and orchards, backdropped by sparkling ocean and rolling hills. Not for the first time since arriving, Ramsey wondered why Jonathon wanted to return to the dreariness of their home.

The cart ambled along, the soft clop of the mule's hooves competing with the trill of songbirds and the faint rustle of a salt-tinged breeze. Mixed with the scent of sun and ocean, a delicate hint of exotic flowers filled the air. Butterflies danced along the edge of the road, competing with bees for nectar. Parker leaned over the edge, pointing to a blue butterfly with long, violet hindwings.

Lost in the enchanting beauty, Ramsey didn't hear Caidon's shouted warning. The cart lurched upward. Parker squealed and tipped over. Without a second thought, Ramsey launched herself over with him, wrapping her body around his as they soared through the air. They landed hard in a thick pool of mud. A rock slammed into her hip and her ribs. Dirty water splashed over her while viscous sludge pulled her under. She shouted Caidon's name before grime covered her face and forced her to hold her breath. Parker thrashed, and then suddenly, he was gone.

Panic hit hard and fast.

The more Ramsey struggled, the quicker she sank. The stench of rot and muck assaulted her senses before she could no longer take in another gasp. A strong hand wrapped around her upper arm and yanked. She ignored the shock of pain and tried to find purchase beneath her to help, but her feet only sank deeper into the mire. An arm wrapped around her chest. Slowly, inch by agonizing inch, the sucking mud released its hold. On a disgusting *plop*, she fell backward onto a hard body. Two arms wrapped around her and squeezed. Ramsey gulped for air and tried not to panic further when she couldn't open her eyes.

"You're okay," Caidon panted, his hold tightening.

"I can't see," she said, proud of the lack of anxiety in her voice. "Where is Parker?"

Little hands grabbed at her, and Ramsey reached back. Caidon sat up, taking her with him. "He's fine, not quite as muddy as you."

"What happened?" she asked, waiting while he used something to wipe her face clean enough for her to see.

"Someone put a rock in the road."

Parker climbed onto their collective laps and shuddered. Tears ran streaks down his grimy face.

"Don't rocks naturally happen in nature?" Ramsey asked.

"Not like this. We need to get moving before whoever set the trap comes to check on their prize."

Ramsey twisted to see his face, ignoring the pinch at her hip and side. "You think someone put a rock in the road for us? Why?"

"Break a wheel? Cause an accident?" He shrugged. "Any number of reasons that leave us vulnerable on the roadside."

Ramsey glanced at the cart. "Nothing happened?"

"No, I alerted the driver in time. He avoided the rock, but not a deeper road groove, which is what sent Parker over when we came out of it." He grabbed Parker under his arms and stood. After settling the boy on his hip, he reached down to help Ramsey. She didn't want to let go, and thankfully, he didn't make her.

"How long do you think we have?" she asked, accepting the driver's hand from across the bench.

"Not long." He handed Parker to her and then swung up into the back on a rapid motion of strength and dexterity. Once behind their luggage, he took out a rifle, painted in an odd, almost messy variety of grays and blacks. "Go."

The driver burst into motion, his mule obeying with a bray of annoyance. Ramsey barely had time to clutch Parker to her chest. He'd wrapped his small body all around her, not caring about the filth that squished between them. They traveled considerably faster than the lazy, sedate pace the driver had set before. A combination of nerves and curiosity had her glancing over her shoulder. Caidon braced the rifle over the top of their luggage, his body half laying as much as he could manage with his larger frame. A cloud of dust billowed out behind them, swirling and sparkling in the sun-drenched breeze, beyond which she could make out very little.

"Is anyone following us?" she shouted over the clatter of wheels and hooves.

"Not so far," he answered without shifting his focus.

The beautiful country flew past without any notice from the occupants this time. Ramsey was too focused on trying to figure out if they were nearing their destination or not, wishing she knew what the Seartavos estate looked like. Tension stiffened Ramsey's already sore muscles, and even after hours of the steady trot the driver managed to keep the mule at, she couldn't relax. Parker had fallen asleep. Ramsey feared his cheek would end up stuck to her dress, drying like thick clay around her, but she didn't dare wake him.

Caidon didn't seem to relax either. Every time she looked behind, he was in the same position. She wondered how he managed. The mule dropped to a slower walk, sweat gleaming off his gray-brown coat. Soft colors appeared on the edges of the clouds, the first hint of sunset kissing the horizon.

"How much further?" she asked their driver.

"A half-hour, no more," he answered in Italyssian, making Ramsey realize she'd spoken in his native tongue.

She didn't quite know how to feel about that, so she ignored the unfamiliar talent and instead tried to figure out which stoned off parcel of land in the distance may belong to her sister-in-law's family. While through Sylphine, Ramsey had become proficient at Italyssian, she hadn't spoken it in almost a year. They ambled up a steeper incline, and at the rise, Ramsey spotted a stunning three-story mansion made of pale-yellow stone that seemed to glow in the setting sun. Flowered vines wound a cheery path up thick columns while huge pots with pruned trees lined a curving drive. Hints of vibrant blue and white fabric fluttered and disappeared from the second and third stories, which appeared to be completely open to the outside, closed off only by balcony railings.

"Is that where we're going?" she asked.

"*Saie*," he said with a nod.

As they drew closer, she noted a variety of bikes, carts, and two-seater gigs without their horses parked neatly at the bottom of the hill leading up to the residence. Faint musical notes floated on the breeze, competing with the rush of ocean waves crashing unseen somewhere nearby. She squeezed her eyes shut and wondered at the chances of being able to disappear into the house unseen by what appeared to be half of Italyssa on the property.

The driver pulled to a stop at the open iron gates. Caidon politely refused the offer to help with their belongings, instead paying him double the agreed upon rate, enough for him to find lodging on the way back to the port city if his mule needed to rest. With Parker still out cold in her arms, they walked up the steep path. Caidon hadn't put his rifle away. Instead, it laid barrel up against his shoulder while he lugged their cases, now tied together, behind him. He never stopped looking around.

Nearer to the house, the music grew louder, and happy conversations added to the noise. Children shrieking and laughing cut through it all. An array of savory food scents and wood smoke drifted by, and Ramsey's stomach growled. Parker stirred in her arms, sending flakes of mud in every direction. Ramsey's hair felt like a hundred pounds, her dress even heavier the more steps she took. Soon she had to stop and catch her breath.

Caidon paused and glanced back at her. "We can't linger, *zlanishka*. I'd take your hand if I could."

"I'll be okay. I just need a second," she managed between labored breaths.

His emerald gaze searched beyond her, and he shook his head. "You're too exposed. Come on."

Shoring up reserves she didn't have but needed to find anyway, she forced herself to start the upward trek again. He fell behind until he was at her back. Whenever she slowed, he encouraged her, and she managed one more step. At the top, she used a pillar to hide behind and lean against while Caidon knocked on the huge, dark-stained front door. The door swung open to reveal a stunning woman who could have been Sylphine's sister, but since Ramsey knew the Italyssian beauty was an only child, that left her mother, Nathalia. Only a hint of silver enhanced her golden, hip length hair. Ocean-green eyes stared in alarm between the three of them. Ramsey could only guess how they must appear, exhausted and mud covered.

"*Ljekairva ilatse*, what has happened to you?" Nathalia opened the door wide, ushering them in with both hands.

"Trouble followed us," Caidon replied. He entered only after Ramsey and Parker were safely inside. "Sorry to disrupt your gathering."

Nathalia waved away his concern with a scoff and frown. "You are no disruption. Trouble seems to find our Sziverian family on our island." Her gaze flickered to his rifle. "At least no bullets this time."

The reminder that her brother had been shot on this very doorstep had Ramsey swallowing and clutching Parker tighter to her chest. "Where is my brother?"

"They are outside—"

Ramsey didn't give her the chance to finish, simply rushed by, searching for a way to wherever the festivities were gathered. To the left, the house opened into what appeared to be a beautiful courtyard with a high, pruned hedge for privacy all the way to a cliffs edge. Paper lanterns in a variety of colors hung from criss-crossing strands over the entire space, which was littered with small personal fires surrounded by padded wooden furniture. A bricked center was filled with dancers, both for entertainment and as couples enjoying the upbeat, exotic sounds of a band playing on a small stage. A buffet lined two tables near the house. Flower petals burst into the air with a shout of excitement and laughter.

As if on a slow wave, guests began to notice her and fall quiet. Or perhaps, they noticed the equally muddied man beside her with a rifle still resting against his shoulder. Two people pushed through the crowd, and Ramsey couldn't stop the tears that sprang into her eyes at the sight of her brother and his wife. Her sister long before she was Jonathon's bride. Family, familiar and safe. They rushed to her, arms outstretched, concern darkening both their faces. No one had the chance to question anything as they ushered her back into the safety of the house.

Jonathon looked different. The dark, rich brown of his hair had been replaced by a sandier shade and longer, covering his ears and falling to the collar of his loose, white shirt. His skin wasn't a pale tone anymore, though not quite as deeply bronzed as his wife's. And Sylphine… she wore the same revealing, striking style as the women at the docks. Flowing orange and yellows, with a silver chain wrapped multiple times around her hips, accenting the fullness of her figure and stunning shade of her skin. They were amazing together, two beautiful people.

Behind them, she noted Sean and Katria. Sean had picked up the same glowing tan as Jonathon, but Katria remained ivory pale. And very pregnant. In fact, she all but waddled, accepting the help of her husband, a hand on the small of her back, the other at her elbow. Her attention seemed entirely focused on Caidon, or rather the rifle he'd allowed to fall barrel down against his thigh.

"I see the Cyranos allowed you into the country," Sean said, frowning.

"They'll let me leave, too," Caidon said.

Sean snorted. "Good luck, there."

"No luck required," Caidon answered, falling back until he was behind the group. "If I need to leave, we'll find a way."

Parker realized who was with them and squealed. Sylphine reached for him as he launched himself at the couple. Uncaring about the dirt and grime, she hugged the boy close and rocked him back and forth. "*Mayi slyazo malche*, what happened to you?"

"I fell off the carriage," he sniffled, his little arms wrapping tight around her neck.

Sylphine's pretty eyes widened. "What?" She looked at Ramsey. "What happened? Was there an accident?"

Caidon filled them in, sliding next to Ramsey when they were safely in the foyer away from the crowd. She leaned into him, thankful when he slipped an arm around her waist and pulled her close. Jonathon's gaze narrowed, but he let Caidon finish. She'd told him about her contracting over the radio when she'd been able to reach them to let them know they'd be arriving.

Sylphine spoke low to Jonathon, who nodded, then she reached for Ramsey and gave her hand a quick squeeze. "I am glad you are here, safe. I'm going to take Parker upstairs and get him washed up." She turned and disappeared near the back of the house, where Ramsey assumed the stairs were located.

Jonathon returned his attention back to them. "I'll show you where you'll be staying. Nathalia and Acrisius will keep their guests from getting too curious before they chase after Sylphine to meet Parker. They've been too excited to wait for long."

"You're Caidon Survaine," Katria said, following them to the back of the house.

"Yes," Caidon answered, more in a question than confirmation.

"Is that a Ruthenian Long-Range Rifle?"

"Class A-seven," Caidon confirmed, releasing Ramsey to get their luggage.

She licked her lips, her vibrant blue eyes locked on the gun. "May I?"

Caidon stared at her for a silent beat and then popped a small lever on the side several times, causing brass casings to spring free. He caught them before one could hit the floor and handed the now empty rifle over. Katria accepted and caressed the gun like a long-lost lover. Sean tilted his head back and stared at the ceiling, a long sigh echoing around him. Ramsey watched her, unable to stop the feeling of inadequacy as Katria went through the motions of positioning, sighting, and testing the rifle in an expert fashion. Her round belly didn't seem to hinder her in the least. A woman like her was much more suited to the lifestyle and skills required to be the mate of an assassin.

"Amazing," Katria said in reverence, handing the weapon back. "My father said if I wanted one, I could go to Ruthenia and petition."

"Your father could. Only a Ruthenian-born can own one. This was my father's. He obtained it right before retiring."

Katria stared at the rifle in longing. "What class are they up to now, do you know?"

"I think nine, which is how I know you need to be a national to own one. I was denied based on my Sziverian citizenship."

"Weapon like that, I can see how they'd want to make sure it was never used against them."

Caidon's smile didn't reach his eyes. "That's how I figured it, too."

Sean wrapped an arm around his wife and held her back at the bottom of the steps. "This is as far as we go. We'll see everyone when you're cleaned up."

Nervous flutters danced in Ramsey's stomach. Jonathon led them to the third floor, not looking back more than once to confirm they still followed. He had yet to say anything to Caidon.

"The house used to hold most of the Seartavos family, so each floor has three suites that are more like small apartments than bedrooms. There's a bathroom, small kitchen, and the living area can double as an additional bedroom if necessary. Their hot water is spring fed, so no concerns about running out. Your room has two bedrooms," he said, growling faintly. "The other two suites are not ready for guests."

Ramsey sighed. "We are married, Jonathon. Have been for weeks now."

"I don't even know this guy!" Jonathon snapped, rounding on them so suddenly Caidon grabbed her to keep her from walking into him. "I don't even know you. Have never heard of you. How in the inhabited world do you know my sister, and what made you think you had the *right* to marry her?"

13

Caidon remained calm, despite his brother-in-law's livid expression. Dark blue eyes flashing, shoulders back, and his spine straightened to reach his full height, Jonathon Hunter looked every bit the dual ranks he held for his nation. In charge and in control of whatever situation he landed in, and currently, he seemed to have decided Caidon's marriage was a situation needing to be handled.

Too bad.

"She said yes," Caidon answered and pushed past to the room with the only open door on the spacious landing.

"Who *are* you?" Jonathon asked, following him in.

Caidon glanced around the spacious rooms if they could be called that. Fireplaces acted as room dividers, but otherwise, everything was open, square columns providing necessary support for the ceiling above. Colorful rugs broke up the creamy stone floor. Curtains billowed from the archways, revealing a breathtaking view of either the ocean's horizon or the farmland beyond. A salty ocean breeze drifted past, carrying the scent of blossoms and crisp spring renewal. For a moment, he was too stunned to do much more than stare. Then he remembered he didn't have the luxury of losing any footing with the man determined to make sure he was good enough.

"Caidon Survaine, Master Guardian Survaine under the First Intelligence Office," he answered while searching for a bed. "I'll be happy to give you more after we're cleaned up."

Jonathon opened his mouth, looked at his sister, and closed his jaw so fast his teeth snapped. He gave a brisk nod and then left, closing the door quietly behind him. Ramsey let loose a shaky breath.

"Sorry about that," she said, stepping deeper into the room, looking around.

"He loves you. If I were still around my sisters, I'm sure I'd do the same to any suitor."

"You aren't a suitor. You're my husband."

"Whom he's never heard of, let alone met," Caidon pointed out. "He's allowed to be a big brother."

She grumbled incoherently. Caidon smiled, looking for the bathroom. He found it in the center of the room, the only completely private space. With an inward smile, he wondered how many babies were made in the space when a family had lived in the suite. Or, perhaps, there were once some sort of semi-permanent walls. He lit several lamps lined along a mirror with another directly across to reflect more light. A huge shower took up the entire back wall with a stone bench on either side, and the water set up to flow from the center like rain. No glass panels or curtain closed it off. Instead, the floor was a step down with a grate drain.

"Wow," Ramsey murmured, brushing past him on the way to the shower. A streak of dirt followed behind her. "This house is incredible."

"Do you need help, or do you want me to go?"

"I know I need help, but…" She pressed her lips together. Dried mud cracked across her cheeks.

"But you'll end up naked in front of me, and this bothers you," he guessed. He approached her slowly and guided her to face the shower. Reaching his arms around her, he undid the row of buttons along the front of her gown in relaxed motions. Not caring about the grit covering her, Caidon nuzzled her ear. "I'll stop when you tell me to."

Her breathing changed and her body relaxed back into his. "And if I don't tell you to stop?"

"I have to," he said, despite the desire to do anything but.

She groaned. "I know."

Dirt chunked and flaked to the floor with every twist and turn she took to get free of the filthy dress. Underneath the dress, a layer of silt covered her pale skin and underwear. A disgusted grumble left her. "How am I going to get this out of my hair?"

"Lots and lots of conditioner," Caidon answered, trying not to stare at the sensual curves she revealed. Failed, because they were his to enjoy. A silk tank top covered her torso to her hips, where silk panties hugged her round butt and drew attention to her thighs. Damp residue weighed the fabric down, exposing the curves of her modest breasts, and made him regret not having paid more attention to them when he'd had the chance. "I'll leave you to it. Just call if you need help."

Before he reached the door, she called in a small voice, "Help?"

"*Zlanishka*, if I stay, it won't be to wash you."

"So?"

Caidon paused, his hand on the doorframe. She looked at him, challenge clear in her gaze. "Would be less than wise with everyone waiting for us."

"You need to wash up, too."

"Yes, and you need to see your brother without me."

A pout pushed out her bottom lip. "I don't want to. He needs to understand I made the choice on my own, as an adult—"

"Which you can do better when I'm not standing there."

She heaved a sigh and kicked the sodden clothes away. The long length of her legs beckoned him, making him imagine how her skin would feel underneath his hands, slick with soap. Mercifully, she spoke and interrupted his musing before he could think about how far he'd go in his exploration.

"He knows you didn't coerce me."

"Yes."

When she reached for the hem of her slip, he left the bathroom. The gentle fall of water cascading on the tile sounded, and he took a deep breath to clear away the fog of desire. He set her luggage on the bed and then went to the huge balcony that looped around their suite.

Trailing a hand on the thick stone rail, warmed by the sun, he walked the length to the ocean side. White-tipped waves crashed into the rocky cliff below. Ocean birds did acrobatics, squawking and fighting with each other over the best air and hunting spaces. Caidon leaned on his forearms and breathed in the fragrant air. Not many places in his travels held such tranquil beauty. Nor, if they did, could he find the time to simply exist and enjoy. So, he did.

"Shower's free," Ramsey said behind him almost a half hour later.

He turned and found her fighting with a comb in her hair. Halfway to reaching for her, he noticed the dirt on his hands and stopped. "I'll be quick."

A disgusted grunt left her, and she stared out over the ocean. "I might just go downstairs looking like rats found a home on my head. This is ridiculous."

"I'll help when I get down there. I doubt your brother will care."

"I have no idea," she said, squinting up as she watched a group of birds squabbling. "I really don't want to go without you."

Caidon pressed a finger under her chin until she looked at him. He brushed a gentle kiss across her lips. "You have to. I won't be long."

She held the comb out to him. "Fine. But I'm holding you to helping me with this mess. I'm sure there is mud still in these tangles."

"Brushing in the shower with the conditioner would have been wiser."

"Well, I've never had a headful of swamp. I will remember for next time."

Comb in hand, Caidon went to the bathroom while Ramsey left to brave her brother. He piled his filthy clothes on top of Ramsey's and showered quickly. Naked, a towel draped over his shoulders, Caidon strode through the spacious room to his small bag still on the floor where he'd dropped it, along with his rifle case. His rifle lay on the bed next to Ramsey's open luggage that looked like it'd exploded from the inside.

Fabric rustled and a shadow moved. Caidon leapt for the bed, raising the rifle only to remember he'd ejected all the bullets. Still, he sighted the barrel as his mind connected with the inanimate object, a flow of information telling him exactly where to position the weapon to achieve his objective. Jonathon Hunter stared him down, all but daring him to make the minuscule movement to the trigger.

Caidon swung the barrel up. "Didn't anyone ever tell you sneaking up an assassin is a stupid idea?"

"I can think of other, equally asinine decisions."

"Marrying your sister is one of the smartest choices I've made."

Jonathon's gaze narrowed. "Yes, I'm sure her talent will serve you well. Does she realize she's just another pawn for the FIO?"

Caidon reared back. "Her talent, while impressive, was irrelevant to my contracting with her. I didn't even know the extent to which she possessed one when she agreed to be my wife."

"Then why did you marry her?"

"That is part of a lengthy discussion I will share with everyone."

"*Jonathon Hunter*," a woman screeched. Jonathon swung around while Caidon craned his neck to see the door to the suite. Ramsey stood in the frame, her cheeks brilliant pink, her eyes blazing. "No, no, no. Absolutely not. Out of our room, right this instant."

"I'm speaking to your husband."

"You don't get to see him naked before I do!" she shouted on a foot stomp. "Out!"

Jonathon gaped, his attention shifting between them. Ramsey moved from the entrance and swung a pointed finger toward the hall. He snapped his mouth shut and strode from the room. Huffing, she slammed the door closed after him. A rapid pound shook the door.

"I'm going to wait for you in this hall!" his muffled bark came through the wood.

"You can wait an hour for all I care!" she answered, hands fisted. "I am a married woman now!"

Caidon took the opportunity, while she continued to have a shouting match with her sibling through the closed door, to wrap his towel around his waist. Cold droplets of water raced each other down his back. He went to a tall chest dresser situated at an angle on a bright square rug and set his rifle on top. Wood vibrated, and Caidon glanced over his shoulder to see Ramsey lifting her foot to kick the door again.

"I don't think your in-laws would appreciate you breaking the door," Caidon said calmly.

Her fists tightened, and she growled. "He's just so...argh!"

"He's your brother."

"And I'm his sister. I didn't stand outside his door and insist he keeps his hands off his wife, now did I?" She glared at the closed door. "How ridiculous would that have been?" Her lips turned into a flat line. "And I could have too. It's not like those two were quiet."

Caidon released a huff. "Not something I needed to know."

Another brilliant flush bloomed across her cheeks. "Sorry. I'm frustrated. He's being unreasonable."

"Perhaps."

She shook her hands open, her nostrils flaring. "I told him I made the decision to contract with you on my own, that you didn't force me. I also explained we discovered how my talent works together and that I'm still learning what it means and how it works."

"And he didn't believe you?"

"I don't know. I guess not since he disappeared, and I found him in here."

Caidon went to his bag and hefted it onto the bed. He dug around until he found a pair of pants and a shirt. A familiar heat sizzled along his nerves, flowing thick like honey through his veins. The taste of desire not his own yet met without a single touch. With a yank he couldn't stop, his towel disappeared.

Masculine lines and beautiful muscle shifted in the sun streaming through the open walls. Ramsey licked her lips, tracing the very firm curve of his rear around to the harsh dip of his hip bone. A ragged breath left him, one she echoed.

"What are you doing?" he asked, his hands fisting in the clothes.

"Seeing... touching," she murmured, leaning close and pressing a kiss between his shoulder blades. The warmth and texture of his skin proved more a temptation than she could deny, and she touched the tip of her tongue to his flesh. "Tasting."

Her name left his mouth on a groan. "We have to get downstairs."

She sighed and ran both hands up his back, exploring the smoothness of his muscled flanks. "I know, and I don't have a bracelet yet. I'm getting one soon, so I can track my cycle after my next monthly."

He took a large step away from her and slipped into his pants. Ramsey pouted, wishing she'd seen his front, knowing he was likely as impressive from that angle as his back. Perhaps more so.

"A conversation for another time," he said, pulling his shirt on over his head.

"Tonight?" she asked hopefully.

He laughed and shook his head. "No."

"But we can—"

"*Sirin-sya*, I can only take so much."

Siren? A temptress of mythical times? Her? She blinked. "I am tempting to you?"

He held his arms open and gave her a questioning stare. "What do you think? I barely managed to get these pants on."

The bulge at the buttoned seam of his slacks attested to his state. She chewed on her bottom lip and then met his gaze. "I can fix that for you."

His jaw flexed. "If we aren't even going to *discuss* sex, why would I agree to more?"

Ramsey sighed, figuring she had crossed some boundary she shouldn't have. "I will learn to balance my desires and the appropriate times to voice them."

Caidon brushed a finger down her cheek to her mouth. His thumb teased her bottom lip, his gaze darkening. "I wish I could appreciate your needs more fully. But I won't throw caution to the wind. Having a child grow up without a father isn't a generational path I want to follow."

Her heart kicked hard, and she wrapped her hands around his wrist. "You grew up without your father?"

"Until I was ten, I only saw him once or twice a year. My mother did the best she could, but she was essentially single. Because of their bond, they couldn't move on from each other." His touch drifted along her jaw and down her neck to trace her collarbone.

Delicious sensations danced along her nerves and heated her stomach at his feathered caresses. She had to think hard to focus on anything else. "But they made their marriage work?"

"Yes. Once my father could remain home, they were able to find love." His lips curled into a crooked smile. "They had four more children, after all."

She returned his smile. "We'll make us work, too."

His hand fell away, and she instantly missed the intimacy. "It won't be easy."

"I know. We're already to our first difficulty. My brother."

He laced their hands together and tugged her toward the closed door. Smudges of dust covered the white paint where her feet had kicked. She bit her bottom lip. After the conversation with everyone, she'd take the time to clean the dirt away. Once out of the room, Ramsey guided him down the three stories to the ground floor.

Her small family was gathered in a spacious sitting room. White wicker furniture with colorful stuffed cushions were arranged around a glass table set on a large piece of driftwood. Curtains in a variety of vibrant shades drifted lazily in the ocean breeze. The crash of waves echoed up from the cliffs. Lemonade, water, and a faint golden tea sat arranged in the center of a circle of glasses on the table. Small cakes, sliced fruit, and cheese were on a tiered serving tray.

Parker sat on the floor in front of the table, stuffing a cheese square into his mouth and reaching for a strawberry. His eyes lit up the second he spotted her. Jonathon leaned forward, loaded Parker's plate with more food, poured a glass of lemonade, and handed both to Sylphine.

"Will you see if your parents will watch him while we talk?" he asked his wife.

Sylphine took the food and smiled. "They will be excited." She pressed a kiss to Jonathon's lips and then stood. "Come on, Parker, let's go see your grandparents."

Parker skipped off with his mother, seeming to have already adapted to the serene new environment like he did everything else. A sense of melancholy arose in Ramsey. She wondered if he'd adjust to her leaving as easily. Caidon seemed to detect the dark emotion. His hand left hers to settle on her back, rubbing in a gentle sweep of comfort. Jonathon motioned to the only settee not occupied by a couple. Sean and Katria took up the largest couch, Katria positioned between Sean's knees, which she held onto, her eyes closed, while he rubbed her low back.

Sean's amber gaze caught Ramsey, and he smiled. "Won't be much longer, but she insists on being anywhere the action is."

Ramsey gasped, her attention shifting to Katria. "You're in labor?"

"Sean seems to think so. I just know I'm uncomfortable and restless," Katria answered. She squirmed, grimaced, and finally settled with most of her weight against one of Sean's raised legs. "And yes, we've been stuck here for seven months. I'm ready to know what's going on back home. I *need* to know."

"Voklane hasn't kept you updated?" Caidon asked, his focus on Sean.

Sean shrugged. "Radio communications have been sporadic. He basically just wanted to know if we'd found a way home once the ice thawed. No one at any of the docks would give us a ticket. Sylphine's father has been trying to get any of his ships home that have passenger quarters. I was to the point where we'd sleep in a hammock with the crates, if necessary, but then Katria's pregnancy became too far along for us to travel safely."

"And now we'll be here until the baby is old enough to take the voyage. We'll probably stay with my father for a couple of weeks when we finally do arrive in Sziveria before taking the MagnaRail back to Haven City," Katria said, her eyes closed, her face pinched. She let out a shuddering breath. "Okay, that was new."

Sean straightened, his hand moving around to his wife's round belly. "What?"

"An uncomfortable sensation. The baby didn't seem to like it either."

Sean closed his eyes and rubbed her stomach. "No, she's not happy, but if it was a contraction, it was an early one." He opened his eyes and looked between Ramsey and Caidon. "How about we get this going."

"What would you like to know?" Caidon asked, sitting on the small couch and pulling Ramsey down next to him.

Sylphine returned and took her place next to Jonathon. Sean waited until she was situated before answering. "Anything you can tell us."

"Why are you married to my sister?" Jonathon asked.

"I received orders on her," Caidon stated calmly, his arm draped across the back of the couch, his fingers playing in the damp, tangled strands of her hair. The action was so similar to the first time they'd met Ramsey had to blink away the memory.

Surprise crossed Jonathon's face. "And you didn't carry them out?"

"No."

"Why?"

"Because she's mine."

Darkness replaced the surprise in Jonathon, and Ramsey spoke quickly. "Caidon saved my life. Six years ago, after…" She cleared her throat, hating the heat of embarrassment that arose anytime she remembered being used so thoroughly by Tobyn Fenster. "After everything that happened. Back then."

"Mom and Dad," Jonathon supplied quietly.

"My brother," Sean growled.

"Fenster," Caidon added.

Ramsey looked at her hands and sighed. "Yes, all of that. I didn't handle any of it well. Caidon kept me from being stupid. In ancient cultures, it was believed if you saved a life, you owned it, so he isn't wrong in saying I am his. But more importantly," she lifted her head and met her brother's fierce stare head-on, "he is mine."

"Who do you suspect sent you the false order?" Sean asked, his demeanor once again shifting to calm.

Caidon's touch moved from her hair to the sensitive skin at the back of her neck. He traced small, irregular shapes, and Ramsey tried not to shiver. "Your brother at first, especially after learning he's been freed. However, Voklane and I have formed a new opinion. Someone learned Ramsey has been translating the manifest codes."

"From the Cyrano manifests?" Sylphine asked, eyes wide. "You finally broke the code?"

Ramsey fidgeted. "Yes. Caidon helped me figure out how my talent works, and I was able to translate. The code was just a scramble of Markinish dialects."

Sylphine sat forward, her aqua eyes intent. "What did you find? Is it what we suspected?"

Unsure how to answer, Ramsey glanced at Caidon. "I didn't find anything that seemed to relate to human trafficking, more toward smuggling."

"Voklane is going to meet with Immetana to see if perhaps items were being used in place of describing specific types of people," Caidon added, saying what Ramsey couldn't bring herself to. "If there is a pattern of the same types of goods being used over and over, it'll be likely."

"Especially since we're positive Cyrano has been part of trafficking prisoners or kidnap victims," Jonathon said. "The evidence has to be there."

Caidon nodded. "I agree, and I think it's the main reason a false order was put out on Ramsey. She was getting too close to helping Voklane find it."

Jonathon's gaze narrowed. "She wasn't supposed to be helping him at all."

Irritation slid through Ramsey. "Wasn't your place to say."

"I am responsible for you," Jonathon said slowly as though his patience were thinning. "You were broken once by doing the right thing. What do you think would happen if you attempted to do the right thing again, only for it to go sideways?"

"I'd deal," Ramsey stated, her body tense. "I'm twenty-four, Jonathon. At some point, you have to let me make choices, good or bad, and let me suffer the consequences."

"Like you suffered before?" He waved a frustrated hand in their direction. "Someone else had to pick you up, Ramsey! What if he hadn't been there? Would I still have a sister? Or what if he'd been as bad as what you'd helped lock up? Or what took—" He bit off his words and looked away. Sylphine sucked in a breath and laid her hand on his thigh. "These people aren't playing fair or even civilized. They're ruthless and cruel. No, I didn't, and I still don't want you involved."

A heavy silence settled over the room, everyone remembering, even without Jonathon having spoken the words aloud, the brutal lengths the V Alliance had already taken to achieve their goals. Some a healing wound, others still painfully fresh for those involved.

"If I hadn't helped, a teenage girl would still be missing," Ramsey said softly. "Probably forever."

"Not forever," Caidon stated, grabbing her hand and sliding their fingers together. "Lucianna Castien would have shown up in a few years, a product of likely brainwashing. A weapon they would have managed to fashion to their needs."

Katria twisted until she half faced her husband. "Castien. Weren't they on the assassin list with my family and Caidon's?" Before Sean could answer, she pinned her vivid blue gaze on Ramsey. "What happened?"

Ramsey took a deep breath, glancing at her brother

before focusing on Katria. "Vayden Dossett is close to Henry Castien. When Castien's family was murdered, his daughter was kidnapped in the chaos of the event."

"All the evidence went missing," Jonathon said. "I brought the case to Voklane's attention before Sylphine and I left."

Ramsey nodded. "Yes, so Castien asked Vayden Dossett to find her. Melody Ericksen was assigned the case at HCES. They worked together. They found a list that Voklane brought to me to be translated. So far, that list is the only proof he has that the V Alliance is indeed involved with the missing persons in Haven City. Neither the FIO nor SNID have been able to link anything to Cyrano, other than the shipping date on the list matched a day Cyrano was supposed to be in port."

"But so could any dozens of other ships," Sylphine said with a sigh.

"Yes. Not enough so far."

Katria moved until she faced her husband. Anger blazed in her eyes and molted her cheeks and neck red. She shoved both palms against Sean's chest hard. "I told you! I said they'd be in danger."

Sean grabbed her hands and held them to his chest. "It wouldn't have mattered if we said something to them or not."

"But—"

"He's right," Caidon said. "Castien would have believed he could keep his family safe, just as he always had. My father knew about what happened to your family, and it wasn't until Castien that he realized a threat was real and he might not be able to protect my sisters. The V Alliance is desperate to have a Gen-Heir sharpshooter, and they're taking extreme measures since none seem to want to work for them. Not even my father knows if his daughters have inherited his gift. Knowing I did was enough. He doesn't want that for any of his other children. He sent my mother and sisters to Ruthenia."

Katria rubbed her belly, her cheeks still pink, but her anger seemed to slide into concern. "No one wants their child to be choiceless in their future."

"I agree. However, the group doesn't know about all the children, if they're talents or not, which means they may grab what they can and cut their losses if their victims turn out not to be genetic heirs," Caidon explained. "By now, though, as small of a community as we are, they've made two mistakes that will no longer be ignored. Everyone will be on alert. They have a mediocre assassin running around out there that I guarantee will be found if your father, my father, and Castien decide to find him."

"Or her," Katria chirped.

Caidon smiled. "Or her."

"You don't think they'll try again with another family? Maybe even in another country?" Katria asked.

"Who's to say they haven't?" Caidon asked. "Lucianna was a recent failed attempt in Sziveria, so we know, as of last fall, they haven't succeeded. And they've been trying for over five years."

Katria sniffled. "I hate these people, whoever they are." She turned to look at her husband again. "When the baby is old enough, if they're still looking for this assassin, I'm going to help. The V Alliance won't come after all of us."

"We'll discuss it later," Sean said, his mouth a tight line.

Ramsey took a deep breath against the sudden tension in the room. Sylphine shifted uncomfortably, and Jonathon took hold of her hand, kissing her fingers before pressing their clasped hands to his chest. The flash of anger at their comfortable public display of affection took her by surprise. What right did he have to happiness that she didn't? She looked away before she said something regretful. If she thought too hard about Jonathon disliking her marriage, she'd ask him why he wanted her to remain alone and unhappy. Since she didn't think he meant such a malicious outcome with his objections, getting into a fight would solve nothing. Either he'd learn to accept her husband, or he wouldn't.

"Is that everything?" Sean asked, unfolding himself from around his wife.

"That I can think of," Caidon replied.

"Do they have a thread on my brother?"

"No."

Sean braced his elbows on his knees, his shoulders sagging. "I keep trying to think of where he'd go. If he was in Westica when Cora was there and if he had anything to do with her death. Or if he's somewhere else, and how his influence is benefiting all the awful happening in Sziveria. Someone must know something."

"I think the consensus is he's not wreaking havoc in Sziveria. Therefore, he's not an issue to be concerned with right now. There are other, more immediate issues needing to be dealt with," Caidon said.

Sean shook his head. Ramsey's stomach clenched when his amber gaze lifted to meet hers. "Not for me."

Ramsey offered an encouraging smile. "You could

do your own investigating while you enjoy being a new parent."

"Maybe learning he's an uncle will bring him to us," Katria said between labored breaths.

"I'd rather our child didn't act as a lure," Sean said, frowning. He stood and helped Katria rise. "Let's get you somewhere comfortable."

"Do you think I'm close?"

"Labor is unique. You could be, or we could still be waiting until this time tomorrow. Either way, I'd rather be ready."

<h1 style="text-align:center">14</h1>

A FAINT COMMOTION TRAILED THE BLACKBAINS UP THE stairs. Neither Ramsey nor Caidon went after the couple like the rest of the house seemed inclined and excited to do. Ramsey scrunched up her face, staring at the empty space where everyone had disappeared through.

"Do you think we should have followed?" she asked, leaning against his side, content.

"I don't know them. We can if it's important to you."

"No. I don't know them very well, either. Seems like a private thing anyway, the birth of the next generation."

He shrugged. "In many cultures around the inhabited world, birth is something an entire village, or even town, participates in and celebrates. It's a reminder that humanity is still thriving, that one more generation will carry on life."

"I wonder if Italyssa is one of them."

"Likely. The throwing of the flower petals when we arrived is a blessing in this culture, for fertility."

Ramsey smiled and imagined what living in such a romantic society would be like. No wonder very little seemed to affect Sylphine. She'd been raised in sunlight and love. Not just from her family but from the very people who lived on the small island nation. "I wonder what crime is like here."

He raised a brow. "That's a random subject change. But, it's fairly low, all things considered. No one is immune to crime, however."

"Sylphine said they were having issues with magic lily dust and kidnappings, too," Ramsey said. "I wonder if it's as bad as Sziveria."

"Yes, the people near revolted over it."

A faint memory of a newspaper article from over two years ago came to her mind. "Oh yes, that's right, they thought their government wasn't handling it. I wonder if the Cyrano's were foolish enough to help steal their own people or if another shipping venture handled the trafficking from here."

"All good questions," Jonathon said from the door. "Ones I've been asking, which is probably why we're stuck here. I started snooping over the winter, working with the investigative team assigned to handle the smuggling of the drugs and the individuals addicted enough to literally kidnap and sell people for their next fix. By the time the channel opened up, someone had barred us from being able to travel."

"And you're waiting on Sylphine's father to get a ship in port, right?" Caidon asked.

"Yes, that's the goal." Jonathon hitched his thumb over his shoulder. "Did you want to come upstairs with me?"

"No, we don't know Katria well enough to stand

around her room while her labor progresses. If it were Sylphine, I'd be making you make room on the bed," Ramsey said.

"It's tradition here. Once she starts pushing, they start celebrating, so the baby is born to excitement and joy. This is the third birth we've been involved with. Two of Sylphine's cousins had babies over the winter, and one house staff."

"They just hang around until then?" Ramsey asked, curious.

"Pretty much. You'll see. If you want anything to eat, you'll have to come up there. Aside from giving her any privacy she demands in their bedroom area, their suite will be where we'll take meals until after the baby arrives."

Ramsey grimaced. "I can't imagine that. How very different from the family only we have when our children arrive."

"Sean isn't too happy about it. The emotions of everyone in the room can make it difficult for him to focus on his wife, but we're guests in this land."

Ramsey considered the alpha couple in question. "I think if things become too overwhelming, they'll listen to him."

Jonathon smiled. "I do, too. Or they'll listen to Sylphine. She's become fairly close with Sean and Kat since we've been here."

"Is there a radio in the house?" Caidon asked.

"Yes." Jonathon motioned with his head out of the room. "I'll take you to it."

. . .

CAIDON FLIPPED ON THE RECEIVER, CHANGED THE transmission type, and input the correct frequency to radio Ryan Voklane. Jonathon lounged against the doorframe to the only small room in the house, Caidon figured. Ramsey had gone upstairs, too curious in the end to see how things were progressing with Katria.

Static filled the silence, and then a tinny male voice came across the waves. "Office of the Arch Guardian Synintel, Voklane speaking."

"Survaine checking in," Caidon answered into the small handset.

"Is the child safe with his parents?"

Caidon glanced at Jonathon. "Yes."

"Good." A faint crackling sounded. "Do you have a pen and paper?"

Jonathon pointed to a row of drawers above the radio. Caidon stood and collected a pen and sheet of clean paper. "Yes, go ahead."

"The *Trinity Rising* will leave port at high tide, around five in the morning. You and Ramsey need to be on it. The captain will have your papers for when you make entry into Thanzia, along with your directions from there."

"What's going on?"

"The ice drifts are still too dangerous for any ships to dock in Mark Inland, but we've identified a ship laden with potential traffic victims. If we're correct, they left Port Tabria before we could get anyone from Immigration and Import to board the ship."

"And since they can't dock, they'll sit in the ocean until they receive word it's safe to make port."

"Yes."

"You need us to get to Mark Inland before they do."

"Correct."

Jonathon straightened and went to the desk. He braced one hand next to the radio. "And you expect my sister's talents to pave the way, don't you?"

A heavy sigh crackled over the waves. "We have real-world situations your sister can provide essential support for. She's willing, and she's with the best."

"Did you fabricate the assassination order on her to bring all this about?" Jonathon asked, his jaw tense.

"No, absolutely not."

Jonathon's midnight blue gaze locked on Caidon. "Because you couldn't trust he wouldn't carry it out?"

"Caidon doesn't execute targets he hasn't personally verified. It's in his contract. We can only recommend an elimination. He conducts his own research on the target. Anyone who knows him, knows how he works, and would have known Ramsey Hunter was never in any danger from Master Guardian Survaine. Someone was desperate, didn't know the rules, and decided to gamble. Thankfully, they lost."

"And you won."

"An unexpected advantage, yes."

Jonathon hung his head, eyes closed. Caidon remained silent. From what he understood, an advantage in the ongoing, complicated intrigue plaguing Sziveria was needed. From the First Intelligence Office to the Sziverian National Investigative Division, all parties involved were one step behind the V Alliance. While the underground group didn't seem to be progressing in a manner they wanted, they were still creating enough havoc in secret to be an issue. Any means to foil a plan of theirs was a desperately needed win.

"A ship full of people have no hope right now, Jonathon," Ramsey's quiet voice said behind them. "You won't put me above so many lives. Not when I can possibly help."

Jonathon's shoulders hunched further.

Ramsey touched a hand to his back. "Please, let me do this."

Caidon didn't think it would help to mention she didn't need her brother's permission or even his approval. Not anymore. However, he knew Jonathon seeing Ramsey as someone capable was important to her. "I could do it alone, but the chances of my being able to learn where the ship will dock are slim to none without her language skills. I'd possibly be able to learn some of their network, but no lives would be spared the horrors of being sold to the whims of whomever makes the purchase of a human being."

"There are no other teams?" Jonathon asked.

"Not that could achieve what the Survaines could. They won't have to try to be convincing as a traveling couple being newly married, and their unique skill sets will achieve results," Ryan said.

Jonathon stiffened at the plural use of Caidon's family name. A reminder that Ramsey now belonged to a new family. Ramsey wrapped her hand around Jonathon's forearm and pulled him closer to the doorway but not out of the room.

"You have a family now," she said softly. "And whether you agree with my decision or not, I'm married now, too. I'm someone else's responsibility, just like he's mine. I don't know how we'll do as a team, and I know a stressful mission isn't ideal for testing out how well we'll work together, but I want to do this. I *need* to do this."

Jonathon met Caidon's eyes. "You will keep her safe."

"If any harm comes to her, it means I'm dead," Caidon said honestly.

Ramsey sucked in a sharp breath.

Jonathon switched his focus back to her. "This is the world you want to play in. Life and death."

"I'm not playing in anything," she said, her body tense. "I know this is very real. Just like if we don't help, the very real future for many Sziverian's is bleak. You and I both know there are children on that ship, Jonathon. Parker was destined for the same fate before you rescued him."

Jonathon growled and looked away. "You had to bring that up."

"It's the truth."

"I know." He ran a hand down his face. "Fine. Chances are you won't be able to reach me while you're on this mission. I don't know how much longer we'll remain in Italyssa."

"If I get the chance, I'll try here and the house in Haven City, I promise."

"You'll want to leave around midnight," Jonathon said. "A horse will be faster than the mules they prefer to use for travel here. There's a stable used by law enforcement at the docks that you can leave them with."

"What about a bicycle?" Caidon asked.

Ramsey shook her head. "I don't know how to ride one. Only the brave commute Haven City on a bike."

"The Seartavos' do have a passenger tricycle. There

would be enough room for Ramsey to put the luggage at her feet and next to her on the seat. That would work. You'd definitely get there faster," Jonathon said.

"Could I leave it at the stable as well?"

"No. There's bike parking, you'll just lock it up."

"Perfect," Caidon said.

Ramsey stared at him. "You're going to cycle us to port?"

"I cycle in most nations. Only a handful have Ariot's or rail lines suitable for passengers. It's via horse or bike. Bikes are cheaper and faster."

"Great," Ryan's voice chirped from the radio, earning a startled look from Ramsey. "Radio me when you get to New Jordon in Cairo."

A faint *click* sounded, signaling the end of the conversation. Caidon replaced the handset and flipped switches to conserve the magnetically stored energy so, hopefully, the next user wouldn't have to power the unit. He stood, the information Ryan had asked him to write down in hand.

Jonathon glanced at the clock hanging by the door. "You both should probably get something to eat and then get some sleep. There's only a few hours now before you'll need to leave."

Ramsey rose on her tiptoes and hugged her brother. "I love you, and thank you."

Jonathon returned her embrace. "Listen to your husband, and don't make any rash decisions."

"I'll do my best."

Jonathon's gaze locked with Caidon's over the top of her head. "You're in for it, you know."

Caidon nodded and gave a half-hearted smile. "Yes, and I can't wait."

15

Anyka Margaret Blackbain entered the world at eleven forty-three at night to the loudest celebration Ramsey had ever heard. A roaring cheer echoed around the house and was likely heard by the distant neighbors unless they were also present and helping in the merriment. To Ramsey, it felt like the entirety of Italyssa had crammed into the wide hall in front of the second-story suite. Whomever didn't fit in the hall spilled over into Jonathon and Sylphine's room across the corridor.

Colored paper lanterns were lit and launched from the nearest balcony, announcing to anyone who'd see them that a new, magnificent life had been birthed into the world. The tradition and symbolism brought Ramsey to tears. Made her want to be in Italyssa if she ever had a baby, or at least adopt the tradition in Sziveria.

After she'd assured herself mother and infant were doing well and very healthy, Caidon took her up to their rooms to repack their belongings. She couldn't believe they weren't getting even a full day in the country. According to Caidon, she needed to get accustomed to the constant change in scenery, language, and culture. They wouldn't be staying put until they arrived in Mark Inland.

While Caidon double-checked their belongings, Ramsey snuck off to find her sister-in-law. She knew he wouldn't give her the chance if she asked. Sylphine was in the kitchen, overseeing preparations. Ramsey pulled her to the side.

"I need a favor," she whispered as she hugged her sister tight.

Sylphine returned the embrace. "Anything. I wish you were staying longer."

"Me too."

"But I'm so proud of you." Sylphine leaned back, brushing her fingers down Ramsey's cheek. "Jonathon needed standing up to, even if he ranted for a bit. He needs to know you are grown and ready for your own life adventure."

"Thank you."

Sylphine grasped both Ramsey's hands and squeezed. "You are much stronger than he gives you credit for. Now, what can I do for you?"

Heat bloomed across her cheeks. She ignored the tinge of embarrassment. "I need a bracelet."

Sylphine's gaze narrowed. "Why do you need jewelry to help save people?"

"Not a decorative bracelet. A, um— you know...." Why couldn't she say it? Sighing, she squeezed her eyes closed when Sylphine continued to stare at her in confusion. "An ovulation bracelet."

"Oh. Oh!" Sylphine covered her mouth, giggling. "Oh, of course. Yes. I have extras upstairs, in my room.

Jonathon asked me last month to start tracking to help know when my fertile window is."

Relief filled her, along with excitement. "Perfect. Thank you. And congratulations."

Still holding Ramsey's hand, Sylphine led her out of the kitchens. "Thank you, I'm nervous and hopeful. You know how to use the bracelet, yes?"

"I'm not sure. Is it complicated?"

"I'll give you the entire kit. There are instructions. They're in Italyssian."

Ramsey shrugged. "That's okay. I'll be able to read it."

"Your talent has really grown."

A sense of pride made her smile. "Yes, Caidon has been very helpful."

Sylphine squeezed her hand. "He seems good for you. I'm happy you have found each other."

"I wish Jonathon shared your enthusiasm."

"He's your brother, of course he isn't happy another man has stepped in to fill his protector shoes. He'll manage, though. It's been hard for him, these seven months, knowing you were alone with Parker and there wasn't anything he could do. He wants all his family safe under one roof again, and now…." Sylphine shook her head, her golden hair sliding across her back. "He won't ever have that again."

"That's depressing," Ramsey muttered.

"But the truth."

Ramsey chewed her bottom lip. "I suppose."

Sylphine stopped near the stairs and faced her. "Life is nothing but seasons upon new seasons, Ramsey. We accept them and live because we cannot change what is to be. I am ready to get to Sziveria and see what being

Key Guardianess Asherwick holds for me. What supporting my very amazing investigator husband will be like. I am ready to be a mother. You have so much in front of you, just like us, only different, and that's okay."

Ramsey kissed Sylphine's cheek. "Thank you. I don't know what I'd do without you."

"And I without you. I can't wait until you are back home." Sylphine released her hold and bounded up the stairs, layers of orange and yellow silk trailing behind. "Come on, let me get you that bracelet so you can enjoy the intelligence life without worry."

Without worry. Somehow, Ramsey didn't think that was going to be possible. Already doubts crept in. What if she encountered a language she couldn't help with? How quickly would Caidon come to rely on her skill? At what point would she disappoint him? Puffing out her cheeks, she tried to quell the uncomfortable twist in her stomach. Whenever she was involved, failure became an inevitable conclusion. Too many times, she'd proven her inability to handle stress. Caidon seemed confident he could, and would, help her grow, but what if she couldn't?

She slowed on the stairs. "Maybe I should stay here, with you."

Sylphine turned on the step, her hand braced on the thick, stone rail. "You are being ridiculous. You can't stay here and help your husband. You need to be where he is."

Ramsey pressed a hand to her stomach. "What if I can't help? What if all I do is get in the way?"

A frown of disapproval darkened Sylphine's beautiful face. "Jonathon should have been working on helping you build self-esteem instead of sheltering you."

Ramsey blinked. "What?"

"You've already been told how valuable you'll be. You've argued for your place at Caidon's side. What else do you want, Ramsey? I can't give you conviction."

Ramsey squared her shoulders in a show of confidence, while inside, she shrank like the coward she knew herself to be. She couldn't deny she'd fought to be able to travel alongside Caidon, nor could she back out after agreeing. Whatever happened, she'd deal with the consequences. Hopefully, any mistakes she made wouldn't cause Caidon to be hurt, or worse, cost his life or that of an entire group of people.

Pressing her lips together to keep from whimpering at the enormity of the task before them, she followed Sylphine up to her and Jonathon's suite. The room was laid out similar to the one Ramsey and Caidon had been given but held the personal touch of a home. Dark furniture filled the space, contrasting with the pale floor, walls, and the airy environment outside. The room *felt* like Jonathon.

Ramsey raised a brow. "You let my brother decorate?"

Sylphine smiled a dreamy sort of smile. She brushed her fingers along a mahogany chair with padded cream upholstery. "Back in December, when Haven City is usually buried in eight feet of snow, we had heavy frost at night and chilly enough days we had to close in the balconies and burn fires, but no snow. Jonathon was very homesick. I took him shopping to make our space feel more like home for him. He agreed to do the same for me when we return to Sziveria."

A home that would truly belong to them and no longer be hers. Ramsey cleared her throat against a sudden lump. "Put all my things in the attic. I don't know when I'll be— when we'll return for me to get them. You'll need the space more than my things."

"Oh, Ramsey," Sylphine sighed and then pulled her into a tight hug. She rocked back and forth, and Ramsey returned the strong embrace. "That will always be your home. I don't know if Jonathon will be able to just pack you away."

The hug grounded her. "But if you have a baby…"

"We'll figure it out. He may put the wall back up that you had torn down. Who knows? But I do know, until you tell him otherwise, there will always be a bed for you." Sylphine pressed a kiss to her forehead and pulled back. "Marriage doesn't mean separation from family. It means growth of the one you already have. You will see this. Your family has expanded by mine and by Caidon's."

"A lovely thought," Ramsey mused.

"A true one." Sylphine patted her cheek and then crossed the room to a tall chest dresser. She rummaged around in an ornate shell box. When she didn't find what she searched for, she opened the top dresser drawer. "Ah, here we are."

Ramsey met her halfway and accepted a small, sturdy, smooth lavender-painted box. She opened it and looked over the contents. An unstrung bracelet, colored beads in amber, jasper river stone, and onyx were divided neatly into little glass squares, a thermometer, and a folded sheet of paper. "You weren't joking about a complete kit.

"You can't do the bracelet properly without one. I

haven't used this one. I wanted to have different color options."

"How many did you buy?"

Sylphine shrugged. "A couple. Would you like to have some other bead colors to take with you?"

Ramsey closed the box, which latched neatly by a magnet. "I'm sure I can find more options in our travels if I want them. These are beautiful, thank you."

"Of course."

They left to search out Jonathon and found him sitting on the bed holding a newborn loosely wrapped in a bright blue blanket. Sean helped his very slow-moving wife from the bed. Her hair hung in tangled clumps around her shoulders, and while she wore a dressing gown, she didn't much care what anyone present may see since she made no move to adjust as she slid from the mattress into her husband's waiting arms. He didn't bother to help her, just swept her into his arms and carried her to the bathroom. Moments later, the sound of rushing water competed with the ocean outside and the murmur of dying conversation as the crowds wandered back to their homes.

Ramsey watched her brother touch a tiny palm, which trembled and widened at the unexpected sensation. Fussy sounds, impossibly small, brought a smile of wonder to Jonathon's face.

Sylphine wrapped an arm around Ramsey's upper chest and pulled her back, resting her chin on her shoulder. "He doesn't know it yet, but we're going to be like the Ruthenian's during my fertile window," she whispered.

Ramsey wrapped her hands around Sylphine's forearm. "What's that?"

"We aren't going to leave our bed for three days except for necessity's."

Ramsey laughed. "What about Parker?"

"That's what my parents are for." Sylphine sighed, a long sound of yearning. "We are ready for a baby, while Parker is young enough to still enjoy the wonder and old enough to be careful but not too old to be annoyed."

Their hushed conversation caught Jonathon's attention. "She's amazing." He looked back down at her, touching her palm again until she wrapped her tiny fingers around one of his. "They're going to call her Nyka after Katria's sister."

"She'll be Anyka Margaret only when she's in trouble?" Ramsey asked with a grin.

Jonathon returned the gesture. "Something like that."

Sylphine's arm fell away. Ramsey went to her brother and peered down at the small, scrunched face of a new life held in his arms. "They did good."

Jonathon nodded. "They did really good. She's beautiful. I already told Sean he's in trouble."

A dusting of black hair covered the crown of her head. Dark, fathomless eyes blinked without focus, their color a mystery to reveal itself in the months to come. Ramsey brushed her fingers along the petal-soft skin and urged away the yearning to hold something so precious and miraculous of her own. Their time would come, but not for a while. Until then, she'd have to be content with holding her future niece or nephew and spoiling the one she already had.

"If I can radio, I will," Ramsey said softly, her hand falling away.

Sylphine reached for the infant when she let loose a

bellow bigger than her. "Someone is ready for another feeding." Jonathon handed her over, the goofy, wistful expression still on his face. Sylphine shook her head and laughed. "We'll have one we can keep soon, Jonathon dear."

"I hope so, Sylphine love." When Sylphine went out of view, Jonathon shifted on the bed, his feet swinging over the edge. "Caidon is already waiting downstairs with the trike. I helped load it before I came up here, and Sean asked me to hold the baby while he helped Kat." His dark eyes searched hers. "Are you *sure* you want to do this?"

Ramsey ignored the doubt still settled like a stone in her stomach. "Yes, I'm positive. Will you tell Parker goodbye for me? I don't want to wake him. We'll radio or write to him as soon as we can."

"Of course, I will. I won't be able to talk you out of this, will I?"

She shook her head.

A long, heavy sigh escaped him as he stood. "All right." He pulled her into a possessive hug. "If anything happens, you radio the moment you can. I'll figure out a way to get to you, okay?"

"Okay." Ramsey hugged him back. Hard. Tears burned her eyes.

"Promise me."

She buried her face into his chest. The scent of home and family assailed her, and when a tear escaped, she used his shirt to wipe it away. "I promise."

16

Despite the bitter cold permeating the air, the outdoor market, with faded rugs draped over thick ropes for cover, thrived. Ramsey bundled deeper into the fur-lined cloak Caidon had purchased for her on arrival. The climate was as brutally cold as she'd heard the Northern Boundary was rumored to be. She suppressed a shudder at the knowledge they'd be heading even further north. The chill of the arctic winds held on longer for the Continental Midland countries.

To the natives, the temperature appeared downright mild. The women were draped in colorful gauzy layers that flowed from a choker around their neck, over their arms, and trailed down their bodies to their feet. Leather shoes adorned with beads and embroidery peaked out with each step. Ornate belts or beaded strands wrapped around their torsos to emphasize whatever part of their body they wished to draw attention to. Some crisscrossed under the breasts and over their stomach to tie at the hips. Others simply draped a thick scarf or metal belt around their hips. Either way, the effect was stunning and undeniably feminine.

Maidens wore flowered or metal combs at their crown with a thin layer of silk draping down their backs like an elegant veil. Like the Italyssians, their unmarried women were easy to see in a crowd. She'd learned Thanzia and Cairo also had distinctions, but for their married ladies. In Cairo, married women of influence and wealth had long embellished fabric trains, and attendants often trailed behind carrying. While in Thanzia, married women wore arm bands with family colors draping from them, despite if they matched what she wore or not. The cultural differences and customs fascinated Ramsey.

"An interested male will steal a woman's veil in a market setting like this," Caidon said, having to lean close to be heard over the constant shouting of vendors for customers attention. "If she's been being courted already, she'll come here in hopes that her suitor will declare his intent publicly for her hand."

The crush of shoppers ebbed and flowed like a river, jostling Ramsey into Caidon. "How would she ever know who? There's so many people."

He pointed to square pedestals positioned every few booths. "Keep an eye out. He'll jump on one of those and wave her veil."

Ramsey eyed the nearest one, where an old man sat smoking a dark brown cigarette. The fragrant spiced tobacco curled sweet blue smoke into the air. "What if she doesn't agree?"

Caidon wrapped an arm around her waist and guided her around a congested stand. "She pulls an extra one from her handbag, has her friends put it on, and walks back into the crowd."

Ramsey made a sound of dismay. "She shuns him?"

"What else is she to do? No different than a man announcing his promise to marry in Sziveria and the bride-to-be rejecting his proposal."

"Now I know why we're a bit more private. That would be horrible," she mumbled, shaking her head.

"In most nations, marriage is permanent. Sziveria is unique with contract limits. Here in Syrinad, the couple better be sure, or the family arrangement strong, because there is no going back after their binding ceremony. If the couple are well known in the area, the crowd will react positively or negatively to the future union. Like most inhabited lands, community is important, and this is a way for them to be involved in the pairing. It's a colorful, fun tradition I've always enjoyed witnessing."

A brisk wind howled down the lane. Canvas snapped, and jars filled with goods rattled. A wave of startled sound emanated from the collective crowd as women grabbed their veils and men their hats to keep them from soaring free. Everyone stopped moving as gritty sand blasted through. Caidon pulled Ramsey into the shelter of his body, and she huddled close, pressing her face into the warmth of his neck. His scent and the sensation of his skin sent a tremble through her belly, an elemental reaction she couldn't control. Her cloak whipped out behind her, and she imagined she'd have taken flight if not for Caidon's tight hold. Then silence.

The multitude returned to their business like nothing strange had occurred.

Ramsey blinked dust and grit from her eyes and glanced around. "What was that?"

"They call it a sandburst. They happen once or twice a day and are more intense here in the market because of the tight corridors."

She touched her hair and grimaced. "I will never get all the sand out of my hair."

He laughed and ruffled her curls at her shoulders. Grit puffed free, and she sneezed. "It's not as bad as the mud bath you took in Italyssa."

"True. But twice a day? I'm surprised women aren't covering *all* their hair," she said.

"Wouldn't work. It'd just blow up underneath the fabric. A cap or full wrap would be the only defense, and I've only seen the elderly do so."

They pushed their way through the next two rows, searching for easily transported, premade food goods. The train ride from Syrinad to Mark Inland would be long, slow, and without many options for purchasing goods, Caidon had warned. They had to go prepared, and the Visiroth market was the best place to find a decent selection for their needs. With the wind finally settled down, Ramsey looked around at the vibrant civilization around her.

The cloak she wore wasn't the only thing that set her apart from the native population. Her pale-as-snow complexion did as well. The women were exotic, with shades of skin that varied from warm caramel to rich cinnamon. Caidon's golden tone fit right in. Only his green eyes set him apart. Since Italyssa, where the men and women were also bronzed and beautiful, Ramsey had been firmly placed in the *tourist* category, with no hope of blending. She hoped Mark Inland would be different. She didn't imagine they could accomplish much with her garnering stares everywhere she went.

With each step, they traveled deeper into the market. The local language coalesced in her mind until she understood each word as if it were her own tongue. A woman sang the praises of her silk, the highest quality to be found for all your needs, the dye guaranteed not to run or fade. The colorful samples danced in the breeze and teased the imagination of what they could become. A young girl called out about sweet pies, easy to carry and eat while walking, too sweet and delicious to pass up. The sugared scent of fruit, fresh pastry, and an unknown but delicious spices made Ramsey's mouth water.

Riotous laughter sounded from a tall, hairy man as they passed by. Vibrant powders in clear glass jars filled his tiered table. He elbowed his companion in his round gut and pointed. "Ah, look at these waytrippers, the husband doesn't even know how to keep his woman warm!"

"Perhaps she is too cold to warm," the round man laughed. "Maybe she's like the fish at Melaxi's booth, frigid and a lump in his sheets."

Ramsey's cheeks warmed. She attempted to ignore their vulgar discussion. Unfortunately, Caidon stopped at a smoked meat vendor at the next table. Hairy man snickered, his beady black eyes looking her over. He licked chapped lips and pulled the crotch of his pants loose.

"I would put pink in those cheeks. Make them

match the fresh fruit between those thighs." He slapped his leg. "I bet they wrap real tight around her man."

A crude smile showed the round man's rotting teeth. "She'd probably be thankful for a real man in her bed. Her little husband is probably tiny all over!"

Hairy man burst into laughter. Ramsey blinked slowly. They thought Caidon was *little*? Then again, they were both giants, and a solid fifty pounds overweight, if not more. Compared to them, perhaps her husband could be considered lean. Broad shouldered and fit, she couldn't bring herself to consider him small. Not when she knew there wasn't anything little about him.

Disgust and anger slid through her, and before she could bite her tongue, she looked the rude vendor up and down, and said, "The only tiny thing I see from here is you. Does a woman even know when you're in her bed except for the mattress sinking from your weight?"

Several gasps and sniggers had Caidon looking up sharply. He glanced from the purple-faced vendor to Ramsey's glare and sighed out a sharp curse. "Did you just insult a local?"

"He called me a cold fish and said you had a tiny penis!" she answered, exasperated.

The meat vendor sputtered and glared at Hairy and Round Man. A thick piece of jerky flew across the distance and hit Hairy in the middle of his forehead. Grabbing her elbow, Caidon yanked her into the crowd just as Hairy bellowed out profanities too fast for Ramsey to catch most of them. Caidon made several quick turns and cuts between tables before slowing.

"You can't draw attention to us, no matter the insults from the natives."

"I'm sorry, he just—"

"I know he disrespected you, then me, and you have no filter, and limited self-control. You couldn't help yourself. I get it."

His green eyes blazed with an impatience he worked hard to curb. She wanted to grasp his face and taste the passion she knew he'd explode into if she did. Instead, she clasped her hands together and proved him wrong. See? She had *some* self-control, and when she wanted to, she could contain herself. Though she knew this was one of those moments she needed to take seriously.

"I'm sorry," she said.

He ran a hand down his face and searched the crowd. "We can't stay here. There's another market at the second train stop, we'll get off there."

A niggle of guilt made her rub her arms. "How long will we have to wait for the next train if we get off for the market?"

"I don't know." Pulling his shoulder bag around, he dug inside. A piece of paper crinkled as he adjusted the bag. "Okay, looks like the train runs every six hours along the eastbound track. Cargo has right of way, and if I remember, that causes mid-route delays, but we'll still have to be at the station at the scheduled time."

"So, six hours?"

He refolded the paper and shoved it into the pack. "With a possible hour or two of waiting tacked on."

Until now, Ramsey hadn't realized the importance of how easily they'd slid around crowds and traveled through lands unknown. Like shadows, Caidon had taken them from one destination to the next without any interactions that would leave a memorable impression. If she'd been paying attention, she would have known the necessity of his actions. Instead, she'd been too excited taking in all the foreign sounds, sights, flavors, and textures.

Caidon pulled her close. "It's your first mistake. You're allowed to make them."

"Yeah but—"

"No. We've been traveling for two weeks. You've ensured we weren't swindled, had the right food placed in front of us, and went to the correct destinations because you can speak like a local." He kissed her forehead and pulled back until she met his gaze. "The vendor was a scab, and I should have noticed you were getting upset and pulled you out of the situation."

Frustration made her huff. "I'm not your child to correct."

His thumbs caressed along her jaw. "No, but you are my wife to teach. Covert living isn't an ingrained knowledge. You must understand why things are important. We had a lot of time to discuss everything on the ship voyages, but doing everything in real life is different."

Ramsey quelled the self-reproach and wrapped her hands around his wrists. The ovulation bracelet she'd *finally* been able to start yesterday glinted in the bright sun streaming between gently swaying canopies. "I will bite my tongue from now on."

He brushed an index finger along her bottom lip and smiled. Her stomach trembled. "Or just ask if they speak Sziverian. If the answer is a confused look, then feel free to insult away with a pretty smile on your face."

She laughed. "Deal."

Returning her smile, he pressed a far too quick kiss to her lips and then guided her back through the crowded market stalls. Ramsey glanced in longing at several pastry vendors.

"Are you sure we can't grab things here?" she asked.

"We can't linger. If someone was looking for or following us, you made too big a scene to remain anonymous. We have to get to the station and onto the next train, which," he took a fast look at his wristwatch, "should be arriving at any moment."

Ramsey perked up at the information. "We won't be too far behind schedule after all, then."

"No, we should be fine. When I spoke to Voklane on arrival, the ice sheets were still too thick along the Mark Inland shores to dock."

"A race against the ice flow. How exciting."

Caidon squinted as they cleared the market and walked into the brilliant sun. "Actually, it is. We *have* to get there first, or those people are gone forever. No one will ever find any of them again."

The familiar sense of urgency riding them the entire trip returned. She couldn't make another novice mistake. Lives were depending on their ability to make it to Mark Inland without issue. The only other time she'd made a choice that affected anyone else was when she'd gone against Joel Blackbain. In the end, her decision had created a shock wave upsetting some of the wealthiest people in Sziverian society. Since justice had been served, she hadn't taken the time to care much about lost investments. She did, however, care deeply about lost people.

Nerves danced in her stomach. She admitted being level-headed wasn't a strength she possessed. "I don't want to mess up again."

Caidon took her hand and led her down a sandy brick sidewalk. A family ahead walked their dog, and an elderly couple fed small hopping birds at their feet. No one seemed bothered by the persistent chill in the air.

"Then don't," he said, shrugging.

Ramsey opened her mouth to ask how exactly he figured she could accomplish the impossible when she remembered Sylphine's words on no one being able to give her confidence. She snapped her jaw shut and wrapped the cloak tighter around her shoulders. Returning home wasn't an option. For better or worse, she was part of the mission. Caidon had spent long hours on their ocean voyages giving her a rapid course in First Intelligence Office training. The responsibility fell to Ramsey to behave and be a partner to him, not a hindrance.

"Okay," she whispered. "How long to the train station?"

"Not far. Hopefully, we don't hear the train because that'll mean we're missing it."

Spurred by the threat of being left behind, they picked up their pace. Ramsey ignored the huffed complaints of those they sped past, and shouts to enjoy the beauty of the warm day. She pressed her lips together to keep from asking what warmth? Not even the sun broke through the dry cold.

The soaring brick and glass station came into view,

and Ramsey's steps faltered. The stunning architecture spoke of a society so much more advanced than the canopy-covered market had led her to believe. A curving roof of glass covered a brick structure with arched stained-glass windows and open, wide rectangular entryways. Polychromatic brickwork set intricate patterns into the walls and openings. The train shed was by far the most beautiful she'd ever seen.

Inside proved to be as spectacular. Two rail lines ran along the outside edges of the station, both east and west bound. The center housed a garden, with benches for waiting passengers, and stone pathways weaving throughout. Birds flitted about the interior, adding a sweet sound to the hum of humanity. Ivy climbed brick pillars and hung from iron crossmembers soaring high above. A ticket counter with five tellers kept the lines from getting too long, while a handful of shops offering books, small games, souvenirs, and snacks, kept patrons from suffering boredom.

Ramsey spoke to the female teller, ensuring they received tickets until the end of the line. In all, there were nine stops, and she received two tickets for each, as they'd be required to show an unpunched pass at each destination. The total travel time would be almost two days. She thanked the cashier and hoped her disappointment didn't show at the news.

Handing the tickets to Caidon for safekeeping, she voiced her frustration. "Two days? There are only nine stops. How can it take two days?"

"The trains basically only stop for more fuel. Being a big country, the nine available stops naturally happened because people learned they could hitch a ride at those locations. Passenger cars eventually had to be added, and of course, commerce grew up around where people gathered, and stations were built. The passenger trains follow the same route, but as I said earlier, cargo has right-of-way. Any cargo train encountered at switches gets to go first on the line, adding to travel time."

Ramsey stared at him. "How do you know the history of every place we've gone to?"

"Our world is a lot smaller than it used to be, and I've been to almost all the inhabited places. How a society developed and thrived is fascinating to me, and the more I know about a location, the easier it is to fit in with the indigenous people." He glanced at the tickets in his hand and then motioned for her to walk forward. "The loading area is at the very end of the station."

"We're the first stop, right?"

"Sort of. There is a loading station at the docks near the Siber border. Since we arrived at Jordan Pointe, this is our first access to the rails. There will be some passengers that disembark here and some who get on the train to head toward Siber. There is a rumor Syrinad is trying to connect all their docks to their rails."

Jordan Pointe had made Ramsey wish she had an artistic skill. The docks were situated at the bottom of an immense cliff with a breathtaking waterfall named Jordan Falls. "Would be wise if they have the commerce to support the expense."

"Syrinad is one of the leading exporters in glass, both clear and stained."

Ramsey looked up at the complicated glass designs patterned in the arched ceiling providing shelter and sun for all the life below. "And the entire world is a consumer of glass."

"Yes, like wood, it's a vital necessity for survival."

"This place is… I never thought I'd see anything like it," she said. "Land of cold sand, sun, and patches of green wonder. And not a single Ariot, only horses, carts, and bikes, like Italyssa."

"Italyssa doesn't have a rail line."

"That's true, but still, why don't they have vehicles like we do?"

"Only a handful of nations have the wealth for Ariots. Ruthenia does, but only the most affluent own them because they're only practical for three or four months a year, not long enough to be useful to the average person." He sat on a bench inlaid with a botanical mosaic. His fingers brushed the small glass tiles. "Give them time. The wealth will arrive in the nation. Too much talent."

The distant rumble of the inbound train made people meander to their area. Soon the ground vibrated with the power of the engine's arrival in the shed. Iron ground on steel as the brakes screamed in protest and the hulking weight of the cars screeched to a stop. The hiss of the brakes locking seemed an unspoken invitation that the train was ready to board. Everyone lined up, tickets out, belongings waiting at their feet. Ramsey noted what they carried didn't vary much from what others had. A variety of bags, purses, satchels, and cases.

Everyone entered the first car and walked through to their seats or private cabins. Ramsey frowned when she realized she'd asked for two seats in their elite class, giving them some space for the long voyage but nowhere to sleep in privacy.

"I didn't know they had cabins," she said, searching

the brass alpha-numerical combinations for seating assignment as they walked down a narrow aisle.

"They are new."

"She didn't ask if I wanted one."

"Probably because they were already sold out."

Ramsey found their seats. A spacious padded bench with spring-loaded footrests faced the wall. Neatly folded blankets and pillows were piled in the corner. Caidon stowed their belongings in bins above the seats. He took the aisle side, leaving the huge window for Ramsey.

"For the best anyway," he said as she sat.

"What is?"

He plucked at the bracelet wrapped three strands deep around her wrist. "That we didn't have a private cabin."

She stared at him, confused. "Why? We had private cabins for most of our ship voyages."

Leaning in close, his lips brushed her ear, and he whispered, "And we slept in separate births all the same. I made sure of it. Now, you're a temptation I don't have to ignore. Train walls are thin." He kissed her long and deep, until everything in her trembled, and she strained not to climb onto his lap. "I don't think you'd appreciate the entire train knowing how you sound."

"And if I don't care?" she asked, unable to tear her gaze from his mouth.

"Doesn't matter," he murmured. The warmth of his breath sent a shiver through her. "Some things will only be for us."

• • •

MIDNIGHT FELL IN INKY DARKNESS NOT EVEN HANDHELD lamps could cut through. Caidon chose their path carefully, his hand tight around Ramsey's as he guided them across the Syrinad border into Mark Inland with a small group of brave travelers. No guards patrolled, no official welcomed them or asked about their business. Those who ventured into the lawless country did so of their own volition.

"The signs say turn back," she whispered into the soundless night. Not even animals scurried about.

"This town is mostly safe, but beyond isn't. We'll be able to find a room for the night with running water and a meal served in the morning. After that, we'll mostly sleep in abandoned buildings," he answered.

Her hand tightened. "Like trespassers?"

"Close to the docks, we can't afford for anyone to know where we are. Even if we could risk it, there's nothing. Mark Inland is barely this side of the primal wars. The reason they have a hundred languages is because they have a hundred factions still fighting for the land claimed under one ruler twenty years ago. Syrinad, Siber, Latanus, and Gaula were all quick to stake their borders, wanting to ensure the infighting stayed where the useless king now claimed."

"They didn't oppose the borders?"

"They might in the future if Mark Inland finds a precious resource along any of the borders. Right now, the land is lawless, and no one wants to claim any responsibility or else they'd have to help stabilize the area they demand."

"So, it's easy to do illegal things here. No one cares."

"It's the perfect place to funnel smuggled goods," he agreed. "From here, their manifest can be changed if the country of origin doesn't allow the product or can even be sold from here and transported to the nearest country with a rail system and smuggled in that way. From Sziveria and Ruthenia, it's a good half-way point to the southern regions of the inhabited world."

"If it's ungoverned, how does anything get handled?"

"Factions own specific docks and will take care of a ship if they claim or lose the income or product."

He helped her over a deep rut in the frost-crusted mud trail that counted for a road. Up ahead, lamps swung, highlighting the occasional beady glow of eyes, and thick foliage of a forest. Her hand trembled in his and he wished they'd arrived in the daylight instead of frightening darkness. Alone, he never had to worry about what lurked in the unknown depths.

"And you're certain we can find a warm place to sleep tonight?" she asked, teeth chattering.

Caidon pulled her close and kissed her cold cheek. "I'll make sure you stay warm."

A spark ignited along his nerves, dispelling the chill and constricting his breath. Not even the long ocean voyages, where they'd been constricted some days to their cabin, had he managed to become used to the sensation of her emotions sliding under his skin. The longer they were together, the more he experienced. The heat of her anger or frustration, the sparkle of her joy, and the sizzle of her desire. All of it filtered along an ever-strengthening strand between them.

"How far do we have?" She adjusted her bag on her shoulders, pulling the edges of her cloak that had bunched under the weight of the straps.

Careful to keep her hair from catching, he helped

settle the heavy weight of her possessions along her back. Transferring what she could carry from a chest to a pack had been a necessity. The moment they found a clothing vendor, he'd get her clothes more suitable to the current culture. A thick jacket, pants, and boots. Easier to walk in and far warmer than the dress and cloak she wore. Sziverian women dressed more on the feminine side of fashion in dresses and skirts, whereas Mark Inland women had to work along with the men to support their families. The artic climate meant layers that were easy to move in. In a dress, Ramsey would stand out more than she already would with her violet eyes and creamy skin.

"Another half hour, at the most," he answered.

"Should we stay with the group?"

The wariness in her voice said what she didn't. Small circles of light bobbed and grew weaker in the distance. "You mean stay with the light?"

"That, too."

He chuckled. "I have a lamp."

"Why aren't we using it?"

"We'll draw more attention as bright, shiny prey than if we wait for our vision to adjust to the ambient light of the stars and moon."

"Can you see in the dark? Because I can't," she fussed, grabbing his arm as she tripped.

"My night vision is stronger than yours, yes."

"Part of being Ruthenian?"

"Likely. Or part of my genetic talent."

"Which comes from Ruthenian genes," she stated dryly.

Caidon clenched his jaw to prevent himself from replying to her snappish comments with one of his own. She was cold. Tired. Completely out of her element because he, and her country, had asked more of her than most guardians were expected to achieve. Tolerating her condescension was a small price to pay. Unpleasant weather, poor sleeping conditions, weird food, and sometimes even weirder people were all things he'd become accustomed to and had learned how to function around. In this situation, he needed to be the bigger man.

Taking her elbow in hand, he guided her around holes and wheel ruts, always alert to their surroundings. The flicker of lamps soon disappeared, leaving them alone in darkness. Caidon stopped. Ramsey made a sound of dismay and tried to tug him back into motion.

"Wait," he whispered.

"For what?" Another huff of exasperation left her. "And why are we whispering? No one is around to hear us."

"Sometimes nature deserves our silence," he said, his words still muted. "Look up."

"I don't..." Her words died on a gasp.

Slowly, as if appearing for them alone in the hushed stillness of night, stars twinkled into existence. More and more colors shone against an endless sky the longer they stared. Blue, red, orange, white, and yellow, distant fires burning in colors witnessed by their ancestors since the beginning of time.

"I've never seen anything like this," she whispered in reverence. "It's unbelievable. They go on forever."

"Yes. I would have shown you on the ships, but almost every night was cloud-covered. See the brightest yellow one?" He leaned his head against hers and pointed to the left of the moon.

"Oh, yes, I see it. Wow, it's so much clearer than the others."

"That's the planet, Venus. Some nights a really bright red star can be seen under the moon, and that's Mars."

"Amazing."

"Ruthenia has an observatory where they study planets and stars. I've been once. They use these giant glass lenses to see into the sky."

"What are they trying to learn?"

"I don't know. We have some information about astronomy from before the Cataclysm, but most is a new science, like medicine, since we don't have the technology anymore. I guess we'll always wonder what's beyond our skies."

He shifted his focus to her, taking in the wonder of her face, cast in colorless shadows from starlight. A sense of satisfaction filled him that he'd given her this moment. On an impulse, he leaned in and pressed his mouth to hers. Delight filled her eyes before they closed, and the warmth of her tongue touched his lips. Caidon opened, enjoying the slide of her tongue along his, the intimacy of a stolen moment under the canopy of stars. He kissed her until the chill of night settled deeper around them, and a shiver not from passion trembled along her body pressed close to his.

Reluctantly, he broke their kiss and took hold of her cold fingers. "Come on, we should be able to see better now."

Their breath left them in silver vapor trails. Frost crunched beneath each step. Trees framed the road in black silhouettes against a gray night. Caidon had to keep guiding Ramsey, her attention on the heavens rather than the pitted road in front of them. The faint glow of civilization appeared, and each foot closer dimmed the celestial lights above. Soon they faded completely as the road shifted from dirt to laid stone, and meager streetlamps provided enough illumination to see nearby buildings.

Caidon found them a suitable inn after bypassing two. Long ago, he'd learned to look at the pride the owners took in the exterior. Even if paint chipped, stairs sagged, and windows were cracked, if it were devoid of trash collected in front or passed out people, chances were the same could be said for the inside. The front door creaked open when he pushed. A quick glance around didn't show any dangers as he ushered Ramsey into the warmth. She let out a shuddering breath and rushed to the woodstove burning in the gathering room corner.

A short, thin man appeared from behind a swinging door. He pushed silver glasses up his nose and smiled, revealing a gap where a tooth used to be. Unknown words tumbled from his mouth.

"Ramsey?" Caidon called, bracing his forearm on the counter almost as tall as the man standing behind it.

"What?" She looked from him to the waiting hotelier. A flush blossomed across her cheeks. "Oh, right. Sorry."

With a sigh of longing, she left the warmth of the stove and returned to his side. Caidon removed her pack from her shoulders as she spoke, and he recognized the language to be Syrin. The proprietor nodded, enthusiasm brightening his face.

"We are in luck," she said, smiling. "He speaks Syrin. I'm not sure what I'm going to do the deeper into this country we go, but we'll figure that out later."

"Perfect." Caidon conveyed their needs, which she translated. Minutes later, they had a room and a promise of hot breakfast before they left in the morning.

Loaded with all their possessions, Ramsey carried his rifle case while he handled the rest. They headed to the third floor. She unlocked the door and waited while he went in. A small room with a sink, counter, and table with two chairs took up one room. To the left, a narrow doorway led to a bedroom with a bed. He wondered how they'd both fit to sleep on the small mattress. Very close. He swallowed against the imagery of Ramsey plastered along his body all night. Forcing the thought away, he did a quick check of the bathroom and closet. At his nod, she closed the door and locked them in.

The case made a *thump* as she set it down and looked around the dark room. "This is a lot nicer than I expected."

"I think they see a lot of traveling merchants, who expect a level of finery. The room wasn't cheap." He glanced at the silhouetted furniture and shrugged. "Then again, the sun may reveal a different perspective."

"Are we leaving the lamps unlit?"

"I can light the one in the bathroom, if you'd like. It should provide enough light for both of those rooms. The pellet stove will, too."

She rubbed her arms under the cloak and gave a muffled sound of chill.

"As long as there's pellets, I can light the stove," he said, reaching down for his rifle case.

"I wasn't worried," she whispered.

Warm honied desire spread through his veins and ignited the lust he'd been trying to force away. Found he no longer could. His grip tightened on the handle, and he looked up, wishing he could see her expression in the darkness. "No?"

"You promised to keep me warm."

Grabbing the front of his jacket, she yanked him to her, not giving him the chance to respond. The rifle case clattered over between them. Caidon's feet caught along the edge, and he fell into her, slamming her back into the wall. Her mouth captured his, fervent in her demands. The thread between them burst into focus in his mind, like a thick strand of shimmering gold, increasing in ties until he felt wrapped in a web of her making. Without breaking the kiss, she shoved his jacket from his shoulders. Untangling his arms, he tossed the leather away. The flutter of her cloak followed. His tongue slipped into her mouth, taking control, tasting all the yearning they'd kept in check far too long.

Her hips arched. On instinct, he pressed into her, pushing her tighter against the wall. Fabric bunched and twisted between them. Annoyed, Caidon yanked her skirts up while she shoved her underwear down, using her toes to finish the task. Warm, supple skin met his fingers, and he caressed up her thighs, hefting her upward. Without hesitation, she anchored her legs around his hips.

The loosening of his belt made a sliver of reality penetrate his consciousness. He tore his mouth from hers. Ragged gasps left his mouth, and he rested his forehead against hers. "I—" Words lodged in his throat, and he swallowed and tried again. "I don't know if I'm going to be very good at this the first time."

Metal clanked, and in seconds, his belt hung loose against his thighs. The buttons along the front of his trousers went next. "I've never been any good," she breathed, pressing her mouth to his.

Doubt at her lack of confidence made him want to argue because he knew firsthand the depths of her passion, and she hadn't been lacking in anything. But he had to remember, he wasn't her first, and the idiot who came before him had clearly made her feel less than. The almost desperate need for control vibrated along their bond and trembled in her limbs. Caidon took a deep breath and then kissed her, slowly, compelling her back into a moment with him instead of lost in the mire of her perceived inadequacy.

Removing one hand from her rear, he took hold of her hand and threaded their fingers together. He lifted their joined hands to the wall above her head. An uneven breath left his lungs and caught in her mouth as she shifted position. The tip of his erection glided into her slick, welcoming heat. In unhurried thrusts, he pushed deeper inside until she enveloped him, surrounding him in sensation and pleasure.

"You're perfect," he somehow managed to utter. He flexed his hips, moving in a deliberate rhythm, wanting to feel everything. A hushed curse of surprise left his mouth. "You feel very, very good."

"You do, too," she said between gasps.

He tightened his grip on her butt and the hand he still held. His muscles burned and shook from the strain of holding her while he moved to a rhythm focused completely on what made her feel good. What made cries of pleasure rise from her parted lips. A whisper of need for more, for harder, deeper, filtered along their bond, and Caidon responded.

Increasing his pace, he moved faster, driving in powerful thrusts to bring them both toward a release just out of their grasp. Sweat trickled between his shoulders and met his tongue when he licked her throat. She came on a broken cry, her body arching from the wall, every muscle tense. The incredible reaction within her left him no choice, her body requiring him to join, milking him into his release.

Trembling, he sank to the ground. She followed with him still buried deep inside her. Boneless, she melted against the wall, her legs falling open along his thighs. Sucking in lungsful of air, Caidon laid his head on the cushion of her breasts. Her heavy breaths moved her chest beneath his cheek, and he hugged her tight.

The delicate thread of their bond surged into a solid cord. Caidon groaned, and Ramsey gasped and jerked.

"What was that?" she asked, her words unsteady.

"Our bond." Lifting his head, he grasped her jaw in both his hands and kissed her. "You're mine now. Forever. There's no going back from this."

She returned his kiss, taking it deeper. "You're mine now, too."

"Ah." He ran the tip of his tongue along her bottom lip, reveling in the shudder she gave that he felt inside and out. "I've always been yours, *zlanishka*."

Between kisses, soft caresses, and the leisurely shed of their clothing, they made it to the bathroom. After showering, Caidon lit the pellet stove and then climbed under the soft sheets with Ramsey. Her naked body snuggled along his. Drawing long strokes across her back, he soothed her into a calm state until she fell asleep half sprawled across his torso. Tiny orange flames danced behind the small glass plate of the stove. Caidon stared at them, the erotic memory of their coupling mixing with the anxiety of caring for his mate.

His fingers rolled the cool beads of her ovulation bracelet along her wrist. The strength of their bond took him by surprise. He figured it'd be stronger by faint degrees, not a near tangible energy between them. In the shower, she'd stubbed her toe, and her pain had filtered to him as distress. At one time in his ancestor's history, this trait had likely protected a mated couple, allowing one to come to the others aide when in trouble. Caidon saw this attribute as trouble in the making. A distraction in his field could kill him. Forcing calm, he willed the concern away for now and slipped into a light sleep.

A featherlight touch eased him from slumber. He buried his face in the crook of Ramsey's neck. Her back pressed to his chest, her butt nestled between his hips, her leg was thrown over his, and her fingers coaxed him to life between her spread thighs. Without a spoken word, he slid his hand along her stomach to her damp curls. Slick need coated his fingers as he carefully sank them into her heat and caressed her until she writhed, panting and whimpering for more.

Like the sun cresting the horizon, they found the beauty in a slow coming together. Gentle, undemanding, giving her the tender moment neither had been able to manage earlier, he eased into her an inch at a time until he filled her. Groaning as she accepted him fully into her body, once again awed at how incredible she felt, he loved her in the quiet stillness of dawn. He splayed a hand across her stomach, and she threaded her fingers between his, her grip flexing with each deliberate roll of his hips.

Caidon pressed kisses along her neck and traced her pounding pulse with his tongue. Her release came on a ragged hitch of her breath. Only once he'd heard the sweet, soft sound again, felt the delicate tremors along his shaft deep within her a second time, did he allow himself the same. They fell back asleep locked together, content and satisfied.

Hours later, brilliant light speared through a crack in the curtains across Caidon's vision. Grunting in annoyance, he threw his arm over his face and rolled onto his back. The hazy remnants of waking to pleasure and falling asleep sated had him blinking grit from his eyes. In the harshness of morning, he realized how easily they'd come together without thought or worry. Frowning, he eased from bed and wondered how they'd refrain when the day of the month mattered. The creamy expanse of her naked back drew his attention, and he couldn't help but slide his hand along her silky skin. She murmured and buried her face into the pillow. Caidon sighed. Sleep fully clothed, that was how he figured.

Donning his pants, he went into the living area and searched for coffee. He found premade cotton pouches for steeping and a metal canister for boiling water on the pellet stove in a small cabinet. A newspaper was shoved under the door, a convenience he would not have expected for a conflicted country like Mark Inland. He picked it up and unfolded it, looking at the drawn pictures to go with articles that he didn't understand. A quick flash of light in his peripherical caught his attention, but he made no indication he'd noticed.

He checked on the water, found it hot enough for his needs, and poured the steaming liquid into the cup waiting with his coffee. After adding a small jar of preserved sweetened cream, he sipped the dark roast and resisted the urge to walk to the window.

The bed frame creaked, something he hadn't noticed last night, despite their early morning lovemaking. Naked and unconcerned, Ramsey appeared in the doorway. He was careful to keep his expression and reaction neutral.

Taking another sip of coffee, he said, "Don't come out here."

She froze, her hand on the inner frame. "Why? What's wrong?"

He set the paper on the small table and returned to the counter, pulling down another cup. "In my pack, there's a small scope. Get it. Put something on, anything, and then carefully go to the bedroom window and look across into the other building without moving the curtains. Tell me what you see."

The faint scuffle of movement told him what he didn't dare check to see, that she'd obeyed. Patiently, he waited to learn what she'd discover, though he figured he knew.

Someone had found them.

17

EXCITEMENT AND NERVOUSNESS FOUGHT FOR DOMINANCE, and Ramsey tried to ignore them both. She knew what Caidon asked of her was important. Never mind that her body still hummed with remnants of pleasure she didn't know could be achieved. The temptation to give into distraction, to try to figure out how he was so different, made her clench her jaw. She had to focus.

Slipping into a navy button-up shirt he'd had rolled in his pack, she didn't bother with the closures, instead kept looking until she found the scope wrapped securely in padded leather. On her way to the window, she unrolled the bundle and threw the leather on the bed. She pressed her back to the wall and eased around until she could see through the slits created by the curtain. She found the windows across from them, most broken, the building looking decrepit enough to collapse if a bird landed on it wrong.

The importance of her task wasn't lost on her. For whatever reason, Caidon couldn't perform the request. Being needed beyond speaking a few words felt foreign and almost uncomfortable. Circumstance had left her without the pressures of expectation in life. Ramsey had a weakness in longing to return to said careless existence. Steeling her nerves, she took a deep, calming breath and slipped the scope between the curtains.

A cursory search revealed a figure hunkered down and staring through a scope of their own. Anger sliced through her chest. If she had to guess, she figured the observer watched Caidon through the curtainless window. The glint of sun off something made her look harder and a rifle barrel came into focus. Gasping, she fell back in shock, landing on her butt. Dusty wood met her bare skin and she rolled onto her hands and knees, the scope clutched in her hand.

"Caidon!" she screeched in panic.

"I know," he replied, his voice calm. "Everything is fine for now. He's waiting for you."

Anxiety increased until she struggled to catch a decent breath. "How is that fine? How is any of this fine?"

"This is life with me, *zlanishka*," he said, the quiet words filtering through the haze of her fear.

Terror he likely felt along their bond and was having to deal with, on top of a would-be assassin lurking in a rundown building across from them. Ramsey attempted to bury the angst churning in her stomach and swallow back the dryness coating her throat.

"What are you going to do?" she asked.

The rifle case came sliding into the room. "In thirty seconds, I'm going to come to you and you're going to tell me where he's positioned. I'm going to get set up and then we're going to give him a little show so he stays nice and comfortable. You'll come out here, alone, and I'll eliminate our problem."

Ramsey's heart raced. "What if he—"

"No chance," he assured. "He's not better than me."

"You're willing to risk my life on that?"

He entered the room casually, sipping the cup of coffee like a murderer didn't watch them. "Ramsey, he will be dead before you set foot in that room."

Her breath hitched, and she blinked. "Oh."

"Yeah." The coffee cup clattered as he set it on the pellet stove. "Now tell me exactly what you saw."

Taking his request to be literal, she told him how many windows from the left and the top of the building she saw the assassin. Then, in fascination, she watched as he removed his rifle and assembled the parts in expert fashion. He was shirtless, muscles flexing with each precise move he made. His pants weren't fully buttoned either, and her brain went places it had no business going considering the situation. But go there, she did, remembering in vivid detail how she'd explored all those muscled planes underneath the spray of water.

Something must have filtered along their bond because his head snapped up, and green fire blazed in his eyes. "I wish," he whispered.

Heat flooded her body, and she pressed a hand to her belly, now fluttering for a new reason. The floorboards creaked under his weight on his way to the window. Kneeling, he set the rifle against the wall and then held his hand out. Took her all of a second to realize he wanted the smaller scope not attached to his weapon. She closed the distance and dropped the heavy instrument onto his waiting palm.

"I see him," he said, peering through the slit. "Perfect." He rose, carefully setting the scope on the bed. "Walk out into the living area."

Her eyes widened, and she stared at him. "Now?"

"Yes. Trust me."

Swallowing, she nodded and shuffled toward the doorway. Before she stepped through, he caught her, swept her into a huge hug, spun her around, and into the sunlit room, his mouth finding hers. She laughed and wrapped around him. His hands gripped her bare butt, and he groaned. The wall met her back, and she gasped, her fingers digging into his hair.

"Is this the show?" she asked between kisses.

"Yeah," he said, his voice deep and husky. "You should have put more on. I'm having a hard time not giving him something to watch for real."

Unable to stop from teasing, she smiled, her hips moving along his abdomen, reminding him in an entirely different way she wore nothing but his shirt. "Some things are only for us, remember?"

He groaned. "Do you?"

"If you'll recall," she whispered into his ear, "I never had an issue with anyone knowing I was claiming my husband."

"Woman," he growled, "you are going to be my undoing."

A thrill raced through her, welcome and irresistible. "You give me too much power."

He kissed her, seducing with each exploring stroke. The danger watching them faded from her mind until all that mattered was Caidon and his wicked tongue. He shifted just enough to drop her center over the bulge straining the buttons of his trousers. Ramsey gasped at the oddness of equal parts discomfort and erotic sensation.

"You should know I will give you anything you want," he breathed into her mouth.

An orgasm almost took her right then. "We need to stop, or I'm not going to be able to."

"Agreed."

Slowly, he let her slide down his body. Her feet touched the floor, and he had to steady her. He kissed her again and walked her backward into the room, his hands still on her butt, keeping her trapped to his frame. In the shelter of the bedroom, they separated, breathless. Ramsey waited while he positioned himself at the window, and then, with a flick of his wrist, he gave the silent order for her to move back into the living area.

Ramsey squeezed her eyes shut, searched out some unknown courage, and then stepped a single foot out of the bedroom. A faint *pop* made her jump and squeak.

"Done," he said from behind her.

"But…" She let out a mutter of confusion. "How did you… I barely moved."

He walked past her, slipping a long-sleeved cotton shirt over his head. At the door, he stopped and yanked on his boots. "I told you, not many are better than me."

"He could have been," Ramsey protested.

"No. If he had been, we never would have seen him."

Well, she had no argument against that. "Where are you going?"

"To see if he has anything useful on him. While I'm gone, pack up everything. Don't open the door for anyone. I'll use the key to get back in."

He grabbed said key from the table, pocketed it, gave her a quick kiss, and was gone before she could speak another word. Ramsey stared at the closed door and blew a curl from her eyes. In a twelve-hour window, she'd seen the wonders of the universe, discovered her body was capable of immeasurable pleasure, and helped her assassin husband eliminate a threat. The urge to sit on the floor and gaze at the wall to process everything nearly overwhelmed her. Instead, she changed back into her warmer dress, put shoes on, and then organized the few possessions they had out into the packs.

Caidon still hadn't returned. She resisted the urge to go to the window to see if she could spot him. A sense of vulnerability still filled her when she went into the living area, so she sat on the bed and waited for him to return. Her gaze landed on the rifle braced casually on the windowsill edge. What would the weight of holding it feel like? She remembered Katria holding the weapon expertly, a strong equivalent to the man she worked beside. Ramsey sighed. She'd never be that woman.

Rubbing her damp palms on her knees, she watched the door. What felt like eons passed, but was probably only a half hour, he finally returned. A paper-wrapped package crinkled in his arms as he kicked the door closed with his boot. Ramsey rose and met him in the living room.

He handed her the package. "Change into this, then we're leaving."

"What did you find?" she asked, unwrapping the brown paper to reveal a soft pair of thickly woven cotton pants, two long-sleeved shirts, and a fur-lined jacket. She brushed her fingers along the supple fabrics. "Pants?"

"Pants are what everyone wears in this country. We can't stand out." He dug into his inside jacket pocket and pulled out a slip of paper. "I found this icon inked on his forearm. Does it mean anything to you?"

Ramsey took the drawing and looked at the traced image of a nasturtium flanked by wings. "No, I've never seen it before. He didn't have anything on him?"

"Just a few bullets," he said, breaking down his rifle. "No orders or identification. Not even a change of clothes, so he wasn't planning on staying long."

Long enough to put a bullet in her. Caidon didn't speak the words, but she knew they were the truth all the same. A niggle of anxiety threatened to pull her under. Caidon drew her into his arms and hugged her tight.

"Nothing is going to happen to you," he whispered.

The scent and warmth of him soothed and grounded her. "You can't make that promise. Bad things happen, and we're after some bad people. How did they find us?"

"Like I told your brother, if anything happens to you, it means I'm already dead. And I meant that."

Ramsey shuddered. "How about neither of us die."

He squeezed and then released her. "Deal." After he helped her into her new clothes and secured her pack, he picked up his own possessions. "He probably learned of our trail in Syrinad. This is the first city and the only one with decent lodging, it wasn't a stretch to find us here. All he had to do was ask about a couple with our looks and then figure out which room we were in."

Ramsey touched her chaotic hair. "I could braid it and wear a hat."

The unexpected light feather of his finger down her nose made her twitch. "Your eyes, your skin." His hand ventured further to her collarbone and slipped between her breasts. "Your beautiful body. Everyone will notice you no matter where you go."

Her breath hitched. "And your eyes, too."

He smiled and dropped his hand. "Yes, there isn't much hiding for us if someone is really looking."

"How do you blend in?"

"A man alone doesn't attract much attention. Women are different."

She frowned. "That doesn't seem fair."

"It's not. It's another reason the FIO often attaches a female guardian to a male partner. They can travel easier, and safer."

An odd sliver of jealousy made her frown deepen. Jealousy she had no business experiencing, considering as of last night, she'd become Caidon's sole lover. "I'm glad they didn't do that with you."

He threaded their hands together. "Wouldn't have mattered. I'd still have chosen you."

Pain throbbed in Ramsey's head. She pressed two fingers to her temples and rubbed. A grimace twisted her face. All around her, voices chattered in at least seven different dialects, flowing in and out of her mind in a constant stream of information she struggled to process. Caidon had left her in a secluded alcove, sheltered from the cold wind sweeping through the cramped city.

People bartered on the street for food, fabric, and even farm animals. Refuse crunched and squished underfoot and permeated the air with a stench Ramsey had never experienced. For a market, the environment was crowded and unsanitary. Yet, glancing around, she knew the area wasn't capable of better. The cramped trader's row had likely sprung up from necessity. The items for sale were a lifeline for some of the people begging the merchants to accept a handful of beads or strips of leather. Currency seemed to be whatever the supplier was willing to accept.

How anyone managed to understand or even know who spoke their version of Markinish, Ramsey didn't know. She figured the longer she remained in the country, the nuances of the culture would become apparent. Right now, she found herself too overwhelmed by the poverty, and signs of violence within the population, to determine how they knew who communicated in what dialect.

A shadow fell across the alcove, and Ramsey jumped. Relief rushed through her when Caidon's familiar form registered. He gently pushed the fur-lined hood of her jacket down and then covered her ears with thick muffs. Silence descended around her, and Ramsey almost cried from the alleviation. She wrapped her hands around the muffs, breathing away the anxiety.

"Thank you," she said.

He nodded and took her hand, leading her back into the foray of the market. She wrapped her hand around the strap of her pack and held tight in an attempt to feel some semblance of control over the situation. Caidon remained unphased by the chaos, avoiding circumstances she wouldn't have even noticed if she'd been on her own.

Two streets over, the crowd dissipated to manageable levels, and they were able to walk between cyclists and mule-pulled carts on the narrow, packed gravel road. Someone tossed slop from an upstairs window, causing anger to erupt up the street. Caidon pulled them down an alley that crossed over to the next avenue to avoid the congestion caused by the shouting.

"Did you find where we cross the river at?" Ramsey asked, sliding the muffs to her neck.

"Yes, I found an old man who spoke Ruthenian and was able to help."

Guilt assailed her. "I'm sorry I couldn't help."

"We knew Markinish would be a problem. Some areas are worse for how many dialects are spoken, and some are better. I'm sure once you know five or six, we'll be able to make communication work."

Knowing she'd return home to Sziveria, likely knowing a dozen or more new languages, almost overwhelmed her. Her talent still seemed an impossibility, despite the evidence proving otherwise. "I hope so. Did speaking to the old man expose us again?"

"I doubt it, since we spoke Ruthenian, which honestly, he was too pleased to be conversing in to care about anything concerning me."

"What's the plan, then?" she asked.

"He suggested we barter for a bike with a slate of wood over the back wheel for you to sit on. Otherwise, it's a two-day walk to the crossing point."

Ramsey had seen plenty of women, or even children, riding precariously in such a manner. She questioned her ability to balance and not fall off, but a two-day walk didn't appeal. "All right, I guess we should find a bike."

"At the next town. The population is less, so hopefully only one or two dialects. A bike is a commodity in this country. We'll need all the help we can get to afford one."

RAMSEY SHIELDED HER EYES AGAINST THE BRIGHT SUN glaring in the sky and off the water. In the distance, she could just make out the large rickety wooden ferry that would take them across the wide river. Brown water churned and frothed, bobbing the floating raft about on the thick ropes keeping it on track. Two men tugged along on the ropes, shirtless. Light glinted off their sweat-soaked, rich brown skin. A small group of patrons waited patiently in the center; their belongings tied down around the edges.

As the ferry inched closer, the activity on the unsteady, floating dock grew restless. Caidon kept his arms wrapped around her waist, preventing anyone from jostling into her. The protective intimacy made Ramsey's heart flip, despite the odd behavior around them.

"Why is everyone acting like this?" she asked.

"The best place to sit is in the middle. There are a lot of us. The line is subjective, and it becomes a rush for who can get onboard first."

Ramsey eyed the narrow dock, moving with the gentle swell of water beneath. "We're going to fall in."

Caidon laughed. "We won't, we'll be fine."

Once again, he proved her concerns unfounded, a habit she was more than happy he continued to make.

The crowd surged forward, but Caidon was ready, and they moved seamlessly to the front, being helped onboard. Caidon secured their possessions with one of the many ropes provided, all but his rifle case, while Ramsey sat on a rug big enough for two. Caidon joined her, turning to settle her between his legs. The raft filled up, and the ferrymen cast off.

Ramsey sucked in a breath as the river flowed and swelled around them. Water sprayed over the edges and bubbled up between boards. She tried not to worry or imagine being tossed and carried downstream in the turbulent waters.

"Remember this is the safest crossing. The brothers have worked hard to provide a reputation for delivering their patrons safely across Thunder River. People travel for an extra day just to use their service."

The damp rug beneath her butt soaked into her clothing. Water spray beaded along her jacket. She had to work hard to shore up anything other than dread and frustration. After the second day of no shower and sleeping on any cold, hard surface they could find that provided some shelter from the freezing night temperatures, the illusion of excitement had fallen from Ramsey's eyes. She was done. Done smelling offensive. Done being exhausted. Done with the tasteless food because no one could afford even a basic spice like salt.

"How do you do this?" she asked, more to herself than to him since the rushing water drowned out any sound.

He rested his chin on her shoulder and tightened his arms around her waist. "Soon, you'll learn to sleep anywhere, and you won't be so tired. You'll be hungry enough not to care that the flavors aren't what you're used to. You'll notice no one notices you, and you can enjoy the sights and sounds of a new culture. I did warn you my life was difficult."

Yes, he had. And secure in the strength of his embrace, Ramsey knew despite all the awful, she didn't want to be anywhere else. She sighed and leaned back into his warmth. "I'm just whining. I'm sorry."

"You're allowed to whine."

"You don't."

He chuckled and kissed her cheek. "You didn't see me my first year. I threw up more than I ate because the country they first sent me to used this nasty spice in *everything*. I kicked a hole in a wall when a mouse kept crawling over my foot while I tried to sleep. I hated the first solid ten months of my job and seriously questioned my sanity about accepting."

A trickle of hope made her straighten so she could look at him. "It gets better?"

"A lot better. We'll go somewhere truly amazing, and you'll be thanking Voklane every radio transmission. That is if you decide to stay after this assignment." He tucked a stray curl back under her hood. "There's also the feeling after you've successfully completed the job. Of purpose and accomplishment."

She settled back against him, thankful to see the opposite shore edging closer. "I'll take your word for it."

18

THE FULL MOON ILLUMINATED ENOUGH FOR CAIDON TO sneak around without tripping over an object or person. Cold puffs left his mouth, and he squeezed Ramsey's hand, waiting for the return gesture letting him know she was still fine sleuthing along behind. Natveha was the first city they'd come to since leaving Syrinad that had any sort of government structure. Caidon had scouted the town in the daylight and had found a radio center used by the officials. If a local could afford the exorbitant rates, they could send a message. Since Caidon refused to help support a likely corrupt office or be heard speaking a language the officials may have been told to watch out for, creeping around in the middle of the night was his only option.

Caidon led them down an alley barely large enough for them to squeeze through to get to the back of the building, also almost touching the structure behind. The fire hazards the city posed made a shiver race along his spine. Mud slipped beneath his feet, emanating a stench. A muffled gagging cough sounded behind him.

Ramsey slipped and slid on the slick ground, her fingers tightening around his while her other hand grasped his back to catch her balance. He waited until she was stable before moving around to the back door.

The lock was easy to bypass. A pitiful, rusted mass of metal. Caidon set it on a table inside the door. Moonlight filtered in through the dirty windows, casting the room into navigable shadows. He found the radio and motioned for Ramsey to close the door. Setting his bag on the table next to the unit, he dug around inside for a small vial of vicious liquid every FIO guardian was given to carry for covert situations. Another small tube provided the catalyst, that when mixed, emitted a soft green glow. Ramsey gasped and drew near when the jar radiated a growing green light with each shake.

"Hold this for me right in front of the radio," he said, handing her the glowing glass.

"This is awesome," she whispered. "I had no idea you've been carrying this around."

He studied the radio, unsure of its capability to cross the ocean. "I only have one more for this trip. We need to use them sparingly. The good news is, in a colder climate, that little jar will glow for two or three days."

Caidon set the dials and then took a breath of hope. He waited while the line hummed and crackled.

A weak but audible voice replied, recognizable as Ryan Voklane. "Survaine, finally."

Caidon dropped his head to the wall and let relief take over for a second. "The land is wilder than we expected. What can you tell me?"

Ramsey snorted, and Caidon shook his head. She pressed her lips together and looked contrite. They were both exhausted, filthy, cranky, and ready for a trip to be over that wasn't even halfway to being accomplished. Caidon could handle the extremes of his job but asking Ramsey to suffer the same was a difficulty he'd considered, yet found the reality to be much more challenging.

Which only added to his overall stress.

Previous to taking a mate, compartmentalizing had been a proficient skill of his. Now, her care came above all else, including the mission. He knew Voklane's head would pop off if he knew Caidon's inner struggle. One life was not supposed to come before the multitude. And yet, he'd abandon the ship full of people if Ramsey's life were in jeopardy, and the only way to keep her safe was to walk away.

He rubbed his hand down his face, wishing he could pinpoint the moment everything had changed. Probably when he was deep inside her and losing himself in her perfection. Yep. Sounded about right. An experience he couldn't wait to repeat. One they'd had to place on hold due to a lack of basic hygiene. One way or another, he was going to find a way to remedy that tonight.

Ramsey wrote in quick scratches on a slip of paper, and Caidon realized his little venture into his mind had almost cost them vital information. This time he cast her the contrite apology. She smiled and blew him a kiss, and continued to write the information Voklane transmitted.

A distant, muted *pop, pop, pop* had Caidon's head snapping to the window. He motioned for Ramsey to take over and crossed the small room. Pressing his back to the wall, he peered through the hazy glass. Aggressive shouts joined the distinct sound of rifle fire. Small orbs of light danced as far down as he could see. A flash of intense light made him duck and curse.

"We have to go," he said, rushing back to her side. He took the transmitter from her hand. "I think a rival faction is attempting to take over Natveha."

Voklane cursed. Caidon wasn't happy either. He hadn't been able to inform Ryan about or get information on, the assassination attempt their first day in Mark Inland.

He cocked his head, listening to the angry crowd getting closer. "Yeah. We have to go. Someone probably jumped the plan and set a fire before they were supposed to. This radio station will be their next stop."

"Ramsey has everything. Remember to… a radio a…oon as possible… Subail, either the… or the port." Ryan's voice crackled and faded in and out.

"Understood," Caidon acknowledged. "Will find the broadcast center and radio when we're in location."

Voklane signed off, and Caidon changed all the transmission codes. Ramsey folded the paper and slipped it into his pack before he tied the closures into place. He stuck the small glowing jar into his inner jacket pocket, not willing to leave it behind or be a moving green target for those heading their direction.

"We need to go. Now. This place should have been destroyed before the attack started. Someone is either going to show up to make a distress call or to burn this place to the ground. We need to be away before either happens."

"I guess I should feel lucky we haven't experienced any unrest until now," she said, picking up his rifle case while he donned his pack.

"Yes, we've been fortunate." He went back to the

window and took a quick look. The lights were nearer, as was the crowd noise, which had grown as citizen's awoke to a raid. "Up the stairs in the back."

The darkness didn't reveal her expression. She didn't argue with his odd request, leading the way to the second floor. He pressed on her back, urging her up the narrower flight of steps to the third level. Barren of anything but dust and animal droppings, he moved ahead of her to a warped, empty frame where a window once blocked out the elements. The buckled floorboards protested his weight but held.

Caidon sat on the thick frame, ignoring the sharp pokes into his backside. He held out a hand and motioned. "Come on, you're going to step from here to that rooftop."

She balked. "What? No. I can't do that."

"It's literally a step, Ramsey. You won't fall. I'll have you the entire time."

A shadowy movement below caught his attention, and he clenched his teeth and pressed his fingers to his lips. When he motioned her forward again, she shook her head and stepped back, but not out of his reach. He snatched her wrist and pulled her close enough to whisper.

"There are hostiles below. You don't have a choice. We have to stay high to avoid the skirmish. The buildings are close enough together that you can walk across them. Now, go."

She trembled beneath his fingers, but her quick inhale and forward movement let him know he'd convinced her. In movements so slow he figured the entire town would be breached by the time she managed to get one foot across, she slid over to the next roof. Once he was positive she was stable, he tossed her the rifle case and leapt over. Her mouth gaped open, but he didn't give her time to marvel at his building hopping skills. Taking her hand, he ran across the flat surface to the next top, not allowing her the chance to be nervous about the jump.

He took them across the city's upper level to where he'd stashed their bike. Thankfully, the city was still quiet along that street. A hole in the roof, widened by his boot, gave them quick entrance. Ramsey dropped down into his waiting arms with only a faint squeak of alarm. He hugged her tight and pressed a swift kiss to her lips, proud of her.

Outside the building, Ramsey took her place on the back of the bike, modified to allow her to sit pressed against him, her feet braced on pegs near the rear tire. The side-seat wooden slat most common hadn't worked for her, so he'd found a parts vendor and bought a second seat. With her more secure, and comfortable, their travel had become much easier when they found roads, or paths, capable of bike usage.

Caidon took them to the outskirts of town, along a ridge that showed the hills and city below. Taking out his scope while Ramsey held the rifle case, he did a cursory search of the homes outside the city proper. One showed no chimney smoke, and he smiled with satisfaction, moving his attention to the progress of the city takeover below. Faint gunfire and an occasional scream loud enough to carry on the wind drifted to them. Fires glowed an intense orange against a midnight sky. Sighing, he put away the scope and situated his possessions in the basket on the front. The ride to the home he'd found was strenuous, mostly up hill, but rewarded his efforts when they did indeed find it to be unoccupied.

"Where do you think the owners are?" Ramsey asked, taking his hand as he led her through the backdoor.

"I saw five other houses this size vacant. Some of the wealthy were probably tipped off about tonight's escapade and are somewhere else, safe."

Ramsey crossed through the spacious home to large front windows overlooking the valley below. The fires had spread, making the horizon an eerie, smoky, yellow-orange. She hugged her torso, the soft glow illuminating her dirt-streaked face.

"Are we safe here?" she asked.

He joined her at the window. "Yes. If the faction is successful, they'll come looting, but not tonight."

She shuddered. "We'll be gone by then, right?"

"Right."

Caidon went up an elegant curving staircase to scout the second floor while Ramsey raided the kitchen. Her excited exclamation made him smile halfway up the steps. The upstairs revealed plush beds with soft sheets, showers, and actual toilets. Most of the clothing, and all the personal effects worth any value, were gone. A few books written in Westican and Eastern Tongue made him raise a brow. He set them to the side for Ramsey. After checking to ensure the shower worked, he went back downstairs.

"There's running water upstairs. No heat, but it felt like it's fed from a roof source, heated by the sun, so it's warmer than room temperature," he said.

Ramsey paused mid-cupboard search. A small pile

of crackers, dried fruit, and spices littered the counter near where she'd perched. "A shower?"

"Yes."

Slowly, she climbed down. "Was there soap?"

"Yes, but if you don't like the way it smells, I have some in my bag."

"No soap could smell bad at this point," she huffed, rushing to the stairs. She paused, hand on the banister. "Are you coming?"

"I will if you'd like, after you've had time to clean up a bit."

"I would, and deal to my shower first."

The sound of her boots racing up the stairs echoed in the quiet space. Caidon shoved his hands in his pockets and took a deep breath, returning to the wall of windows. Potted plants were spaced evenly along each framed seam. He touched a leaf and noted the firm texture. The occupants hadn't been gone long enough for a lack of water to affect the foliage. Fires raged in the city beyond, and likely would continue, considering how close together all the buildings were. He didn't know what the invaders hoped to do with a burnt-out husk of a town. Not the first time he'd witnessed a lack of planning and execution by a group.

Smoke billowed into the night sky, the firelight drowning out any stars. The columns rose like wavering black flags of surrender. He was thankful Ramsey wasn't close enough to hear the cries of anguish and human suffering from the wicked, surely taking advantage of such chaos. Somehow, he'd have to spare her the sights in the morning.

He grabbed a few jars of food before heading

upstairs. After lighting the woodstove in the room they'd occupy, he set the jars to heat and then went to find her in the shower. Despite the lukewarm temperature, she was immersed in the fall of water, her face tilted to the stream, her hair falling in gleaming wet curls down her back. Rivulets of soapy suds chased each other down her perfectly round butt, full thighs, to the silt-covered stone floor. Arousal awakened in him, but he ignored the primal urge as he disrobed, still too filthy to touch himself, let alone her. He shifted around her into the spray of water, surprised to find it comfortably warm.

"I never want to get out," she groaned. "I don't know when we'll get the luxury again."

"I know, so enjoy. The water will eventually run out."

"Will the water freeze overnight?"

"Depending on how much is left in the tub, probably. And that cold of a shower would be most unpleasant. Enjoy it tonight. I'll braid your hair for you once it dries."

She ran a bar of cedar and lemon scented soap over his chest, her fingers straying further down. He sucked in a breath as hot pleasure glided through him.

"I'd rather you do something else with your hands," she whispered, rising on her toes to kiss him.

He sank his fingers into her thick, wet hair. "Yeah?"

A teasing smile toyed with her full lips. "Yeah."

"Can't argue with my beautiful wife."

Her tongue slid along his bottom lip. "I knew you were a smart man."

Subail, Mark Inland

Two days later

A BULLET ZIPPED BY AND SLAMMED INTO THE WOODEN building behind Ramsey. Splinters exploded in the shattered, dry paneling. Caidon's arm snagged around her waist, twisting and sending her flying around his body and into the shelter of an alley. A colorful string of curses left his mouth.

"Damn it, this city is volatile," he muttered, rushing her down the narrow passageway.

"Why would anyone send anything here?" Ramsey asked, breathless in her attempt to keep up with the quick pace he set.

Another round of gunfire erupted behind them, along with angry shouts and taunts. "The port itself may not be as bad."

"Even if it's not, how can anything get from this city to a border nation to move a product?"

A little boy scurried past, arms loaded with bread. A heavy-set man chased him, waving a spatula. At the corner, a man caught the boy, swinging him onto his hip, pointing a short-stock rifle at the merchant. The baker stumbled to a stop, hands raised, speaking a variant of Markinish the gun-toting man did not, and didn't seem to care, waving the gun and backing away. When the two disappeared, the merchant found his courage again, spewing livid words at the now empty sidewalk. Only once he turned away with a disgusted wave of the spatula did Caidon leave the shelter of the alley.

"Based on what you've seen and heard since entering this forsaken city, how many factions are we looking at?" Caidon asked, edging onto the sidewalk, looking in all directions before ushering her down the now quiet street. A disparity she would have found unbelievable a few hours ago. Subail was turning out to be a city of contrasts.

Ramsey struggled to form a coherent thought, let alone a sentence. She swallowed against the dry dust in her throat. "I don't know, at least five, probably more. Voklane was positive the port was in *this* city?"

"Yes."

Disbelief filled her, and she shuddered. "How do people live with all this violence?"

"They don't know anything different."

He guided her into the little bakery the poor man had been robbed from. A bell tinkered to announce their entrance. The sweet, delicious scent of fresh baking bread and pastries filled the warm air. Glass cases displayed small cakes and pies. An empty basket next to a full one of long bread loaves made Ramsey bite her bottom lip. The baker hadn't even bothered to redistribute the remaining loaves. Caidon grabbed two and set them on the counter, along with a pack of crackers, cookies, and dry noodles. A young woman rushed out from behind a swinging door, wiping flour from her hands. She greeted them in a dialect Ramsey didn't know. Smiling, Ramsey tried one she'd heard and knew when they'd entered the city, hoping it wasn't a rival faction that would get them kicked out of the establishment.

The woman hesitated for a moment, glanced over her shoulder, then leaned forward and whispered in the same dialect. Ramsey sighed in relief. She motioned to the goods on the counter and to a few items in the glass cabinet Caidon also wanted. Meat pies, fruit tarts, and some odd little square confections covered in powdered sugar. He asked for several of those, in a variety of colors that Ramsey figured meant different flavors. Everything was wrapped and placed in a large paper bag for them.

Caidon paid with Subail's preferred method, beautiful glass beads. Ramsey hoped some were left when their adventure was finished. The artistic glass varied in color with a rainbow sheen that glimmered across the surface. Never in any other place they'd visited had she seen anything so unique or beautiful. She wanted to ask Raina if the textile would hold any trade value. Maybe if the city found any peace, the glassmakers could find a means to export and bring a crucial industry to the area.

Ramsey accepted the bag, wrapping both arms around it to hopefully prevent anyone from snatching their food before they arrived at their destination. Wherever that happened to be.

"You bought a lot," Ramsey said.

"The temperature stays cold enough to keep the food from spoiling. The pies and tarts will last us two or three days."

Decent food for days... Ramsey's stomach rumbled at the knowledge. They'd packed what they could from the house in Natveha, but jarred fish and crackers only tasted good together when she was too hungry to care what went into her mouth. Granted, most nights after riding on the back of a bike all day or walking trails too rough to ride, any food made a difference. But a good meal? Saliva pooled in her mouth.

Licking her lips, she swallowed and held the bag tighter. "Where are we staying?"

"At the port, in a suitable abandoned building, like we have been." He adjusted the straps crossed over his back, his attention constantly shifting. "I'll need to find the radio station tonight, if possible. We need someone's help from Subail. Hopefully, Voklane has a contact we can reach out to."

Caidon kept to empty streets and narrow side roads, Ramsey following close behind, holding his hand when he asked, clutching the bag of provisions when he needed both free. The sun was setting over the cresting waves by the time they reached the docks. Long, wide rows of rough wooden planks jutted out into an angry ocean. Caidon paused for a moment, shielding his eyes from the glare of light off the water.

"A storm is coming in," he said over the rush of crashing water spraying over the seawall.

Ramsey tried to see anything beyond the spectacular blazing red and orange clouds. "How can you tell? The sky is clear."

"For now."

He turned his back to the water and surveyed the line of dilapidated wharf buildings. The port was mostly inactive, with ice flows still making passage dangerous. Ramsey didn't notice a single slab of ice, though, when she searched over the ocean. Perhaps the arriving storm was clearing the way. A sense of unease rippled through her. Reality hit her like the waves battering the shuddering stone embankment beneath her feet. Dozens of individuals were relying on them.

If they failed…

Bile rose in her throat. She covered her mouth and took a centering breath. No. Negative thoughts would get her nowhere.

Caidon motioned for her to follow as a small group of laughing men rounded a corner between buildings. Ramsey secured her hood and her hold on their bag and hurried to his side. He found a recessed door and had her take cover while he watched the men from the sheltered vantage point. Their good-natured ribbing faded, and Caidon led her along a narrow passage between structures, watching the sky. At a slim gap between buildings constructed back-to-back, he asked her to wait for him.

"I'll return as fast as I can," he said, handing over his pack but keeping his rifle case.

Ramsey searched in the cold shadows for something to sit on and found an overturned half-broken crate. She kicked it into a suitable position and plopped down. The scents of food wafted from the bag, and she groaned. A rat scurried past her foot, followed by a slinking cat, chattering after its prey. She bit off a shriek and lifted both her feet.

Golden light waned to blue, and the temperature faded from cool to outright cold with the last rays of the sun. A brisk wind whistled past her little shelter, and the boom of waves made her tremble. No more rats or felines, disrupted her space. Bored, she pushed a pebble around with the toe of her boot. Something scraped behind her, followed by rubble falling. Ramsey gasped and twisted on her seat. Caidon dropped down on a crouch.

A delicious shiver raced through her. In the dense, gray light, he was all sensuous motion and deadly grace as he straightened and closed the distance between them. He helped her stand and then retrieved his bag from her feet.

"I found a place just a few buildings down. Hopefully, the roof won't leak on us tonight."

The wind rushed through the alley they stepped into, and Ramsey shivered. "As long as we're warm, I'll be happy."

"I'll have to go find a merchant for blankets after we get settled."

He checked the street before they stepped out of the safety of the alley. A few quick turns and a short walk later, he pulled her into a huge, empty building. Three stories of space rose above them, disappearing into darkness cut only by rectangle windows. Most had holes, but some of the panes were still intact. Weeds grew through the sagging wood floor. Dust covered every inch and held the scent of mildew and time. A stairway wide enough for one led to what Ramsey assumed had once been office spaces and would now be their new home while in Port of Subail.

Confirming her hunch, Caidon trekked to the stairs, leading the way to a door barely hanging on hinges. One push and the slab of wood broke free and tumbled below, splintering fragments of rotted floor upon landing.

Ramsey cringed. "I hope the floor we'll be sleeping on is in better condition."

Not for the first time in their adventures, an expression of regret and resignation tightened his handsome face. Ramsey caressed fingers along his stubbled jaw to his chin, smiling.

"We're safe, yes?" she asked. He nodded. "Then let's look at our new home."

"You deserve better than this."

She rose on her toes and kissed him. "Then so do you, and I'm not fussing about it."

"Wouldn't do you any good even if you did," he grumbled.

Laughing, she kissed him again. "See? Guilt doesn't do you any good, either. I think if I noticed that far corner over there correctly, I'll even get some running water tonight if your storm predictions are correct."

Shock widened his eyes, and he recoiled. "That water will be ice cold. You'll freeze if you stand under it."

Ramsey dropped her hand from his chin to his chest, sliding a trail down his stomach. "Then you'll have to find a way to warm me up."

19

Lightning flashed a sporadic dance outside, followed almost immediately by a boom of thunder close enough to shake the building. Ramsey jumped, her gaze seeking out Caidon's silhouetted form at the window across the room. She burrowed deeper into blankets on the mattress. They'd discovered an unused foldout bed in one of the other offices and had pulled the mattress to the smallest space. The fire wavered in the small, brick fireplace as wind thrashed at the roof.

"We might have to put the fire out until the winds die down," Caidon said, kneeling in front of the hearth. "I don't want to set the building aflame."

Ramsey agreed that would be bad. "All right. You're not still planning on going out, are you?"

"No one can see in this, and that includes when I leave. You're safe alone tonight, and I'll be faster moving on my own. I need to let Voklane know we're in position."

The building trembled again, and Ramsey's stomach

clenched. "You'll be swept away by a rogue wave or something."

"I know how to get around in a storm. I'll be fine."

"You'll freeze," she said, anxiety rising.

"Trust me."

"I do trust you. I don't trust the weather."

"Valid point." He slipped a sheathed knife into his boot and hooked another to his belt. "I won't blow away, or melt, or even freeze. I located the radio tower when I was up on the roofline looking for safe housing. The station shouldn't be far from it."

"I still think it's a bad idea."

"Noted." He handed her a sheet of paper. "Directions to the position of the radio tower. You can find the station on your own if you need to."

The page crumpled in her fist. "Why do I need instructions if you're perfectly safe?"

"Regardless of tonight, you still need to know how to reach someone if an emergency happens and I can't."

Sighing, Ramsey folded the paper and slipped it into her jacket, laying under her head as a pillow. "Please be careful."

He knelt on the mattress and captured her face. The warmth of his breath caressed her lips before he took her mouth in a slow, sensual kiss. His tongue worked hers until her toes curled into the soft blankets, and a heated flush made the fire unnecessary. She clutched at the thick fabric covering his biceps and tried to pull him closer. Chuckling, he broke the embrace.

"I have a lot of reasons to return." He stood, straightening his jacket. "Try to get some sleep."

Right, like she'd be able to get any rest while visions of him swept away by gale-force winds, or zapped by stray lightning, flitted through her mind. He left silently. The pound of rain on the roof and crash of waves close enough to concern her made her burrow under the blankets until only a fluff of hair stuck out the top. She squeezed her eyes shut and tried to force a sense of calm. Her cozy, dark cocoon lulled her into a dozing slumber.

Something damp and freezing shocked her awake. She squealed and bolted upright. The mattress trembled and she gasped, glancing down. More gray than golden, Caidon lay naked beneath the mound of blankets she'd been burrowed beneath. His arm banded around her waist and yanked her back down, settling the covers back over them.

"Are you okay?" she asked, worried by his lack of color and body heat.

"C-cold," he chattered.

Ramsey braced herself, putting her back to his front. He wrapped around her completely, scooting them to the center of the mattress. Only the thin shirt she'd worn to sleep in separated them. The fire blazed bright. She noted the pounding of rain had changed to a gentle tapping.

"Did you reach Voklane?" she asked, unable to stop a shiver from racing through her.

His hold tightened. The chilled skin of his cheek rested on her shoulder. "Y-yes. We're to m-m-meet a contact tomorrow evening at a t-t-tea house." He paused as a violent shiver wracked his entire form. Ramsey grabbed his forearm around her waist. "L-located in a more st-stable part of the city."

Ramsey stared at the ever-shifting flames. She waited until his shivers, and occasional chatter of his teeth, stopped before attempting to talk again. Anger threatened to make her snap at him. Clearly, he'd been out in the elements longer than he anticipated, and the wet cold had stolen all his body heat. What would have happened if she hadn't been here to provide him with a safe means of warmth? Would the fire have been enough to bring him to a safe temperature? The quiet pop of wood and crackle of flames added to the gentle patter of rain on the windows. Slowly, Caidon's trembling ceased.

"There's a stable area?" she asked.

"Supposedly, the locals have formed a sort of militia to protect themselves from the other factions. Since they're organized, the other groups aren't able to get a foothold to take anything. It's not worth the loss in numbers to attempt."

She relaxed a little at the promise of something normal. "That'll be nice, to sit down to tea."

"That's the attitude you need to keep. We should look like we belong. Like we know him, know the establishment."

The iciness of his skin dissipated into warmth, easing the rest of her distress. He was going to be okay. "Please don't do anything so dangerous to yourself again."

"I can't make that promise," he whispered. "My job is the definition of unsafe and requires risks be taken. I thought you understood by now."

Ramsey trembled and slid a leg between his, needing more contact. "Aside from roof jumping, we haven't had to do anything really hazardous yet."

His breath fanned her neck beneath her ear. The firm tip of his tongue glided along her pulse point. Heat flared through her, settling low. A throb of demand deep inside only he could answer. Need shivered along the invisible ties between them, igniting her blood. His growing erection pressed into her butt, and her breath quickened. Oh, what this man did to her. Almost an addiction to how good he could make her feel.

Knowing she alone laid claim to him, the only woman to experience the pleasures of his body, the sensation of his bond when he took her, served to fuel her possessive lust to near frenzied heights. He never seemed to have to do much. A touch, a certain look, a tender kiss at the right spot on her neck, and she was a puddle in his hands. His self-control wasn't much better. If they were clean and isolated enough, and desire rolled across their bond, they stopped and indulged in each other. The memory of being introduced to the joy of his mouth bringing her to climax in the middle of a forest had her arching against him.

He rolled, forcing her onto her back, covering her. The muscles of his shoulders shifted beneath her fingertips. She pulled her knees in and spread her legs to make room for his hips. A groan escaped him as he dropped his forehead to her shoulder, his hard length discovering without a touch necessary from him how ready she was.

"I need to feel your heat, *zlanishka*," he murmured.

Words escaped her as he eased inside her on a smooth, slow roll of his hips, filling her, stretching her, until her world faded from cold to intense heat and the pleasure he alone coaxed to life.

• • • •

"Relax," Caidon whispered into her ear. The weight of his hand settled on her bouncing knee and squeezed.

Ramsey took a deep breath and forced herself to still. "Sorry," she said, her words low so no one sitting near would know they spoke a foreign language. "Where is he?"

"We're early." He nuzzled her hair, appearing to anyone watching that he spoke words for his lover alone. The tactic always made her long for inappropriate things. She squished the desire, not wanting to distract Caidon with her errant hormones. "I wanted to make sure we weren't followed."

Ramsey licked her lips and reached for the steaming cup of floral tea, sweetened by the syrup of a native fruit she'd never heard of. Caidon had chosen a more robust drink, of black tea, pepper, cardamon, and a spicy root plant she'd read about but never tasted called ginger. She'd tried the beverage and had wrinkled her nose at the strong, competing flavors. She much preferred her more mild roses, jasmine, and white tea. She'd wanted her favorite, vanilla and orange, but citrus was a luxury Mark Inland had not advanced to yet. Same with vanilla orchids. The shop owner hadn't understood Ramsey when she'd asked or even described the warm, sweet flavor.

A bell chimed through the teashop, followed by the billow of cold air as a shorter man walked in. He stomped his booted feet and blew on his hands. The storm had brought down cold arctic air with a dusting of snow. Light glinted off a small glass jar with a stopper sitting on the corner of their table. The man glanced at the jar, then at Ramsey and Caidon. She took him for around her age, but it was hard to tell with a black, full beard covering the bottom half of his darkly tanned face. Deep brown eyes crinkled with his smile. He reached out, his fingers poking through maroon knit fingerless gloves. Ramsey accepted his hand, rising as he greeted them both like old friends. He motioned to the counter, and she nodded, returning his kind smile. Bowing, he took a step back and then spun, heading to place his order.

Five minutes later, he returned to their table, a tall cup clutched in his hands. The strong scent of coffee drifted across the table. He picked up the sweetener and dribbled the thick, brown liquid into his drink.

"Do you understand me?" he murmured, glancing at Ramsey.

"Yes," she answered in his dialect of Markinish.

Relief sagged his shoulders as he returned the stopper to the jar and pushed it to the center of the table. "Wonderful." He took a tentative sip, grimaced, and reached back for the sugar. "What can I do for you?"

As they'd dressed this morning, Caidon had gone over the information she needed to obtain from their contact. Ramsey laid her forearms on the table and smiled. "Your name? We are friends, after all."

He laughed and swiped a wool hat from his head, revealing a shiny, bare scalp. "Ah, yes, of course. Avi."

"Thank you for agreeing to meet with us, Avi. I'm Ramsey, and this is my husband, Caidon." Ramsey rubbed her sweaty palms on her thighs. Caidon grasped her hand and laced his fingers through hers. Grounded by his support, she met Avi's warm gaze. "We need to know everything you can tell us about the factions running the docks, how shipments work, and how we can learn about one."

The rim of his hat twisted through his hands. His attention shifted around the room, taking in the few patrons huddled at their tables, reading, or drawing, paying their group no mind. He set his hat on the table and wrapped his fingers around his steaming cup. "All right. The port falls along the dominion of three factions. The True Descendants of Subail, The Fair People, and a group the locals simply call The Power. The entire port is supposed to belong to the city of Subail. However, those three groups have taken control of the sections falling along their contested borders."

"How does anything safely get into the port if they're warring over the docks?" Ramsey asked.

"The conflict is mostly sabotage in nature. One faction will steal the cargo from another or even go so far as to sink a ship of valuable cargo if they learn of it and the other group refuses to pay extortion. Now, most ships with anything of worth onboard come in under guard."

Ramsey contemplated the information. Under guard was good news for the victims, bad news for her and Caidon. If the ship came in protected, she and Caidon couldn't do anything on their own. "How do we learn about a ship and cargo? Does each group have their own dock master?"

"No, one master for the entire port. Like I said, Port of Subail is technically under the control of Subail, but our official governing body is too weak to stand up to The True, The Fair, and The Power, along with the other two or three groups trying to rise in influence. The port master is an authority all on his own. He tolerates the squabbles because they're usually harmless, but he has his own men he pays well to keep the docks safe. That part of the city is *his*."

Caidon leaned forward, his eyes sharp. Ramsey had been quietly translating for him. "Would he hear a petition about an incoming ship full of kidnap victims being brought into Mark Inland for slavery?"

Avi recoiled as Ramsey conveyed the question. He looked around again before leaning over the table. "No. He'll be aware of the contents of the ship, but our country is a no-questions-asked kind of place. Lots of dubious cargo comes through here on its way to other destinations. I believe it's one of the only reasons this city hasn't burned itself to the ground. The money generated by the port allows the factions to keep their followers in their boundaries fed and safe."

Ramsey recalled the child stealing bread to feed a family and sighed. "Maybe not as well as you think."

"No, only stability will do that," he agreed and then sighed, sadness pulling at the corners of his mouth. "And as long as our port accepts all the things other countries are trying hard to stop, no one will agree to trade with us for legitimate goods."

"What is it you do, Avi?" Caidon asked.

Avi tugged his hat closer. "I make hats. I own a shop about two blocks from here."

Caidon said nothing after Ramsey translated, just smiled and waited.

"Yes, okay, right," Avi said, clearing his throat, a flush darkening his cheeks. "We, the Subail Authority, can't do anything to stop the gangs as a whole. However, if we discover they are committing atrocities against their followers, we step in and eliminate their leaders. If it happens again, all of those in any positions of power are removed, either by arrest or assassination. I gather intelligence on all the factions."

"But you allow slavers into your nation?" Ramsey whispered, anger making her fist clench on the table. "How is that not a crime against persons?"

His hands opened in regret. "They are not our people. All I can do is give you information. For Subail to get involved in another countries conflict…" He sighed and shook his head. "We can't afford to lose what few trade companies utilize our country."

"As you said, if your shores weren't profiting from the forbidden, perhaps you'd see more income."

He shook his head again. "I am one man, Miss. I cannot change the ways of my country or even this city. I must be going soon. What else can I tell you?"

Ramsey wanted to argue that throughout the history of humanity, one man or woman had always proven to have been brave enough to stand against impossible odds. In her nation, men and women did it often, and sometimes not even for their fellow Sziverian's. Avi perhaps was not that kind of man. A glow blossomed in her chest. She had, however, married such a man, and he was making her see she could be such a woman.

"How do we learn about an incoming ship and the cargo onboard?" she asked, taking a sip of tea.

"The dockmaster will have all that information." Avi reached into his inner jacket pocket and pulled out a folded slip of paper. "You can find his office here."

Caidon motioned for them both to wait a moment while he rummaged through his pack. He pulled out a folded paper of his own. "Have you seen this before?"

Ramsey asked as Caidon showed Avi the drawing of

the tattoo from the would-be assassin. The hatmaker shrugged and shook his head. He answered more questions she posed, offered information they hadn't asked for to help them, and then left with a few extra beads from Caidon tucked into the lining of his hat.

They stayed behind for an additional cup of tea and some crumbly cookies with chunks of dried fruit. Ramsey nibbled on hers, trying not to bounce in her chair.

"Now what?" she asked, sliding her thumb over her fingers to remove crumbs.

"Now we wait until dark, check in with Voklane, and find out how he wants to proceed."

Ramsey lifted her brows in surprise. "You're taking me with you this time?"

"We aren't returning to the docks until after dark."

"What do we do until then?"

He stacked all their dishes together. "Pass time in shops and places like this, see if we can learn anything else without drawing any attention to ourselves."

Ramsey purchased a small tin of tea satchels, thanking the owner again, and they headed into the cold afternoon. Caidon tightened her fur-lined hood under her chin, kissing her nose. She scrunched her face and batted his hands away. "I'm not a kid."

"I know. I've told you before, I like taking care of you." He took her gloved hand in his.

Her heart turned in her chest. She blinked snow from her eyes and tried to think of something witty to say. Nothing came to her but a useless, "Oh."

Smoke curled out from pipes and chimneys, adding a haze to the dusting of falling snow. A boy chased a small dog, leaving a trail of melted footprints, avoiding a bicyclist racing down the street by inches. Ramsey shuddered, thankful when the mother swooped in and collected her child, who wailed at losing his chance at catching a pet. Caidon stopped in front of a small shop window, and Ramsey looked, curious as to what could draw his attention. Rings of dyed wood gleamed in the cool light. Blue, purple, shifting shades of brown to yellow, smoky green, and pale pink, they sat nestled in black painted wood.

Touching the glass, he pointed. "That one is the same color as your eyes."

"It's very pretty," she agreed, liking a rich green band not far from the purple one. "And that one matches yours."

He held her hand tighter and pulled her into the modest store. A small bell tinkered. A stooped old man sat at a counter, peering at them from behind thick glasses. Ramsey figured the small segment of Subail was safe indeed if the aging merchant could keep his wares from walking off. The merchant's voice was gruff, hard to understand, and he kept shouting for her to repeat herself. In the end, Ramsey gave up, and Caidon used a form of sign language to communicate what he wanted. She meandered around the small space, taking in the pretty jewelry, most made of solid gemstone carved into bracelets, hair pins and sticks, and rings. Ten minutes later, they left with two small boxes stuffed deep in his pack.

Curiosity and anticipation made her antsy. She resisted jumping around him like Parker did when he wanted to know something. "What did you get?"

"You'll have to wait until we're back at the docks."

Squeezing her hands together, she yielded to temptation and sprang in front of him. She wrapped her arms around his neck and hung on, grinning when he hugged her close. "What if I don't want to wait?"

He kissed her and then swung her to his side but kept an arm around her waist. "You don't have a choice, do you?"

She blew a raspberry at him.

His arm shifted to her shoulders, tucking her in close enough for him to touch his lips to her ear. "Later."

She threw her head back and laughed.

RAMSEY'S LAUGHTER STILL ECHOED IN CAIDON'S MIND AS he picked the lock to the dockmasters office near midnight. Along with the not-so-shocking realization he was, without question, completely in love with her. She'd stolen every part of him, and he had no willpower to take any of himself back. He couldn't afford either distraction. If they were caught, he doubted they'd get any sort of fair trial, or even offered an option to go back to their home country. All the love in the world wouldn't save her.

The lock popped, and he cracked the door open, listening. Nothing but silence filled the dark interior. He held the door for Ramsey to slip inside. Two steps in, she shifted to the side and waited for him to make sure they were truly alone. Moonlight speared into the shallow room. The office was single-storied and didn't contain much more than a paper cluttered desk and a couch that looked to be a common napping spot for the dockmaster. Drawn portraits of happy, chubby children hung on the wall behind the desk, along with scribbled art.

Caidon set his backpack on the desk and dug around inside until he found the glass jar containing his glow kit. He slung the bag back over his shoulders.

Ramsey leaned close to the pictures, squinting in the low light. "How cute. Not what I expected from a man who everyone in this area seems to fear."

"He has a lot to protect," Caidon commented, mixing the compounds to make the light source. "A weak man's family would become targets."

"Guess that's true everywhere," she mused. Papers shifted underneath the faint glowing jar. Ramsey hummed. "He speaks and writes in one of the dialects I know. I was worried."

Caidon glanced over the desk, layers deep with sheets of multiple-colored papers. "All of them?"

She moved the clutter around. "Yes, appears so." Sighing, she reached behind and pulled a worn chair forward. "It's going to be a while. How long do we have?"

After setting the light on the desk, he moved to one of the small windows near the door and glanced out at the sky. "A couple hours. I want to be gone before sunrise."

He braced a shoulder against the wall and kept watch while she shuffled through papers. Every few moments, she muttered, set something off to the side, and dove back into the mess. Caidon shifted from one window to another, listening, watching. Drawers opened. More papers shifted. Outside, the waves curled in soft, white rises. A steady oceanic breeze whistled against the clapboard exterior. No shadows moved from buildings. No one walked the wharf, empty of any ships.

The sky was beginning to lighten to gray when Ramsey leapt up, gasping. "I found it," she whispered and then jumped, a book held in one hand, papers in another. "Stars above, Caidon, I found it!"

He went around the desk and took the spiral book from her hand. "What is it?"

She tapped the book. "This is the ships name, where it's been scheduled to moor, and it's anticipated cargo load." The papers in her other hand crinkled. "These are the manifests, the true manifests, not the doctored ones Sziveria has. Look at this one."

The yellow sheet trembled in her fingers. Caidon noted that while most of the manifest was penned in Markinish characters, some were Sziverian, including the name of the shipping company. He took the paper from her, cursing. "Cyrano. Hunter was right."

"No, Sylphine was right. She suspected them first. Leone Cyrano is insanely jealous of the Seartavos fleet. He's willing to do anything to try to grow the power of his family's business."

"And now we have the proof Sziveria needs to keep from ever using our ports again."

She beamed, and he wanted to kiss her. "Yes. How do we copy these?"

"In a minute," he said, setting the book down. "Help me understand this."

"Oh, right." She set the papers down and leaned close to him.

Sharp and sweet, her scent flowed over him in a wave of sensation. His nostrils flared, and his eyes widened, taking her in. A primal thing rose inside him.

Growled. Glowed. Demanded. Caidon shuddered and grabbed the edge of the desk. *Not now.*

"The ship's name is *Wave Rider*, the dock number is seventeen, and this long line here is the expected cargo," she said, running her finger along the ledger. She took a deep breath. "As of the last communication, there were three hundred and six passengers on board. It's been crossed out many times. They started with three hundred and seventy-two."

Caidon forced his brain to engage in something other than the enticing scent of his wife. Or that all he had to do was spin her around, lift her up, and with a kiss and touch, have his wild way with her right on the paper littered desk. The sweet lavender and vanilla scent of her surrounded him, and he shook his head like a dog dislodging something unpleasant.

He pulled the ledger closer, focusing on the line of numbers she touched. "They weren't prepared for so long in the ocean. They're starving to death."

A strangled sound left her. Despite knowing better, he wrapped an arm around her waist and pulled her close. Even through the layers of clothing, her body was soft and supple against his side. Inhaling deep, he pressed his nose into her neck. His body vibrated with the knowledge she was ready to create the next generation.

"Are you okay?" she asked, her fingers brushing his cheek.

"I should be asking you that," he managed, a tremor wracking his frame.

"Caidon?" Concern laced her voice, and she twisted to face him. "What's wrong?"

Putting the problem into words would force him to

acknowledge her place in her cycle and he didn't know if he had the self-control to keep himself in check. Sweat beaded along his hairline and dampened his chest. He ignored the desire and forced himself to focus on the dock master's ledger. "What else is there?"

"There are three other ships expected to make port around the same time as *Wave Rider*. One from Ravenna and two from Westica."

"What's their cargo?"

"Westica is timber, coal, and natural rock, unspecified. Ravenna is..." She tapped her fingers on the book and frowned. "I'm not sure. I've never seen this word before. I'm not sure how to translate it."

Caidon looked at the odd glyph. "Could be there is no translation. It's a resource specific to Ravenna that we don't know about."

"How could that be?"

He shrugged. "Remember peanuts? Maybe a certain food, or type of lumber they have a special name for. Copy it just in case we can learn something along with the information for *Wave Rider*." He eased away from her and placed the desk between them. "And copy all the Cyrano manifests you can. We're taking the originals with us. We have less than an hour."

She nodded and sat back down, opening drawers. She found a pen and a book of blank manifests and went to work without question, though worry still pinched her beautiful face. Caidon's shoulders sagged in relief, and he pushed away from the desk and back to the window. Her scent seemed to follow, to tempt and entice. He bit the inside of his bottom lip and forced his attention to the world outside, brightening by the second.

"Done," Ramsey proclaimed fifteen minutes later. Drawers banged shut, and the chair creaked. "I doubt he'll suspect anything since this desk is a disaster, but I made sure everything was in the same place as when we started."

Outside, Caidon made sure the lock was secured and then took her hand and led her through a less visible route to their warehouse home. "I'm really proud of you."

A pretty flush crept along her cheeks, competing with the pink from the cold air. "That's what I'm here for, right? You wouldn't have been able to get that information without me. I doubt Avi would have agreed to help you beyond what he provided."

"No, I would have been intel gathering based on what I could see if I'd been on my own," he agreed. "Voklane would have to send someone else to do the actual rescuing."

She sniffled and rubbed her nose. "He's still going to, I think. We can't take on an accompanying armored guard. Can we?"

"Maybe," he mused, his mind already calculating how he'd manage. Rooftop position. The ship arrives, and guards stand out from the captives. By the time they realized their comrades were falling over dead, they'd already be too late to react in time. "But we couldn't get three-hundred to safety on our own."

"I'll have to look at the manifests more closely, but I don't think everyone on that ship was from Sziveria."

"Make's sense. There were more than I was expecting."

"I can't imagine... what they must be going through. Almost four hundred people crammed onto one cargo ship. I wonder if any of them died from the cold, too," she said, her voice soft.

Caidon stopped and grabbed her upper arms. He waited until she met his gaze. Her sorrow glimmered in the silvery light of dawn. "You can't dwell on this. Understand? You can't. We're doing everything we can to rescue them, and that has to be enough." He smoothed an errant curl from her forehead back under her hood and whispered, "It's enough."

She squeezed her eyes shut. When they opened, resolve livened the amethyst depths, and she nodded. "Okay."

He almost told her. Almost opened his mouth and declared his love. Lack of experience, and if he were honest, a fear of rejection, made him return her nod and continue on their walk, keeping his feelings to himself. The two rings he'd bought yesterday afternoon lay nestled in his pack, safe, seeming to add an impossible weight.

The alluring scent of her still surrounded him in a cloud of temptation. For twenty-nine years, he'd managed to avoid all things female, only to be caught by a burst of light named Ramsey. She'd turned his existence inside out and upside down, and the journey was far from over. In the space of a few weeks, she'd become his entire world. And as a sharp pang of need flared through his veins, an urge to seduce and create life, he knew he had to protect her from more than the conflict surrounding them. He had to protect her from him.

20

DROPS OF SWEAT RACED EACH OTHER DOWN CAIDON'S temples. He went ahead of Ramsey with the intent of ensuring their location hadn't been compromised, but in the end, had been for the sole purpose of not attacking her on the stairs. Nothing appeared disturbed, and no one waited in the shadows of their small space. Somehow, he managed to light a fire before dropping his bag and lying down, curling in a ball, and willing his irresistible wife to stay away.

"Caidon?" she asked, papers rustling. "Are you okay? Are you sick?"

Sick… that was a word for the pull she had over him. Not her fault. Biology and his damn genetics were to blame. She knelt at the edge of the mattress, her fingers slipping into his damp hair. He shivered, wanting to arch into her touch like a cat. The primal beast inside him roared with a fury Caidon felt like piercing fangs in his brain. Unable to speak, he plucked at her bracelet. Pretty stone beads marking the moment of his misery.

She gasped and wrapped her hand around her wrist. "Oh no… *Caidon*."

Fingers trembling, she reached for him, and Caidon rolled and rose into a crouch on the other side of the mattress. The soft pad bowed beneath him and made balance a challenge. He focused on staying upright. In staying away from her. "Don't."

Her knees touched down, upsetting the balance. "Let me help you."

Fisting his hand, he pressed it into the crumpled blankets and stared at her. Letting the full force of his crazy shine through his gaze. Shock, and a little trepidation, widened her eyes. But she didn't back down. "I *will* get you pregnant right now. There is no maybe. I'll sleep in the other room tonight. Just… don't touch me. Don't come near me."

"You aren't alone. *We* made the decision…" She lifted her hands, palms facing him. "Okay, I may have made most of the decision for us to be intimate. If we hadn't, you wouldn't be feeling this way, right?"

"Right, but we did, and you didn't—"

"I did a lot of reading." Her hands moved in a manner he figured was meant to assure but had him narrowing his gaze. "And this can be fixed, temporarily. If you just ignore the urge, it'll get worse, and you really might end up seducing me without even realizing."

"How could I do something like that without being completely aware?" he asked, falling on all fours and inching closer to her. He inhaled, pulling her sweet scent in deep. *Mine.*

"While you're sleeping. If I'm close enough for you to catch my scent, you'll sleep walk to me."

"I said I'll go to the other room."

"Might not be far enough," she argued, her jaw jutting in defiance.

She was so beautiful. So his. Caidon crept closer. "No, you aren't far enough."

A heavy swallow drew attention to the creamy line of her throat. He wanted a taste, a little one. He crawled closer. Without warning, she barreled into him, sending him flying back onto the mattress, sprawled. Straddling him, she pinned his shoulders down. Her mouth captured his. The sweet taste of her burst across his tongue. A growl erupted from him. Need drove a spike through his body. If he grew any harder, he'd shatter.

Faster than she could react, he had her pinned beneath him. He ground his hips into hers. Every nerve in him begged to touch her, sink into her wet heat, lose himself until he was spent. Her breathing grew ragged. A whimper he'd come to recognize as a plea for release escaped her. Under him, her body writhed. They'd been here so many times before, and it'd always ended the same. Both of them sweaty and satisfied.

"Ramsey," he groaned, fighting for control and losing.

"Shh." She smoothed his hair from his forehead, kissed his chin, his jaw, his throat.

"Trust me," she whispered against his collarbone. "Trust me to take care of you." She pressed a fist between them to her chest. "I can feel here, Caidon, how much this is hurting you." Her hands returned to his face, stroking his cheeks, his jaw, searching. She pulled him close, pressing the sweetest kiss to his lips. "Let me love you, like you love me."

Disbelief made him jerk back. Laughter and yes, love, danced in her eyes.

"Silly man, did you think I couldn't feel that? Could you never feel how much I love you?"

"I didn't..." Her face swam before him, her scent stronger. "I don't..."

"How about we have this conversation after your sanity returns, hmm?"

She shimmied down his body, her fingers making quick work of buttons and buckles. Breathless, struggling not to undress her, Caidon rolled onto his back. He stared at the cobweb lined beams above and fisted his hands in the covers. Anything to keep from touching her. Cool air shifted across his stomach, and when she pulled him free, her hand sliding across his straining flesh, he almost came. She seemed to know.

Their bond wrapped around him, a blanket of desire and comfort. She loved him with words, with her mouth, with her hands, until the primitive hold his heritage had on him loosened with his release.

Ramsey laid on his stomach, her fingers swirling in the trail of hair from his navel. "Better?"

He concentrated on how he felt. "I can still smell you more than usual, but I no longer am out of mind with wanting to... mate."

She flipped her head around. Her hair slid along his hips, her nose scrunched. "I smell?"

Able to touch her again without fear of ripping her clothes to shreds, he sank his fingers into her thick hair and smiled. "Like lavender and vanilla. Sweet."

She blinked. "Oh. That's nice."

"Yes, I agree."

Sitting up, she smoothed her hair from her face. "Okay, we need a plan for tonight."

"I said I'll sleep in the other room."

"And I said I didn't want you sleeping in the other room." A rebellious glint brightened her eyes and tightened her jaw, daring him to argue.

Caidon rose on his elbows, uncaring that he was half-dressed. "*Zlanishka*—"

"Don't *sunshine* me, Master Guardian Survaine." She popped off the bed, hands fisted. "Would you leave me to face this alone?"

"No," he admitted, sighing. If she'd had any Ruthenian in her beyond her Gen-Heir talents, they'd be in some serious trouble. One of them mindless to reproduce, was bad enough.

"Then don't ask me to do the same."

"All right."

Some of the fire died from her eyes, and she eased back onto the mattress. "Thank you."

"We have until dark tonight to sleep and compile all the information we found today to tell Voklane. I suggest we sleep first."

She nodded. "Okay. I will sleep fully clothed, you sleep naked."

He raised a brow.

Laughing, she tugged on his shirt, slipping it down his arms. "In a couple hours, our reprieve will be over. It'll be easier."

Closing his eyes, he grumbled. "Very well."

Sympathy softened her face. "I'd say I'm sorry, but I'm really not. I don't regret being intimate with you. We can manage two or three days a month."

"Says the woman not going through it."

She laughed again. "Okay, true."

He slipped his boots and pants off and then climbed under the covers. "But I don't regret anything either."

After taking off her shoes and jacket, she joined him, laying her head on his chest, over his heart. "So, you love me?"

Caidon should have known she wouldn't let the subject go. Not that he wanted her to. "I bought our rings. I realized we're running around this forsaken country with no visual ties to each other, and the rings in the jewelry shop were perfect. Simple, bought in the midst of our first assignment. Afterward, you were so carefree, as though none of the danger, or craziness of humanity we've been through affected you. It was just you and me on a street, enjoying an afternoon, like we were back in Haven City. I've never had that before I met you."

The weight of her palm supporting her body landed in the middle of his chest and forced air from Caidon's lungs on an *oof*. She stared down at him, eyes round. "You bought our rings?"

Before he could answer, she leapt from the bed, blankets flying. A rush of cold air swept in around him. He grasped for the sheet, rolled onto his side, and supported himself on one elbow, watching her in amusement. "I said all that and you only heard *ring*."

She dug around in his bag, her head practically stuck inside. "I heard everything else."

"But?"

A sound of triumph sounded a second before she emerged with two boxes in her hand. "But nothing. I couldn't wait."

She bounced back onto the bed, setting the boxes in front of him while she yanked the thicker blankets back over them. Legs crossed, her toes wiggling against his bare stomach, she stared at him with expectation. Love hit him like a punch to the solar plexus. He grabbed the boxes in one hand and wrapped an arm around her hips. She tumbled across him with a squeal of laughter. Laying her body along his, she propped her chin on her hands, her eyes smiling.

"You want to see them," he guessed.

Her knees framed his ribs as she sat up. The fabric of her pants rustled against the sheets. She made give-me motions with her hands, and he laughed. Behind her back, he opened one box and removed the rings. He let the other one fall back onto the mattress. He brought his hand around front, fist closed, and held it over her waiting palms. Stone chimed together as the rings tumbled from his grasp.

A chortle of happiness sounded, and she wiggled her butt on his hips. He clenched his jaw, forcing himself to concentrate on the moment and not her lush body. Ripe for the taking. Literally.

"They are so beautiful," she proclaimed in wonder. "Solid stone, I've never seen anything like it before. I thought all the rings for sale in his shop were wood."

"The ones on display were, because those are what most who come to his shop can afford. These were hidden behind the counter," he said. "They're fragile. I have wooden ones to wear when we're doing heavy traveling across a country or engaged in an assignment."

She inspected the smaller ring of dark green jade. "What about metal?"

"If you prefer, we can get metal ones when we're in a country that offers metals. What alloy do you think you'd prefer?"

"I like copper," she said, rolling the amethyst ring between her fingers. "And silver."

"I can afford gold," he said softly, slipping his pinky into the small, jade ring.

"Gold is pretty, but I like the warmer tone of copper and the icy beauty of silver."

"Contrasts."

"Yes." She pushed the amethyst ring onto her thumb. "I love these. I don't want to replace them. They're part of our story, part of this adventure."

Caidon slipped the ring off his finger back onto her palm. "We could have them encased in metal, to protect them."

"Like a plating along the underside and outer edges?" She examined his ring, the color of her eyes.

"Something like that."

"They will look very nice in silver or copper."

"I agree."

She smiled. "They're perfect. Thank you."

"Do you want to wear it?" he asked, his fingers smoothing along the sleek curved stone.

"Yes," she whispered. She trembled as he slipped the ring onto her left hand.

While she admired the dark green against her creamy skin, Caidon slid the amethyst on and then laced their hands together. "I wish I could make love to you."

Her thumb brushed along the edge of the ring near his palm. Longing turned her gaze smoky. "I wish that, too."

Then she yawned and scooted down his body, sliding off to rest along his side. "But I'm tired, and we only have until sunset to rest and compile what we know for a quick briefing."

He squeezed her tight. "I know. Rest, we'll worry about everything else when we wake."

Two breaths later she was out, her cheek resting in the hollow of his shoulder. Caidon stared at the pink light brightening the ceiling. Anxiety curled in his stomach. If he didn't need to be alert enough to keep her safe while they navigated a treacherous city at night, he'd force himself to stay awake. Their first test could have disastrous consequences if he lost control in his sleep. Even though they both understood the risk sex had on the strength of their bond, he hadn't been prepared. How could he have been? All the verbal and written warnings in the inhabited world couldn't have told him how desperate he'd be to touch, to taste, to experience all the pleasure his wife had to offer and give the same.

Caidon closed his eyes and kept his breathing shallow. The stage would pass in one to three days, he just needed to keep his urges contained.

RAMSEY CONTEMPLATED THE ROWS OF MANIFESTS SHE'D laid out, trying to decide where the one in her hand would fit in the chronological order she sorted for them. If the Cyrano name was on the page, she'd snagged it, not looking beyond the ship owner's name. Shafts of bright light cut across the empty floor. She sat in the other room, the door to their sleeping area open to help ease some of the chill. Caidon had disappeared downstairs to make use of collected rainwater to wash. Her hair was still damp from her turn.

Sliding thin sheets of paper around, she placed a few more manifests. The stairs creaked, and she leaned back to peer through the doorway. Caidon walked in, shirt open, pants unbuttoned, hair hanging in a thick wet mess. Ramsey swallowed. Not even the exhaustion pulling at his face could detract from how sexy he looked to her. She drew herself together before he could detect her desire. She rested her elbows on her knees and looked over her work.

Sleep had been elusive for Caidon, something she regretted. When the tension on their bond became excruciating, she'd awoken to find him curled into himself, trying to handle something she thought she'd made clear he was never meant to deal with on his own. They'd fought. She'd won, but not how she wanted, with his trust. While she never considered herself a sexual creature, she'd had to become one to get her way. So, she had. He claimed to love her. She believed him because the sweet, hot warmth of his love had flowed through her like whiskey from his bond. Unique. Undeniable. But at some point, he'd have to understand love wasn't a solo situation.

"How's it coming along?" he asked, the floor vibrating beneath her with his heavy steps. He stopped beside her, buttoning his shirt.

The subtle scent of leather and sandalwood, mixed with a hint of smoke, made her heart race. Hours of relieving his pressure had only served to make her near exploding. She figured one well-placed touch, and she'd unravel. She shoved the need deep, deep down. "Very well. There are almost seventy manifests spanning six years."

He hunched down next to her. "I didn't realize you'd grabbed that many papers."

"They're very thin and were surprisingly organized when I'd found them. The dockmaster kept them separate," she said, laying another down in a row to her right.

"Interesting."

"Yes, along with three other shipping companies. We didn't have time to copy them all."

He picked up several closest to him, flipping between them. "I can't believe you were able to copy all of these."

"Well." She tucked a curl behind her ear and laid out the last sheets. "To be honest, I only copied the ones from this year perfectly, the others, I wrote down the pertinent information that would satisfy a cursory glance."

"Still impressive," he muttered.

Pride blossomed warmly inside her, and she smiled. "Thank you."

"We'll leave two hours after sunset. Will we have enough time to get all the information compiled by then?"

Ramsey glanced at the windows and the blinding orb of the sun shining through the glass. "Yes, we have hours until sunset."

He rose with a groan and disappeared into the other room. He returned with a notebook and a pencil. Crossing his legs, he plopped down beside her. "All right, let's get started."

Hours later, with the light golden and soft and shadows darkening their workspace, Ramsey stretched and took a deep breath, trying to alleviate the dread balled in her stomach. The manifests had told a horrific story of ever-boldening shipping companies making a profit off the lives of others. From infants to middle-aged, no one appeared safe from their clutches except the elderly.

"What are they doing with them?" Ramsey asked, unable to stop the morbid curiosity to an answer she knew she didn't actually want to know.

He sat back against the wall, letting a handful of manifests slide to the floor, and crossed his ankles. "You know of the Servants of Cairo?"

"Yes, sort of. Sylphine explained they're not what people think. Education isn't free in Cairo, so anyone who can't afford to pay is indebted to the country for the length of their education and can be hired out to anyone in the world."

"Right, it's a form of indentured servitude. However, Cairo is very specific about how their people are treated. For instance, I couldn't hire a caretaker for my kids and expect her to also have sex with me. I'd have to hire a woman from Cairo who agreed to that as her service."

Ramsey raised a brow. "There are women who do?"

"Of course. Male or female, they bring in a lot of money for Cairo and only owe half the time. Again, however, if Cairo learns they were mistreated, depending on the severity, the person who took out the agreement may find themselves being visited by a Cairoen Sentinel. Cairo has worked hard to provide a service to the inhabited world *and* maintain safety for its citizens." He waved his hand over the manifests. "Not everyone wants restrictions on those they pay for."

Ramsey's stomach clenched. "And the children?"

"Some will go to homes where they'll be raised as

someone's treasured child. For whatever reason, they were unable to have kids of their own, or find a suitable means to adopt, so they purchased a child. Others..." He shook his head. "There are bad people out there, Ramsey."

The children would not be spared the depravity of perverse adults. Some may have been stolen from loving homes already, and parents were desperate to know their fate. Ramsey swallowed bile. "We can't fail."

"We won't."

<h1 style="text-align:center">21</h1>

URGENT VOICES SPOKE INTO RADIO RECEIVERS, WHILE harried receptionists didn't bother with manners. Rude appeared to be a prerequisite for the job. Delanee gritted her teeth and waited in line, figuring the civilized endeavor was useless. The First Intelligence Office didn't tolerate unauthorized visitors. Yet here she stood, wondering if perhaps she'd be an exception when all the others were turned away with little more than a flick of annoyed fingers. No appointment? No entrance.

Her turn arrived at the desk, and she placed her hands on the cold, gray marble. "Hello, I'm here to—"

"Your last name and the guardian you have an appointment with," a man ordered without bothering to look up.

Delanee cleared her throat. "Well, I don't—"

He glanced up. Gray eyes flecked with green observed her in irritation. "Last name and guardian."

If she weren't concerned about breaking her teeth, she'd have clenched them harder. "Ralston, Guardian Voklane."

He flipped through a wide book in front of him. "I don't see you here." Wheels squeaked as he rolled to the nearest radio. He flipped switches and picked up the receiver.

Delanee's heart jumped into her throat. She didn't know if there was some sort of punishment for showing up to see an FIO guardian without an invitation. And if the guardian in question knew the reason for her arrival, he'd for sure deny her. The sudden urge to sneak past the chaos had her fingers curling into the marble. Not knowing where she needed to go was the only thing keeping her feet rooted in place.

The receptionist spoke into the radio and then cast her another irritated glance. "Your first name?"

"Delanee," she stated with a calm only surface deep. She may be young, but her job as a journalist had taught her to keep all feelings inward. Sharks bit at prey, and she never wanted to be such. She much preferred being the predator, as her beast master heritage demanded.

"He will see you," the man announced, much to her shock. "Office five-sixty-eight."

A visitor badge was filled out for her, and instructions for how to get to the office were carefully explained. Delanee listened intently, though she figured she'd get lost at least four times and ask directions twice. A sense of direction was never her strength. She took stairs wide enough for a crowd to the fifth floor, never trusting being alone in a lift. Too many horror stories of people getting trapped when someone with Human Rabies Syndrome went into their active phase and gnawed on people. She shuddered. No thank you.

The landing on the fifth floor was spacious, transitioning into a maze of cubicles to rival the tiny work-spaces at the *Haven City Chronicle*. Perhaps her employer had visited First Intelligence when deciding on how to squeeze as many people into a space as possible. Three corridors branched from the central room. Delanee chewed on her bottom lip, trying to remember which one she was supposed to take.

Four turns and three hallways later, Delanee was hopelessly lost. Every time she attempted to stop someone to ask where she was in the grand maze known as floor five, they muttered and rushed past. Visions of wandering the halls, starving and thirsty, exhausted and crawling in desperation while being ignored, had her increasing her pace. Panic set in. How much longer until everyone left to go home? Anxious, she followed someone to their office, then another, and another until she was so lost she almost sat on the floor and cried. Perhaps if she screamed—

"I wouldn't advise it," a soft, deep voice whispered behind her.

Delanee spun around with a startled gasp. Piercing, silvery blue eyes stared down at her. She stumbled back a step. Even in the drab light of the windowless corridor, he was as gorgeous as she remembered. Damn it. She'd hoped she'd mistaken the strong jaw, high cheekbones, patrician nose, and a physique that betrayed he didn't spend countless hours sitting on his butt behind a desk like he wanted everyone to believe. He was supposed to have a huge mole on his nose. Or a wart. A bad haircut, and be thick around the middle, not in the shoulders and arms. But no. Perfect cropped short hair. Perfect body. Delanee sighed.

"Would anyone even notice?" she asked, crossing her arms.

He motioned for her to walk forward. "Maybe."

Not even a twitch of a smile. "How did you know what I was thinking?"

"Body language. You looked about ready to do something rash. Screaming seemed the best probable option."

Delanee blinked. "Body language?"

"Yes. One can learn a lot from the way a person moves, stands, micro-expressions they make that they think no one can perceive." Hands behind his back, he fell instep beside her. "Stand next to me at a social event and I'll tell you something about every person present."

"Interesting, and a dangerous offer to make to a journalist who writes the social page."

His smile held no mirth. "Perhaps some need to be exposed."

Uneasiness shifted in Delanee's stomach. Ryan Voklane wasn't a man who played games. Each move he made, either in his life or concerning his operators, was likely calculated and precise. He wouldn't appreciate her questioning his decisions. She lifted her chin, undeterred. Well too bad.

They walked down two corridors and made more left turns than she thought possible for a floor. She glanced over her shoulder, positive she'd passed the same odd blue door when she'd been trying to find his office. "I think I went this way."

"Maybe. The blue doors are admin, each sector has its own administrator, and they're all located on this floor," he said. "The blue was supposed to make them easier to find. I think having them all in one place would have been wiser, but then that would make sense, and why would anyone do that in a government building?"

Delanee couldn't stop the bubble of laughter. Okay, so maybe he didn't take himself, or his job, as seriously as she feared. "They should definitely give out maps when a visitor arrives."

"I agree, except for the security risk. I should have met you at the stairs, I apologize. Most of us meet our visitors, but I wasn't expecting anyone today."

A faint hint of juniper, cedar, and citrus notes drifted to her, and she resisted the urge to breathe in deep. The masculine scent did odd things to her inside, made her want to learn how he'd smell closer to his skin. The ridiculous vision of her leaning close, sticking her nose in his neck and sniffing him, and his subsequent reaction of looking at her like she'd lost her mind, had her taking a careful side step away. Already she figured her getting lost and needing to be rescued had diminished any respect he may have had for her. She didn't need to add anything else. No, she *needed* him to take her seriously.

He stopped in front of an office and ushered her in. Three windows lined the back wall, overlooking the shorter buildings beyond. An immaculate desk sat surrounded by filing cabinets against both walls. She looked around. Not even dust collected on the radio unit tucked behind his door.

The small space allotted between the chairs before his desk and the cabinets forced him to squeeze by. His fingers brushed hers, and a jolt of electricity sizzled up her arm, fracturing through her entire body. She inhaled sharply, caught by surprise at the sudden sense of cold, as if he'd held her hand instead of just touching her. Damn it. The responses to him had to stop.

The sun slashed a brilliant path of light through the windows, turning his pale hair nearly white as he settled behind his desk. "What can I do for you, Miss Ralston?"

Delanee tried to determine her best option, to stand and be assertive, or sit and be respectful of his position. She must have dallied in her head longer than she realized since he cleared his throat and motioned at the chairs. Heat bloomed across her cheeks, and she dropped into a seat, clutching her small purse dangling from her hip on her lap. "I want to know why you sent my brother off land."

"Which brother? You currently have four serving in a supportive capacity."

Her heart lurched. She didn't need the reminder her elder siblings were off playing hero in a foreign land. Again. "Deklan. You know, the Arch Guardian Wolvenguard? The one the crown-elect begged at nineteen to take the position, and who's still somehow managed to survive over an entire decade? I'd think he'd be far too valuable to send away."

"Did you know, before your brother, no one in Ruthenia had been able to bond with more than a single wolf in two centuries?" he asked quietly.

"And they still haven't. Deklan is Sziverian."

"His wolves are not. He bonded with them in Ruthenia. What he can do, the command he wields, makes him an asset we can't afford not to use." He pulled a folder from a drawer. "Are you like him?"

Delanee kept very still. "No."

For long seconds, he didn't say anything, his pale

gaze calculating, as though he willed her half-truth, and the secret she buried deep inside to the surface. Her mouth went dry. Then he stood, and she had the crazy urge to hiss at him and bolt. However, she wasn't the sum of her baser instincts, and she refused to even hint at their existence. She squeezed the purse in her hands until something popped within the satin pouch. Despite her efforts, her breathing deepened, and her pulse raced.

He rounded the desk, his movements easy, non-threatening. With a quick flip of his wrist, the folder popped open, and he laid sheet after sheet on the desk in front of her. "What I'm about to tell you can't be shared outside this room. You can't write an editorial about it."

Curious, she shimmied to the edge of her seat and somehow managed to unstick her tongue from the roof of her mouth. "And you trust me to do this?"

"I trust..." he laid out more papers, making even lines, "the honor of your family."

Well, she couldn't argue against that. She gritted her teeth, sensing with the keen training of a journalist the story of the season unraveling before her. The one to elevate her from lowly gossip writing to actual matters of importance.

"Do I have your promise?" he asked, crossing his impressive arms over his equally impressive chest.

"Yes," she said, rising to look at what he'd laid out. Rows upon rows of names with small numbers written next to them greeted her. "What is this?"

He glanced down at the sheets. "From what I've been able to gather, this is the name and age of every Sziverian awaiting the sale into slavery off the shore of

Mark Inland. They're a valuable commodity, one the local gang tasked with their welfare won't give up. I have two operatives in the country, but they aren't enough. I sent your brother a week ago with the hopes of him being able to meet the couple in place and provide some much-needed assistance in the rescue effort."

"These people were kidnapped?" She picked up a sheet, reading the names and ages, ranging from two years to thirty-two, on the page she held. Heart pounding, she grasped another. "Who would do this?"

"People who see the value of human life in raimarks."

Disbelief had her meeting his stare. "For money?"

"You're surprised?" He leaned against the desk and regarded her. "You have a brother who works for the SNID. He helped me comprise this list. Your mother was the top investigator when she worked as a guardian with the help of your father. You must know the depths of human depravity."

"Darius doesn't speak about his job often, and my parents never talked about their cases."

He considered her words, his jaw working. "I guess I could see that, not wanting to bring the negative aspects of their work home. Still, I'd have figured they'd want you to know about the evil so you can possibly avoid it."

"They've always advised us to be cautious, but my father is…" Delanee waved her hand in an attempt to drum up the word best suited to describe her beast master parent. "Arrogant? Confident? From my understanding, he has never doubted his ability to protect my mother or his family."

From her peripheral, she noted his narrowed gaze and refused to look at him. "But you aren't always home."

"True."

"And your father doesn't appear to doubt *your* ability to protect yourself." He rubbed his chin, his searching gaze making heat climb along her neck. "Interesting."

The subject needed to change. Fast. Clearing her throat, Delanee set the sheets down. "Are these kidnappings related to the magic lily dust kidnappings?"

"I think some are. I think others are a matter of opportunity. Once people learned they could offer an annoying relative, an unwanted child, a homeless vagrant no one would miss for money, they did. Others are clearly a specific want, like all these four- to six-year-old boys with pale brown hair."

Frowning, Delanee looked at the sheets closer. "That's very specific."

"Yes." Ryan sighed. "They were, in fact, the only specifically listed passengers on the manifests. The rest were simply gender and age."

"Haven City Enforcement Services hasn't caught on to serial kidnappings?"

"Not that I've been able to tell."

Her mind spun. She tapped her fingers on the desk. "So that means they're kidnapping from places no one will notice missing children or places no one bothers to report because no one cares."

"Like the Old City Ruins or the Rows."

"And orphanages," she added. "I bet if you ask local orphan houses, they'll tell you they've had runaways."

"And if I'm really lucky, they'll have names I can match up."

Delanee's frown deepened as she touched a row of names belonging to youth. "What will change when they return home? They'll be placed in the same situation."

"I'll talk to my contacts at HCES and see if I can't convince them to check on the orphan houses."

The resignation in his voice said what he'd left unsaid. No one cared about the forgotten children. Once their parent passed, society placed them in homes, donated food, clothes, and raimarks, and then promptly went on with their lives. She might not be able to write about the disappearing kids, but she *could* bring awareness to the neglect of society to take part in their care. Perhaps if more people volunteered, showed the youth mattered, they'd notice when some went missing and take action.

"Does this have anything to do with the reason I had to help Primary Guardian Kynhaven draw attention to his wife last year?" she asked.

"Maybe." He gathered the pages together. "We aren't certain yet."

Another unspoken message. When Delanee had helped Mason Dandridge learn the truth about his Westican born wife and her Sziverian father, she'd learned nothing afterward. The whole situation had been wrapped up in a bow that she hadn't been allowed to touch. Maybe when Deklan returned home, she'd be able to weasel more information out of him.

"Stay out of it, Delanee," Ryan whispered, once again surprising her with his perception. "This isn't your fight, and they don't care who they hurt."

"They?"

He shook his head.

Delanee raised her chin. Fine, she'd leave it alone for now. If her brothers were involved, she wanted to know what they were up against. One way or another, she'd find out who *they* were.

"THEY'RE WAITING UNTIL THE NEW MOON."

Ramsey looked up from her notebook and frowned. Caidon stood with his back to her at the window overlooking the dock they expected *Wave Rider* to arrive. "Who?"

"The True Descendants," Caidon answered, allowing the frayed curtain he'd been holding to the side to ripple back into place.

Three nights ago, they'd learned who claimed this section of the port and would therefore be providing security to the incoming ships. Ramsey had been hoping for The Power to be in charge since they didn't seem to be as organized as the other two factions. "Why?"

"Darkness will provide coverage for the nature of their shipment."

Ramsey unfolded from the mattress that they'd managed with effort to move to their new location. "Won't that make it more dangerous for them, too?"

"Not if their guards know the area well."

She joined him at the window, peering four stories below. They hid in the attic space of a seasonal warehouse used as a distribution point by an Eastern Isles shipping company. While they'd been able to discover the dock to be used, they hadn't been able to find the warehouse where the victims were to be stored. Conducting surveillance, they hoped a process of elimination would help them figure out the location.

"Wolvenguard should be here soon," she said, wrapping her arms around her waist. "I still don't know how he's supposed to be inconspicuous with three Ruthenarc wolves."

"His wolves are crated. He'll arrive looking like he's an employee of this warehouse getting ready for the shipping season to start," Caidon said, still peering through the slit in the curtains.

"Does Eastern Isle know we've appropriated their warehouse?"

"Eastern Isles has generously offered us the use of their space," Caidon said in sarcasm. His lips flattened into a tight line. "I'm sure we'll be taking a trip there in the near future."

"Say no," she said.

"If I don't agree with the assignment, I will."

Ramsey blew out a frustrated breath. "Okay."

He reached over and squeezed her hand. "You'll learn how things work and adjust."

"I don't like that you're something to be traded," she admitted before she could stop herself.

"My services have always been offered in trade when necessary. Not every country is equipped to deal with their monsters on their own. And some people? They're really bad, Ramsey."

"I understand that," she said, taking a step closer to him. "But I don't have to like you being used as judge and executioner as a means of payment."

He leaned against the wall next to the window, a smile toying on his lips.

"What?" she asked when he remained silent, regarding her as she fidgeted.

"I've never had anyone want to protect me before. I'm not sure what to think."

Ramsey gnawed on her lip. There it was, the problem of his inability to rely on her for anything more than a professional capacity. He didn't understand her love, or her desire to care for him, her need to see him as safe and treasured as he saw her. "Well, I love you. I'm allowed to want to protect my mate."

He tilted his head, his emerald eyes brilliant. "You love me?"

She closed the space between them, touching his jaw. "I told you as much when you were out of your mind."

"Ah," he said, his face scrunching like he tasted something bad.

"I know it's all a haze now."

The subtle brush of his fingers along hers a moment before they wrapped around her hand had silly little butterflies dancing in her stomach. She wondered if he'd always elicit such whimsical responses from her or if, in twenty years, she'd become immune to his touch. Lifting her hand, he twisted the green-stained wooden ring on her finger.

"Not everything is a haze," he said, kissing her palm.

Mischief bubbled up within her, and she raised a brow. "Just my confession of love?"

His gaze narrowed. "Is this going to be one of those female things I'll never be able to live down?"

"Maybe," she admitted, laughing. "Or maybe I'll

never let you forget because I always want you to remember I love you."

Movement below pulled his attention back to the window. "I doubt I'll ever forget," he murmured, brows drawn tight.

Ramsey shifted until she, too, could see outside. "I've heard it's a possibility for both of us."

"To stop loving?" He worked his jaw and angled his head, still intent on watching the men loitering about below their window.

"Yes."

"Only if we choose."

Ramsey pursed her lips at his declaration. "Choose to fall out of love? Who would d—"

He held up a hand, and she fell silent. "They're having a very involved conversation. We need to hear what they're saying."

Once again, their professional life intruded on the personal. She forced away the annoyance, having to remind herself she wanted to be part of all aspects of his life. More than her feelings were at stake. "How? If we open a window, they'll hear."

"These windows don't open." He moved from the window and motioned for her to follow. "Second floor. I saw a liquor set in one of the offices."

"Gutsy, leaving anything of value in these rooms."

Rusty hinges creaked as he opened the floor hatch from the attic. "More likely they pay a decent sum to the True Descendants to make sure they have their belongings to return to."

She didn't have time to respond as he slid down the ladder, a feat she'd been envious of the first time she watched him tackle the rungs without a footstep.

Courage had failed her when he'd offered to teach her the technique, so she was much slower on her descent, having to run to catch up to him on the stairs. Only a hint of light three stories below offered any illumination in the stairwell. Carefully, she set one foot in front of the other, hands bracing the wall and guardrail.

"What's the plan?" she asked, proud she only sounded a little winded. Weeks of physical exertion had helped her gain new muscle and endurance.

"We need to see if you can understand any of their conversations. Could just be a group of guys catching up, or…."

"Could be they're planning for an incoming shipment," she finished for him.

The faint clip of his boots on the wooden floors mingled with the rushed, less elegant clop of hers as she struggled to catch up to him on the second floor. He turned into the first office they came to on the right, the floor shifting from bare floor to plush maroon carpet. Fine dust coated every surface and danced in happy little glittery motes through streaks of sun from the windows on two sides of the room. A view of the ocean and docks competed with an open view of the city beyond. None of the buildings rose above the Eastern Isles warehouse on this end of the docks. Someone important must use this office, Ramsey mused.

Sunlight gleamed off polished oak furniture. A desk, two bookcases, padded chairs and a padded couch, and coffee table. Caidon went behind the desk and leaned over. The squeak of wood sliding along wood filled the room. Glass tinkered and a second later he rose with a small glass perched on his palm. He offered the tumbler to her and pointed to the dockside windows.

"Use the couch to kneel on so you can try to stay as low as possible and not be seen. If we're seen, we'll have to relocate."

And that would be bad. Ramsey swallowed against the dryness coating her throat. Her fingers trembled as she plucked the glass from his hand. He positioned himself angled near the farthest window from the group of men. Ramsey's knees sank into the plush, embroidered gold, and maroon cushions. Keeping her mass low, she shimmied to the window and slowly placed the tumbler in the lower left pane. She pressed her ear to the cold glass and waited for her nervous brain to connect the sounds she was hearing with recognizable words.

Bits of conversation floated to her, muffled. She closed her eyes and willed her mind to clear. In a concise manner, she repeated what she could understand. Caidon returned to the desk. The sharp snap of paper was quickly followed by the scratch of a pen. She didn't allow the relief of knowing they finally had the break they needed, overhearing something of importance to affect her. After a few minutes, the conversation drifted away on the wind, and Ramsey glanced out the window.

"They're leaving," she said, straightening.

"Okay. We're going to stay in this office tonight, I think they'll be back after dark. They want to decide which dock would be best for *Wave Rider*, the one assigned isn't satisfactory. They'll give instructions to the dockmaster once they've made a decision."

Ramsey held the cup between both her hands on her lap. "They didn't mention where they'd be taking the people."

"No, that's something I hope we can overhear tonight, if they return."

She gnawed on her bottom lip. "I hope the arch guardian doesn't arrive tonight. They'll probably opt to change the dock if they suspect the warehouse is occupied and opening soon."

"Don't worry about Wolvenguard. He has enough experience to make sure his arrival has minimal notice, if any."

Ramsey couldn't stop a snort of disbelief. "I've never met him, but I've heard he's huge, and no one in this country is over much over five-foot-five."

A lopsided smile curved on his face. "I'm tall for this country."

"He'll be a giant."

"And he'll know how to be an invisible giant. Trust me on this."

Ramsey blew out a nervous breath. "All right."

She sagged against the plush cushions and stared out over the endless blue sky and calm waves. Perfect weather for sailing. Ice drifts were officially gone, and the arctic winds wouldn't freeze anything more than plants, if any, swept through over nights. *Wave Rider* no longer had to hide out in the middle of the ocean. Once they were given instruction, they'd arrive at the port with their precious shipment. Lives needed to be rescued.

Caidon crossed the room and joined her on the couch, gathering her into his side. The strength of his frame wrapped around her, and Ramsey closed her eyes. "When will I stop being so edgy?"

He squeezed her close. "Nerves keep you aware, keep you alive."

Ramsey settled into the comfort he offered. Into the warmth of his body pressed along hers. "You aren't nervous."

"I've had longer to learn how to hide my concerns, but I do have them. I've never had to keep anyone safe or have anyone rely on my talent in the moment. This is new for me, too."

All of the instances when he'd whispered praise into her ear or smiled at her in encouragement when she'd wondered if she were capable, filled her memory. "I..." Her voice failed. She licked her lips and tried again. "I wouldn't know what I could do, that I could be useful, without you."

"Your brother would have come around, eventually."

Ramsey shook her head. "No, I don't think he would have." She grasped his hand draped over her shoulder and laced their fingers together. "I wouldn't have even known I could fill a guardian role without you. I'd have stayed locked up away from life." She brought his hand to her lips. "Stayed a coward."

He gathered her onto his lap, his mouth hovering over hers until she thought she'd go insane waiting for him to kiss her. A loud bang echoed from downstairs. She barely had time to squeak out a surprised yelp as Caidon tossed her onto the couch and leapt from the room. He reached behind his back and pulled a pistol from underneath his shirt that she hadn't even known he'd been carrying. Anxiety sent her heart straight into her throat.

"Wh—"

"Back upstairs. Now. Pull the ladder when you get to the attic."

Quickly, her mind ran through scenarios, none of them ending well. "But—"

"Ramsey," he bit out with a hiss. "No questions. Go."

Another boom echoed from below, and she flinched. When his jaw clenched on a hard stare, she nodded that she understood. He returned her nod, and then vanished from the room. Ramsey licked her dry lips and stood. Everything in her rebelled at leaving him on his own. Stupid as the thought was, because really, what could she possibly hope to do to help? Obey. The answer was simple. He trusted her to do as he asked, and she would do no less.

Slow to try to be silent, she crept back up to their attic room. And as she pulled up the wooden ladder, she couldn't stop the silent plea of hope to make sure he returned.

22

A STEADY SENSE OF CALM FILTERED THROUGH CAIDON. His hand wrapped tight around the matte-black pistol, the metal and innerworkings seamlessly connecting with his body to relay information in a way only a Gen-Heir talent like himself could fathom. He would never miss a target. Distance, environmental factors, trajectory, all of it sifted through his mind to make him the perfect killer.

The first time he'd touched his father's rifle, the flood of data had almost made him pass out. At the time, Caidon hadn't understood his father's anger, nor had he realized what acknowledging that part of his heritage would mean. What embracing his genetically inherited talent would cost? Gripping the gun, moving on stealth feet, he knew he wouldn't change anything. The rarity of his talent served his nation well.

Using his shoulder, Caidon eased open the door that led to the narrow balcony overlooking the vast warehouse floor below. Sunlight spilled across the floor from the back entry. Caidon dropped to one knee and sighted along the pistols narrow targeting line. Wheels clacked over the lip of the floor as two cloaked figures pushed in a huge crate. An exceptionally tall, broad-shouldered individual followed in behind, and Caidon lowered his weapon with a sigh of relief.

He straightened, pressing the gun to his thigh as he stepped out onto the landing and called down, *"Ts mesti dsi, Vok-lup Kot Strazhran?"* Are you the Wolf Man Who Guards?

The tallest figure snapped to attention, his hooded face lifting to find Caidon at the rail. The hood fell, revealing burnished skin, long dark hair pulled back at the sides, and eyes of an unknown color from the distance. *"Dak,"* the Wolvenguard answered.

Caidon touched two fingers to his brow with a nod. Wolvenguard returned the gesture. Caidon slipped the weapon back into his safe place and turned to go collect his wife. If he met the Wolvenguard team without her, she'd be upset. He ran up the steps to the third floor, smiling when the trapdoor didn't even open a crack.

"It's safe. Send the ladder down," he said.

Wood clattered and screeched while she opened the hatch and sent the ladder sliding to him. He made sure it was stable before she stepped onto the first rung.

"What was it?" she asked.

"The Wolvenguard team has arrived."

Her eyes widened, and she paused halfway down. "Really? I don't hear the dogs."

"They're still crated."

She resumed the journey down. "We'll have to be careful. If they make lots of noise, those men will know the warehouse isn't empty."

"I know."

She hopped down the last rung and rubbed her palms on the front of her pants. "I'm sorry, of course you know. I'm… nervous."

Caidon grasped her hand and pulled her close. "It's real now."

"Yes." Her fingers trembled in his. "We could fail."

"I told you we won't."

"You have no control over that."

Caidon tugged her toward the stairs. "More than you think. They'll make a plan with multiple contingencies that we will fit into. While I haven't worked on a team, I know how they function from training."

She frowned. "From training?"

"I've been solo since my guardianship, but during training, I had to do team field exercises."

Ramsey cast him a look of doubt. "You won't be in charge."

"I take orders for everything I do," he pointed out.

"And carry them out how *you* decide is best."

He paused on a step and turned to face her. An unwelcome and unfamiliar sense of hurt coiled in his chest. "Are you worried about my ability to work with a team?"

"No, I just…." A line pinched her forehead, and she turned her gaze away. "I'm not sure what good I'll be."

Ah, not doubt over his ability, but her own. Caidon grasped her shoulders and squeezed until her beautiful amethyst eyes lifted. He brushed a curl from her forehead and pressed a kiss to her lips. "You are the reason any of this is possible. You have done your part. It's time for the rest of us to do ours."

She licked her bottom lip and nodded.

"The night of, you can stay here," he said. "I think you should."

"You might need me to translate."

Damn, he hadn't considered that. Shaking his head, he took her hand and started back down the stairs. "See, you're extremely useful. I doubt any of us would have thought about needing to be able to communicate with the victims."

Voices reverberated around the open space below, garbled and indistinct. Three people worked on the crate, while the other two crouched. A huge animal shot out of the enclosure the moment an opening appeared. Ramsey gasped, yanking on his hand. They stopped halfway down the balcony and watched a golden Ruthenarc wolf with gray-tipped fur dance around a man. Three more beasts stepped free, and unlike the excitable canine before them, walked calmly to their master. The man stood, his tall frame unfolding. As a unit, the wolves sat and looked up at him.

"Is that Wolvenguard?" Ramsey whispered.

"Yes."

"If you saw them at home, you'd think they were different beasts," a deep voice boomed, his back to them.

"They are well-trained," Caidon said, venturing onto the stairs leading to the ground level.

Ramsey leaned close enough to murmur in Caidon's ear, "He could hear us?"

Caidon turned his head and ignored the close temptation of her mouth. "Yes, he's bonded. He hears what they do when he wishes."

Her eyes grew wide. "That's a lot of information to process."

"Come on," he said, tugging on her hand to get her moving again.

Wolvenguard met them halfway across the expansive warehouse. Light filtered in from windows three stories above. The wolves' nails clicked on the dusty wood floor. Caidon pressed a hand to Ramsey's back when she tried to hide.

"Caidon Survaine," he said, offering his hand and then motioning to Ramsey after Wolvenguard accepted. "And this is Ramsey, my wife."

"Deklan Ralston." Closer, Caidon could make out the teal shade of Deklan's eyes. A startling contrast against his milk-in-tea skin. Deklan swept a hand behind him. "My wolves are Neva, Izia, and Nikita."

Caidon raised a brow. "Old world names?"

Deklan smiled. "Yes. Tradition, and not creative, I know, but they fit their elegance and royal bearing." His face twisted into a grimace. "Well, almost. We're still working on Nikita."

"Did you have any issues getting here?" Caidon asked.

"No, none. I think we somehow managed to take the most volatile route here. Everyone was too busy fighting with each other to notice strangers passing through."

"Which shocked me since we were pushing a huge crate," a woman said, coming to stand beside Deklan. She held her hand out. "I'm Sabrie."

Two men joined her and introduced themselves as Tate and Galvin. Next to Deklan, both men appeared short, though Caidon figured they were close to his own height. The fourth man remained in the shadows with his wolf.

Caidon nodded his direction, a sense of unease prickling his nerves. "Who is he?"

"Hollis Lenard, a Ruthenian beast master. No formal military or civilian rank. There's over a dozen unsolved kidnappings in his country. When Ruthenia learned about the ship sitting in the ocean with possible kidnap victims, they wanted to confirm," Deklan answered.

"At least five nations may have citizens on board," Ramsey said. "Why would Ruthenia be the only other one to care?"

"The others likely haven't learned about it yet," Deklan said.

"Ruthenia doesn't trust you?" Ramsey asked, her gaze sliding from Deklan to his small wolf pack.

"I'm Sziverian first, much to their disappointment," Deklan said, shrugging. "They want one of their own, I guess."

"How did they learn about the ship?" Ramsey asked, shifting closer to Caidon, her fingers sliding into his. Caidon squeezed her hand.

Deklan rubbed the back of his neck. "I'm not sure. He was waiting for us when we made port in Syrinad."

The uneasiness from earlier returned. Caidon stared at the stranger, who remained separate from their small group, his wolf still running around. "Interesting. You trust him?"

"Not at all," Deklan answered, his smile all teeth. "But when I radioed Voklane, he knew of Hollis and asked us to be diplomatic."

Ramsey's scrunched her nose. "Politics."

Caidon squeezed her hand again. "All part of this life you have chosen to live with me."

A heavy breath puffed from between her lips. "You keep saying that."

He bumped his arm into her shoulder. "You keep making me remind you."

Deklan's focus shifted to the narrow balcony running the length of the second story. "How many floors are there?"

"Three," Caidon answered. "The second floor is office space. The third appears to be storage rooms, or room for additional office space if the warehouse requires it. The fourth floor is attic space and where Ramsey and I are staying."

"I will look at the third floor for us, then. My wolves need room to get some energy out without being heard. The ground floor won't work, but their running won't be heard from the third floor outside, not with the ocean so close."

"I will take an office on the second floor," Hollis said in Ruthenian, making no effort to come closer.

"What will your wolves need?" Caidon asked both the masters.

"I will get what my dog needs," Hollis replied, his voice dry and thin from the distance where he spoke.

Caidon shifted his attention to Deklan, brow raised in question.

"I brought most of what mine will need. It's in a compartment in the crate. Anything else, I'll send Tate or Galvin."

Sabrie rolled her eyes. "Yes, because the danger is too high for a woman."

"We talked about this on the voyage," Tate growled. "A lone woman attracts more attention than a lone man, especially when you don't look like a local."

"There is a stable section of the city a couple of blocks from here," Caidon said. "I recommend going there for any supplies."

"After I get the wolves settled, we can go over plans," Deklan said, making a sharp motion. The dogs stood, their pink tongues hanging out of their mouths, eyes bright with attention and a sort of hopeful happiness only a canine could manage. "*Sesay ursla'viti.*"

The change was immediate. The dogs fell in line and followed behind Deklan, Neva in the lead, Izia and Nikita flanking her on either side. Caidon took a moment to appreciate their majestic yet deadly beauty. Their full height made apparent as they passed by Ramsey, reaching her waist, and she gasped, squeezing in tight to Caidon's side. The russet tips of Neva's fur trembled in response, her fluffy tail flicked in agitation. Izia was gray to her golden, while Nikita was midnight with startling blue eyes, making his pelt seem more sapphire than black. Large triangular ears, thick with fur, twitched. Their moist, black nostrils flared, and Nikita sneezed. Deklan glanced back in question. Caidon gestured that all was well.

"Do not show fear," Caidon whispered, taking her hand. "They are predators to their bones."

"I didn't know how big they were," she replied, her words hushed, reverent. "They are... astounding."

"They are beasts," Hollis rumbled, his words thick with his Ruthenian accent. "Trained to kill with well-placed teeth to throat." He snapped his fingers against his palm close to Ramsey's face. "Never mistake their purpose."

Caidon made a low sound deep in his throat. A

primal warning not to be ignored. Hollis jumped back, gaze narrowed. His wolf whined.

"*Do not*," Caidon rumbled in Ruthenian, "*come near my mate again.*"

"We are not here to fight amongst ourselves," Deklan said, his words quiet yet authoritative. His intense gaze focused on Hollis. "*You* are a guest on this mission."

Hollis glared and shoved past to take the stairs first. Wolvenguard's pack growled, showing teeth. Caidon itched to free the pistol resting against his back. The moment Hollis disappeared from sight through the narrow upstairs door, Ramsey let loose a tense exhale, her palm sweaty against his.

"Do you want to include him in the plans?" she asked Deklan.

The arch guardian considered her question, frowning. "I think we'll have to. Everyone needs to know what is expected of them or we'll fail."

"Not an option," Caidon said.

"Agreed," Deklan said. "I will handle Hollis."

They followed the team to the third floor, waiting near the stairs while the wolves and humans explored the various empty rooms. Deklan closed his pack into the largest room and then joined them in the hall.

"All right," he said on a sigh. "What's the plan?"

"THIS IS WHERE THE WAREHOUSE THEY WILL USE IS located," Tate said, pointing his finger to the crudely drawn map of the port in their area.

Ramsey stood on the couch, trying to peer over everyone's head to see the plan, but even the additional height didn't help. Huffing in disappointment, she dropped onto the cushion, bouncing lightly on the stuffed seat. Early morning light, warm and bright, spilled into the office. Late in the night, the expected group of men from The True Descendants met and discussed their plans in detail. In the darkness, the moon was nothing more than a sliver in starry sky. Ramsey hadn't feared being spotted while she translated the conversation for Caidon and Deklan. The meeting had revealed so much more than they'd expected, and no one had slept waiting for the sun to rise to make plans for the night to come.

The strategy was simple, easy to execute if everything went according to plan. Ramsey didn't have the courage to ask how often something actually happened as designed. Since they had a plan B and even a plan C, she figured not often. Once everyone seemed happy with the arrangement, they retired to try to get some sleep before sunset.

Back in their small space, Ramsey tried to calm her nerves. Hypnotic shadows and reflected light from the ocean below danced across the vaulted ceiling. On his stomach, his arm thrown over her, Caidon slept, having fallen into a deep sleep moments after landing on the mattress. Ramsey wished she could do the same, but the culmination of their journey was almost upon them, and she wasn't sure if she was ready. She figured she likely never would be prepared for something so important. However, if she didn't sleep, she'd be useless.

Adrenaline faded from her system, and she dozed. Hours later, the warmth of the late afternoon sun filled the room. The teasing warmth of Caidon's breath along her shoulder eased her from sleep. A moan escaped her, and she twisted toward him. His arm tightened around her hips, pulling her close until he half laid across her. He lifted a sleepy head and glanced at the windows. Sighing, he dropped his cheek to her chest. She feathered her fingers through his hair.

"We don't have enough time," he muttered against her breasts.

A delicious thrill went straight to her toes. "I'll beg if I must."

Deep laughter rumbled in his chest. "Everyone will hear."

"I'll put a pillow over my face," she said.

He settled between her thighs and rocked his hips, tormenting her needy body. She still marveled at how easily they fell into passion. How quickly desire flared between them. How *right* they were together. The flex of his muscles beneath her palms had her breath hitching. She arched into him, her feet hooking around his thighs. His hand slid under her shirt, seeking and finding the fullness of her breast.

Muffled laughter followed by the deep rumble of a man's voice filtered up from the floor below. Caidon sighed and rolled away from her. Ramsey sat up, growling, and resisted hitting the floor and shouting to the group below. The distraction of her husband, of the pleasure he alone knew how to bring, would have been welcome. Instead, Ramsey found herself fighting nerves. Caidon squeezed her thigh before rising to dress.

"It's going to be fine," he said, pulling on a shirt.

Ramsey forced herself from the warmth and safety of their bed and went to dig through her bag for clean clothing. She didn't have much, which made choosing a dark pair of thick pants and knitted navy sweater easy. Using a black ribbon, she gathered her unruly curls into a ponytail. Caidon set his rifle case on the table at the back of the room and built the weapon with expert hands. After checking over every inch, he loaded several small cartridges and placed them in his pockets. He handed her three as well, just in case. Ramsey draped her cloak over her shoulders before following Caidon down the ladder.

They met the group on the main floor. After a quick conversation reminding everyone of their roles, they separated. Hollis ran his wolf along the huge room. Deklan and his team returned to the third floor to prepare his wolves, while Caidon and Ramsey slipped out the back door into the alley. Chilled evening air, salty and thick with the scent of fish, swirled her cloak around her ankles. She followed close behind Caidon. A tremor of anxiety made her entire body tremble. Caidon's fingers wiggled behind him, and she grasped his hand. A sense of calm warmth whispered along her nerves.

"Thank you," she whispered, not releasing him.

"You will do everything I say, no matter how ridiculous it sounds or how much you disagree," he said, low, his tone inviting no argument.

She squeezed his fingers in understanding. Danger and shadow games were not anything she claimed to know about. To disobey him would be to put herself, and their objective, in jeopardy. Too much rode on their success for her to even consider defiance.

The port was quiet. In less than a week, all that would change, the docks becoming accessible to all nations who used Mark Inland as a halfway point to other destinations. Keeping to the back alleyways, they didn't encounter another person on the way to the warehouse. Caidon made quick work of the heavy padlock and then waited while Ramsey found a window low enough for him to enter so he could re-lock the door. Inside, birds who'd somehow managed to find enough to survive the winter indoors took flight at their sudden arrival, squawking and flapping high above, their little wings beating an echoing flutter.

Caidon sighed and looked upward. Tuffs of hay, small branches, and fabric covered the beams. "Great, we get to sit among bird crap."

Ramsey scrunched her nose. "As gross as that sounds, I'm glad they found shelter and lived through winter."

"I imagine it's the reason we still have many bird species, they found places to hide during the worst weather conditions. Resilient little things."

Shifting the weight of his pack and the rifle slung across his shoulder, he made his way toward a narrow ladder leading to a loft. Ramsey figured they'd find more little resilient critters up there and suppressed a shudder. Chasing away curious and hungry mice had become something of a skill in Mark Inland, one she could have done without. She was developing many talents she never figured she'd need. She waited at the bottom of the ladder while he investigated the loft. Once he deemed it safe, he motioned for her to join him. The thin rails creaked beneath her weight and wobbled. Holding her breath, she climbed. Caidon helped her over the last few, and she exhaled the moment she made it safely onto the platform.

Caidon dropped his pack to the dusty floor and rummaged through until he found a tightly wound bundle. A rope ladder. Better than scaling a rope hand-over-hand, but still not stable. There hadn't been any time to allow her to practice, and she hoped she didn't embarrass herself falling. After several unsuccessful attempts, he managed to hook the ladder onto a thick beam overhead. He secured his pack and rifle to his back and then climbed up, making the entire process look easy. Ramsey frowned. Somehow, she figured she wouldn't look graceful *or* sexy finagling her way up.

Caidon straddled the beam, looked around, and then motioned for her. Ramsey swallowed, her throat scratchy. She shook out her sweaty palms. "You can do this," she whispered.

The ropes shuddered and swayed with each step up she took, forcing her to cling, sweat breaking out all over her body. She squeaked when the entire thing attempted to swing her in an arc. Caidon grabbed the top to steady the momentum.

"Easy," he said.

"I've been trying," she bit out, beyond frustrated, bordering on tears.

"You're almost here, only a few more. You can do it," he encouraged, leaning down until the tips of his fingers came into sight.

Ramsey steeled her nerves and slowly, muscles protesting, lungs struggling to pull in enough air, managed to reach his outstretched hand. With his assistance, the remaining section went much faster. He helped her swing onto the rafter. When she was steady, he repacked the ladder.

"Do you see those boards laid out over there to the

right?" He motioned behind his shoulder, and Ramsey shifted her attention. Planks were arranged in a haphazard manner across several beams.

"Yes."

"That's where we're going."

She blinked. Words failed. Maybe if she didn't look down, she wouldn't think about how awful the fall would be if the meager boards failed to support them. His fingers brushed hers before he twisted around.

"We have to move carefully. If we send too much debris onto the floors below, they'll look up."

Ramsey followed behind him, mindful of how he progressed, and tried to match each slow slide, picking up and replacing nests each time he did. At the boards, he moved them around with caution until they were arranged close enough together to comfortably support two bodies side by side. He laid on the slats first and then helped her. The pack settled between them.

The small flock of birds settled. Delicate bird song chirped and twittered through the open space. Golden light filtered in through the dirty windows, turning dust motes into dancing fragments of glitter. Ramsey used the serene moment to calm her anxiety. Nothing would happen for hours until the darkest part of night arrived. Then they'd learn if all the planning would make a difference.

23

Long waits were not an uncommon theme in Caidon's life. He'd once spent a week laying on a filthy mattress at a low window across from a visiting dignitary's hotel room while waiting for the man to prove his guilt of luring young women to his room with the intent to rape and murder them. A serial killer masquerading as a protector of his county wasn't welcome in Noreden. Hours meant little to Caidon.

Ramsey didn't seem to share his ease of laying still for an extended amount of time. Her foot ticked. Her shoulders rolled. Her fingernails tapped a quiet rhythm on the wood beam in front of them. At one point, she'd even attempted to lure a little yellow bird over. The skittish creature had bounced close enough to see the tiny black feathers along the edges of its wings before losing courage and flying away. The dried berry Ramsey had been luring it with likely remained close to her fingers, though all the birds had fallen into a silent sleep. In the inky darkness, he couldn't even see his own hand in front of his face.

"Should be soon now," Caidon whispered.

"I'm trying not to think about it."

Caidon filled his nose with mildew-scented air and breathed out slowly through his mouth. He regretted Ramsey would see men take their last breath today. Either by his hand or the Wolvenguard's, men would die tonight. Unavoidable, if not regrettable. He could not bring himself to lament the end of men who stole safety.

A faint, golden glow bounced beyond the windows, breaking through the absolute blackness. An uncomfortable tightness tingled along his bond. He shifted his weight, brushing his fingers along the back of her neck. Under his touch, her muscles relaxed, and her soft exhale let him know she once again reigned in her anxiety. Pride filled him. The light drew near, as did the shuffle of feet in chains and muffled voices.

Metal boomed and reverberated seconds before a wide door slid open. Two men entered ahead carrying lanterns. They searched the area, not leaving any corner or crate unsearched. Mice scattered and squeaked. A few birds flapped in protest of their disrupted peace. Not once did either of the guards look up. Caidon smiled.

One of the men exited while the other waited at the far end of the warehouse. The first set of captives hobbled in, shoulders hunched, hair shorn to their scalps, their clothes no longer a discernable shade. Children clung to the legs of the adult closest to them. Ramsey grabbed his forearm and squeezed until her fingers bit into his skin through his clothing. Four more groups followed, guided to a location in the warehouse by the guard holding a light. Not one person attempted to stray. They huddled in their assigned location, unspeaking, trembling.

Caidon flexed his arm, and Ramsey understood, releasing her hold. While he regretted making her lose the contact that helped her hold the horror back, he needed complete use of his arms. Silent, in controlled motions, he positioned the rifle against his shoulder and searched through the scope for his target. The connection to his weapon was immediate. A flood of information processed no different than vision or hearing by his brain. Accepted and utilized. He adjusted the rifle, the view through the scope focused on the small space between the eyes and above the nose of his target. Thick, black eyebrows framed the spot so prettily for him.

The moment had to be executed at the perfect time. Too early, and Deklan's wolves wouldn't be able to do their appointed task. Too late, and they'd lose the element of surprise. Everything hinged on him choosing the correct instant. Patience. Each breath an exercise in composure. A man sauntered in, flanked by two burly men sporting dark beards down to the middle of their chests. Anticipation curled within Caidon. Here was the man he'd been waiting on— the leader.

Meager light from lamps gleamed on their bald heads. Leader man rubbed a hand along his naked scalp, glaring at everyone. If not for the long facial hair on the muscle, Caidon would have believed the ship had been cursed with lice. But the parasites didn't care about scalp or face, they bit and made a home either place. Unless the men refused to shave and hoped to treat the ailment shoreside. The loathing in Leader's dark eyes made Caidon surmise he blamed those around him for the lack of hair.

Leader barked orders, pointing to two groups. Caidon leaned close to Ramsey.

"He's speaking New Columbian," she said, voice low. "He wants the groups with children and teenage girls separated."

The silence of the captives broke like a wave. Small children screamed, holding tight to the legs of those they'd come to trust. Women begged. The teen girls made wild grabs for anyone brave enough to help as they were yanked from their party. Objections rose, requiring action from the guards, who seemed more than eager to suppress the show of defiance. The groups not affected shrunk away, whimpering, useless to offer any help. Leader shouted, impatience clear in his voice and jerky movements. If he were already sorting, they had something planned soon.

Caidon leaned over the rifle and shifted his focus to Leader. With accuracy born of his father's genes, Caidon sighted in his target and pulled the trigger. The man's bald head snapped back a split second before his body followed, flying off his feet and back toward the spray of blood and bone that had exited his skull before anyone realized what had happened. A stunned hush filled the warehouse. The signal Deklan had been waiting for. The back door screeched open and a new sort of chaos unraveled.

IN THE NEARLY FIFTEEN YEARS DEKLAN RALSTON HAD BEEN running wolves, he'd seen a lot. Nothing could have prepared him for the desolate fear of hundreds, beaten and reduced to husks of humanity. The stench of their fear added to the stink of their unwashed, waste saturated clothes and skin. Of infection and the sickly-sweet aroma of starvation. Through his wolves, he shared in the misery of experiencing the overwhelming horror of degradation. Nikita was the first to make his complaint vocal, sneezing and whining through their bonded link.

I don't like the smell, I don't like.

I know. He didn't have time to appease their discomfort or even his own. *Sesay oksepa'nat.*

Their collective *Yes, Alpha, yes* flowed like a chorus through his mind. They darted off, obeying the instructions of Neva, his canine alpha. They separated the first guard from his charges, taking him down with a vicious growl and jaws latched onto the back of his shirt. Izia stood on his captive, keeping a low menacing growl while Deklan swept in and hogtied the man's hands and feet, leaving him unable to do much more than squirm like the worm he was. Neva took down the next guard, and Tate handled the securing. One guard tried to be bold, slashing a knife at Nikita. The reward for his effort was a bullet to the brain from above. The rest of the guards surrendered without any further effort required except rope restraints.

Deklan wound the final strand of rope around the last guard. A sharp slice of anxiety cut through his attention.

Wrong, hurting is wrong! Nikita cried through their bond. Neva and Izia joined in his distress, yelping and barking.

Deklan snapped his attention around the room. Hollis's wolf tore into a young man. Agonizing screams mixed with shouts of terror to echo around the cavernous space. Deklan lifted a hand and signaled to Caidon not to shoot, knowing the sharpshooter would be inclined to stop the carnage of an apparent wolf gone mad. But Ruthenarc wolves weren't prone to fits of rage, or bouts of frenzy. Battle didn't excite them. One-hundred-percent reared to bond with a beast master, their merged link alone controlled their actions. Deklan crossed the distance, his focus on Hollis.

"What are you doing, *maestur zvarelor*?" Deklan asked, his focus completely on the attacking wolf, who, even while tearing into a new victim, quaked. And not from eagerness but from fighting his nature to do no harm.

"*I am being a master!*" Hollis snarled in Ruthenian. "*They are weak! Useless to Ruthenia. Kidnapped because of a drug they could not resist. Baited. Sold. They are not fit to return to their mother soil.*"

"*There is no honor in this!*" Deklan roared.

"*There is only honor! Removing a blight that no one can know about. My country will not be seen as weak from their mistake.*"

Wrong! Wrong! Wrong! His wolves yowled, echoing the sentiment burning in Deklan's heart.

Deklan reached deep, far into his consciousness, to the threads binding him to his wolves. Gold, silver, and sapphire, the lines connecting them shimmered beautiful, iridescent. Pure. He sank deeper into himself, pulling on the genetic gift of his father, allowed to blossom into something once common, now mythical among his kind. The angry red glow of the bond between Hollis and his wolf flared into Deklan's sight.

Focus intent on the warped bond, Deklan held his

hand toward the sick thread. *"You are not worthy of your wolf. You are no longer Alpha."*

Deklan snapped his hand closed. Fist tight, he tore the thread from the beast master. Hollis's wolf yelped and fell sideways. Panting, he stayed down. Deklan's wolves went silent and flattened to the floor. Blood dripped from Deklan's nose, hot and thick.

Brother, what is your name, brother? Neva asked, her voice a soft whisper of calm.

The answer came to them, weak, distant, but heard, *Zhenya.*

Safe, Zhenya is safe.

Deklan sat, ignoring the blood dripping down his face to plop onto the floor between his crossed legs. He held his hand out and waited. Zhenya shimmied across the floor on his stomach, eyes darting away from direct contact with Deklan. Hollis rumbled. The faint *ping* of a bullet hitting wood let Deklan know the former master wouldn't be interfering with the bonding. He placed his trust in the sharpshooter. Everything faded around him. The sniffling and crying of those once destined for slavery, now rescued. The quiet murmur of Tate, the medical scientist on his team, seeing to the injured first. None of it mattered. None of it could intrude.

Zhenya reached him. He was beautiful, with black tipped red fur, and copper eyes that betrayed his shame. The cold tip of his wet nose brushed Deklan's fingers. Closing his eyes, Deklan slid his hand up Zhenya's nose, between his eyes and to soft coat between his ears. He sank deep into the pelt until he contacted skin.

Wolf Zhenya, will you accept me as your Alpha? Deklan asked.

Behind him, the collective anticipation of the answer flowed from his pack.

Accept, I accept, Zhenya replied.

The wolves howled in welcome.

Deklan built the bond. A magnificent copper thread flared between them.

"How?" Hollis croaked, his fingers flexing into his chest.

Deklan slowly opened his eyes. "I am the Wolvenguard."

RAMSEY HAD NEVER HAD TO WORK SO HARD NOT TO CRY. If life did things to make her sad, she embraced the need for tears. Now, however, tears would only make the situation worse. Each person she spoke with, defeated and unable to accept they were free and hadn't been captured by a new owner, broke her heart a little more. Caidon had taken to holding her hand, pulling her close when she needed the additional contact, and giving her space when she managed to somehow reign in her emotions.

All the guards had been trussed up and carried back onto the ship they'd once used to steal away freedom. Their captain lay dead, along with two others who refused to surrender. Ramsey kept her gaze averted from where they'd been laid, the blood pooling under them viscid and dark, soaking into the wood floor.

She also had to work hard not to dwell on the impossible she'd witnessed. Beast masters were a mystery to her, and what had happened was foreign and a little scary. The wolf who'd been forced to attack lay curled in a dark corner away from everyone. Deklan cast him worried glances every few minutes but never imposed on the wolf's solitude. The pack stayed close to Deklan's legs, to the point of being underfoot. If Ramsey thought too hard on the whole incident, she started to feel slightly unhinged.

Tate, the Wolvenguard's medical scientist, sat on the floor wrapping the ankle of a little girl. Sabrie had found a list of gender, age, and country of origin on the ship when they'd taken the guards and had brought it back for Ramsey. Using the list, Ramsey wrote names next to the information of every person she interviewed. So far, twenty-seven people were unaccounted for, and aside from six or seven who other victims knew for certain died at some point while waiting in the ocean, no one could say about the others. They would remain missing, likely nameless.

One country remained for Ramsey to process. She'd met and tried to assure those from Westica, Monaco Sands, Sziveria, and Ruthenia. New Columbia was the largest group, which Ramsey figured made an awful sort of sense since that's where the Cyrano ship made port when under the now dead captains command. Easier to find victims when you were in charge of the operation. Ramsey wrote down names next to ages and gender and asked the same question she'd posed over and over again in whatever language required, changing the destination as necessary.

"Are you willing to return to Sziveria on the ship that brought you here, where you'll be returned to New Columbia?" she asked in the woman's native tongue, writing down the name of the woman next to her age of twenty-three.

"*No*," the woman answered, so quiet Ramsey almost missed the answer.

Pen frozen halfway to writing *Yes*, she'd written the word almost two-hundred times now since no one had disagreed with the plan, she figured she'd misheard. "*I'm sorry? Are you willing to return to the ship and to your home?*"

"*No*," the woman stated again, louder, her chin lifted and dark brown eyes defiant. "*I am not going back.*"

Ramsey hesitated, glancing down at the woman's name. "*Makaria, I understand if you're worried about the ship. It's been cleaned, and everyone will have full access. You aren't returning as a prisoner. You're safe now.*"

Color infused Makaria's cheeks. She looked around and then leaned close enough to Ramsey to keep their conversation private. "*I have nothing to return to but bad friends and bad choices.*" Tears shone in her dark gaze. "*They addicted me to the coca, and when I was useless, helped carry me onto the ship for a handful of leaves and a purse of coin. If I returned… I'll be too weak to keep it from happening again, do you understand? I can't. I can't go through the missing low again.*"

"*But you can't speak the language here. You have no money, no clothes, and nowhere to live. What will you do?*" Ramsey asked, fisting her hand to keep from touching the woman, her nature urging her to offer some sort of comfort.

"*I will learn, and I will find what I can. I'm not without some skills. I'm an excellent seamstress, and I can embroider. Before…*" She choked on the word, licked her lips, and tried again. "*Before I tried the coca, I had a steady hand. After…*"

After, her life had become all about the soonest

moment she could slip another leaf into her mouth. Coca wasn't common in Sziveria, the leaves needed to be fresh to get the potent effects, meaning it had to be grown somewhat locally. From her limited understanding, the plant was a distant relative of the pre-cataclysmic coca plant, only instead of needing to be dried to get the addictive high, users just chewed a fresh leaf. Instant rush.

Caidon moved forward and held out his hand. Colorful beads rested on his palm. "Pick the ones you want to keep for memories, and she can have the rest."

"You understood her?" Ramsey asked, shocked.

"Not the words. Her body language."

Of course, how could she forget that skill of his? Ramsey looked over the beads, trying to remember which ones held the most value. The blue ones that shone with an inner rainbow, or the yellow ones, sparkling even while laying still. Or maybe the green ones shot through with shimmery red threads. Or even the purple ones with flecks of silver, such a rich hue that only in the clearest noon light could their true color be revealed, making them appear like the night sky captured in a tiny sphere. Ramsey dallied. All of them were unique. No single bead the same.

Caidon smiled. "I'm teasing. I have one of each color in a small pouch for you."

Ramsey shook her head and gently smacked his arm. "Give them to her, and I will explain their purpose." She translated as Caidon described the value of each color and then told Makaria the safest part of Subail and the many languages and factions within the city borders. *"I have nothing else to be of help. We don't know a room for rent or any seamstresses in need of help."*

Makaria rolled the beads around on her palm. *"This is so much more than I could ever hope for. Thank you. This is my decision, and everything is mine to worry about now."*

The comfort of Caidon's arms wound around her waist and pulled her against his chest. "You are a good woman," he said as Makaria slipped from the building and off into her new life.

Ramsey wrapped her fingers around his forearm and let her weight settle into his frame. "And you are a good man. You gave her what likely amounts to six-months in wages in Subail."

"She'll require every bead to get a new start."

"I hate to break up such a sweet moment," Gavin drawled, and Ramsey startled in Caidon's arms at the sudden intrusion. "But Deklan has asked me to get you both. If we don't leave soon, whoever was expecting to obtain some new property of the human variety will be disappointed to learn they've been cheated, and we'll have a new problem to handle. He figured you both had things you needed to collect from the Eastern Isle's warehouse before we lifted anchor."

Ramsey glanced around the warehouse, surprised to find them alone except for a few stragglers. A group of children were having to be convinced about boarding the ship they'd finally been freed from. The clipboard with over two-hundred rescued suddenly felt heavy in her hand. Disbelief made her weak. "We did it," she whispered.

Caidon's arms tightened around her. His chin rested on top of her head. "Yes, we did."

EPILOGUE

PORT SCARBROUGH, SZIVERIA
  One week later

BRIGHT SUN GLARED OFF THE WATER, BLINDING RAMSEY. Having never been away from her country before, returning brought a level of excitement to almost rival the night Caidon had taken her against the wall for the first time. Almost. Only the blinding wash of light kept her from seeing anything except a haze and the blue sky above. Seagulls cawed, dove, and landed on whatever surface they figured they wouldn't get chased from.

Deklan piloted the ship to the dock. Lucky for them, as the Arch Guardian Wolvenguard, he'd been required to learn how to operate every form of transportation known to man in the inhabited world. Trains, ships, Ariot's, and carriages, he could manage all of them.

Ramsey tried to relocate, but the constant play of sun on water continued to deny her what she wanted to see most. Her home shores. Defeated, she sat at the rail, the noon sun heating her hair and making her scalp tingle. Caidon joined her, squeezing her knee.

"Almost there," he said over the constant noise of water and birds.

"I wanted to see," she said, picking at a rough piece of wood near her foot. "I bet Sziveria is beautiful when you get to see it for the first time after being away."

"Port Tabria is, with the mountain range rising like a giant. As is Port Ice Hollows with the cliffs. Here? Not much different than any other port you've seen, with the exception of Syrinad. Buildings, wood, and people."

"Our people."

He squeezed her leg again. "That's true."

The niggle of discomfort she'd been fighting returned as the ship rocked, turned faintly but continued course. Ramsey rubbed her collarbone. "What happens now?"

"I don't know. Voklane said there'd be officials waiting for us when we docked. I'm assuming we'll either get a few days to rest, or we'll be informed of our next destination."

Our. Ramsey didn't think she'd ever get tired of hearing that. She leaned against his side, pleased when he wrapped an arm around her and dropped his cheek to her head. "Still want me tagging along?"

"Wouldn't go anywhere without you."

Caidon's finger brushed along the back of her neck, spreading a familiar, comforting warmth through her. She smiled up at him. "I love you, too."

He brushed a kiss across her lips. "You know none of this would have happened without you, right? Not unless an entire team went in."

"Risky," she murmured against his mouth.

"Especially in a country as divided as Mark Inland. The translation of vital information, being able to find necessary documents, all of it crucial to rescuing this ship."

"A ship that will never again carry human cargo," she said with satisfaction.

"Yes, and the Cyrano's won't ever trade in Sziveria again, at least. Perhaps, for a time, we've made a difference in our country."

"The victims will take their account back to their homes, and maybe things will change there, too."

He hugged her closer, his focus through the slats to the shimmery water beyond. "We can hope."

Ramsey studied his face. He hadn't shaved since before the rescue and had heavy stubble. She'd delighted in the textures against her palm and other sensitive places on her body. She feathered her hands against the bristle. "I like this."

"Then I'll keep it." He scratched under his chin, his nose wrinkling. "For now."

Long shadows passed by. Thick ropes followed, flying overhead. Ramsey gasped and scrambled to stand. The rocking motion beneath her feet made her stumble. Caidon steadied her and she grasped the thick wooden rail. The port edged closer, visible since the shade from the ship cut through the glare. A small group waited. Among them, she noted familiar faces, and she jumped in excitement, grabbing onto Caidon's arm and pointing. He laughed and moved behind her, wrapping tight around her as the ship swayed and lurched to a stop. The secured ropes groaned with the weight of the vessel but held.

Ramsey took Caidon's hand and pulled him to the

footbridge being extended to the ship from the dock. She didn't care how rude she may be, insisting on being off first. The moment she'd spotted Jonathon, Sylphine, and Parker, she couldn't wait any longer to be on home soil. Gavin and Tate locked the wide plank into place and then gave the safe signal to disembark. Ramsey let go of Caidon and flew down the walkway. Jonathon met her halfway, catching her when she launched into his waiting arms.

Her brother squeezed her tight. "You made it. You're okay." He released her and stepped back, taking her cheeks in his hands and looking her over. "You're safe."

Tears burned her eyes. "We did it, Jonathon. We rescued them."

He brought her back in for another tight hug. "I know. I'm so proud of you."

"Aunty Ramsey! Aunty Ramsey! Aunty Ramsey!" Parker chimed, bouncing next to her and pulling on the bottom of her shirt. "Look!"

Ramsey looked down at her little nephew. He pointed a finger at a gap along his bottom teeth. Ramsey gasped in shock, her eyes wide with an appropriate amount of surprise. "Oh, my stars! You lost your first tooth!" She knelt in front of him and took his chin between her fingers. "What is it to become?"

He clasped his hands to his chest and beamed with pride. "I planted a baby orange tree. In years and years, my tooth will help baby oranges grow!"

Ramsey glanced up at Jonathon. He laughed and ruffled Parker's hair. "He had trouble saying clementine, so baby oranges."

"A good choice for your first tooth," Ramsey said.

"My next one is gonna be tomatoes!" he proclaimed

and wiggled the tooth next to the vacant space in his mouth. "Thats was my first momma's favorite, and Momma Sylphie said my momma would have loved me planting a tomato, so I'm gonna plant one."

Ramsey hugged Parker. "I think that's wonderful, and Momma Sylphie is right."

"And then green beans, because babies eat lots and lots of green beans, and I want to help the baby eat lots and lots." Parker puffed out his chest. "Big brothers are helpful, you know."

Ramsey blinked and stared at Sylphine, who nodded. "Really?" Ramsey asked.

Sylphine nodded again, tears in her eyes. "Really."

Ramsey squealed and launched herself at her sister-in-law. After giving her a big hug, she tackled her brother again. He laughed and hugged her tight. "Congratulations."

"Thank you," he said. Sylphine joined them, and Jonathon wrapped an arm around her waist. "We're pretty excited."

"Me too!" Parker said, jumping in a circle. "I love babies!"

Sylphine chuckled. "He says that now. I don't know how he'll feel after the first month."

Ramsey grinned at them. "I can't wait to find out. Caidon will have to make sure to find me a radio station if we aren't home when the time arrives." Realizing her husband wasn't around, she turned and sought him out in the growing crowd as the ship fully disembarked. "Where is he?"

"I think I saw him over with Voklane," Sylphine said, pointing to a small group that included the Wolvenguard team and a man that resembled Deklan so much Ramsey figured they must be related. "I know he had something he needed to talk to you both about."

"Probably our next assignment," Ramsey said with a sense of pride. And, if she were honest, a sense of importance. They'd made a difference, and already she could tell the feeling would become addictive, as Caidon had once told her.

"Or the reason you needed to leave in the first place," Jonathon said, the words so low she almost missed them over the noise of voices, ocean, and ships.

All of Ramsey's excitement faded, replaced by anxiety. Caidon turned her direction, catching the tall man who'd been speaking by surprise. The man's gaze flickered to Ramsey, and a glimmer of understanding crossed his expression. He said something. Caidon nodded and left the group.

"What's wrong?" Caidon asked the second he reached her, his fingers lacing between hers.

"I mentioned Ryan wanted to speak with her, possibly about the reason she'd needed to leave," Jonathon answered.

Caidon lifted his chin. "Ah. Perhaps he does. We've been busy discussing our findings from Mark Inland. Darius Ralston, he's a guardian with the Sziverian National Investigative Division, will need everything we gathered in the dockmaster's office."

"After copies have been made," Jonathon said, frowning. "In triplicate."

"Voklane mentioned that," Caidon said.

Jonathon's expression went flat. "Disappearing documents are a problem. Annoying in that they've almost cost lives and mysterious because we can't figure out who is stealing evidence."

"The V Alliance?" Caidon asked, voicing the obvious.

"Well, yes, but who specifically? We don't know who they are until one of them dies. Again, annoying."

Ryan joined their little group. He looked at Ramsey and she moved closer to Caidon. "Tobyn Fenster is dead. He was part of the V Alliance, and we believe connected to the false order sent to assassinate you."

Sylphine made a happy noise of distraction and swept Parker into her arms. She walked to the edge of the dock and occupied the little boy by pointing at something in the water.

Ramsey's heart skipped a beat. Tobyn had been in her home. Right in front of her, close enough to have hurt her if he'd wanted. "Why?"

"Someone learned you were able to translate the manifests like we suspected. They couldn't afford for any more information to be learned. Not after the children were rescued last Wintervail. I believe when the assassination order didn't move as fast as they wanted, they sent Tobyn, who had a history with you, to make another attempt," Ryan explained.

"Thankfully, he failed," Jonathon said, sighing. "I never liked that guy."

Ramsey swallowed. "He had two kids."

"His wife has already re-contracted," Ryan said. "We aren't sure if she's involved. Her quick marriage raises some questions."

"They didn't marry for love," Ramsey said, thankful when Caidon wrapped his arms around her. Memories of Tobyn telling her about his wife approving his desire to make Ramsey his mistress had her wondering if perhaps the primary guardian wasn't part of the plan after all.

"Either way, she's being investigated."

"How did he die?" Ramsey asked.

Ryan frowned. "Human Rabies Syndrome."

"As an outbreak or in a facility?"

"Outbreak, in a store."

Ramsey covered her mouth in horror. "Oh no."

"It's okay, no one else was infected. The storeowner acted quickly, evacuating the patrons, and locking Tobyn in until a containment unit arrived." Ryan ran a hand through his hair. "The real problem arose when no one else in the city or surrounding towns had an episode within two weeks or turned themselves into the facility. His case was isolated."

"How is that possible?" Caidon asked.

"By infecting him with an active strain of the virus via injection or another means. I've seen it before," Ryan answered.

Silence settled among them, and Ramsey blew out a nervous breath. "What an odd way to punish someone for failing."

"Common for the V Alliance, unfortunately."

"She's safe from Joel Blackbain, then?" Jonathon asked.

Ryan shrugged. "I don't know. He doesn't seem related to any of this, but he's still missing, and I strongly suspect part of a plan we don't know about." He met Jonathon's stare, and the tense energy between them seemed a tangible thing. "The best place for your sister is still at her husband's side."

"You only say that because she's useful to you," Jonathon said, anger darkening his words.

Caidon sighed. "We have been over this, Asherwick. Ramsey goes where I go because she's mine to care for, as I am hers. No argument."

Jonathon's jaw worked, but he kept his mouth closed. Ramsey cast him a thankful smile. Her guardian brother understood. He had a wife of his own to protect.

"Is there anything else?" Caidon asked. "We're filthy and tired. I'd like to get us to the room for the night we're in Haven City."

"Where are you going next?" Sylphine asked, rejoining them with Parker on her hip. He fiddled with a vivid blue feather in her hair.

"They don't know," Ryan answered.

Ramsey and Caidon said their goodbyes. Darius Ralston caught up with them and scheduled to meet them for dinner at the hotel they'd been assigned for the duration of their visit home. Ramsey wanted to bathe, eat familiar food, and sleep. In that order. Caidon gathered their meager possessions from the ship, and then they walked to the train about to depart for Haven City.

Hours later, on the fourth floor of a room that was downright luxurious after a mattress on a dusty floor, Ramsey looked out over the city. The familiar, simple brick buildings, peppered with glass tops or greenhouse balconies, were such a welcome sight she almost cried. Carriages shared the road with Ariot's. People wearing known fashions bustled along the sidewalks. Caidon called to her from the open bathroom door.

"The water is hot, and clean clothes will be delivered for us." He stood shirtless, his pants unbuttoned. Her heart kicked, and a new hunger, unrelated to the need to taste food, rumbled through her. "You can go first."

Ramsey pulled her clothes off on the way to him. "How about we go together."

He gathered her against his chest, his fingers burying into her chaotic curls. "Always."

THE END

THANK YOU FOR READING! ENJOY THIS TITLE? DON'T forget to leave a review and let other readers know.

KEEP READING FOR A SNEAK PEEK AT THE NEXT TITLE IN the series - *WOLVENGUARD*

WOLVENGUARD PREVIEW

A strange scratching pulled Cia from unconsciousness. Throbbing pain bloomed from her jaw and her throat ached. Beneath her, a hard surface pressed into her bones. She blinked, the empty room an unfocused blur. Where was she? Grit met her palms when she tried to push herself up. Weak, everything hurting, her first attempt to rise failed. Grunting, Cia tried again, managing to get onto her hands and knees. Her hair fell in a tangled mess around her face. Her tongue a swollen dry mass in her mouth. She smacked and tried to swallow, willing her memory to return.

Vague flashes of violence and fear made her draw in a ragged inhale. Everything came back to her on a rush. She gasped and grabbed at her chest, feeling for the strap of her messenger bag. The thin leather belt crossed over her chest and she followed it to the compact leather satchel. Patting at the contents, she let out a breath of relief when she felt the books still inside. The man who'd punched her in the face when he'd dragged her down the stairs, literally, and apparently thrown her into some kind of prison room, hadn't bothered to search her. Why, she didn't know.

The odd, shallow scrapes caught her attention again and she crawled across the cement floor toward the sound. Only a narrow window near the high ceiling allowed any light into the room. Heavy shadows surrounded her and she felt her way through the darkness. Her fingers bumped the edge of a wall a second before her forehead did the same. Scowling, she sat back and tried to force her eyes to see the edges of the room. A *snick* echoed through the hollow space. Cia froze. Waited.

When nothing more than another round of scratching happened, she continued her journey around the perimeter of the room. A faint breeze against her fingers made her stop. She touched cool metal. The scoring was louder and vibrated across the surface. Another *snick*. Cia spread her hands across the smooth plane, searching for a handle and found only steel. Then nothing. The door fell open and she stared into the most stunning set of golden eyes set against slate fur she'd ever seen. A massive wolf gazed back at her.

She didn't get the chance to figure out why a wolf was in front of her. The world trembled and bucked. A deafening roar filled the air. The dog launched into the room past her. A huge body followed, taking Cia along. She slid on her back across the floor, screaming as the room tilted and groaned. Heavy weight settled over her, shielding her as they continued to slide. The thunderous noise pulsed in her head, pulling another scream from her. They crashed into the wall in a heap of bone and muscle and Cia succumbed to the darkness once again.

Gasping awake, Cia attempted to rise, but something hefty and far too warm draped across her body. A wet tongue lapped at her cheek and she swiped it away.

"Stop," she croaked.

The tongue disappeared, replaced by a cold nose. Cia turned and blinked. Amber eyes came into focus. The wolf from earlier. The dog whined and nudged at her again. Cia pulled her arms out from underneath… a man. Oh summer sun, a man laid on her. Heavy and solid muscle. She rose enough to try to see him.

Bright light filtered in from above. The night had come and gone. The scent of smoke curled in the air. No noise, of nature or human, sounded. Cia pondered that for a moment before trying to scoot back enough to try and wiggle free. The wolf made another low cry of distress, nudging at the man's arm laying limp at her side. She moved carefully to allow his head to remain cushioned by her body. Dark, wine-red hair, long without a hint of curl, covered his face. She figured the length fell at least past his shoulders. Cia brushed the strands from his face and jerked her hand free in shock.

Deklan Ralston.

"Stars above," she whispered, her heart jumping into her throat.

Trembling, she pressed her fingers to his neck. A steady pulse met her touch. Still shaky, she smoothed more hair from his handsome face. Wisps caught in the dark stubble covering his jaw. He'd found her. And she had no doubt with the beautiful wolf and him picking the lock for her prison cell, *she* had been his target. She clenched her jaw. Had Joel Blackbain escaped after all?

The acrid stench of smoke hit her again and she glanced up. Haze floated in front of the barred opening.

She kept one hand on Deklan and reached for the wolf. "What happened, I wonder?"

The dog had no answers to give. Cia sighed and continued to smooth her fingers through Deklan's hair. She took him in. Relaxed in unconsciousness, she traced his strong jaw, up to his temple and over his brow. Everything about this man was perfection. She remembered the first time she'd seen him at Shield Guardian Terravine's annual Wintervail party. A force of his own, standing across the room, tall and imposing, she hadn't been able to stop staring.

Her Uncle's wife, Melody, had noticed her ogling. Cia had blurted out how gorgeous he was. At which point her aunt-by-marriage had burst her bubble by telling her exactly who she'd developed an instant crush. An Arch Guardian. *The* Wolvenguard. Who Melody also felt was too old for her. Well Cia disagreed on the age bit. Her own parents had shared a gap. Age didn't bother her. The ranked guardianship he held however...

Cia was the daughter of a notorious assassin, raised in secret, only venturing into ranked society once a year before winter set in. Deklan's world was as foreign to her as her little secluded one would be to him. Working for the First Intelligence Office was a perfect fit for her. The organization was notorious for their secrecy, Cia would never have to reveal her guardian status unless she wanted to. And she didn't. She had zero desire to be thrust into the glitz and snobbery of ranked society. Once a year was enough for her, thank you very much.

A sigh of longing left her as she traced the angles of his face again. Disappointment filled her. She was bold enough to ask for what she wanted, and she definitely wanted to know this man. Before her mother's instant death, Cia hadn't been so audacious. But realizing in a single horrific moment how fragile life was had left an impact. Tomorrow wasn't promised. Leaning forward, she pressed a kiss to his warm temple.

"Too bad, wolf man," she whispered against his skin.

Tingles spread across her lips and she resisted the urge to taste the skin beneath hers. She frowned at the odd impulse. His scent filled her nostrils and she inhaled deep, replacing the pungent odor of smoke with his unique aroma. The woodsy musk of juniper and sandalwood mixed with warm notes of cashmere wood. Masculine and comforting, Cia rested her forehead to his temple and allowed herself to be surrounded.

Deklan stirred and she straightened. His wolf stiffened, staring intently. Groaning, he braced himself on his arms and she scooted away from him. He fell back on his butt in an ungraceful heap, grabbing his head between both hands.

"What in the artic happened?" he asked, his voice gruff and raw.

"I'm not sure," she answered, looking up at the window. "Nothing good."

He released his head long enough to follow her gaze. "I remember the ground shook and I saw something…" He pressed his fingers to his temples. "I don't know what I saw."

Cia eyed the barred frame. The bars weren't part of the metal, rather part of a grate that appeared to lift from the narrow rectangle. "How high do you think that window is?"

Using the wall to brace himself, Deklan slowly rose to his feet. He wobbled for a moment, found his balance, and eased across the space. His arm slid along the wall toward the window, coming short by at least two feet. "Maybe ten feet. I can jump it."

"But can you fit?"

He took a step back and titled his head. "Nope."

"Didn't think so." Cia rose and dusted off her hands and butt. "Okay. I think I can fit."

"What about the…" he looked at the metal and cement wall and finished his sentence on a sigh, "door."

"Yeah," she drew out. "Not much of a door from in here."

One hand braced on the wall, he dropped his head, his shoulders tense.

Cia reached for him, hesitated and pulled back. "Are you okay?"

The wolf nudged his leg, whining. Deklan reached down and spread his fingers between the dog's ears. "My head is killing me. I don't know if it's all this smoke, or… maybe I hit it or something."

"Let me see," she said softly, closing the distance between them.

For the first time since he awoke, he lifted his head and looked at her. Cia forgot to breathe. Deklan had a unique shade of skin, not quite brown, not quite bronze, but some beautiful in-between shade only his family seemed to have. His mother was pale brown, his father a cinnamon bronze, and together they'd made stunning children. The tone brought the expectation of dark eyes, in shades of brown. Instead, he looked at her with vivid ocean green irises, startling in their contrast to the rest of him. Even his hair was so dark without the sun or another bright form of light it looked dark, maybe brown, maybe black. With enough light, the red highlights appeared.

Cia forced herself to focus and took in his face. He towered over her and had to lean over for her to reach his head. A thin line of blood ran down his jaw from by his ear. She touched his jaw and turned his cheek to look closer. A small cut marred his skin, and a bruise discolored his temple. She brushed her fingers under the contusion and he flinched away from her.

"Let me see your eyes," she said.

He met her gaze. This time Cia remembered to keep breathing. She moved them until he stood in a beam of light and checked his pupil reaction.

"I don't think you have a concussion, but I'm not a medical scientist," she said, checking his pupils again by covering and uncovering his eyes. Long lashes brushed against her palm.

His brows drew together as he closed his eyes. "All my wolves are still part of me, no broken bonds, so it's not that."

Cia brushed his hair away from his temple. "You're going to have a nasty bruise here."

Frowning, he touched his temple and winced. He straightened and she took a step away. "Did you see my bag?"

She shook her head. "No. I only woke up a few minutes before you."

"Maybe it's still out there. I have something that'll help with the headache."

Cia looked up at the narrow window. "Did you get Blackbain?"

He tilted his head to the side, his stare unfocused.

"No. They're stowed away on his train, which has been traveling all night. My logistics expert believes they're heading to a port."

"How do you know that?" she asked in disbelief.

"I told Neva to alert my team that I'm linked to her and can hear them if they speak to her."

Cia's eyes widened. "You can do that? Hear what they hear?"

"Yes, and see and smell. Thankfully I can't taste, and I can't feel, either." He braced his hands on his hips and looked around the small, empty cell.

"That's incredible," she whispered.

"All beast masters share the same connection with their animal," he stated, as if his skill were a boring, average fact.

"I know beast masters are more common in Ruthenia than in Sziveria, so maybe to you it's perfectly normal that you can talk to animals. I have never met anyone like you," she said.

A shallow smile tilted his lips, revealing the beginning of a dimple in his right cheek. "Then we're even. I've never met anyone quite like you before, either."

Cia frowned and pondered what he could mean.

He didn't make her ask. "We're trapped in a cement cube. Something is clearly burning out there. I hear no sounds of life." He touched under her chin, titling her head back to expose her neck, and her heart attempted to leap out of her chest. "And it looks like someone tried to choke you to death at some point. I have no idea if you're even okay. Yet here you are, calm, making sure my brain isn't about to leak out of my ears."

"Oh no. Should I be crying? Or freaking out? Or just

generally making this situation more difficult?" she asked with big eyes.

He laughed, and yep, the smile launched him from gorgeous to devastating. "You're what? Twelve?"

"Nineteen," she corrected with a glare.

"Right." He waved a hand as if nineteen and twelve were the same age. "Most girls your age would doing all the things you said."

"Most girls didn't watch their baby brother and mother die," she bit out and turned her back to him, looking at the window. "Most girls don't know how useless screaming is when the worst has already happened and freaking out fixes nothing. Dead is still dead."

"Lucianna, I didn't mean—"

"Cia," she said to cut off an unnecessary apology. "My family calls me Cia."

He turned her around to face him, leaning close so their gazes were level. His mouth, full and so, so tempting, was *right there*. Cia clenched her jaw and dug her fingers into her hips to keep from touching him.

"I'm not your family, Guardian Castien."

Oh damn, he knew her position. She blinked at the stupidity of her surprise. Of course, he knew her position. He'd been sent to drag her sorry, betraying butt back home. "How much trouble am I in?"

"I have no idea."

Worrying about the unknown, yet inevitable return home, was useless. Time for a subject change. "I think I can fit through that window."

He moved to stand beside her, arms crossed. The sleeves of his shirt pulled taut over his biceps. Cia worked with fit men, sometimes on a daily basis, and yet she appreciated the flex of his strength on a different level than she did the men she trained around. Height-wise, he matched Kevin. Tall. If Cia were to rest her head on his chest, she'd be able to feel his heart beat under her cheek. But where Kevin was lithe, Deklan had the same bulk as Mason. Big arms. Big chest. She glanced down at his boots. Big feet. She doubted there was much *small* about the beast master.

"I won't," he said.

Cia shrugged. "That's okay. I can pick the lock on the door like you did last night."

He glanced down at her, brow raised. "You have the tools?"

Grabbing the leather strap across her chest, she lifted the bag from her side. "Everything I need is right in here."

His attention shifted back to the window. "All right. Do you want me to hoist you up there, or…?"

"I can climb up you and stand on your shoulders."

His head snapped around. "You can what?"

Cia pointed to the ground under the window. "Stand right here. I'll climb up and stand on your shoulders. Easiest, and steadiest, way. I'm going to have to pull the grate free, so you'll have to anchor my feet."

He stared at her. "I don't think—"

Cia grinned. "So don't think."

A specific mantra had taken residence in Deklan's brain. *She's too young. She's too young. She's too young.* Over and over, he repeated the phrase, the reminder, like the life-line it had become. He could not, would not, feel anything but professional civility for the woman, *girl,* standing in front of him. Not exactly the picture of innocence with her challenging gaze full of attitude.

In living color, she was more stunning than the artistic rendering he'd stared at for days. Eyes a peculiar shade of gray, bluer rather than steel. At one point her long hair had been braided, but an obvious struggle and whatever had happened in the night had left the golden brown frayed and dust-coated. Underneath the grime, her rosy beige skin looked touchable. Soft. He tightened his crossed arms to keep from giving in to the impulse. Her full lips, a natural lush pink, were another temptation he had to look away from. Summer sun, but she was beautiful.

Deklan returned his attention to the high window. One way or another, they had to get out of here, and the small opening seemed the only option. He growled. Izia mimicked the sound and Deklan uncoiled himself enough to soothe his wolf.

Cia took a small step away. "Is your dog all right?"

"He's fine," Deklan said calmly. "He sensed my agitation, is all."

"He's beautiful. What's his name?"

"Izia."

"And you're bonded to him, too?" she asked, her stare curious.

"I'm bonded to three wolves."

Her mouth fell open. "I... I didn't know that was possible."

"Generations ago it was common for a wolf beast master to bond with a small pack. Now? It's unheard of." He shrugged. "My father made the controversial choice to accept a bond with my mother. Her Sziverian genetics served as a blank canvas for my father's stronger, more dominate Ruthenian traits."

"My parents were both Ruthenian," Cia said. "My father never spoke of why he left there to serve Sziveria."

Everything in Deklan stilled. He wanted to flee to opposite side of the room and not allow her to touch him again. Under any circumstances. Cia had the ability to forge an unbreakable connection between the two of them with little more than attraction and thought. He wanted to know how much her parents had taught her about their genetics before he allowed her into his personal space. But they didn't have the time. They had to get out of this box and somehow find a way to follow his team.

He'd have to be careful on his end of the emotional spectrum. Not allow any errant desires to manifest. Deklan shoved all his feelings down deep and locked them away. He was being overly cautious, he knew. At no point had she given the impression she wanted anything from him in any capacity. And he refused to acknowledge the hint of disappointment.

"All right," he said. "Let's do it your way. The locks outside are tricky, but I can walk you through it to make it faster."

"Great." She grinned at him. Her teeth were white and straight, only adding to her overall beauty.

Deklan unwound one of many leather straps from his wrist to tie back his hair and moved closer to the window, looking up. "How do you want to—"

Her hands gripped his shoulders a second before her weight landed on his hips. Her bare toes dug into his side. She climbed him like a tree, rising onto his shoulders, using the wall in front of them to steady herself.

"Oh good, it's not locked. Whew." Her weight shifted and Deklan reached up to wrap a hand around her calf to ensure she remained stable.

The warmth of her skin seeped through the thin fabric of her pants. Her muscles shifted and flexed beneath his palms. Deklan stared straight ahead at the gray wall, his gaze tracing hairline cracks in the surface.

"All right, I'll need your hands to get higher," she said, slightly breathless.

Deklan inverted his hands and helped her balance on his palms. Looking up, he slowly lifted her. His biceps strained more from making sure she stayed steady rather than from her weight, which was less than one of his wolves. When her shoulders cleared the window, he gave her a push, helping her launch the rest of the way through. An odd sound left her, but before he could inquire, her hips, then legs disappeared through the opening. Deklan let out a breath and took step back.

"Ready to get out of here, Izia?" Deklan asked, petting his wolf. The dog sat, tongue hanging out. "Yeah, me too."

Deklan picked up Cia's discarded shoes and moved to the door. "Are you out there yet?" he asked.

"Yeah," she answered, her voice muffled.

Deklan guided her through the process of navigating the heavy tumble bolts. The last one clicked and the door fell open. Smoking ruins as far as he could see greeted him.

Cia stood, a singed bag in her hand. "I think the door protected it from the worst."

Deklan stepped into the harsh morning light. "What in the arctic."

"I know." A frown marred her pretty face. "The alarming part is there's no bodies that I can see. Do you think they evacuated them?"

"How many people were here when you arrived?"

"I don't know, it was nearly dark, I only saw a few."

Deklan looked around again, turning. Ash floated in the air and covered the ground in a thick, gray blanket. Only the smoldering squares of what once used to be foundations attested to anything ever having existed in the location at all. What had that amount of power? Bombs blew things to pieces. Fires burned, but didn't leave a fine coating of ash behind. He turned and looked at their building. Scorch marks scored the exterior, but the structure remained strong.

"A volcano?" Cia asked, facing the forest, her eyes shielded from the sun.

Deklan followed her gaze. The trees stood, though the ones nearest were covered in the same fine powder as everything else. "We would have baked to death if it'd been a volcano, and none of those trees would be standing."

She wrinkled her nose and wrapped her arms around her waist. "I don't like this."

Deklan agreed. "There's a reason the UZ's exist."

"Last night, this was practically a swamp. They had boardwalks in place."

Cautious, Deklan pressed a boot toe where the walkway used to extend. His shoe met solid ground. He took a slow step forward. Izia whined. Deklan held his hand back and Izia touched a wet nose to his fingertips.

What do you smell? Deklan asked across their bond.

Too much smoke, too much.

"We go slow," he said. Apprehension curled through him. Whatever had caused the odd destruction could have originated from the UZ, of which they stood within the boundary. He wanted to be far from here as soon as possible. "Single file, step where I step."

"All right."

A faint breeze tugged at his clothing, warm and balmy. Deklan glanced up at the cloudless, vivid blue sky. "I think it's going to be hot today."

"Hot? Does anywhere get truly hot?"

"There's still a desert in what's left of Africa, but I don't think like it gets hot like it used to, pre-cataclysm. But for us, yes, it'll feel quite unpleasant." He tested the ground before each step, managing a steady pace. "I was uncomfortable yesterday walking during the day."

"I was warm, but not enough to take off my jacket."

"Today you probably will."

Thirsty, Izia whined.

I know, but nothing here will be safe.

In fact, he didn't know at what point water would be safe. Not until they reached civilization or rain fell from the sky. They eased along the barren landscape. Burnt plants and cracking mud crunched under their feet, mingling with their heavy breaths. The eerie lack of nature only added to his uneasiness.

After an hour of walking, he shrugged out of his jacket and handed it to Cia to stuff into his pack. She'd tied hers around her waist at some point. Her damp hair clung to cheeks and throat. The flush of her skin and glistening layer of perspiration had Deklan's throat constricting. He imagined she'd look very similar after a strenuous round between the sheets. A bead of moisture snaked from her collarbone down between her pert breasts, where her once white tank stretched tight. Deklan turned away from her, his heart hammering in his ears and in another, more uncomfortable part of his anatomy.

"You weren't kidding," she huffed behind him. "I hope we clear this soon. I think the ash is making it hotter than normal."

"And the lack of shade."

"Oh wow, do you think we'll burn? I've heard of sunburns." She grunted. "I've heard they hurt. Do you think they hurt? Have you ever had one?"

Deklan shielded his eyes against the glare of sun coming off the ash. "Why so chatty all of the sudden?"

"I don't know. I'm boiling and covered in sticky. We're heading in the opposite direction of the city all my things are in. I'm trying not to panic, if you want the truth."

"You're an operative for the First Intelligence Office. Panic isn't an emotion they usually accept for their guardians in the field."

"Operative in training."

"And yet, here are you," he said, unable to keep the reproach from his voice.

"Were they upset?"

Deklan didn't pretend not to know what she asked about. "Yes. Did you expect them not to care?"

She blew a raspberry. "I don't know."

"Funny thing about teams," Deklan said, stepping over a large chunk of smoldering wood, "they tend to care about what happens to each other."

"I'm aware of team dynamics."

"Really?" he asked skeptically.

"Yes, really."

Deklan clenched his jaw and looked over his shoulder at her. Some of his frustration must have shown in his eyes, for she gasped and took a hasty step back. "And yet, here you are," he said softly.

Her already red cheeks deepened in hue. "I don't expect anyone to understand."

"They might have surprised you if you'd tried."

Her lips compressed in a tight line. Deklan went back to navigating the unknown path.

"You know," she began, "the tracks ran on the west side of the forest between the two mountain ranges. I bet they form a loop between the two cities. If we head in that direction, maybe we'llleeeaaahhh!"

Deklan whirled around on her shriek morphing scream. Eyes wild and wide, she struggled in ash coated mud up to her thighs. Deklan made the signal for Izia to halt, seeing the wolf about to spring in his peripheral. Izia laid sphynx style and remained still.

"Freeze," he commanded on a harsh bark.

Cia stopped moving. Hands raised, she stared at him.

"It's sinking mud. The more you struggle, the deeper you'll sink," he explained.

"How far?" she asked, breathless.

"I have no idea. Some are only a few feet deep, others too deep to ever know."

Color drained from her face. "What do I do?"

"For now, just relax."

"Relax?" She sputtered and waved her arms. "How am I supposed to relax? I'm trapped in mud!"

"If you'd followed directions and stayed behind me,

you wouldn't be, would you?" he said between gritted teeth.

She flapped a hand and looked away from him. "Fine. Be that way."

"What other way exactly, am I supposed to be?" he asked, looking around for long stick that wouldn't turn to ash when touched.

Dust floated in the air around her and she flicked at small, settled piles in front of her. "I don't know, charmed by my youthful innocence? Patient with my stupidity because, poor thing, I've lost so much."

Deklan stared in silence until her gaze rose back to his. Pretty eyes. So much bluer now when surrounded by the colorless world. "Is that how you've been treated?"

She shrugged. "I think my father agreed to finally allow my training providing I was treated delicately."

Deklan spread his arms. "There is nothing delicate about real life, or what this world *will* throw at you."

She held up soot coated hands. "Hey, I get it, I more than anyone know that. I figured the team I was placed with knew that, too."

"Nuh-uh, nope," he said, popping his *p*. He went back to searching for a lever. "Stop trying to blame your team for your inability to follow a simple task. I'm not buying it. You may be young, but you've faced enough horror to have lost naivety. And you aren't stupid."

Using his foot, he brushed away ash and kicked at debris. When he glanced her direction again, he found her staring at him, her jaw clenched.

"Fine," she snapped and looked away on a glare and motioned to her right. "There are rails to the east of here. I thought if we went that direction we'd find them, see if they're still in any sort of usable condition. If we walk them long enough, we're bound to find civilization or a train we can hitch a ride on."

"I know about the tracks. I was heading to them in a safer route. However, even if I weren't, the proper way to have handled that would have been to call a halt and have a discussion, not be a brat and take off on your own."

She recoiled. "Brat?"

He snapped his fingers and tsked. "Forgot to add the spoiled to it, didn't I? Sorry, won't make the mistake again in the future."

While she sputtered, he dug up a half-buried stick with his boot. He tested the strength to make sure it wouldn't break halfway through the rescue. He dropped his pack on the ground at his feet.

"I'm not a brat," she murmured, reaching for the stick.

"Fine, defiant rebel then. Either one will endanger you however, therefore endangering your team." He braced himself. "Grab hold, and when you can reach my hands, take them. Don't let go or we'll have to start over."